EYE OF THE STORM

SACRED STONES BOOK TWO
EYE OF THE STORM

ANNALISE AZEVEDO

Eye of the Storm
The Sacred Stone Book Two

Copyright © 2019
Annalise Azevedo

Published by Ouroborus Book Services
www.ouroborusbooks.com

Cover Design by Sabrina RG Raven
www.sabrinargraven.com

CHAPTER 1

'Concentrate, Laria.'

As Laria Alfero heard her magister's voice within the shadows of the forest, she clenched her fists nervously and focused on her other senses.

'Yer gonna have to learn to rely on yer other senses.' Tahani Rosa's voice continued and Laria suddenly reacted by dodging an arrow. It flew past her face and dug itself into a tree. Finally, Tahani's pale form materialised from behind another tree and Laria recognised the bright glow from her animalistic eyes. Looking at her from afar, it appeared as if Tahani just got out of bed with her untameable raven hair.

'I really don't believe shooting arrows at me will improve my abilities,' Laria commented flatly as Tahani lowered the bow.

'Of course it will,' Tahani replied with a grin. 'Yer relying on instinct rather than sight.' In an instant, Tahani lifted her bow and fired another arrow in Laria's direction. She had no time to dodge; her hand stretched up to snatch the arrow before it dug into her chest.

'Well I've had enough of being shot at for one day,' Laria admitted as she threw the arrow on the ground.

'What makes ya think that I'm done?' the dux questioned and shot another arrow towards Laria. As Laria jumped away from the projectile, it surprised her when Tahani suddenly appeared in front of her to attack with the bow forgotten. It caught Laria off guard, sending her flying back with a burning flare in her ribs.

However Laria had a few tricks up her sleeve.

With her back on the ground, Laria recovered and countered. Tahani's features flashed with surprise as Laria kicked out a leg and hit the dux's gut. The surprise was worth it. As Tahani recovered from the sudden attack, Laria aimed an elbow to connect with her face.

However Tahani grabbed Laria's arm and slammed her into the ground. Laria yelped as she hit the forest floor and ignored the look from her magister.

'Get up kid,' Tahani ordered with a cocky smirk. She raised her fists in front of her face. 'Yer not done yet.'

Shooting a glare towards Tahani, Laria forced herself to stand. Her face felt like it just made impact with a metal pole. She stood back to her feet, however she saw Edward in Tahani's place.

Why was she seeing him? Laria remembered every detail about the shifter and she hated it. In a burst of rage, she charged at Edward's form and he merely sneered in victory.

'You lost Laria, it will come to life.'

Laria's eyes widened and a sharp pain shot through her chest as she found herself on her back. She recognised Tahani's strong arm pinning her into the ground. A new emotion flashed in Tahani's expression, but it disappeared just as quickly as it appeared.

There was a moment of silence. 'Now yer done,' Tahani muttered and offered a hand.

Laria took it, pulling herself up with a wince from the chest pain. *Here I thought I was done with the countless bruises,* she thought bitterly, checking her nose to see if it was broken. As a teacher, or a magister as the shape shifters liked to call it, Tahani taught Laria everything about fighting.

Unfortunately, Tahani had a reputation amongst the shape shifters. As the Ungue Dux, she was chosen as one of the leaders. Truth be told, Laria didn't know much about her responsibilities, but Tahani informed her that it was her job to take out any threats within the shadows.

Not that it made Laria feel safer.

'So what's been bothering ya, kiddo?' Tahani asked as Laria went to pick up her jacket left on the ground.

'Nothing really.' Laria replied flatly, hoping Tahani would drop the subject.

'Don't lie 'bout that,' the dux scolded. Laria flinched from her tone. 'I've been alive for eighty years, Laria, and I've seen that look in someone's eyes before.' Finally Laria fixed her jacket and glared at Tahani. 'So spill – ya need to clear yer mind.'

'Why does this bloodlust feel strong?' she asked Tahani, who remained unfazed. 'It has been like this ever since I killed Edward. Now I can't even fight without seeing him curse out those words to me. Even now – Lux finds a way to meddle in my head and manipulate my mind.'

'Ya know – I know what it's like.' Laria was flooded with surprise. 'I killed a human when I was ten years old,' Tahani confessed. 'I didn't have Sangri controlling me or anything. I was so consumed by my rage that I did it automatically.'

'Is there a point to this?' Laria asked, trying to divert her attention. She knew that Tahani had a dark past, but hearing the details sent a chill down Laria's spine.

Tahani sighed with irritation. '*I'm saying* that ya gotta stop beating yerself up 'bout Edward. Ya keep saying that it was yer fault but yer did it 'cause ya had to.' Tahani's midnight eyes turned serious as they locked with Laria's gaze. 'Just like I did.'

Before Laria could respond, Tahani turned away from the brunette. 'Now let's go – we gotta go to yer Forte's house. Go wish him a happy birthday and to his human brother.' As Tahani stalked through the forest, Laria looked down at her hands.

For a moment, she could've sworn that they were stained with crimson. But as quickly as it appeared, it was gone once again. Laria blinked, but she tried to follow Tahani with deep thoughts. Why would the dux have to kill someone at such a young age?

'Wait.' Tahani lifted her arm up to stop Laria. A scoff came from Tahani as she lowered her arm. 'Well, look what we have here?' Immediately the dux shot out shards of ice from her fingertips and a loud snap echoed within the forest.

'Tahani?' Laria questioned, slowly approaching to see what she had claimed. Peeking over her shoulder, Laria's eyes widened when she saw the metal jaws closed tightly and covered in frost. 'Is that what I think it is?'

'A bear trap,' Tahani confirmed, crouching down for a better inspection. 'This ain't even padded – these bad boys are illegal. If either one of us were caught in this – not even I could've gotten us out.'

'The question is... what's it doing here?'

'Yer guess is as good as mine.' Tahani stood and stepped over the trap. 'I'll tell Nadia 'bout this – go ahead and be careful.'

For a moment Laria hesitated but she shook her worry away. It was Tahani – she was as tough as nails. Slowly Laria walked ahead and made her way out of the forest.

***

Maya Rosa sighed hopelessly as she scribbled down everything that Jenna was listing. Here she thought that they were at Brodie's party – not planning for the Halloween party. But of course, Maya gave up trying to convince Jenna when a notepad and pen was shoved in her hands.

It was impossible to convince Jenna Sommers otherwise. 'And we have to have a scary theme for this year! Last year was terrible and I swore to myself that I would make it so perfect that our grandchildren will eat their veggies when they hear our scary haunted house theme.'

'Alright,' Maya said quietly, trying to dismiss Jenna's last comment. 'Why don't we make the theme based on... prey?'

Jenna paused in consideration, her blonde hair bouncing with each step. 'Prey?'

'You know... sort of inspired by the skin walker jazz,' Maya continued as she gained Jenna's attention. 'I was reading a bunch of skin walker stuff recently and I found out their tribe of origin. The Navajo was filled with witches and to become a skin walker, they had to kill a human, so humans were probably seen as prey.' Of course, a lot of the story seemed true.

The blonde tapped her chin with a thoughtful hum. 'That's interesting... We are the prey... and they are the predators. It could work,' Jenna announced, and Maya almost sighed blissfully. 'But who would be willing to become a skin walker?'

A new voice separated the pair from their deep discussion. 'I wouldn't mind being a skin walker.' Brodie Forte announced his presence, easily identified by his curly cinnamon brown hair and hazel eyes.

Immediately Jenna turned around to face Brodie with a glint in her eyes. 'You would really do that for me?'

'Of course,' Brodie answered with a small smile. 'I have your back. Even if it means dressing up for a ridiculous costume party.'

Jenna's smile was replaced with a frown. 'Come on, you know that I love Halloween – you should feel privileged to be a part of it.' When Brodie rolled his eyes, Jenna turned away from him to dismiss his complaint. 'Now I've got one skin walker – now we have to find a bunch of them?'

'Why not ask Seth then?' Maya asked icily, and she froze when she felt two pairs of eyes on her. She instantly regretted her mistake and cleared her throat. They still didn't know that after discovering the skin walkers, Maya was so angry with herself for being weak, so she pushed Seth away. 'I'm pretty sure you would find someone.'

'What's going on with you and Seth?' Jenna interrogated with a frown. 'Has he said something to you?'

'No,' Maya denied irritably. 'It's not him... it's me.'

Much to Maya's surprise, Brodie was the next to comment. Yet she could see the mocking smirk across his face. 'You know – that's the most clichéd break-up excuse.'

'What are you implying?!' Maya snapped as Jenna agreed with him. 'It has nothing to do with break-ups, so you can get that fantasy out of your head.' She suddenly got to her feet and left the pair on their own. 'I need to get a drink.'

As Maya left the room, she groaned in annoyance at the sight of the familiar faces all around the house. A bunch of people from school were invited to this party for Brodie's sake. Maya recognised most them from his basketball team. While they were done with the finals, Brodie was still well-known for his skills in basketball and people still cared for him.

Well, it was time for her to get that drink. Passing through the people was a pain for her, especially in her already irritated state. Maya didn't know why she was so angry, especially at the teasing of her and Seth. Deep down, Maya wondered if it had to do with the memories of the bonfire night.

He nearly died.

Her irritation grew as she made her way through, but her patience ran dry when someone roughly shoved her. She turned around, anger cooking up her chest, but it halted the second she felt a hand grab her wrist.

It was the one person she didn't want to speak to. 'You seem to be distressed.' It was Seth Laurence.

Maya turned to him, her eyes narrowed as she saw his concern. 'Nothing... just getting a bit claustrophobic. I didn't think this party would bring half the town.'

Without hesitation, Seth pulled her along with a grunt, 'Let's go into the kitchen. There are less people.'

Maya nodded immediately, following Seth along with an uneasy feeling in her gut. She hated the thought of him caring about her after what she put him through.

The scowl became visible as they arrived in the kitchen; a large spacious room with doors blocking the outside noise. Seth let go of her wrist, his dark eyes filled with unspoken words, yet he seemed conflicted.

'How are you feeling?' he spoke after a dreadful moment of silence.

'Honestly...' Maya trailed off. She turned away from him to avoid his piercing stare. 'Frustrated...'

'I apologise,' Seth stated softly. 'You have been through a lot.' In response, Maya tried to not look back at him, but she could feel his presence lingering right behind her. His breath tickled the back of her neck. 'I know you're scared.'

She fiercely turned to face him. 'Stop it,' Maya said stubbornly, and Seth hesitated. 'I'm not one of those people who you can just 'observe' and speak my thoughts out for me. Why don't you yell at me? Or punch the wall? Or something?!'

Seth's gaze didn't waver. 'I care about you... is that too hard to believe?'

'Yes,' Maya shot back and she tried to step away but she met with the bench. 'It is because you don't care about anyone else. You're you.'

Seth winced at her comment but Maya didn't care. She lifted a hand to stop him from getting any closer, recognising the feeling of a racing heart under his shirt.

'Please,' Maya said softly and lowered her hand. 'Leave me alone.' Seth's eyes widened as if he had been slapped, but after what seemed like an eternity, he let her slip past. Just as Maya was prepared to leave, she felt his hand constrict her wrist to make her face him.

'My injuries were never your fault, Maya,' Seth insisted and Maya froze. He knew. 'And I won't stop caring about you — because that is the kind of person I am.' With that he let go and Maya took the opportunity to move.

It wasn't like her to flee, but there was something that felt odd about his confession. Just as Maya left the kitchen, she felt someone bump into her.

'What's wrong?' Laria asked as Maya stared back at her friend. When did Laria arrive?

'Nothing,' Maya said and she forced a smile. It was time to make sure she got out of the party. 'But Grams wants me to come back.' Laria didn't stop her and Maya walked out.

She got in her old, beat up car; Maya turned on the engine and left the Forte Estate.

***

It didn't feel like a birthday for Brodie. He was eighteen, but there was nothing special about it. At least he was legally an adult and Aunt Tara didn't have to check up on him anymore. Brodie kept Jenna company until, shortly after Maya disappeared mysteriously, Laria came along with grave news.

It didn't take long for Brodie to kick out everyone from the estate, the only ones that remained were Laria and Seth. Tahani arrived after Laria, telling Brodie and Seth that she had something to discuss. From the fact that Laria wasn't surprised with Tahani's story, it seemed that she already knew.

'What would a bear trap be doing in these parts?' Brodie questioned with a scowl. 'If there are more of them in this area...'

'I've already scanned the property,' Tahani assured and dismissed the worries. 'Not a trap in sight – there were more in the forest that we were in.'

'I passed a few, but I triggered them with branches,' Laria confirmed. 'Whoever was using them wasn't just hunting for food. Even then, the forests in these parts are protected.'

'Still,' Seth's monotone voice spoke up and the three turned to him. His arms were crossed over his chest with a stoic expression. 'I would recommend more of a search.'

'What do you have in mind?' Brodie asked.

Seth didn't answer the question, but a doorbell came from the front door. A confused scowl formed on Brodie's face as he heard it. The group exchanged a curious glance at each other, before they went back to Seth once again.

He scowled. 'In normal society – I believe that one of you should answer the door.'

'Smart ass,' Brodie hissed and made his way to the front door. Just as he opened it, he instantly recognised the dark hair and blue eyes. Brodie's scowl reappeared. 'Jason.'

Jason looked just as annoyed. 'Seth called us.'

'Us?'

'Happy birthday Brodie,' Heather said, peeking her head over Jason's shoulder. It suddenly occurred to Brodie that they were probably hanging out for the day. The thought of his sweet friend with Jason made him sick to the stomach.

'Thanks,' Brodie replied and allowed the pair in. As they entered, they made their greetings to the remainder of the group. Brodie's attention went to Jason, watching as he interacted with Laria – she said something with a soft smile while he chuckled at her words.

'So... why did you text us here?' Jason asked Seth, getting his attention instantly.

'We need you for a favour, Heather,' Seth said, directing his answer to Heather, but he immediately snapped his head to the front door. Brodie frowned, aware that Seth's mind-reading powers could've gained attention. 'An enemy is close.'

Laria looked confused for a moment as she glanced around the group. 'How did you know that?' It looked like no one had yet told her about Seth's telepathic powers. But that had to wait. Brodie swung his front door open only to see a limp body in his yard. Concern was the first thing that came to mind.

Brodie raced towards the person, hoping that they were alright, when he noticed that the woman had a crushed windpipe. She wasn't moving.

'I thought everyone left,' Laria said, approaching from behind Brodie. He ignored her presence, crouching low to touch her body. Despite being late fall, the grass wasn't cold enough to make her body as cold as it was. It could've been days since she died.

'She looks 'bout mid-twenties or something. Probably human.' Tahani approached the pair, she took a moment to observe the body with a scowl. 'Strange stuff is going on today. We must be cursed or something.'

Laria responded with a question. 'Did someone dump her here? She wouldn't have been at the party.'

While Laria and Tahani discussed the theories, Brodie already knew the culprit. *He had to have done it. The one who murdered my father. Lucien.* The thought of the man became more than a bitter thought in the back of Brodie's mind. After all, Lucien Alfero had no problems with murdering Brodie's father, so how hard could it be for him to kill an innocent woman?

Brodie's arms shook and he clenched his fists. How could he let Lucien do this to another person? In the corner of his eyes, he realised that Laria hadn't moved from her spot. With an unreadable expression, it dawned on Brodie that Laria had improved on her ability to mask her distress.

Why would she want to hide the pain? Brodie asked himself, turning back to the anonymous girl. *We could've done something about it–*

Brodie suddenly felt a hand clamp on his shoulder, halting his thoughts. 'She's dead,' Seth declared calmly. As Brodie glanced back at him, Seth's stare didn't falter. 'There was nothing that could be done about it.'

Finally Heather and Jason reached them. Heather let out whimper as she took in the sight in front of her. She pulled herself away from Jason, crouching next to Brodie with a shaky breath.

'I'm sorry that this happened to you…' Her voice quivered. She reached out to the body, grabbing her hand like it was some sort of comfort.

'We won't let this go,' Brodie promised to Heather. His words seemed to comfort Heather, but Brodie knew empty promises wasn't enough. The guilt was bubbling in his chest as questions flooded his head. Who was she? Why was she here? Did she even have a chance to defend herself?

'I should call the sheriff-' Seth was cut off by a phone ring, but it wasn't a phone that Brodie recognised.

Yet the ringing didn't stop. Laria tilted her head. 'It's coming from that pocket.'

An eerie glow appeared from the hip of the dead girl's trousers. The thought of answering a stranger's phone was unsettling for Brodie. He knew that he shouldn't touch it, however he knew that someone could be looking for her.

Brodie had the phone to his ear when he heard a female voice. '*I will make your world fall apart, Brodie Forte. Enjoy your first gift.*' It was an English accent, one that he recognised. The line went dead and Brodie clenched the phone in his hand.

'I recognise this scent,' Tahani said sternly. Brodie saw her clench her fist. He'd never seen the look in her eyes before — like a beast that was cornered. 'It's not his way of normally killing 'em but perhaps that is his goal.'

'What kind of monster would do such a thing?' Heather asked Tahani, finally standing back on her feet.

Tahani's expression didn't change, her midnight eyes focused on the limp body in front of them. She let out a deep sigh as she made the declaration, 'This scent belongs to Nick Forte.'

CHAPTER 2

It has been done – N

Sitting by the diner of Silver Roots, Charmi Forte's blue eyes went to her phone. The time she spent planning and remained out of sight of the enemies was worth it.

Now that she allowed her brother to send off the dead body to the Forte Estate, Charmi could now begin her plan. First, she would have to remind them that they didn't have the ability to save anyone from their wretched town, not even the strangers.

The desire of vengeance would occasionally slip back into her. Charmi deserted Lucien after he dismissed Brad's death like it was nothing. And Brodie Forte was the reason why Brad was dead in the first place. She was going to make Brodie's world crumble around him.

Bringing the glass to her lips, Charmi smiled wickedly. Hiding out in the cabin in one of the forests was worth the wait. No hunter knew she was around – she was too well-hidden from the world to be caught. This town had improved since the last time she came in, developing technology that can track down their bloodlust – a creation most likely developed by witches no less.

Finally, someone entered the Silver Roots, though the people didn't stop their actions to look at the new arrival. Instantly recognising her blonde-haired brother, Charmi's smile widened. Nick Forte returned the smile as he made his way through the tables to take a seat next to her.

'Good evening Charmi,' Nick greeted, faking an American accent. Charmi scoffed, recalling that this was nothing but a game to him. Her brother used to like the roleplaying behaviour back in London, something that he held with him as he developed into the harsh killer he was today. Perhaps he was doing his best to hide himself, it wasn't unusual for him to pretend.

'I'm glad you could come,' Charmi said, flashing a smile. Nick scowled as it occurred to him that she wasn't playing his game. 'How did they take it?'

The scowl from Nick vanished and took a seat in front of her. 'They clearly weren't happy. It's boring actually… to care for mere strangers.'

'As soon as Brodie Forte is dead, we can do whatever we want,' Charmi promised, meeting Nick's blue eyes. 'However… I do have someone that you can play with.' Nick's smile widened as he looked at Charmi's phone with the photo of a female teenager. 'Jenna Sommers – a friend of Brodie as well as Laria, and the daughter of Clark Sommers, one of the hunters. It would be a perfect message to send.'

'A daughter of a hunter,' Nick mused as he took the phone from his sister's hands. A sadistic grin expanded on his face and he chuckled in delight. 'And this will make you happy?'

For as long Charmi could remember, she was glad that Nick listened to her every order. They had been through enough; it was her time to prove to the world that they were not to be trifled with.

'I know this will make you happy,' she answered and she saw a sinister grin crawl on his face.

A chuckle left his lips as his eyes changed from blue to gold. 'It sounds like fun.'

***

Jenna frowned just as her history teacher finished writing the 30th of November on the board. It was on a Sunday this year. Beside her, Laria looked bored to be writing.

'The Acer Opacare was celebrated due to the treaty that

was once signed by the indigenous people of this land – also known as the founding families.' David Embers gave a pointed look towards Laria who turned away from his encouraging stare. 'Yet, it was suspected that the indigenous people were a part of the Navajo Tribe that disappeared in Utah over six hundred years ago.'

More eyes went over to Laria, who was now glaring at David to stop talking. As a friend of three from the founding families, Jenna thought it was interesting. Was it because of the attention?

'I have said some time ago that they gave themselves European names to hide their tracks. Shortly after the four families were settling down, they came into contact with Europeans and it started off harshly, but it was thanks to an individual from the Rosa family who stopped the violence. Since then, our town has been settled as the one and only Golden Cliff.'

'What's the point of this?' Laria asked flatly, ignoring everyone's eyes now. Her tone confirmed Jenna's suspicion. Laria wasn't a fan of people staring at her, with the teacher mentioning her name – people were bound to look.

David leaned on his desk. 'The Acer Opacare is a special dance for the town – you probably attended in years before, but never knew its origins. It's to celebrate the treaty that happened over sixty years ago.'

With the answer, Laria's looked away and went back to writing which left Jenna to her thoughts. It probably wasn't just the attention Laria didn't like, there was something that seemed off with her. Jenna wanted to ask, but decided it would probably be a better time to talk when she's less moody.

Jenna instead focused on her school diary to the particular date, making a promise to herself that she had to go dress shopping. The best time to go was after the Halloween party, since she didn't have to worry about avoiding the Halloween Candy.

In the background, she could hear the questions from her other classmates about the event. The records of the treaty were rare, only stating someone from the Rosa family was responsible.

Jenna spent the rest of the class listening to David talk. His words seemed to blur into one, distracting Jenna from her concern for Laria.

She didn't realise that her class went quickly until she heard the school bell ring, causing the students began to pack their bags. The sound itself caused Jenna to jolt into awareness, letting out a shaky breath.

Suddenly, she felt a hand on her and Jenna realised that Laria was looking in her direction with a frown.

'Are you alright?' Laria asked, pulling her hand back. 'It's not like you to be so jumpy.'

Seeing that Laria's annoyance was gone, relief overcame Jenna. She seemed better now that they weren't talking about her family history. It always sounded like a sensitive subject for Laria.

'I'm okay,' Jenna replied, finally packing her books. From the corner of her eyes she saw the remainder of her classmates began to leave while David erased the board. 'I spaced out.'

'You shouldn't be doing that. You need to be focusing on your studies.' David intervened and Jenna looked at her teacher with a roll of her eyes. It was strange – out of all of her teachers, David was the only one that preferred to be called by his first name. Apparently, he felt like the students connected better if he knew them on a first-name basis.

'Laria,' Jenna spoke again and clicked her fingers to grab Laria's attention. It took the click to snap her out of the trance and Laria offered a smile.

'Sorry Jen,' Laria said sheepishly and went to pack her bag. 'But I need to talk to Mister Embers about the test.'

'Do you want me to stay?' Jenna asked, blinking curiously at Laria's personality change. Ever since her mother died Laria had been naturally withdrawn and now it was getting worse. What was running through her mind?

The reaction was instant as Laria stood to her feet. 'No,' she muttered curtly. 'I'm fine.'

'Alright then – I'll see you later.' Without another word, Jenna left Laria alone in the classroom with David to get into the hallway. However, Jenna's mind was elsewhere.

Years ago, it was simpler – when they were in first grade. Jenna was picking flowers from the park when a soccer ball hit her head; oblivious to the fact the younger Maya was responsible. With Maya, Laria and Brodie were there checking to see if Jenna was hurt. Brodie back then was shorter than them, with a chubbier face and a goofy grin. Maya was the only one who didn't want to say anything.

Even then, Jenna felt like she didn't belong with her friends, an outcast. Something about them always seemed different and Jenna could never put her finger on it until Laria lost her mother in the fire. Now it seemed like the rest of her friends knew something she didn't, forcing Jenna to watch them from behind with questions.

On the way to her locker, Jenna noticed that Seth stood alone in the corner. Something happened between Maya and him, which forced them to drift apart. He went back to his anti-social ways, stoically standing by his locker as he waited for the lunch break to end.

Finally, Jenna recognised Maya who looked irritated. Just as Jenna smiled and prepared to greet her raven-haired friend, a hand grabbed her arm and pulled her away from the crowds. Jenna screeched as she went into a classroom and expected someone to come at her with a giant axe.

'Calm down, Jenna,' a voice demanded, and Jenna recovered from her shock. 'I thought that it would be better if I pulled you into a classroom.' The familiar voice registered to her and Jenna's alarm dissolved into annoyance.

Yet, she still wasn't pleased. 'Taro,' she said coolly, ignoring the frantic beating from her heart. Two weeks ago, when they were at his bonfire, they got into a small argument. Jenna had been so infuriated with him that she tried to get away from him, but he grabbed and kissed her. It was so sudden that Jenna didn't have time to register what happened, but then Sara turned into a psycho and attacked.

'Look Jenna I'm tired of this... stop with the glares,' Taro said as he crossed his arms casually. 'I said I was sorry, didn't I?'

'That's exactly the problem,' Jenna replied sarcastically as she rolled her eyes. 'You keep acting like you care about me.'

Taro almost growled. 'I keep telling you, I do-!'

'Tell that to yourself when you make out with Sara again,' Jenna replied sharply. After a moment of silence, she gave in. 'What do you want?'

Jenna had spent many years pining for this guy in front of her, despite how he acted mean to her friends. Everyone told Jenna that she was immature, but she ignored them. Even when she saw him with Sara Maraca, Jenna refused to give up. There was something about him that made Jenna believe that he was a good guy – despite his recent actions.

'I need to know something about your friends,' Taro confessed, and Jenna scowled.

'What's going on?' Jenna asked, straightening up cautiously.

He scratched the back of his neck and tried to answer, but Jenna noticed a strange black marking on his bicep. Before Taro could say anything, Jenna grabbed his arm to get a better view.

'Jenna!'

'What's this, Taro?! You have a tattoo?' The ink was strange; it had three claw-like markings to signify some animal scratch and Jenna recognised it. 'My dad has the same one on his shoulder! Taro, you could get into trouble for stuff like this!'

Taro pulled his arm away suddenly and hid the tattoo. 'That's not important at the moment,' he said coldly. 'I'm asking about your friends: Laria, Maya and even Brodie. They've been acting strange, haven't they?'

'Well yes...' Jenna trailed off when her mind went to her distant friends. 'But it has only been a few months since their parents died and Maya had a fight with Seth. Whatever is going on with you, I want no part of it.' She went to turn away when Taro grabbed her.

Jenna was about to snap at him but he cut her off. 'I know you wouldn't believe me, but I care about you Jenna,' he announced. 'But don't tell me that you haven't been thinking about it.' Finally, he let her go and allowed Jenna to leave the classroom.

She glanced back at Taro as she left the room, trying to push the words out of her head. But no matter how hard she tried, she kept going back to his comment.

Halfway down the hall, Jenna momentarily paused to look back in the direction she came from. Taro stepped out of the classroom casually and eyed her from the distance. Everyone was acting strange now.

***

Beads of sweat dripped from Jason's face as he prepared his workout. His fist connected with the punching bag in rapid strikes. The sound of music trailed behind his ears, but all sounds managed to fall deaf on him, as his mind went to the incident the day before.

The kicker was discovering an unknown girl who had been killed and somehow Nick Forte returned to their lives. Jason remembered him vividly, as well as the caramel-haired woman, Charmi. They were both killers, willing to end Jason right in front of Laria like it was nothing.

And he remembered Heather's distraught face. Feeling the small anger stir him, Jason focused on quickening his pace. After the girl's body was discovered, Sheriff Cyler declared the girl wasn't a local. She came onto the investigation and spoke briefly to Tahani.

Jason kept a scowl on his face; the dead girl's face remained in his mind. While Seth went to school, Jason decided to stay back to get his mind set. He couldn't brush away the thoughts of the mysterious girl who just went to the wrong place at the wrong time.

It also didn't help that this was the first birthday he had, without Mae. Instead, he had a brother that hated him and the truth that Mae wasn't his real mother.

A loud knock interrupted Jason from his training and Jason froze. He wasn't expecting any visitors since his friends were at school. Grabbing the nearest knife, Jason held the weapon behind his back and stalked his way to the front door.

The knocking continued as Jason's hand went on the knob and he pulled the door open. As Jason tightened his hold on the knife, he widened his eyes at the sight of Heather standing by the front.

However her expression was different. 'Hi,' Heather muttered softly.

Lowering the knife, Jason leaned on the doorframe and using his free hand, pulled the remote from his pocket to turn off the music. Once it was silent, Jason looked back at the brunette. 'What's going on?' he asked, eyes flashing with concern before he stepped out of the way. 'Would you like to come inside?'

'No,' Heather replied uneasily and shifted the weight onto one foot. 'I think it's better off if I stay outside for this.' Now Jason was worried. 'Jason,' she began and finally met him in the eyes. 'Lately I've been caught up with exams and... I feel like it's been putting some distance between us.'

'I know,' Jason replied gently. She seemed upset about their situation, so much that Jason asked her to come over the day before. 'I'm nearly done with my exams, you should be as well and then we could hang out like before—'

'That's the problem, Jason,' Heather cut off firmly and Jason froze. Now he understood Heather's implication. 'I have plans for my future – and... I can't afford to risk them for you.' Something bothered Jason about what Heather just said.

'You're breaking up with me.' He was surprised with himself when he realised that it wasn't a question.

'I'm sorry Jason,' Heather whispered desperately. 'I can't afford to fail.'

'I know,' Jason repeated his earlier phrase even though he was mentally snapping. There was more to it than failing exams or the future. After all the time he spent with her and it was just ending like leftovers. It was something he wasn't getting.

Heather broke away from Jason's stare, mouthing another apology before she backed away from the door. He didn't chase after the witch when she ran; he wanted to, but a voice in the back of his mind stopped him. The best chance he had was to let her go.

Finally Jason looked down at his hand and realised it was shaking in rage. He hadn't felt this way since he found out that Brodie was his brother. There was a small voice in the back of his mind, mumbling in an unclear language. His eyes went down to the knife as he tightened his hold on the blade.

And just like that, the feeling disappeared.

Jason dropped the knife as if the blade zapped him and it clattered uselessly on the ground. He knew what it was. It had been like this for the past week, bubbling to the surface.

His bloodlust was finally awakening after eighteen years of remaining dormant.

***

David finished writing the important dates on the whiteboard. As he turned back to his class, his gaze met with the blinking faces of students. Some of the faces were filled with interest, eyes directly focused on the teacher while others were threatening to fall asleep.

To awaken them, David cleared his throat loudly and made them flinch. 'As I was saying... Historians widely view the Revolution as one of the most important events in human history, and the events of the end of the early modern period, which started around 1500, are traditionally attributed to the onset of the French Revolution in 1789.' He leaned on his desk and played with the chalk in his fingers. 'The Revolution is often seen as marking the dawn of the modern era, though I believe that with the current government and this corrupt world, we'll repeat history eventually.'

The class of freshmen erupted with chuckles at David's choice of words. They didn't seem to realise that David was being serious.

With a sigh, he drew his grey eyes back to the board. 'Now, for homework tonight–' His voice was drowned out by groans from the remainder of the classroom. There were always students that didn't want to do homework. 'As I was saying, for tonight I want you to–'

Again, David was interrupted but it wasn't by the students. A loud beep came from his phone and David turned back down to stare at the device. The freshmen giggled at the startling sound, but he decided to ignore it. Surely the message could wait.

'I'm sorry.' The history teacher raised his hands and went back to writing on the board. 'So, as I was saying, tonight I just want you to go through your textbooks. There are three chapters for you to read and I want a short summary of the French Revolution.'

Despite the students lacked enthusiasm, they copied down his instructions. They probably didn't want to fail and David's homework helped them, whether they liked to admit it or not.

Throughout the rest of the class, David made sure that he covered topics that were necessary for the next lot of exams. Each question, he made sure he was direct and straight to the point.

Despite enjoying his day job, David certainly felt relieved when the bell rang and each student began packing their bags. It was exhausting to keep up the act like everything was okay.

'See you Mister Embers!'

'Alright – have a good afternoon.' Once all the students left, David let out a deep breath before checking the new message on his phone from the mayor, Susan Cana.

Our meeting has been pushed forward. Come after your class to Town Hall.

Then they would probably suggest more silly things that seemed impossible. He straightened his position and eyed the clock, seeing the second hand was almost at the twelve.

He packed his own bag, shoving the books away as fast as he could before he rushed out his room. He stood in his doorway and sent an immediate text to Tracy Ladas, saying that he had to rush out of school, before he tried squeezing through the crowd.

Since the school day was ending, David had to push through the countless students. He spotted his silver SUV as he fumbled with his keys and unlocked the door.

As soon as he turned on the car, the phone rang lightly and David read the ID from his phone before switching it on speaker. 'Hey there, Diana,' he spoke to the phone and began to reverse out of his park.

'*Hey.*' the voice brought a smile over his face. His wife always had a calming effect over him, ever since they met. *I know you're at work, but I was just calling to see if you would be home in time for dinner.*'

'It's alright,' David replied, keeping his attention on the road. 'I was just going to Town Hall – I'm not sure if I'll be home on time but don't wait up for me.'

'*I see.*' The disappointment was clear. '*Listen David, if you don't feel comfortable doing this, then you shouldn't have to.*'

David spared a glance at the photo of the ID with a soft gaze. It was a woman in her early thirties with long brown hair and chocolate brown eyes. Deep down, he knew she was right – he shouldn't be trying to work with the hunters. They had different views of the shifters that lived in the town.

'I know,' he finally said. 'But I can't let this happen, I shouldn't have let this happen in the first place.'

'*I suppose I can't change your mind no matter what I say.*' She still seemed disappointed. David felt bad, but he knew that it was for the right reasons. He had to protect his family, even if it meant taking risks. *I love you.*'

Diana never said it unless she was worried about him. 'I love you too, Diana.' The phone let off a small beep to announce that had Diana hung up from the other line and David returned his gaze to the road.

Once again, he was forced to deal with the empty silence.

The day itself didn't seem strange. Only Laria's distant nature, even from Jenna but after talking to Laria, David learned she came across a dead body after Brodie's birthday. He wasn't sure if they knew the deceased, but it was still a devasting impact, nonetheless.

If he'd had the time, he would've consoled Laria during her free time. It was only recently when he learned that she wasn't human, despite knowing her family name. He simply assumed that she took after her mother's traits rather than her father's.

Because of Laria's situation of being a late bloomer, the hunters were targeting anyone who held the same name as the four families. So far they hadn't attacked anyone – at least David assumed. The only thing he was aware of was the beartraps and that was only from Laria when she told him.

David heard an alert from his phone and he quickly checked it. It was an alert that a shifter was in town. He set his eyes on the road once more when his heart jumped out of his chest and slammed his foot on the breaks. A curse slipped from his lips, the car spun out of control and crashed into a pole. David raised his hands to protect himself from the sudden airbag.

Luckily the most damage that he had was done to his car. David pushed back the airbag and looked out the window to see the cause of his crash. Someone stood out in the middle of the road, slowly turning and flashing an eerie grin as his eyes glowed.

Well, at least he found the shifter.

But David had no time to think about that. The shifter stalked his way to David's car with a snarl and the teacher reached for his glove box, but in the next second he let out a yell as his car flipped over. The shifter lifted and threw the car with relative ease. Something hard smacked against David's skull and his body seared.

David's body hung upside down and his recovery was slow as the shifter approached the destroyed car. He could see that the shifter was filled with bloodlust and wore an ugly sneer of amusement to see David's position.

David fought viciously to get out of his seat. His belt

refused to co-operate with him. A silver glint on the roof caught David's attention and he recognised it as the pocketknife he used whenever he had to cut open something at the last minute.

'Damn it,' David growled in agony and grasped the knife with shaky hands. He felt his fingers tremble as he pulled out the blade and used it to slice the belt. With a quick slice of the belt, gravity forced his body to drop like a rock.

Glass cut into his skin as David landed among the shards, but his hope faded as soon as his door ripped open. He felt a cold grip around his ankle drag him out.

'This is fun – I should do this more often,' the shifter sneered in gratitude and slammed a foot into David's ribs – a sickening crunch was loud enough for a human like David himself to hear. 'Now time to tear off your head and show it to your petty organisation!'

David suppressed the shudder, and the shifter tried to reach for David but a hand shot out to stop the shifter. The shifter's eyes widened and pulled his upper lip back like an animal.

'Takon,' David said in shock, recognising the Mandati Dux disguised as the school councillor.

'Just hold still,' Takon Falls replied calmly as the attacking shifter suddenly pulled away with a grunt. 'It's my responsibility as a dux to take care of humans, even if they're hunters.' In one swift motion, Takon shot out his fist against the shifter's jaw.

The impact was enough to knock the shifter out and hit the ground with a cold thud. It took David a moment to compose himself, but he saw the swell from Takon's punch.

A hot flare in his ribs returned as David wrapped an arm around himself. He slowly pulled himself to a seated position and watched as Takon pushed his glasses back.

Takon then faced David, running his fingers through his dark hair. 'I take it that you have a meeting with your little group?'

David nodded. Takon was one of the few shifters that

knew what was going on behind their backs. Of course, he hadn't notified the rest of the shifters since it would only result in chaos. David was working with Takon to come up with a co-existence between the shifters and hunters.

If the humans were safe, David would not have to worry about the shifters turning their backs on the hunters.

'Come on.' Takon helped David to his feet and removed the gun from plain sight. 'Let's discuss an alternative and come up with an excuse.' As the dux brought out his phone to call an ambulance, David wondered if they were ever going to succeed with their treaty.

CHAPTER 3

'Cheers,' Haroni Ladas said as he downed the drink. He nodded softly for another, making the waiter pour the contents in his glass.

If anyone had observed him, they would've assumed that he was some important businessman, with his expensive black suit and paperwork. However, Haroni's attention was focused on information regarding strange cases around the area. Of course, it came from his recent offer.

'Sir, you look like you're stuck in something.' The bartender spoke and reminded Haroni that he was still at the Silver Roots diner. 'What's got you drinking in the afternoon in the middle of the week?'

'My life,' Haroni replied with a heavy sigh and took a gulp. 'A colleague skipped out of town and ditched me with all his work. His best friend – a very pretty girl – is trying to track him down so he can come back to finish his work.'

'What about this girl?' the bartender wondered, leaning forward with the towel in his hands to clean a glass. 'You like her or something? Is that why you're drinking?'

Wait... what?

The fallen angel felt the drink go down the wrong pipe and he coughed out the drink with alarm. He spluttered the drink out of his system before he silently considered what the waiter said.

Tahani Rosa? No, that was beyond foolish. It was wrong on so many levels, especially considering the nearly thousand-year age gap. His intentions weren't to settle down. But the most important reason of all – Haroni couldn't turn into a hypocrite. After blaming Tracy for falling in love with Abeytu all those years ago, Haroni swore to himself that he wouldn't be bound by love.

After turning away from the possibility of romance, he used humour and a charming mask to get by his day. He was often polite on the outside, but he could be as cruel as the rest if he wanted to. Normally he would have his good time with anyone that had an eight-figured body, but he would never develop feelings for any woman.

Let alone the Ungue Dux. Tahani was nothing more to Haroni than a friend – drinking buddy would be accurate.

His silence finally drew him into reality and Haroni shook his head in dismissal. 'Don't you have a job to do with other people?'

'Sorry – that must be a sore subject,' the bartender muttered as he refilled the drink. 'It's my job to keep interactive with my customers and give them drinks.'

He felt like a ticking time bomb with this guy. 'There is no subject to discuss.' Haroni went to his drink. 'Just fill up the drinks and that will be all for me this afternoon.'

'Alright then.'

Haroni felt satisfaction as the bartender left him to work. This was beginning to pick at his brain like a seagull going through the trash. Looking through the hospital records, Haroni was tracking down Zanobi and Lucien but so far nothing revealed them. The least that the skin walker pair could do was something to get their attention.

So far, they'd been hiding their recent actions. But then again, there were a few stray skin walkers that had been roaming in town. Such as the outsiders that attacked the girl the other night; Nadia had yet to find the skin walker that was responsible for that. From the random nature of the killing, it was safe to say that they were no longer going for the descendants' bloodlust.

'What are they after?' Haroni asked himself, staring at the condensation of his drink.

Then there was something that haunted him. A few days ago, he received an email from an old friend with an image attachment of a dead body. He was surprised to receive the picture until he saw the scarred markings on the body. It was then, when he realised that it hadn't been a skin walker kill, that Haroni had to double check.

If it was who he thought it was, then no one in Golden Cliff was safe.

'Fancy seeing you here – drinking and waiting for someone to warm your sheets.' It was a sarcastic tone from his favourite sister.

A smile came upon Haroni's lips, making eye contact with the matching cerulean eyes. With a lazy wink, Haroni raised his glass and smirked in her direction. 'Nice to see you too, dear sister.'

Tracy Ladas barely changed throughout the centuries. Her face was still filled with cold and sharp features with her long blonde hair hanging over her shoulders, her gaze lacked interest as she made her way to the bar.

She didn't make a sound as she crossed the room to Haroni and acknowledged his presence. Like the professional she was, the blonde-haired woman took a seat and spared a glance at the paperwork.

'Your search is pointless,' she told him. 'You are searching for someone who's been in hiding for fifteen years. The only way Lucien gets found is if he wants to get found.'

'I doubt that, Tracy,' Haroni replied, genuinely honest, before focusing on his work. 'And besides – I wanted to find the skin walkers that have been lurking around – maybe they know something.'

'I wouldn't have suspected that,' Tracy responded, taking a peek at the work. 'But I guess that you plan to track the skin walkers down – then question where Lucien and Zanobi are hiding?' As Haroni didn't answer, he heard a light scoff from his sister. 'I don't believe that you're doing this because you're bored.'

'You're right, dear sister.' Haroni pushed himself to his feet and sent a serious gaze in her direction. 'I want to do this because of me; Laria was nearly taken. I nearly broke my promise. If you don't believe me for that, then it is your own problem.'

Tracy remained quiet for a moment. She turned back to her drink and played with the straw. 'I was informed that Laria went to go searching for the traps.'

'Again? After another night without sleep?' Haroni raised a brow in suspicion, wrapping his fingers around the cool glass. He knew about her insomnia. It had to do with the bloodlust. She shouldn't be roaming around, especially while exhausted. 'That does not sound right – have you spoken to her?'

Tracy replied, 'She headed out before I could reach her.' She took a sip from her drink. 'I think you may need to bring Christopher to Golden Cliff.'

'Christopher...' Haroni thought back to Laria's older brother and fidgeted with his phone in his pocket. 'I will consider it,' he decided as he moved the phone away from his grasp and left it in his pocket. 'So, do you know where she ran off to?'

'No idea,' Tracy huffed in annoyance and shot a glare towards her brother. 'And I already told you that she isn't my responsibility.'

'Never said that, dear,' Haroni responded and finished off his drink. Just as the bartender came back to Haroni, he shook his head and placed a couple of bills on the counter, including the tip. Tracy raised an eyebrow towards Haroni as he stood to his feet and collected his paperwork. 'Well, if you'll excuse me, I need to head out.' Unfortunately, Tracy could see through his transparent smile.

'You really are a fool.' She spoke softly and turned away from him. 'Why must you help any woman, but when it came to me – you refused to help?'

It felt like the Silver Roots went silent. Haroni refused to look back. His smile dropped, and his eyes were staring off into space. The tension between the fallen siblings felt like moving through water.

But Haroni didn't choose to say anything. Instead, he hardened his resolve and moved his way past the other people. Once again, the sounds returned to the diner and as Haroni stepped out of the room, he grabbed his phone and dialled a number.

The phone rang and rang, but Haroni felt suddenly worried when it clicked onto voicemail.

'Hi, this is Laria speaking, sorry that I can't take your call right now... Just leave me a message and I'll get back to you as soon as possible.'

After the beep, Haroni hung up the phone and cursed lightly. He sighed in frustration and dialled the next best number. It had only taken a few rings until the phone was answered.

"Sup, Haroni?'

'Good.' Haroni felt himself nod when he heard Tahani on the other end of the line. 'At least someone knows how to pick up their phone.' He felt his mind wander back to the earlier conversation to the waiter before angrily dismissing it. 'I heard from Tracy that Laria got out of school and I was wondering if she found you.'

'Sorry.' Tahani's voice sounded breathless. She must've been training from where she was. *'I hadn't seen the kiddo since class – I just thought that she went back to the house. I'm at the pits right now if that was gonna be yer next question, then I'm going on a search for one of those traps I was telling ya about.'*

But then why would she miss her call? Laria always had her phone with her, and she barely ignored calls unless she... 'Thank you dear – I'll talk to you later,' Haroni replied and he hung up before dialling Laria's number again.

It was voicemail.

'Laria dear – listen to me,' Haroni muttered seriously. 'With the skin walkers around, you have to inform me of whatever your actions are because I'm worried. Call me back.' And with that, he hung up the phone.

***

The trees towered above Laria, making the shadows loom over the path. If it hadn't been for the constant ringing from her godfather, Laria knew the only sounds that would've been heard were the sounds of her boots crunching against the dirt.

She didn't even realise her current location until recently. She had already made it this far, and Laria felt that she couldn't back out.

Since Edward's death, she had constant nightmares that reminded her that the bloodlust was slowly taking over like a parasite. Lux, the personification of her bloodlust that dwelt inside her, put her on edge – one of the reasons why Laria felt so afraid whenever she was alone. She feared the day that she snapped.

Every time she thought back to the death of Edward, Laria felt her mind go back to her best friend's words. Brodie was right. Everyone killed. Even though he was drunk, he managed to state the truth and every time she went back to it, it tore her up from the inside.

The last time they had a proper conversation was at the bonfire, when he told her that Jason was his brother. Yesterday, at his birthday party, she felt like all they spoke about was the bear traps and then the body they'd found on the lawn.

Laria recognised Brodie's large estate and told herself it was too late to back out now.

The chilling breeze stopped her as she stepped up on the porch. They'd had their differences the past few weeks and Brodie seemed different each time she saw him. Brodie was her best friend who had always been there for her. Now it was her turn to help him.

Her knuckles brushed the door softly and for that moment, Laria felt her hesitation kick in. Ever since they lost touch, Laria could feel Brodie slipping away. But again, Laria told herself that she wasn't going to hesitate and she raised her fist to let out a stern but confident knock.

Laria tried to not show her disappointment when there was no response from the other side. As Laria dropped her fist, she turned away and flinched at the sight of Brodie standing behind her.

The Forte heir himself smiled. 'Hey there...' His brown shirt was half-buttoned, showing the top half of his chest, and his face was covered in dirt, meaning that he had most likely shifted recently. 'What's going on?'

Unable to hide her emotions, Laria felt a smile return to her features. 'What reason do I need to see my best friend?'

For a moment, Laria would've sworn that she saw hesitation in Brodie's features. The cheerful glint in his dark hazel eyes was gone and the smile dropped before they all appeared again in an instant.

'Good point.' Brodie reached forward and opened the door for her to enter. His face turned rather serious as he looked to her. 'There's something you need to know anyway. I'll get you a drink-'

'That's fine.' Laria found herself cutting him off as she walked into the building. She could remember every detail. The dark house made from oak and the comfortable leather couches that Laria nearly fell in love with. Despite Brodie not flaunting it, he inherited a lot more than just an estate. Of course, his Aunt Tara had a part of the inheritance as well but she probably had less interest in it than Brodie.

'I just came back from the police station.'

Instantly, Laria knew. 'Any information?'

'The girl was a Jane Doe – no records, no ID, that phone that she had was a burner and we still don't know who killed her. The only thing we can figure out is that she was strangled to death, it wasn't done by Nick or Charmi. Since she isn't a local, the sheriff assumed that Charmi found her dead body outside of town and used it to spook us. That's all we have at the moment.'

Laria wasn't even sure how to react to that. 'Who else knows?'

'Excluding us, Tara only.' Brodie answered after taking another sip. 'She told me that she would get to the Mandati Dux as soon as possible.' Finally, his hazel eyes locked with her gaze and Laria felt like he burnt a hole through her head. 'You're being surprisingly calm about this.'

'I'm just trying to understand,' Laria said and she avoided his intense stare. 'Why get a body? Don't they usually kill on a regular basis?'

'Your guess is as good as mine,' Brodie confessed and he clenched his fist. 'It was quiet for two weeks and now she's attacking. I have a feeling that this is just the beginning of the bad things – especially from her.'

'Me too,' Laria admitted and ignored the bitter burn in the back of her throat. 'But we'll figure it out,' she declared and Brodie offered Laria a strange look. 'We've been through enough – but whatever is going on, I know that we'll pull through.'

As he finished his drink, Brodie sat next to Laria and she naturally leaned into him. From her position, she felt his muscles tighten. Eventually Brodie's arm drape over her shoulders. Just like the rest of his body, it was warm and comforting. Her mind went back to the days when she would huddle to him for warmth whenever it was cold.

'Yeah...' he softly agreed and his fingers lightly traced patterns on her arm. 'I do too.'

They fell into a comfortable silence and Laria smiled once again. It was normal again. Lux remained locked in the cage in solitude and Laria wasn't afraid whenever she was with Brodie. In her pocket, she felt her phone vibrate and she remembered that she was meant to be helping Tahani with the bear traps.

'I need to leave now,' Laria realised. Brodie moved his arm and she grabbed her bag to leave. Before she exited the room, Laria stopped in her tracks and turned to him. 'I won't allow Lucien or Charmi to get away with what they've done.'

It was like Brodie sobered up in that instant. 'Laria...'

And Laria continued, 'They don't deserve forgiveness – for that girl and for your father... I promise that I will help you whenever you need it.' Brodie was unable to respond and Laria understood.

He was speechless, even when she opened the door and spared him another glance. Even though he couldn't respond, Brodie had a look of understanding which she accepted when she left.

***

Tahani looked around her as she left the building. The pits were situated underground, however to enter them Tahani had to make her way through a building that led to the basement.

The pits were in a secluded place mostly because of the police. Nadia Cyler knew the location, but she also knew that most of the pits' crowd consisted of shifters. As long as no one was killed then Nadia kept to her word about keeping off the pits. After all, it was great for controlling the Rosa bloodlust.

Every time Tahani left the pits after a match, she felt great. She was occasionally met with a challenge, but in the end the dux managed to swipe him off his feet and win the match. There were times when she did have to use effort when she was fighting.

But it seemed like yesterday when Tahani was literally spending her nights there. Society wasn't a fan of unnatural phenomena such as youthful appearances, so Tahani spent years away from the human eyes. Aging was something Tahani never really thought about since it was slower than humans.

Not all shifters were slow agers, however. It was determined by their bloodlust oddly enough. The more a shifter killed, the slower they aged. Before Tahani found herself living in the pits, she and Kaeylin, her late sister, were manipulated into killing humans. The killing hardly bothered Tahani, but it traumatised her little sister.

Nowadays, Tahani stayed at Haroni's training Laria. Since her arrest, she decided to stay out of the schooling life. It had never been her style to read books – it was amazing that people thought she was at the schooling age. Laria did occasionally make the comments that she definitely didn't belong in high school.

Maybe I'll think of sneaking into a college. Parties would actually be fun. Tahani thought to herself with a snicker.

Unfortunately, Maya had tried to keep her distance from Tahani ever since she broke into her house and demanded answers from the girl's grandmother, Adelle. Laria informed Tahani that she told mostly everything to Maya, so she was aware that Tahani was a shifter from the Rosa family.

It would be better for Maya that she stayed in the dark anyways. While Maya had no fear, she was also a human who happened to have many shifter friends – one of them being Seth Laurence. How she managed to get his attention was beyond Tahani.

Then there was the situation of Azu. It should've been handed to the daughter, but Maya didn't know anything about the stone.

Honestly, Tahani had no idea on where to start her search for the stone. It was Kaeylin, who oversaw the stone, after Tahani entrusted her with it. Kaeylin was one of the four that sealed up the rectocs, the creators of the shifters and origin of the bloodlust.

By then their bond was severed and Tahani went to live in the pits away from Kaeylin while she went to start her new life with her 'other half'. If Tahani could, she would do everything in her power to see her sister once more. Tahani had to confess that Kaeylin had a good reason to believe in humanity.

There were some decent people.

The fall breeze brushed Tahani's face. She loved the cooler weather. Tahani remembered back in her younger years when she, Kaeylin and Zanobi would go outside and play in the snow at the first signs of winter. All those years ago, they were so happy.

Zanobi...

Tahani's mood dropped at the thoughts of her best friend, wherever he was. Two weeks had gone by and there was still no sign of him. Sometimes Tahani wondered if he even left, if his betrayal had only been a dream.

At first, Tahani tried to deny it as much as possible. Zanobi was her best friend; they'd known each other for decades. But she knew what his power was; the ability to body jump and learn of anyone's information. He took over her body to find out about Azu and if Tahani knew about it. Then when he realised that she was useless, he used her body to kill Seth's parents.

Angrily, Tahani clenched her fists. If she ever saw Zanobi again, then he was going to hear it.

As she strolled alone into one of the forest shortcuts, Tahani stopped when she recognised one of the activated bear traps. It was the only thing that she needed, and with the trap, she could find out who was responsible. With observant eyes, Tahani scanned the trap and frowned when she spotted the familiar marking.

Takon informed her about the hunters, but she didn't expect them to set out illegal traps for them-

'It looks like someone is having ugly thoughts.'

Tahani recognised that voice. Her body tensed as she looked behind her.

Midnight eyes locked with the bright blue as Tahani got to her feet. 'What the hell do ya want Charmi?'

'Is that the way you greet your dear friend?' Charmi wondered innocently. 'Oh wait. You don't have any friends.'

'I probably have more than ya think, bitch.'

The look on Charmi's face turned dark. 'That's right; I only have my family now. What happened to yours?' Tahani felt her body go stiff with rage as she saw the images in her eyes. The memories she forced herself to block out of her mind as they resurfaced to the present.

She remembered the smell of rotting flesh as she gazed at their figures. Her parents had their clothes stripped off with humiliation, but their dead, bleeding bodies hung with nooses around their necks, right in front of town, which only meant that they bled to death. The last thing that Tahani was told to do was to protect Kaeylin, before the siblings went into hiding and lost their parents. For days, the sisters searched without rest, and they succeeded.

Tahani recalled the tears stinging in her young eyes as she stared at her parents and the loud horrified screams from her little sister. The humans had heard them and chased them into an alley, where they were saved by Zanobi.

'Get out of my damn head!' Tahani growled, snapping herself out of the recurring nightmare. 'I've already asked ya, Charmi – what the hell do ya want?'

'I want what every Forte desires,' Charmi answered simply with a shrug. 'I want to feed my bloodlust with vengeance. Remember when we were friends, but you ran and hid the second that your parents told you to? What happened to me?'

'How should I know? Do I look like a bloody mind reader?'

The look on Charmi's face indicated that she was ready to murder. 'You know what happened to us. Humans treated us like vermin and wanted to exterminate us.'

'We all have our problems,' Tahani declared with a snort as she crossed her arms. Charmi returned a similar glare with confidence. 'I'm just not gonna stick around here without gaining my own information. So ya gonna tell me? Where's Lucien and Zanobi?'

When Charmi fell into a deadly silence, Tahani felt annoyance lick her spine. Tahani knew Charmi better than most people – Charmi had the fearless attitude of a Rosa. Something that was dangerous and admirable at the same time.

Finally, Charmi smiled darkly. 'I haven't seen them since I ditched them. Even if I did tell you of our hideout, it would've been long deserted.'

Tahani glared at the woman. 'Perfect,' she muttered sarcastically. 'What a coincidence that ya ditched them after Zanobi revealed himself.'

'But honestly – your goals are nothing but a lost cause,' Charmi admitted simply as she shrugged her shoulders. 'Zanobi and Lucien are searching for the remainder of the stones, so they can reunite the Corvena... They already have

Viri – it won't be long until they find Rel and Verm. They need you for Azu.'

'So they can unleash the four rectocs? That sounds like the dumbest plan ever.'

'Well who am I to judge the greatness of Zanobi and Lucien?' Charmi questioned sarcastically, sparing a glance at her red polished nails. 'I'm against them as much as you are – but it doesn't mean I'm on your side. I'm simply finding Rel after killing Brodie Forte and his miserly band.'

'Brodie...' Tahani scowled. 'What the hell do ya have against him?'

'Don't you remember that the Forte brat was the reason Brad died?' Then it clicked. Zanobi had told her about the day that Charmi and her brothers came to attack Laria.

'Of course, you're lucky that you don't really have the connection with Brodie.' Charmi turned away from Tahani and walked away harmlessly. 'However, you didn't help us when we needed you most, Ungue dux – you're just as bad as Brodie Forte.'

Suddenly Tahani could remember it all in a flash.

'Get out of my head Charmi or I swear that I will tear yer throat out!' Tahani snarled at the other shifter's back as the memories flashed in her mind again. Her dead parents, the smell of flesh killing her senses and she remembered the screams of Kaeylin.

Charmi turned away, leaving Tahani trapped within her thoughts.

For a moment, Tahani thought it was happening to her again. The forest and Charmi's retreating form melted away and she was back in that place. She let out a startled yelp when she turned to see that little Kaeylin was at her side, crying for the loss of their parents. She felt the sickening thrill of alarm as she looked back to see her dead parents.

'No, this can't be happening again,' Tahani said, shaking her head madly. As she tried to deny it, she felt the familiar tremors that she felt on that day.

'Tahani?!'

The dux found her vision of her history fading, but it was only replaced with darkness. Uneasiness was in her system when Tahani felt someone lift her in the air. She shuddered at the darkness, recalling every detail of her little sister's frightened features. 'Kaeylin...'

CHAPTER 4

'So tell me, what's got you in a weird mood?'

Jenna raised her head out of hiding from the table and her brown eyes met with the pair that made her heart flutter. So much for hiding in Silver Roots, the most public place in town.

'You've got me in this mood,' Jenna replied numbly and went back to hiding. 'Now, I'm going to mope here like I plan to, and you are going to go away-' When Jenna stopped, she saw that Taro's attention wasn't on her, but rather on something behind her.

She was alarmed when he took the seat in front of her. His eyes hardened as he addressed to her. 'How long has that guy been watching you?'

Jenna had to confirm this herself, turning slowly to see that there was a man sitting in the back of the Silver Roots. He looked like he was a few years older with sandy blonde curls, lightly coloured skin and his eyes seemed blue. Slowly the man noticed that Jenna was looking back at him and flashed a smile, showing of the dimples in his cheeks.

The female forced a nervous smile before turning to Taro. 'I don't know...' she admitted with concern, refusing to look back. 'I've been here since I finished school – I'm not sure about him.'

'Come on – I'm taking you home.' Taro stood up to his seat and grabbed Jenna's hand. As Taro dragged her out of the diner, Jenna's curious gaze went back to the mysterious male. He was still watching. The man didn't make any movements to follow along, calmly remaining in his seat.

Jenna returned her attention to Taro's new attitude. She still didn't trust this personality change. They both slipped out of the Silver Roots and Taro led her to an old truck.

As Taro pulled out the car keys from his pockets, Jenna was stunned into silence and watched. What about her car? Her eyes briefly landed on her car at the front of the Silver Roots, almost refusing to leave. Taro opened the door of his side and impatiently glared at her.

'Jenna.' His voice wasn't angry with her, she realised. He was angry at her hesitation. 'We'll pick up your car in the morning.'

She entered the car and flinched as he slammed the door. He started up the truck and drove with a grunt. Taro drove a bit too recklessly for Jenna's liking. When he went through a red light, Jenna started to panic.

'Taro.' The quarterback didn't respond to her. 'Taro, stop and look at me!' she snapped, forcing him to look over at her for a second. 'You're scaring me.'

'We had to get away from there,' Taro retorted curtly. 'That man wasn't hu-!' In an instant, the car jerked in another direction. With panic, Jenna looked up to spot a canine figure in the middle of the road.

Taro cursed and swerved out of the way with his foot slammed onto the brakes. The truck lost control of its steering, running off the road and grazing a tree. A loud bang rang off in the background and Jenna cried out. They both waited for a jerk of an impact, but instead the vehicle rumbled to an abrupt stop, just short of the trees ahead of them. Taro was silent beside her. He looked over, his blue eyes flashed with relief to see that she was unharmed before he looked down. Jenna was almost tempted to ask about his confusion, then realised that she had her hand wrapped around Taro's forearm.

'Are you alright?' Taro asked after what seemed to be an eternity of silence.

Jenna pulled away as she nodded. 'Yeah,' she whispered

and the memories of the wolf suddenly flashed in her head. 'Taro – that wolf!' She turned to see where the animal was, but it was gone.

Scanning his surroundings from his seat, Taro cursed again. 'Damn mangy mutt.' It seemed that this newfound anger was a common thing for the quarterback nowadays. 'Where the heck did it run off to?'

'I don't know...' Jenna whispered and settled into her seat.

'Hey,' Taro whispered and took her hand again. Jenna wanted to pull back, however she was frozen. It was strangely comforting. 'We're alright – that's what matters.'

He was right. That could have been a lot worse. Finally, Jenna pulled away from Taro's hold and she frowned. 'About before... when you said something about the man...'

Instantly Taro moved his face away. 'Forget about what I said,' the quarterback encouraged, and Jenna was tempted to protest. What was Taro hiding?

***

Maya flicked through the pages of the old book carefully. Her body was stretched lazily on her bed with a bored yawn. Each page she scanned was with a keen eye, but it mostly said nonsense.

Nothing got her attention.

After scanning another page, Maya gave up. All she wanted to know was more about the shifters and the way that they become one. Ever since realising that she was a descendant of skin walkers from the Navajo tribe that could have the potential to transform, Maya had been researching ways to do it, but little of what she'd found could be called reliable information.

It may have been two weeks since Maya learned about the supernatural world, but she was miles away from understanding it. She was meant to be a shifter, like the rest of her friends. But being a shifter... or having the instincts of one made her frustrated. She wasn't afraid of it or of her friends – not one bit, but it stuck to her.

Her mind went to Seth, who was a part of it ever since he was born. Before they became friends, he kept away from other people and Maya never questioned why. Maya didn't know how she felt; she wanted space and she hated being useless. If she hadn't turned then her life would be in constant danger.

Now that she knew he was a shifter, it made a bit more sense that Seth stayed away from them. Maya remembered the day they were assigned to be partners on a science project. They were awkward together at first but then Maya opened up to him. She was struggling to figure out the missing link and she worked up the guts to ask him.

After Seth helped her, Maya began to push for conversation and surprisingly, he replied to her. They were short and curt responses, but she was determined to figure out the mysterious, anti-social boy. She didn't spill out her life story, but she managed to have a decent conversation with the guy.

Since then, Maya learned that Seth wasn't a jerk; he was just distant and withdrawn from human contact. All this time, Seth had truly been alone.

'Maya!'

Her grandmother's voice came from the living room. Maya rose up from the bed, closing the book with a lazy sigh and grabbed her hooded jacket. As she exited the room, Maya noticed that Adelle was standing from the front door.

Her formerly white hair was dyed black, with obvious wrinkles on her aged face. Her stony grey eyes were filled with wisdom and the familiar warmth.

'What's up?' Maya wondered. She paused when she saw that past her grandmother, there was a familiar face standing at the door. Slowly her smile dropped.

Seth stood by the front with a calculating look in his eyes. 'Maya.'

In return, Maya felt alarm bells ringing in the back of her head. 'Seth.' The whisper unknowingly escaped her lips as she met his dark eyes. 'What are you doing here? I thought I told you to leave me alone.'

'And I thought I told you that I'm not that kind of person,' he responded in a cool tone and Maya glared. Why was he stubborn now of all times? A small smirk formed on his face for a moment before it dropped. 'May I come in?'

Before Maya could refuse his request, Adelle chuckled lightly. 'Of course, you can.' Her grandmother offered a smile to Maya who glared back. 'He is such a pleasant boy, Maya. Why haven't I seen him in a while?'

'He was busy,' Maya told her, and crossed her arms. 'And I thought after the whole Tahani incident – you would be less trusting.'

'But Seth was there to help us!' Adelle told her and Maya felt exhausted. Ever since Seth first came to Maya's house, Adelle had been fascinated with him. It was a strange behaviour; she wasn't like this with her other friends.

'It doesn't mean I want to talk to him every minute of the day!' Maya exclaimed, throwing her arms up in frustration. In the corner of her eyes, she saw Seth flinch at her sharp tone. A part of her felt bad, pushing him away. It wasn't like he did anything wrong, she just couldn't help it.

'Did he hurt you?' Adelle's features turned stern. 'If that's the case then-'

'It's not that.' Maya cut her grandmother off. 'I just… need to read.'

As Maya looked at Seth, she saw his raised eyebrow and questioning stare. It was almost as if he was questioning her newfound hobby. Little did they know, she was telling the truth. However Maya didn't blame him for questioning her reading, it was something she hardly did unless the book was interesting enough. Not many books were interesting to her.

'It won't be long,' Seth finally said and Maya tilted her head. 'I promise, it's important.'

That got Maya's attention. Seth only referred a few things as important – unless it had to do with their friendship. If it had to do with their current situation, Seth would've mentioned it at Brodie's – but there was only way to find out.

A soft groan left her lips. 'Fine, come in.'

Maya led Seth to her room, ignoring the unsettling stir in her gut. She peaked over her shoulder to see him observe the photo frames by the walls. That was when she felt lightheaded.

The night of the bonfire, when his eyes were predatory and filled with anger. It was a side of him that she never thought that she would see. She was shocked that he was able to hide the rage with such a calm persona. Seth was like he was a different person when he was angry.

She wasn't afraid of him despite of it. Then again, she wasn't one to fear much, except for the people she cared about.

When they entered her room, Seth hovered around the books with a raised eyebrow.

'I wouldn't expect for this to interest you,' he declared and flicked a page. 'You won't find anything in these books, shifters intentionally wrote lies. Proper journals would be the best way to go.'

Leaning on the wall of her room, Maya scoffed. 'I doubt that's what you wanted to talk to me about.'

'You are correct,' Seth answered and sat on her bed. 'A girl was killed last night. We found her in Brodie's front yard,' Seth announced in a cool tone and Maya froze. 'We don't know who killed her yet.'

'This was the same party I left?' Maya asked, realising how lucky she was. She couldn't imagine how Brodie felt upon finding a victim in his own home. He nodded and Maya wished she was sitting on the bed at the moment. 'I'm sorry for you to see that.'

For a moment, Maya thought she saw a change in his emotionless expression. It disappeared before she had a chance to confirm it. 'It was not the first and it certainly won't be the last.'

Was he referring to his parents?

'I just wanted to let you know – just be careful,' Seth said after a moment of silence. 'I apologise for antagonising you. I get why you want to push yourself away from me, and I understand what it's like to be powerless.'

'Then you probably know what I want to know,' Maya told

him and this time, she caught Seth's expression morph into shock. 'Laria told me about shifters living in this world, but she never told me how to become one.'

'Maya-' Seth tried to speak.

'Just listen,' Maya said and approached him. When she sat next to him, she gestured to the books with her. 'This is why I'm reading. I just want to know if there's a way. I'm not a damsel in distress, I don't want people to get hurt because of my powerless state. Just tell me what you know.'

Seth let out a deep breath with a shake of his head. 'And they call me stubborn.' His mutter confused Maya. Asides from her, who called Seth stubborn? 'I'll help you.' That caught her off guard.

'Wait, I have still at least a minute of my speech,' she said before dismissing it. 'It's really important to me Seth, I hope you know that.'

'I know,' Seth replied to her, 'The only person I know who's in your situation was Laria and she suffered through her mother's death. I will try to see if there's another way because I couldn't bear to harm an innocent person.'

Maya offered the best grin she could muster, yet it failed miserably when she found herself trapped in Seth's dark eyes. Leaning away from him, Maya stretched her arms.

'I guess this means I can't be a jerk to you anymore,' Maya told him. 'It was fun while it lasted.'

Seth narrowed his eyes. 'That's not funny.'

Instead of dismissing the comment, Maya realised her opportunity to enjoy every bit of it. 'Hey, you barged into my home and wouldn't take no for an answer – this is the least you deserve.'

He didn't seem pleased, but seemed to accept it. 'I am sorry. I should have considered your concerns earlier.'

'Water under the bridge,' Maya told him with a shrug. If Seth was willing to teach her, she would let it drop. For now. 'But I won't let that slide a second time, so if I tell you to back off – you back off.'

***

Laria answered the mansion door and swung it open for Hugh Salve, the Medicinae Dux to enter.

'Good afternoon, Miss Laria,' Hugh greeted and spared a glance into the mansion. 'You have a beautiful home – the angels are very lucky.'

'Thanks for coming over,' Laria replied and she gestured for him to enter the building. Hugh followed along with her wishes, his medical bag hanging over his shoulder from a strap. 'I don't know what happened.'

'Show me,' the dux insisted and Laria went to one of the lounge rooms. On one of the leather couches, Tahani was lying unconscious with a blanket over her body. Behind her, Brodie and Jason hovered over her, but they were silent. Who could've hurt Tahani so easily? When Laria tried to head back to the mansion, she found Tahani's body in the middle of the forest floor.

It took Laria a while to get her to safety of the Ladas mansion. While Laria knew some shifters were naturally stronger, her powers weren't at that level. Instead, she went for plan B – calling Brodie and Jason. Convincing the brothers to help her together was a miracle but it was done.

As they reached the mansion, Laria went through Tahani's phone to call Hugh. It was a good thing that he was one of her most common contacts.

Hugh frowned and went to approach the unconscious dux as he unpacked a torch. Just as he reached out to touch his patient, Tahani reacted first and lunged for Hugh. She went for his throat but he was faster.

'That's enough, Ungue Dux,' Hugh said evenly as he held her wrist back. Laria was stunned to see Tahani pull her hand back to apologise for reacting. 'It's fine – just a natural reaction from you as usual. If anything, your common attacks have improved my reflexes.'

So this wasn't the first time Hugh found her unconscious?

Slowly, Tahani regained a sense of her surroundings, and a curse left her lips. She sat back on the couch and placed her face in her hands stressfully.

'Tahani...?' Laria asked curiously and Tahani silently looked at her. 'What happened? I called Hugh in case there were internal injuries.'

'I'm fine,' Tahani confessed and she looked at her hands. They were shaking. 'But I had a run-in with Charmi.'

It was like a bucket of icy cold water dumped itself on Laria. Tahani had encountered Charmi? Laria was familiar with her. In the corner of her eye, she realised Jason clench his jaw and look away from her.

A lot happened that day, Laria wondered if the thoughts of that kept him up at night.

It was a day of discovery, of Lux and Brodie's first kill.

'Did she tell you want she wanted?' Brodie broke his silence and he got close to Tahani. The annoyance overcame Tahani's face. 'Tell me!'

'Calm down hothead,' Tahani grumbled back without hesitation. It caused Brodie to falter, but his face remained as a scowl.

'Well, as a Forte, Charmi is all into the vengeance stuff,' Tahani explained curtly. Laria knew that. 'She wants you guys dead.'

'So she's after me?' Laria asked, with disbelief. That day haunted her mind when she saw Brodie mercilessly kill Brad and dump his body. The girl from the party was just a message that she was beginning her plan. She could still remember the angry voice of Charmi in the back of her mind.

This is not the last of us Brodie Forte — I don't care if the leader killed your father, I will be the one who kills you.

And it wasn't only Laria. 'We have to warn our friends,' she declared with a serious glare. As someone who went up against Charmi, she recalled the brutality of the shifter and her brother.

'And we will,' Tahani promised sternly. Hugh looked just as serious as Tahani at the moment. She got to her feet. 'I have to report this to Takon... Human lives are at stake here and even worse...' Tahani's voice trailed off and her eyelids fluttered as she struggled to retain her focus.

Laria reached out for the collapsing dux and yelled out for her. 'Tahani!' Hugh beat Laria to the punch and he grabbed Tahani as her body fell. 'What's wrong with her?'

'Argh...' Tahani grunted in protest and tried to fight against Hugh's hold. He kept still, patiently holding her upright. Tahani chuckled in denial and showed a faint grin. 'It's nothing, Hugh I can handle a bit of a dizzy spell.'

A frown deepened on Laria's face. 'Dizzy spell?'

'You weren't told?' Hugh asked, and he shook his head with a deep sigh. 'I suppose I shouldn't be surprised, she has been unwell lately. Sleeping patterns have been off, she hasn't been watching her health.'

'So much for the right of my privacy,' Tahani grumbled, and rubbed her face. 'Being a doctor means ya don't go spilling anything to do with my issues.'

'You may have that right to privacy, unless I have reason to worry about your safety.' Hugh replied, as he assisted her to the couch. 'You've been through a lot, I'm surprised you haven't gone to the specialist I referred you too.'

Tahani's eyes narrowed and she avoided Hugh's stare. 'I don't need any help... I'm fine. I got shot, happens all the time in this country.'

'You know I wasn't referring to your physical injuries,' Hugh told her. The idea of Tahani suffering mentally never occurred to Laria, especially since she had her own issues.

Much to Laria's surprise though, Tahani rolled her eyes. 'I said I'm fine, I don't need to talk to anyone about how I nearly died while my best friend ditched me. We have other issues to get through – like Charmi.'

Hugh's expression became unreadable and for the life of her, Laria couldn't tell what he was thinking. The only thing Laria could see was the unconvinced expression in his dark eyes.

'As your doctor and friend, I don't believe you. Unfortunately, I cannot force you to go – but my door is always open.' Slowly he turned to face Laria. 'I do appreciate you calling me, if anything else happens – let me know.'

'I will,' Laria thanked him. Seeing Tahani on the ground was a reminder that a lot had happened with them. While it seemed like Tahani wasn't going to get herself help, the best thing Laria could do was support her. 'I'll see you next time.'

'See ya, Doc,' Tahani muttered and waved a hand. 'I owe ya one.'

Hugh paused, but did not say anything. The pause was brief, and with that he left the group on their own. As soon as Laria heard the door close, she clenched her fist and tried to keep civil.

She had to walk on eggshells, Laria was perfectly aware of how easy it was for Tahani to snap back. 'You should've told me about it, Tahani…'

'What difference does it make?' Tahani said, meeting Laria's stare. 'Ya know that Charmi is our current issue. She's hunting the rest of ya down because of what ya pal Brodie did to her brother. If she's around, and so is Nick – so ya must be careful.'

'I don't regret my choice,' Brodie told Tahani. 'The man mocked my dad, he had to pay.'

'For once I agree with Brodie,' Jason added with a shrug. 'The guy was about to kill me, who knows what would've happened.'

'And the rest of these people's blood are on yer hands,' Tahani responded and Brodie flinched in shock.

However the shock shifted into anger as his eyes brightened. 'I won't let that happen-!'

'That's enough!' Laria cut her friend off. 'It's unfortunately happened. For now, we need to rest up – because it will still be a problem tomorrow. We'll talk it about it later.'

'I guess,' Jason said, 'I need to go back anyways – my day has been long as hell.'

Brodie grunted. 'I know we'll get to the bottom of it.'

'Thanks again for coming,' Laria told them as they went to leave. Jason was the only one who turned to Laria with a brief smile while Brodie waved. Once the door closed, Laria suddenly remembered that she still had to give Jason's present however decided to wait.

Something was bothering him.

'Since when did ya act like a leader?' Tahani wondered and Laria took a deep breath.

'We're not talking about me,' Laria told her firmly. 'I mean it, you went through something a while back.'

'Seriously? This chat again?' Tahani shot Laria a look of disbelief. 'Come on kiddo, I ain't one to crumble so easily. I told ya we need to worry about Charmi. She's the threat at the moment.'

Hesitance coloured Laria's tone. 'But what if-?'

'Don't worry about me!' Tahani cut her off, scowling. Staring at Tahani with bewildered expression, Laria had to resist arguing back. Why was Tahani the stubborn one? 'If I had to worry every time I had an issue, I wouldn't get anything done.' Finally she stood up again.

'Where are you going?' Laria asked, seeing that Tahani was stretching her arms and heading towards the door.

'Out for a run.' The answer seemed so obvious. 'Yer welcome to join me.'

The last thing Laria wanted was to find an unconscious Tahani once more and she knew convincing Tahani to rest was only going to be a waste of energy. Laria got to her feet with a grumble and followed after the dux.

CHAPTER 5

Jason shot back a glass of whisky, recognising the taste in the back of his mouth. No wonder Brodie enjoyed the drink. Finally comfortable on the couch of Seth's living room, Jason kept his cerulean eyes on the ceiling. Finding the stash that Seth's parents once owned, Jason took advantage of it and drank. His mind was still on the breakup.

Sure, they only dated for two weeks and it wasn't serious, but Jason still cared for Heather. Maybe the true reason for his depression was because he felt so clueless; like he had when he was trying to figure out his father.

Just as Jason prepared to take another drink from his glass, he heard someone knock on the door. He knew it wasn't Heather – but Jason wished it was. With a sluggish groan, Jason pulled himself to his feet and went to the door, only to open it to recognise Laria.

She tilted her head in a confused manner. 'You don't look like yourself.'

Jason noticed that she was eyeing off the drink before he moved it away. 'I just needed some time to think.' He didn't know why she was watching the drink, but he didn't like it. 'Heather and I broke up.'

Taking her attention off the drink, Laria's eyes widened. 'I'm sorry for that. What happened?'

'No idea,' Jason replied, and he took another sip from his drink. Laria's attention followed the glass with a hint of wariness. 'What's with you?'

'Nothing,' said Laria calmly, still eyeing the drink. 'You look like Brodie drinking that.'

'It was my first one, Laria,' Jason confessed and finished his drink. He realised that even underneath the dark trench coat, Laria was shivering. 'Do you want to come inside?'

'Sure,' Laria answered instantly, her eyes darting outside. 'It's starting to get cold.' As Jason allowed her in, he noticed the Laria's cheeks were flushed from the colder weather. Once he closed the door behind her, he went into the kitchen to place his glass in the sink.

He turned to face her. 'Do you want a drink?'

'Look at you,' Laria teased lightly and Jason perked a brow. 'You're sounding more and more like Brodie. Does Seth know about this?'

'Don't say that – if Brodie got word then I would never hear the end of it,' Jason muttered in annoyance. As he pulled out a can of soft drink, she accepted the offer.

'Why are you two so distant?' Laria wondered and it made Jason frown.

To be honest, he didn't know why he was different around Brodie. As a kid, Jason always thought it would've been cool to have a brother. However there was something about Brodie that Jason didn't understand.

'We just don't get along,' Jason finally answered. 'It was like this when we met, remember?'

When she put down the drink, a smirk formed on her face. 'I remember, *Newbie.*'

Again with the teasing tone. He let out a huff and returned the smirk. 'I thought we were over that nickname when we became friends.'

'Nonsense,' Laria cut him off. 'Even in the distant future, you won't be losing that nickname. To me, you'll always be the newbie that knocked me off my feet every time we met.' Slowly, her smile dropped and was replaced with a curious glance. 'Where's Seth? I thought he would've been here with you.'

'He went out to see one of the shifters or something,' Jason answered and borrowed Laria's drink. He needed something sweet after the whisky. She protested with a frown, and Jason chuckled before taking a good mouthful of soda. As soon as he placed it down, Laria snatched the drink back with a glare. 'Besides... couldn't you just check my scent like other shifters do?'

Then Jason noticed the odd response. He raised a suspicious eyebrow as Laria's cheeks flushed in embarrassment. 'I try to not focus on people's scents unless it's important because... Well... it's complicated...'

'How complicated is it to smell someone?'

Laria nearly spat out the drink as her response. Instead, she straightened up and awkwardly cleared her throat.

'Okay,' Laria muttered calmly and exhaled instantly. 'Let's just say... I've gotten a trace of your scent before and I like it. It's a nice smell.'

Now Jason understood why it was complicated. 'Whoa.'

Laria quickly realised what she said and she raised her hands to defend herself. 'It's sort of confusing... you have this nice guy smell about you, like you smell of several colognes since you used to live in the city and with other people... in one way, Brodie's and Seth's scent is closer to the forest since they grew up here. I like their scents as well – ah... that isn't making this conversation better, I'm sorry.'

'No, its fine – seriously,' Jason said with a laugh, scratching the back of his head sheepishly. 'I sort of had it coming since I did ask.'

'Well, let's change the subject.' Laria went into her coat and pulled out a small box. Jason frowned in confusion and he spared her a look to see her smile. 'I didn't get a chance to say happy birthday – Seth and I pitched in together to get you this. That's why I thought it would've been better if he was here.'

If Seth was willing to work with Laria, then it must've been good. Jason forced himself to open the box and alarm hit him when he saw what was inside. 'You two bought this?!' he pulled out the smart watch, admiring the leather bands and silver, circular clockface. Jason turned it on and marvelled as the smaller device lit up in response.

'Seth said you wanted one,' Laria said with a slight shrug.

'I happen to have a good eye for things like that. It's not the newest one in the market, but now you'll get to speak to it like a spy.'

'That wasn't my first thought,' Jason grumbled and went to fiddling the watch. It was asking him to connect with his phone.

'But it was a thought?' Laria suggested with a grin.

With the roll of his eyes, Jason shoved Laria gently. He didn't realise that Laria thought of him that much – though Seth had a hand in it. It seemed strange, Jason wasn't actively looking for smart watches, but this one seemed right for him.

Dealing with his breakup had shoved him down, yet this actually brightened his day. And all he could do was smile. 'This is great, thank you.'

An alarming ring halted the moment and Laria pulled out her phone. She passed the drink to Jason as she went through with the device, her eyes soft until they read the message. Her mood switched instantly and Laria stepped back sternly.

'I have to go,' she said suddenly. 'You need to call Brodie and Seth – tell them that there's an enemy nearby and stay back.'

Immediately, Jason followed Laria and tried to catch up to her as she left the house. 'Hold on Laria-!' The soft contact of Laria's coat hit Jason, forcing him to freeze. He looked at her coat, realising that she threw it at him. Before he could ask her, her form disappeared and he silently cursed.

This wasn't the first time Laria tried to chase off outsiders and all those times, Jason happened to be with her. And he wasn't going to start letting her go after them alone. He dumped the coat with his new watch on the counter and rushed after her. 'Laria!'

***

'Keep focused,' Tara said. Honestly, Brodie didn't expect that his auntie would train him in the middle of the estate's living room but here they were. 'That is the key focus of training the bloodlust.' She prepared to make a hit towards Brodie, and he reacted with his instinct.

He blocked her attack with a forearm, before he pushed it away and used his free arm to go for her throat. She jumped back from his attack and aimed a roundhouse kick towards his head. Just as Brodie prepared to defend himself, he felt his phone vibrate and halted in his movement.

It was the hesitation that stopped Tara from hitting him. Tara scowled and lowered her leg from her nephew. 'You stopped.'

'I just got a message,' Brodie apologised and pulled the phone from the pocket.

Are you sure it's a good idea being relaxed at your estate when your worst nightmare is around?
-C

A grunt of annoyance escaped Brodie's lips. It was like he couldn't lower his guard for a moment. His eyes brightened at the thoughts of killing them and he suddenly headed out of the house.

'Brodie,' Tara spoke warningly and Brodie stopped as he heard his aunt's voice. 'What's going on?'

'Sorry, Aunt Tara,' Brodie said and started to walk out of his house. The thought of Charmi's dead body put an amusing thought to his mind. 'But there's something I have to do.' He immediately left Tara alone in his house as he took off.

Satisfaction bloomed in his chest when Tara didn't pursue him. Everything around him was a blur as he rushed into the forest. As soon as he hit the trees, Brodie caught a sickly-sweet scent that he recognised instantly.

'Well, Brodie — it seems that you're quicker than the last time we spoke.'

Brodie scowled in annoyance, turning to face the caramel haired woman. 'Charmi...'

CHAPTER 6

I would've sworn they were around here somewhere, Laria thought, slowing down in her tracks before she stopped and listened out for any unusual sounds. With a curse of irritation, Laria was about to pull off her shirt to shift when she heard something within the trees.

'Now what do we have here? I think it's a lost little sheep.' Immediately Laria turned around and hesitated when she saw an unfamiliar man. Had an unregistered shifter targeted her? However she did recognise Jason being held by the enemy.

'Jason!'

Her friend coughed to reply just as Laria clenched her fist together in anger. 'Laria, don't worry about me!' He grunted as the shifter tightened the vicious hold on the throat.

Laria's eyes flashed amber warningly. 'Damn you! Let him go – you have no business with him!'

'You forgot to say please,' the shifter said with a sneer. He let Jason go however, startling the pair with the unexpected action. 'I do not care for the boy at the moment; I just want to fight the last Alfero! No powers, no weapons, just our bloodied fists!'

Laria could hear the bloodlust's laugh in excitement and a chill went down her spine at the thought of fighting once more. She couldn't do it. The best chance they had was to get Jason away.

'I won't waste our time fighting,' Laria said firmly, watching as the enemy shifter's grin morphed into a frown. 'Go pick on someone else.'

'I should be clear,' the shifter said coldly. 'I wasn't giving you a choice!' He ran at her and before Laria could move, she felt his body ram into her. The shifter hit her like a truck, slamming her against a tree. 'You will fight me.'

Let me kill him.

Laria's eyes snapped open. Of course Lux wanted nothing more than to murder the shifter in front of her.

'Screw you,' Laria answered back to the voices. 'I'm not going to-' Before she could finish her sentence, Laria was flung from her spot and sent crashing face-first into the dirt. It was almost like another day of training with Tahani, only that her life wasn't on the line.

'Laria!' She heard Jason call out in the distance, followed by a curse of anger.

'Listen you little brat!' Laria felt the pressure of his boot against her back. 'Charmi paid me handsomely to get me to hunt you and this boy down. She probably thought neither of you weren't worth the time. It's not just the money I just want – I want the thrill of fighting someone, because I want to be the one who kills Lucien's only daughter.'

Lucien.

Laria clenched her fists to the side, silently cursing to herself. She didn't even have to know him, just his mere existence put a target on her head. All the more reason why she had to be the one to stop Lucien.

'I don't care,' Laria answered the shifter as she freed her face from the ground. 'I'm not going to pander to your needs and fight you.' He didn't get the consequences of her fighting. Lux would take over without hesitation – the only thing Laria could do was not fight back, to stop the bloodlust from taking over.

And Luc knew that. *Coward.*

'It seems like I won't be able to convince you,' the shifter muttered in disappointment. Finally the pressure on her back disappeared and Laria got the chance to push herself onto her hands and knees. 'I ain't leaving without my pay, so I will be killing you both here today.'

If not her it meant – 'Jason!' Laria felt her body shift without command. The transformation into the grey wolf was an excruciating experience. The bones snapped into place after Laria felt a strange tickle over her skin. Her body changed shape as her face stretched into a muzzle and her eyes changed from chestnut to amber.

Thankfully her clothes were big enough to slip off her as she transformed. Had she been wearing her summer clothes it would've been a different story.

Her legs sprang from their position and with a growl leaving her lips, the shifter spun around to face her. His grin returned. 'Not what I had in mind, but better than earlier.'

Behind the shifter, Laria glanced at Jason. His jaw slightly dropped and now that Laria thought about it, this was the first time he'd saw her transform. Though being fair, Laria had only shown Tahani this form while she trained.

However she redirected her attention on the enemy in front of her. *I won't let you touch him,* Laria said to him telepathically. If Laria tried to put her thoughts into words, all they would be were growls. She had to make sure that this man heard her.

'If you think that you stand a chance against me, then you're sorely mistaken.' The shifter's eyes brightened into an icy blue. 'But I'll give you points for effort.'

Laria knew he was right. Just like with Nick in the past, she wasn't strong enough to take him on. It just meant that Laria had to survive long enough for backup.

I hope someone will come soon. Laria thought to herself, then forced herself to run. In a blink of an eye, she ran at him with baring teeth. She kicked off the ground for an extended leap and clamped her jaws into his arm.

The metallic taste of blood filled her mouth as she heard a cry of anger. Laria's eyes narrowed and she tightened her grip as the shifter tried to swing her around. He didn't seem like she was holding him down, despite holding his arm down.

'I have to admire your idea of bloodshed,' the shifter confessed, before using his injured arm to slam her against the tree. 'But it's not enough.' The sudden pain caused Laria to release him with a yelp. He used the chance to move his arm away and let gravity take a hold on Laria as she collapsed to the ground once more.

She recovered from the attack to shoot a glare towards him. He was strong, probably stronger than what Edward was. The only chance she had was to make sure she stayed conscious long enough.

Using this chance, Laria dodged a swipe from him. With the shifter's injury, he was slower which was an advantage for her.

I can't underestimate him though. The thought came back to Laria, and he whirled around to face her once more. Maybe I can get him away. Hesitantly, she looked towards Jason. Then again, he followed me out in the first place – so running may be a waste of energy.

'Are you done planning over there?' The shifter demanded with a sneer. 'I hope that isn't all you have, it hardly feels like a warmup.'

Laria growled to colour her irritation. *He's annoying.* It was time to move. As the shifter made a dash at her, Laria sidestepped him and kept her distance. In the back of her mind, gratitude flooded her. She had to definitely thank Tahani for the training lessons, even if they ended with her on the ground.

'This is tiring.' The shifter suddenly redirected his attention to a fallen log. Laria stumbled in her step as she saw him lift the object of his interest. With bark cracking under his hand, the log itself was thick, at least reaching his height. 'I know I wasn't going to rely on the elements around me, but I'm done playing your game.'

With a yell, he hurled it towards her and Laria regained her sense of movement. As she dodged the crushing log smash the trees behind her, the awareness came back to Laria as the shifter was too close for her comfort.

'That's better.'

Before Laria could flee, she felt a hand clamp around the

scruff of her neck. Her legs went limp and Laria gritted her teeth in annoyance. It seemed that being able to transform into a wolf gave her the same wolf weaknesses.

If he hadn't just thrown a log at her, she would've been shocked that he could lift her with such ease.

The shifter met Laria's stare with a grin. 'Got you, little wolf.'

Laria growled, but she couldn't fight against the hold. *Then stop talking and finish it already.*

'Believe me… I plan to kill you now.' Immediately, the shifter slammed her into the ground and Laria let out a yelp. He approached her body and crouched beside her. 'Nothing personal… I'm just doing this for money.'

Laria squeezed her eyes shut, cursing her luck. She didn't want to die, after everything she went through, Laria didn't want it to end. Jason was still with her, she had to protect him!

Then stop being a coward and let me out! Lux shouted from her cage. The thought of allowing Lux out, filtered Laria's mind. This mess could be over before it began and all Laria had to do was allow Lux to be free.

But at what price?

Laria would lose another moment of her humanity. If Lux were to finish the shifter off, the death would be another body that Laria saw each night. The shifter that she didn't even know the name of would haunt her.

But it would save Jason. His safety meant everything to her and Laria couldn't allow anyone else get hurt because of her.

I told you that you need me, Lux continued to talk to her. In her mind's eye, Laria could only see the bloodlust coaxing her. *Unlock my cage, let me take over…*

Laria felt the bars of Lux's cage weakening with each second. The excitement grew from Lux and it return, self-loathing came from Laria.

However a shout of agony suddenly stopped the cage from breaking down. Laria snapped from her trance and shook herself to discharge the previous thoughts.

Had it been a second later…

Laria didn't want to think about it. Her attention went to the source of the cry, when it dawned on her that the shifter that previously had her trapped was holding his stomach with blood pooling from his hands.

Behind the shifter, was Jason with not so human eyes. With his eyes normally blue, they were brown – exactly like Brodie's when he was using his power. The anger was clear in his eyes and Laria recognised the sight.

Jason's bloodlust finally revealed itself.

'You have to excuse the time it took me to step into action,' Jason said coldly. Laria flinched when his eyes flickered towards her. 'But I don't like showing myself, I only do it when I have to.'

The thought struck Laria like a bolt of lightning. This was Jason's bloodlust. Seeing the lack of emotion on his face was a foreign concept for Laria.

'Jason…?' Laria whispered, suddenly realising that she had returned to her human form. It must've been when she was in the trance.

'Jason isn't here right now,' the bloodlust form of Jason told her. 'My name is Ultio, Jason's bloodlust. He couldn't bear the thought of losing you – so now he's taking a break from the action.'

This was the first time Laria witnessed another bloodlust speak to her. Ultio seemed different from Lux – while they broke out when they had to, Lux usually attacked without talking.

'Put some clothes on,' Ultio told her firmly and focused his attention on the shifter. 'I will kill him.'

'Wait…' Laria clenched her fist and scowled. 'I can't let you kill him! This isn't something Jason would want.'

'Do you really think I care about what he would want?' A scoff left Ultio's lips, a strange action coming from someone that looked like Jason. 'Besides, I know Jason better than you do – no matter how strong your bond is. This is something he wants, especially if it means never seeing you in that state again.'

He felt that way? Laria couldn't think of anything to say. If it were true, it meant that Jason's bloodlust was even stronger than hers. Why would he willingly let his bloodlust free if this was what it meant? *Probably the same reason why I was about to.*

'I'm impressed,' the shifter confessed with a snarl. He ripped the branch from his back. 'But it won't be enough – your bloodlust is new. Your power will be weak.' The shifter charged towards Ultio with a yell.

This was wrong, watching Jason – Ultio fight for her. The last thing Laria wanted was for Jason to lose his humanity over her.

Yet she was too afraid to move.

As Ultio promised, the fight was over quickly. He ducked to slip past the shifter's first attack, causing the shifter to spin to face Ultio once more. Ultio immediately stretched his hand out to grab the enemy's throat.

As the shifter choked in Ultio's grip, Laria forced herself to stand with shaky legs. It couldn't be something she allowed, no matter how terrified she felt.

If she managed to get through to him, then Jason could stop himself from making a mistake that would cost him. 'Jason.'

'I told you, Jason is not here.' Ultio didn't look away from his goal. 'Just because I won't kill you, it won't stop me from breaking an arm of yours.'

'I can't let him suffer for my fear,' Laria begged to the bloodlust. 'Please, Jason, hear me.'

Anger flashed in the bloodlust's eyes. 'Jason will not come back until I've done what I promised. Now put on some clothes!'

'Not until Jason comes back to me!' Laria argued and she stepped towards Ultio cautiously. 'Please Jason…'

Ultio didn't answer back to her. The only thing Laria could hear was the weakened wheeze from the other shifter. However it only took a moment for Ultio to redirect his energy to slamming the shifter into the ground.

'No!' Laria cried out, realising that the force crushed the shifter's windpipe. Just how strong was Jason's bloodlust? There was no way it made sense. Why did she allow this to happen?

As Laria cradled her bare body, Ultio turned away from

her. 'Jason can return to you now.'

How could she look at him in the eye after letting him kill without hesitation?

Immediately, Laria saw the boy in front of her turn. Seeing his blue eyes struck a heavy feeling in her chest. It was worse knowing that despite the events that occurred, Laria was grateful to see him alive.

'Laria…' Jason muttered, he glanced at the body on the ground and stepped back with a sharp exhale. 'I did it…' His voice trembled, however he lost consciousness and fell. Before he hit the ground, Laria caught him and she let out a shaky exhale as she made sure he didn't slip from her grip.

'Jason…' How could I let him do this?

***

Charmi felt a wide sneer draw on her face, recognising Brodie's angry features. It would be his turn to suffer the same things that she had. The loss of her family, he was going to realise the true meaning of vengeance.

In silence she watched him curl his fingers into clenched fists. He probably followed in her own path of bloodlust, though his hatred was mostly fuelled towards Lucien. Yet he was so deep that he would go after the closest connection to the Alfero.

As Charmi smiled, Brodie stiffened in his position and his glare made itself obvious. 'What are you smiling about?'

'My success,' Charmi answered simply and folded her arms over her chest. She saw Brodie's fist clench and her smile widened. 'Honestly, do you think that *you* could handle me on your own? You can't even contain the anger bottling up inside you.'

Brodie clenched his jaw. 'Don't underestimate me.' His eyes brightened as if his bloodlust was seeping out threateningly and Charmi felt the satisfaction lick her spine.

'You don't like it? The fact that you are weaker than everyone else?' She enjoyed torturing Brodie. While Laria was whiney and in denial, Brodie had the angry reaction that

Edward once had. She missed that about him, strangely enough. 'The feeling of hate seeping so much that you're flaring at anyone who so much resembles Lucien.'

Brodie snapped, letting out a roar. He ran over to Charmi with his fists out. 'Shut up!'

As Charmi dodged the fist sailing through the air, she snickered and grabbed his arm when it shot past her head. With her arm locked around his, she could easily dislocate it. For a moment, Brodie's surprise stopped him and Charmi pulled him off his feet to slam him into the ground.

'See, Brodie?' Her voice was soft. In a matter of seconds, Brodie had been easily pinned due to his anger. 'No match for someone like me with that anger, you're better off taking out that anger on the one you really hate.'

'Screw you,' Brodie spat and struggled in her hold. 'I want you to die more than the others... and then I will kill Lucien!'

'Really now?' Charmi saw what ran through his eyes. 'You are aware of my power, right? To unblock all those concealed thoughts – do you remember when you were drunk and you had that fight with Laria?' Brodie's eyes narrowed. 'I dare you to look me in the eyes and say you're still not tempted to kill her in order to stop her father's plans.'

Brodie hesitated and Charmi smiled cruelly. Her plan was already locked in motion; if Brodie were to snap then it wasn't going to be in front of her but the last Alfero.

However, Charmi wasn't expecting anyone to approach. She felt something hit her stomach, throwing her off Brodie's form. Charmi growled when she recovered from the attack and she shot up to glare at Seth Laurence.

Seth remained cool and collected, just like the last time they met. The look that he had was rather a neutral glance, like one would give to a mere stranger. His bloodlust wasn't even close to spilling. He lacked Brodie's uncontrolled anger.

'Charmi,' he said calmly. A brick wall had more emotion than this boy.

'And here I thought you'd forgotten me,' she replied with a sneer. 'Nice to see you here.' Her mercenary should've found

Laria Alfero by now… or the human boy at least. She only hoped that he finished them off quickly.

'What are your intentions?' Seth questioned, folding his arms over his chest.

Charmi scoffed at his lame attempts at interrogation. He wasn't the talking type – he should clearly stay quiet. It was strange of how guarded he appeared, despite keeping his distance. Honestly, it was smart – compared to Brodie's sloppy posture. 'Why don't you read my mind? Or is that mind reading crap just all talk?'

'As I assumed,' Seth replied calmly and shared a look with Brodie. As Brodie glared back at Charmi, Seth's position turned more defensive. 'You Fortes have a terrible knack of vengeance. I won't let you hurt any of Brodie's friends.'

A smile twitched on her face. 'You don't include yourself?' she wondered, reading through his concealed memories. Seth stiffened when he realised what she was doing. 'You've felt abandoned, that your parents didn't care about you.' The lack of Seth's response made Charmi continue, 'and that one thing that bothered you... the one thing that they always hid from you.'

Seth's brows deepened into a scowl and his eyes narrowed 'Be quiet.' His stoic tone wasn't fooling anyone. It was easy to see what his mask was failing to hide. He a sharp breath and he took a small step towards her. But Charmi knew that mentioning Seth's parents wasn't enough to push him over the edge.

They weren't the ones he cared for most.

'I know it, Seth,' Charmi taunted, taking a step towards him in response. 'And I also know that I will kill Maya Rosa right in front of you!' She jumped back, interrupted by dodging the strike from Brodie whose eyes flashed warningly.

'We don't want to hear it!' Brodie told her, preparing for the offensive.

She wanted to continue, but she was foolish to go after Brodie with Seth by his side. It was better to target Brodie without anyone to guide his actions. As much as Charmi hated to admit it, she was unable to fight them without Nick. He was doing his own job, going after Jenna Sommers.

'Very well,' Charmi stated with a smile. 'As much as I've had fun here, I need to leave.' She backed away from the pair and she heard a cry of frustration from Brodie.

'Don't go!' he demanded and he stepped after her. Seth also looked like he was ready to give chase if Charmi ran off. She already had an alternate plan for this.

And just like that, Seth suddenly jerked his head towards Brodie. 'Don't do it!' Did he already know her plan? The telepathy was interesting. 'She's baiting you!'

Despite the warning, Brodie didn't heed Seth's words and Charmi scoffed again. As Brodie rushed at her without hesitation, she grabbed his arm and twisted it back. She turned him with her to face Seth, who froze in place, unwilling to attack while she held Brodie as a shield.

'Listen here and listen well,' Charmi said coldly to the boys. 'I demand Rel. If you don't give me Rel then I will start killing off everyone in this sad town.'

Seth's dark eyes narrowed, as if he recognised it. 'You think that taking Rel and our deaths would stop Lucien's chase after the families? You're delusional.'

'You really don't know,' Charmi realised and for a moment she felt like ending Brodie there. He needed to die for his sins against her family. *No,* she told herself. *We need to stick with the plan.* Flashing a smile towards Seth, Charmi tightened the hold she had on Brodie.

The pop followed by Brodie's agonised screams was enough pleasure for her. Her mind was filled with images of more than screams, but she shoved the thoughts away. She pushed Brodie into the ground and Seth immediately went to aid the reckless boy. Charmi felt the smile crawl in her features and left the pair to recover in the forest.

They didn't give chase, but Charmi preferred that. Her plan would have to wait.

***

'Hold on,' Seth said as he placed his hands firmly on Brodie's currently useless arm. At the sudden contact, Brodie felt the stinging sensation and winced. His shoulder felt like it was on fire. He silently swore to himself that he was going to be the one that killed Charmi.

'Hold on?' Seth's comment caught Brodie off guard at first. It took him a moment for the realisation to sink in and he snarled at Seth. 'I can't hold onto anything, it can't move!'

'Stop complaining,' Seth muttered calmly. 'I'm just making sure I get this right.'

Was he for real? 'It's a dislocated shoulder, not the cure for cancer!' He winced again as Seth wriggled his sore arm. 'Cut that out.'

Brodie squeezed his other hand to release the pent-up adrenaline while he heard a deep sigh from Seth. 'Look, I'm not a doctor, just be patient.'

'You said you knew how to do this,' Brodie accused, glaring at the ground.

'I said I *may* be able to do this,' Seth told him. 'I don't do this on a regular basis, the only experience I had was when my older cousin popped my arm. You either can get it done now, or we can drag you to the ER which will take longer. Your choice.'

Cursing his luck, Brodie squeezed his eyes shut. Why did all this crap happen to him?

'Just do it quickly,' Brodie hissed in agony and clenched his jaw. Seth tightened his hold in preparation and Brodie growled in annoyance. 'Seth, I swear just–' Pain exploded into Brodie's arm as Seth roughly shoved his arm back into place. 'Damn it!'

'You have no one to blame but yourself,' Seth stated gruffly and went to check his phone for any other messages. 'You were far too reckless – what happens if she had killed you? Do you think that your friends would've accepted that?'

'She wouldn't kill me,' Brodie grumbled and winced as he massaged his shoulder. It definitely needed a sling after that. 'She needs Rel and if she kills me then there's no one to help with the rock.'

Seth let out a breath and his eyes narrowed due to the annoyance. 'I can read her mind, Brodie,' he explained gravely. 'For a second she didn't care about this ridiculous scheme of hers and she wanted you dead.'

Brodie scowled in return. If Charmi didn't kill him, then it was clear that she had a plan brewing. It was the lack of violence that surprised him.

But killing Laria on the other hand...

'I dare you to look me in the eyes and say you're still not tempted to kill her in order to stop her father's plans.'

When she said those words, it surprised Brodie. He never actually thought about the fact that it would stop her father's plans. All this time, Brodie felt that Laria's presence swelled his bloodlust.

Immediately Seth scowled and turned to Brodie. 'I am not as close friends with Laria as you were, but the old Brodie would never consider killing his best friend.' Damn mind reading powers.

Brodie shot back to his feet, wincing as he moved his arm. 'Do you know what it's like to think that it was her father that killed mine?' He grabbed Seth's collar and pulled him forward, but Seth barely fought against the grip.

'I know what it's like to lose parents,' Seth countered sternly. 'And the murderer of my parents happened to be the Ungue Dux under possession. You don't think that I feel angry that she gets to walk away unpunished?'

'Why would you tell me this?' Brodie wondered after a moment of silence. Seth had a knack for keeping quiet about his true feelings after all.

He hadn't moved when he answered. For a guy that was filled with mystery, his eyes showed off the obvious answer. Just like everyone else, he was sick of the unnecessary deaths.

'Because, I can read your thoughts Brodie, and I know that Leon's been warning you to calm down through Rel.' Brodie didn't bother to hide his surprise, instead he dropped Seth's collar.

It was true. For the past two weeks, Leon occasionally came back to Brodie in dreams about controlling the bloodlust. In fact, Brodie wouldn't be surprised if that was the reason why Tara had been training him more often.

Before Brodie could respond, he heard Laria's yell for help. Forgetting about his current urges to tear out her throat, Brodie turned back to see her. Laria rushed into the scene with her arm around Jason to support him.

At first glance, Brodie wondered how Laria was able to lift Jason when she could hardly lift Tahani, however it took him a moment to see her literally using the bloodlust's power to assist her.

Seeing Laria on her feet was a relieving sight. After seeing Charmi, Brodie feared that she would've tried to target Laria somehow. Thankfully, she was alright.

For now.

Brodie ignored the voice in the back of his mind, his frustration returning as he set his eyes upon Jason, who was unconscious. Seth reacted first and ran to meet the pair. They helped set Jason to the ground carefully while Brodie watched from afar.

But the sight on blood on Jason's clothes caught Brodie's attention, and he knew that it wasn't Jason's.

'Are you two alright?' Seth asked them and his eyes narrowed towards Laria. 'Why is Jason with you?'

'It was my fault,' Laria confessed as her amber eyes faded back into their original colour. She avoided Seth's stare. Brodie didn't move, suddenly uncomfortable as if he was an outsider and focused his attention back on Jason. Asides from being knocked out, he didn't look seriously injured, so why was that making Laria feel guilty? 'I should've been watching out for him and because of me, he... he...'

'His bloodlust came out, didn't it?' Brodie concluded and when Laria didn't respond to him, a scoff left his lips. 'It's about time... now he can stop moping about being just a poor orphan boy.'

'It's not just that!' Laria snapped at him, shooting a glare towards Brodie. Her voice took him by surprise. 'It's because I wasn't able to do what had to be done and now Jason...' She lost her voice again, but they were cut off by a light groan.

Raising an eyebrow Brodie observed Jason bringing himself to awareness. With a startled cry, Jason suddenly pulled himself upright. The panic caused Laria to dodge Jason's head and Seth watched them in a painful silence.

'Laria...' Jason blinked and he rubbed his head. 'I had this dream... you were there and there was this shifter...' He hesitated as the realisation dawned on him. 'I... killed him...'

Brodie narrowed his eyes. 'It looks like you did something useful for once.' He felt the glare come from Laria and Seth, but Brodie ignored it. His thoughts wandered about Jason's scenario.

Why didn't Jason manage to protect Laria the first time she was attacked? Then again, Brodie shouldn't be judging his twin brother after Brodie just considered killing his best friend.

'I'm sorry that I let you, Jason,' Laria whimpered and avoided his stare. 'I should never have let it get that far.'

'It's alright Laria,' Jason reassured her with another groan. 'All I remember is that I couldn't let you down, but I was sudden filled with the thought of revenge. I wanted to make that shifter pay...' Jason clenched his fist.

'The Forte bloodlust is connected to vengeance,' Seth explained to Jason. 'So it's no surprise...'

'Well, since today has ended badly – I'm going home.' Ignoring the pain from his shoulder, Brodie finally regained the strength to keep walking.

Seth was the first to point it out. 'Brodie.' In that moment, Brodie paused before turning towards them. Jason wasn't looking at him, but Seth's neutral expression returned. 'Make sure you get that shoulder checked out.'

With the pain, Brodie had no choice. He nodded and but as soon as he saw Laria's frown, he avoided her stare.

'Brodie...' Her voice was soft. A part of himself wanted to turn, to apologise for being distant to her – of all people, but he couldn't. Biting the inside of his cheek, Brodie forced himself to remain silent.

What choice did he have? She wouldn't get it. If he had looked at her, he probably would've remembered what his bloodlust wanted. He didn't want to think of her that way — like she was a target for his revenge.

'I don't care, Laria,' Brodie honestly said. His attention went to the surrounding trees, anything to keep from looking back at her. 'I don't care for Jason — I only allowed him to train with me because it was what my father would've wanted.'

'But he's your brother,' Laria replied with a hint of hardness. Brodie finally turned to her, recognising the Alfero look of determination that he was used to seeing. 'You don't turn your back on family.'

Brodie said nothing in response, turning to leave the scene. No matter how much he wanted to, Brodie couldn't muster the power to speak back to her.

CHAPTER 7

Tracy scoffed from her desk as Haroni showed her the message on his phone. She took in a deep breath, scowling as Haroni moved the phone away. Judging by her cold glare, she was demanding an explanation.

She crossed her arms and leaned into her seat. 'You should have told me sooner.'

'I wanted to be sure,' Haroni replied and pulled out a folder to slam it in front of her. 'That this message wasn't just from a fool that wanted to anger me.' And Haroni was angry – angry with himself for allowing this to happen. 'I went through the most recent death reports in Cheyenne... and they've all been skin walkers from both sides with a particular symbol on them – one that looks remarkably similar.'

Tracy met his gaze blankly, but she opened the folder to view the photos of the unique marking. It had a crescent-shaped cross, giving the distant appearance of a bird. She studied the image and her eyes turned harsh as she subconsciously reached for her hip. Haroni knew exactly what she felt when she gazed upon the picture; it was the same tingle that he felt on his chest.

They bore the mark. The reminder of their banishment.

'The angels wanted to send a message,' Tracy muttered and closed the folder to cover the images.

Haroni took the file with a glare. 'They've never been this close to us, the day we were banished they vowed vengeance for the death of their kin.'

'Alright then,' Tracy fixed her blouse and brushed back

her hair. 'How do we stop them? They have the powers that we lost. It wouldn't take them long to follow the trail.'

'We leave this town and go to another secluded place,' Haroni replied simply and Tracy sent him a look of disbelief. 'There's a reason why I keep my job a secret from the rest of the world – so that when I move, they don't know anyone that had been contact with me.'

'Then what?' Tracy returned dryly and Haroni frowned back at his sister. He knew that she was just as upset as he was. Golden Cliff was always the place Haroni found himself coming back to. He met Lesley in this town when she was just studying the origins of the skin walkers and how they were connected with the supernatural world. He decided to make it his home with Tracy five years ago and they'd gotten comfortable. 'We take Laria, go over to some new part of the world and pretend that we can move on?'

'Laria's staying in Golden Cliff, dear sister.'

'I beg your pardon? All that time bringing Laria into your house and taking care of her – was that some ruse because of Lesley?'

'I know Laria,' Haroni confessed as he walked to the window of Tracy's office. 'She didn't want to move to Cheyenne when Edward wanted to take her; I doubt that she would go anywhere else because of our enemies.'

'And you believe that she would be safer here,' Tracy realised and she looked down at her paperwork with a hard gaze. 'I apologise Haroni – I don't believe that Laria would be safe here for a second, especially with angels on the way here. I will stay here and protect Laria – no matter the cost of my own life.'

'Tracy, you must be joking.' His eyes flashed with surprise as Tracy gave him a serious glare. 'Why would you suggest splitting up?'

'Because in the end one of us lives,' Tracy replied with a cold gaze. Haroni tried to swallow the lump in his throat as he saw Tracy's loyal stare. 'I am responsible for this curse – the least I can do is make up for the mistake.'

'Tracy...' He couldn't find the words to admit that he was sorry. Haroni wished countless times for Abeytu's revival – but the only way that was possible was with the united Corvena and sacrifice of someone with an Alfero bloodline.

'I will stay here,' Tracy decided boldly and she took the folder in order to hand it to her brother. 'If you wish to stay with me and battle it out – I will fight for you until the end. But if not, escape this place and begin a new life...'

'Then I will consider it for you, dear sister,' Haroni responded and took the folder back. With a simple nod, Haroni left Tracy's office and walked through the school hall, ignoring the whispers from the students around him.

He didn't want either of them to stay behind. It would bring danger to all those lives in Golden Cliff but Tracy was willing to fight to the end. Haroni realised that this decision would be an internal struggle with one of the biggest situations in his life.

If he stayed, it meant that Laria, her friends and Tahani would be up against the only other angels in existence and it wouldn't end well. Just like he was centuries ago, angels were not as tolerate of skin walkers. To them, the skin walkers were an act of sin that didn't belong in this world.

Then again, Haroni understood why the angels felt the need to exterminate them. It didn't mean it was right however.

So he had to leave. They needed to survive and understand that Haroni was doing what was best. If there were angry with him for leaving, he would have to accept it. At least Tracy would know the truth, and Haroni trusted her to not tell anyone.

It looks as if I have made my decision.

***

'Have you seen Laria?' Jenna asked Maya, who had been more interested in writing down notes until Jenna spoke to her. The tomboy raised her head from her work, tilting her head with a curious frown.

'No,' Maya replied and leaned back in her seat. 'I haven't

seen her since Brodie's birthday party.' They were currently in their final class, which happened to be the dreaded math class. It was a Friday afternoon and they were stuck listening about algebra.

If Maya had anything in common with Jenna, it was their mutual distaste for algebra.

In the corner of her eyes Jenna turned to see Taro in the back row. The quarterback didn't have his attention on her, but he looked just as bored as the girls were. For a moment Taro looked away and Jenna exchanged a glance.

'Haven't you noticed she's been acting strange?' Jenna wondered and Maya paused in her writing. Slowly, Maya went back to her work and frowned in consideration.

'I don't know, Jen,' Maya said quietly, trying to keep an eye on the teacher. 'I mean – she lost her mum – grieving just doesn't take a couple of therapy sessions. Believe me.'

'I know that,' Jenna replied hotly. 'It's not just Laria; Brodie, Jason and even Seth have been ditching school more often.'

Now Maya turned to the blonde with a warning glare. It had always been a routine for Maya to glare whenever Seth's name was mentioned. 'Seth's just being Seth. Besides – it's not like any of us are going to figure it out anytime soon.'

Jenna was about to reply when a sharp voice cut them off. 'Sommers, Rosa.' The teacher had a stern tone. As Jenna's blood drained from her face, she heard the warning for their silence. Their math teacher was known to be strict.

Jenna couldn't afford another detention with the teacher. If she got another one, she would never hear the end of it with her parents.

So the pair remained quiet, yet Jenna's head was bouncing with ideas. It was normal for Maya to brush Jenna's comments off, but this time it was different. Something was definitely off to Jenna and for the life of her she couldn't figure it out.

When class was dismissed, Jenna was still quiet while she packed her bag. Beside her, Maya's phone buzzed and Jenna found herself pausing to watch Maya fiddle with the device.

The tomboy bit her lip. 'I've gotta go,' she announced and finally went to shove her books in her bag. 'I've got to do some studying to do.' She scooped up her overpacked bag and waved before leaving Jenna in a quick pace.

Now Jenna knew that Maya was a part of the secret.

'I told you,' Taro spoke from behind and Jenna quickly turned to face him. He was the only student left in the classroom; even the teacher left in a rush. 'You think it's a coincidence now?'

'Why do you keep acting like this, Taro?' Jenna demanded, annoyed at everything. Why was everyone lying and pretending?

'Jenna – we both saw that wolf in the middle of the road,' Taro replied sternly, ignoring Jenna's accusations. 'We both saw the look in its eyes. So don't ask me why... when you already know the answer to that.'

Finally, Jenna felt her eyes sting with tears. 'I'm scared of it, Taro,' Jenna admitted softly and she looked down at her feet. 'No one else knows that I saw it but you.'

Taro stared back at her in silence, his hand in his pockets before he let out a heavy sigh. 'Close your eyes.' A frown deepened in her features when she met his gaze. 'Try something new, called trust.'

'Fine,' Jenna replied hastily and closed her eyes.

She wasn't expecting something warm being pressed against her lips. It was a natural reaction and Jenna opened her eyes to see that Taro was kissing her. His lips were identical to the time at the bonfire, when he kissed her out of the blue.

Jenna went along with the kiss, moving her lips against his with instinct. Her heart was racing in her chest and her head had yet to register the fact that Taro was kissing her for the second time.

'Wait,' Jenna said and pulled away. It felt like her cheeks were on fire. 'Why did you do that? What about Sara?'

'Well, Sara and I weren't that serious,' Taro told her and Jenna stared with her jaw slightly opened. Was she just hearing things? 'Since that night at the bonfire, I couldn't keep lying to myself – I made Sara promise that she would leave you alone. And secondly – I did what I did because I wanted to. It's as simple as that.'

Judging his calm features, Jenna couldn't tell if he was telling the truth or not. She wanted to trust him, but at the same time she was scared of having her heart broken. Even though Taro had been nicer, Taro still had the reputation of the jerk.

'I can't,' Jenna said in a breathless whisper. Taro's frown deepened as Jenna stepped away from him and avoided his stare. Despite her thoughts were telling her she was wrong for pushing him away, Jenna didn't have the courage to stay within his presence. No matter who she saw, they always hid the secrets that she craved to know. Was she not important enough to them? To anyone? 'I have to go.'

'Where?' Taro asked, but Jenna was already leaving him behind. 'What about school?'

Anywhere. 'I need a break.' Jenna didn't look back at him, but she was loud enough for him to hear. 'I'll be back soon enough.'

Thankfully, Taro didn't seem to follow her. Jenna ignored the eyes of the other students as she clutched her bag and left the school building. No doubt someone from her class saw her and would eventually spill the beans about her leaving but it didn't bother her.

She just needed air.

Jenna kept walking until she reached several hundred metres away from the building, safe away from prying eyes. As soon as she knew she was alone, Jenna let out a deep sigh and sat on the curb.

Surely, she was just being paranoid. Jenna chuckled dryly and shook her head. She wished she was, but one thing she knew was that she wasn't crazy. Her friends were hiding something from her and for some reason Taro knew it.

Don't get me started about him. Jenna thought, grumbling under her breath. In her eyes, he was the perfect man with a promised scholarship with his football career, he cared about her – at least she thought he did. He pretended to like her back at the bonfire, then he kissed her out of the blue while dating Sara Maraca, the school president.

Jenna groaned and pinched the bridge of her nose. 'It's so complicated.'

'How so love?'

In a panic, Jenna whirled around to see someone looming over her. The stranger's face was definitely a sight she could recognise. Sandy blonde hair, blue eyes and a smile filled with dimples?

However Jenna chose to remain cautious. There was something about him that made her stomach churn. She pushed herself off the ground, drawing her eyebrows together as she lifted an arm in front of her to keep the distance.

'Who are you? Why are you following me?' Jenna demanded. Why did this stranger choose to find her the day she decided to leave the school grounds? Deep down, Jenna scolded herself. It was a silly idea for her to do so.

'My name is Nick,' he introduced himself, smiling softly. 'I promise you, love, I'm not following you – or at least I wasn't until now.'

'Enough with the love business!' Jenna told him firmly. Despite that he smiled and seemed polite, there was something off about him. She couldn't put her finger on it. 'And answer my question. Why are you following me?'

He was amused. Jenna could see the playful look in his eyes and it still gave her a feeling of dread. She had to make sure he didn't get close enough to her. Luckily, she remembered that if she ever got attacked, she had to scream out "Fire" to get attention.

'I just wanted to tell you something,' Nick continued to speak as if Jenna hadn't snapped at him. 'The truth you've been craving, about your friends, your boyfriend and this lifeless town.'

'Taro isn't my boyfriend,' Jenna muttered, seeing Nick's lips twitch. 'And what do you mean by that?'

'You certainly ask a lot of questions,' Nick pointed out,

crossing his arms. 'I promise I can answer any you have.'

What was with this guy? Jenna narrowed her eyes and made her take a small step back. 'Why? Why should I trust you?'

'Because,' Nick said and he advanced towards her. 'Why not? You want to know about the secrets of this town, don't you? I happen to have the answers you want.'

Jenna wasn't convinced, but she didn't move from her spot. 'Then tell me,' she insisted and she saw Nick's smile widen. If anything, he seemed like the predator kind that would use her trust against her. Desperation overcame her common sense. 'What are the secrets of this town?'

'This town is home of the shape shifters,' Nick answered the question without hesitation, halting Jenna's thoughts.

'Shifters…' Did he mean skin walkers? Those kinds of shape shifters? Immediately, Jenna shook her head. 'Now I know you need professional help.' As she tried to turn around, she felt something grasp her forearm. 'Let me go-!' Jenna struggled to break free, with her heart racing.

'Look into my eyes, love.'

Suddenly, Jenna faced him. 'I told you to knock-!' Her eyes were staring back at something inhuman. Instead of locking eyes with the blue eyes, she was staring into the golden eyes. 'You were that wolf…' Saying the thoughts out loud was bizarre, but Jenna couldn't deny what she was seeing.

Immediately Nick released Jenna's arm. 'I'll be willing to talk more, if you let me.'

Unable to respond, Nick winked in her direction before transforming into a wolf in front of her eyes. It was the wolf that Taro nearly hit with his car. The sandy brown canine picked up the fallen clothes and darted into the trees ahead.

In her shock, Jenna found herself walking back to the school campus. Her breath shook, her body was shaking and her thoughts were flying through her mind. She recognised Taro standing at the front of the building, tilting his head and frowning.

Even when she approached him, she couldn't speak. All

this time, she had been living in a world where wolves didn't just come from Yellowstone. What did Nick want? Why would he reveal himself to her? Wasn't that taboo in their culture?

He stepped up to her, reaching for her arm. 'Are you okay? You look like you've seen a ghost.'

'I'm not…' Jenna's voice was hoarse. 'I just saw a shape shifter.' Taro sharply took in a deep breath, but asides from that, he wasn't dismissing her words. 'Are my friends… shape shifters?'

Taro seemed conflicted, but eventually he settled and slowly nodded. 'Yes. They are.'

***

Laria watched Jason from behind as they walked back to Seth's place. She saw Seth supporting him, but there were no words exchanged since Seth told Maya what happened by text.

Laria found relief as they finally made it to Seth's house. Jason walked in first and as Laria tried to follow him, she realised Seth shot his arm out to halt her movements. His sudden movement caused Laria to step away from him with a concerned frown.

'Seth?' Despite knowing him as a shape shifter, Laria still felt uncomfortable around him. Judging from the wary stare from Seth, he didn't trust her either. She didn't blame him for the lack of trust – they still didn't know each other. He most likely only paid attention to her because they shared mutual friends.

He grunted and moved his body in front of her to block the view from Jason. 'Tell me Laria, what did you do with the body?'

The question caught her off guard. 'I…' She trailed off, her mind blurring with the memory. Her panic for Jason clouded her judgement. At the time, she quickly dressed herself before picking Jason up. 'I didn't do anything with the body…'

Seth's eyes narrowed and he grunted again. 'I suppose I will have to deal with it. I suspect Maya is on her way, I confessed everything to her – about Jason's true heritage. So do not deny it. I'll be back shortly.'

Before Laria could respond, Seth curtly turned away from her and began to head in the direction they came from. With a scowl, Laria crossed her arms over her chest.

Why does he seem to hate me? After she sighed, Laria redirected her attention to Jason. She entered the house, closing the door behind her and saw that Jason was washing his face over the sink. 'Jason…'

Jason pulled his head away from the running tap, ignoring the water droplets that flung in the air. 'I did it…' He chuckled and pulled his hands free from his face. 'I became a shifter – just like I wanted.'

'Look what it did to you though,' Laria whispered and Jason raised an eyebrow. 'I know I'm not one to talk, but your bloodlust seemed strange. It willingly allowed you to take control again, don't you find that strange?'

'I honestly don't understand it myself,' Jason admitted, 'but after all that you've done for me, this was the least I could do. I had to make sure that I had that strength to protect my friends.'

Laria fell into silence. What was she supposed to say to that? While she was flattered that her friend went on a murdering rampage for her, it meant that Jason was forced to live like this forever. To him, it seemed like a dream come true but Jason didn't realise the side-effects. Maybe he did, and was still in shock after killing the other shifter. It was the only thing that made sense, he just didn't notice that he would feel the urge to kill for the rest of his life.

Before they could continue the discussion, Laria could hear Maya calling out for Seth.

'He isn't here!' Laria answered and on cue, she came inside.

'Seth told me what happened,' Maya muttered and she frowned. Laria immediately knew what her frown meant. She stood up and Jason remained on the armchair. 'Did you guys plan to tell me about Jason being Brodie's brother?'

'It wasn't like that, Maya.' Jason replied, losing his focus on Laria and he clenched his fists. 'We kept it as quiet as possible because of the risk.'

Maya sighed but her frown was still visible. 'I know... it's just frustrating that I have to not know anything. I'm sorry... I know you guys trust me but I don't feel like that sometimes.'

'It's because we trust you that we have to be careful, Maya,' Laria insisted and stood up with her friend with a concerned gaze. 'If Charmi is really intending on chasing after all of us, then we have to stay low and keep our secrets.'

'What about Jenna?' Maya wondered as she turned to Laria. 'She's asking questions, Laria – she knows that something's up.'

'Jenna's safer not knowing,' Laria responded curtly. 'It's different with you, you were meant to be a shifter – Jenna wasn't. As much as I would love to tell Jenna, we can't risk her safety. We need to formulate a plan to watch the town.'

'Then we will need to discuss this with the others.' Jason announced to them but he looked at his clenched fists. 'At least now we have the element of surprise on our side. No one else knows that I have the bloodlust...'

'But you still have to control your bloodlust. We can't let you go around untrained – you could seriously hurt someone again,' Laria told him firmly. This couldn't be shock, maybe it a power high. 'I will talk to Takon; he would probably assign you with a Magister... Which I assume would be Tara.'

'I can't imagine that,' Jason laughed at the thoughts. In the few times he met his aunt, Laria knew that it was difficult for him to connect.

'What about me then?' Maya demanded with a scowl that appeared similar to Tahani's. Ever since Laria found out that Maya was Tahani's niece, she began to see similar features. 'I can't be stuck as a human like this! If Jason can unlock it, so can I!'

'Easier said than done,' Jason muttered under his breath and crossed his arms over his chest. Yet Laria had a serious gaze in her eyes.

'Bloodlust isn't a good thing Maya,' Laria warned and Maya

sent a scowl in her direction. 'We have to live with the fact that we killed, and we took pleasure in it... Do you really want that?'

Maya's eyes were hard, and Laria understood what she was going through. If Laria had been in her shoes, she probably would've felt the same way. Maybe eventually she would have no choice and snap like Jason, but until then... Laria didn't want Maya to have anything to do with it.

'Please Laria...' Maya grasped the front of Laria's shirt and tightened her hold. 'If you know a way, then tell me...'

Finally, Laria sighed and decided what to do. 'There is,' she claimed and Maya raised a brow. 'I can't confirm it for sure, but this is what I was told. The Corvena was responsible for our powers before it got separated within the family. Rosa's family stone is known as Azu – if you go find Azu then you will have your powers unlocked.'

Maya frowned and her features showed the annoyance of Laria's request. 'Then where would I search for this bloody rock?'

Definitely Tahani's niece. If anyone was able to find the Rosa heirloom, it was definitely going to be the Rosa descendant. 'Your grandmother knew your mother as a kid – it would be best if you start by asking her since she trusts you.'

'Alright. The sooner I find this thing the sooner I can kick some more ass.'

Jason lightly chuckled and interrupted the moment. 'You do enough of that as a human,' he muttered under his breath, earning a laugh from Maya.

CHAPTER 8

'What's going on?' Tahani asked when she stepped into Haroni's room to see him packing. Ever since recovering from the fever, Hugh ordered her to take it easy. But this was different – she heard Haroni enter and noticed his strange behaviour.

'Leaving,' was Haroni's short reply.

'Alright,' Tahani muttered with a frown. 'So when are ya coming back?'

Finally he stopped packing to face Tahani. 'I'm not coming back, my dear,' he announced with a flat tone. 'I won't be able to help you with Zanobi's case.'

It took a few seconds for the realisation to sink in. That couldn't be true. Haroni went to his bags as Tahani tried to control her rapid breathing. A mixture of emotions boiled to the surface in that instant – yet the most obvious one was her rage.

While she got angered and lost her temper from time to time, it was nothing compared to the explosion from the ticking time bomb that she was. The true extent of her rage was rare, that she only recalled the rage, three times in her life.

The first time was during the massacre when she was a kid with Kaeylin. After their parents' death, it was mostly about Tahani, Kaeylin and Zanobi; even though she didn't trust him at the time. A human kidnapped a boy roughly her age and chained him up for everyone to see.

That day was the first time she killed a man. At the young age of ten, Tahani stole a hunting knife from the butcher and attacked the offender. Kaeylin hadn't judged her actions, Zanobi helped the kid back to his feet and it was the only thing Tahani had done that she considered selfless.

The second time was Kaeylin's death and Tahani was mad with herself. She was mad that she never made amends with Kaeylin and her husband; the man that Kaeylin claimed at the time was the man of her dreams, was nothing but a ghost. Tahani was arrested for vandalism and Zanobi had to bail her out.

The final time was shortly after Kaeylin's death. Tahani remembered going out for a drink at the Silver Roots. A group of drunk idiots heard of her death. They said indecent things about her little sister, and Tahani was still annoyed with her recent outburst so she sent all three men to hospital.

It seemed that this stunt from Haroni was going to be the fourth time she lost her control.

Tahani snarled, clenching her fist until her knuckles turned white. 'We had a promise! We were gonna find Zanobi!'

Immediately Haroni turned back with a smile. 'Things change dear,' Haroni said simply and Tahani growled in response. 'You would've done the same if you were in my shoes.'

A scoff of disbelief escaped the dux's lips. 'That's a lie. I would've never backed out of a promise!' For a moment, she thought she got to him.

'I apologise.' Haroni turned away from her just as he recovered from his shock. Tahani was sure that her eyes stung of tears. She couldn't tell if this was result from Charmi's power of memory lane or her time bomb was about to explode. But once she heard him apologise, that was it for her.

She snapped. Using one hand, she grabbed him to spin his body so that he could face her, and without hesitation, she punched him in the face. The bastard certainly wasn't expecting it; he crashed into the ground.

'Why?' she whispered, her breath escaped with uneven pants. 'Why ya runnin' like a bloody coward?'

Slowly, Haroni's expression went into one that she

couldn't understand. He pushed himself to his feet and looked down at her. 'That... my dear – is none of your business. Just be glad and respectful I'm allowing you to stay here.'

'Shut the hell up,' Tahani spat back. 'Respect is earned buddy, and yer not gonna get it by pushing others away.'

'That's rich coming from you, Tahani.' Haroni wiped the blood from his face harmlessly. 'When was the last time you shared your story to Laria? Or your niece – or even to me? Did you believe that you went through all the hardships as a child? Don't be ridiculous – I have nine hundred years on you.'

That was it. 'Fine! Congratulations Haroni Ladas – yer winning ya battle,' Tahani announced with a glare. Her eyes returned to their original shade and she shook her head. 'But ya lost me... Good luck at for yer future, and thanks for disappointing me.'

Haroni didn't move as Tahani roughly shoved him. He didn't make any eye contact with her. She didn't want to look at him as she left him to go to her room, slamming the door with a burst of anger. Her body began quivering and soon, Tahani found herself staring back at a familiar figure in front of her.

They weren't in the mansion anymore. Instead they stood in a forest, silence consumed the background. There was nothing that made a sound, asides from Tahani's pounding heart.

'Zanobi…' Her voice quivered, trying to get his attention. He wasn't facing her, but Tahani could recognise the shade of auburn anywhere. When he didn't respond, Tahani anger got the best of her. 'Damn it, Zanobi, look at me ya bastard!'

Why was he like this?

However to Tahani's horror, Zanobi began to walk. Tahani tried to move closer to him, but the world faded around her and she found herself back in the mansion.

How could he do this to me? Tahani's thoughts raced through her mind. Her heart pounding became loud enough to ring and it was hard for her to breathe. *I don't know what to do!*

The sound of gunfire caused Tahani to yelp, and she pulled at her shirt to recognise the lump of scarred tissue over her chest. She was told that Hugh had not been the one to heal her, but some human doctor saved her life. As a result, Tahani had been unable to completely heal from the wound.

Make it bloody stop! Tahani heard the gunfire over and over again. Laria's cry followed afterwards. She forced her eyes to squeeze shut and she clenched her teeth. *This isn't real, cut this crap out!*

With her wishes, the noise vanished. As Tahani opened her eyes, she flinched when she realised her arm was sore. Taking a look at it, horror overcame Tahani's expression as she noticed her skin bleeding from a fresh wound. Tahani looked at her other hand, with claws covered in blood and shrinking back into bloodstained fingernails.

The realisation dawned on the dux. Her bomb restarted.

***

There could be a bunch of other things to do on a Saturday morning other than going through her mother's journals in Seth's house. Maya huffed as she chucked the book on the table. Sitting across from her, Jason raised a suspicious eyebrow at Maya's temper tantrum.

'Are you okay there?' Jason asked teasingly.

'Shut up,' she snapped sharply. If anything was going to annoy her, it would be this constant search for Azu. The answers were vague and not enough for her.

And it frustrated her.

'Well, I'm going for a walk,' Jason said with a sigh. He pushed himself off his seat and left Maya alone in the house. Seth went out for another meeting and now Jason was going for a walk. Great, now she was studying alone.

The only one who most likely knew about Azu was...

'Tahani...' Maya realised when she remembered the day that Tahani demanded answers about Azu.

So if Tahani could unlock it, so could Maya. From what the book said, a Rosa skin walker had the bloodlust filled with thrill. Maya loved taking risks and challenges; she loved the adrenaline rush when she did something exciting.

Maya took a break from her researching session and went through her bag to get a snack. All this sitting around and doing nothing was driving her crazy. Just as Maya grabbed a green apple, she frowned when she noticed a small brown book that looked different. Leaving the apple on the table, Maya returned her attention onto the book and flicked through the pages.

This was a journal that Maya hadn't seen before. At least that was a plus side to this pointless day.

Her blue eyes scanned the front cover and read the elegant writing at the bottom of the cover. *Kaeylin Rosa.* It was weird; Adelle gave Maya all of Kaeylin's journals before and Maya read through all of them, once again ending up with nothing but a corny story about how her mother met her dad. If Maya was in the mood, she would've scoffed.

Her dad didn't exactly feel the same when he ditched them.

But maybe Adelle found this journal after giving Maya the others and put it in her bag. With a heavy sigh, Maya opened the first page and let her eyes scan the date. It took her a moment to realise the year of the journal entries.

It was her year of birth. How the hell did she not realise that her mother wrote when Maya was still an infant? She flipped through the pages quickly and she spotted that some of the June dates were in time gaps.

She skimmed through the later dates, noticing there was a doggie ear on Brodie's birthday. It was strange to see that Brodie's birthday was important for her mother to write.

> *Dear diary,*
>
> *Maya is only a few months old and she's been growing rather quickly. Her father is so proud of her and he hopes that she grows up like me. But I believe she's a true Rosa. If she's not grabbing anything that's a hazard, she's rolling around with a cheeky grin on her face.*
>
> *It's honestly times like this when I wish I didn't do it. But I managed to go to Maine, strike a deal and keep the*

'No!' Maya snapped, looking over to the next page but it was torn off. Wherever Kaeylin ended up hiding the stone was probably within the next page. 'Damn it, Mum, you just had to be so damn subtle about these things! This is probably why you died.'

Before Maya could throw the stupid book through a window, a throat cleared and stopped Maya from her mini rage fest. She felt embarrassment flood her cheeks as Seth raised a curious eyebrow and looked at the journal in her hands.

'Jason told me that you were getting frustrated at the lack of answers.' He sighed coolly and took his seat beside her. 'But please don't break my window.'

'Well sorry, princess,' Maya grumbled sarcastically, leaning on the palm of her hand. 'Did you find what you were looking for?'

Of course, Seth didn't change his emotions as he observed the books from his position. 'I'm getting there.'

She gave a dry smirk. 'Will I be expecting the news to report another animal attack then?'

Seth finally glanced back at her, his dark eyes sparked with a hint of amusement. 'I suppose we would have to wait and find out.'

'Speaking of animals,' Maya realised when her eyes took a glimpse of the first book she had. 'The books say that you guys can turn into a predatory species with a pelt of a certain animal. Did you kill some beaver to turn?'

Now it was Seth's time to show a weird look — which was weird to Maya. 'No, an animal transformation has to come with a need. I believe that the pelts are what kept the tribe's scent hidden. I turned into my animal form when I was young and to answer your next question — I haven't killed a beaver before. I can turn into a panther — jaguar to be exact.'

'How does that happen?' Maya asked, realising the question slipped before she had any control. 'Brodie turns into a cheetah, you a panther, Laria a wolf – I don't even know what Tahani turns into…'

'It's mostly about connections,' Seth answered calmly. 'Brodie looked up to his father, who could also turn into a cheetah. I used to watch a lot of documentaries about big cats, but when I saw the panthers for the first time.' The look on his face changed, almost as if he was relishing in the moment. 'I just felt like they were powerful, graceful and the fact they were solitary was something I connected with. I suppose it's the same with many large cats, but the panther was something I felt like it was me.'

It did somewhat explain how Laria was a wolf. Her dream was to go to Yellowstone National Park to study the wolves there. When Maya asked at the time, Laria simply stated that she was fascinated with the research that was put into the restoration of the Grey Wolf.

Seth noticed the look on Maya's face and he returned his blank expression. 'Are you alright?'

She placed the book on the desk and ran her hands through her curly hair. 'I give up.'

Normal Seth would've shrugged off her speech, but this Seth was obviously some other Seth. That was because he actually *frowned* when Maya rested her head on the table.

The brunette didn't ask why she gave up on searching for Azu. He picked up the journal and read through the work of Maya's mother without a complaint.

Finally Seth grunted softly and placed the journal back on the table. 'That's no reason to give up, Maya.'

'What do you mean "no reason to give up"?' Maya harshly replied. 'I'm done – it's clear that Kaeylin didn't want me to know... all of this is her personal life.'

'And what's the thing that you've been reading?' Seth wondered, offering a raised eyebrow when Maya gave a glance back at the books. 'All the entries have one thing in common.' Then it hit her. She looked up to see Seth's small smile, the one that was filled with understanding. The one who knew about the stone was her dad.

A wide smirk formed on her face. 'You're a bloody genius Seth Laurence!' Without thinking, Maya grabbed his face and crashed her lips against his in excitement.

It was only for a second though, since she pulled away and the realisation hit her when she moved her face away from him. Her expression went from excited to horror when she realised that she kissed the boy who avoided human contact. Seth's face was pale, as if he had just seen a ghost... or a rectoc... or maybe his own parents.

'Shit!' Maya cursed in embarrassment and her cheeks went bright red. That saying "she could just kiss him" had sparked in her brain and she didn't even think. Maybe Maya really should start thinking before she acted. Seth still hadn't moved or reacted from her recent stunt. 'Look Seth... I'm really sorry... Seth? Are you with me?'

When she quickly clicked her fingers, Seth snapped out of his funk. But then again, he didn't completely snap out of it. He blinked in confusion, pushing himself off the chair and keeping an arm's length distance from Maya.

'Wait, Seth, hold on – we need to talk about this like two normal people,' Maya tried to plead but who was she kidding? She hoped that they were still friends and not known as the awkward pair.

'Do not worry...' Seth said awkwardly, trying to avoid her stare. 'We are still friends and we will always be...' Maya was almost tempted to ask how he was able to take the words out of her mind. But they've already made things weird as they were – Maya had no right to demand the question.

'I'm sorry, Seth,' Maya whispered in a gentle tone. Honestly, she didn't expect to hear her own voice drop to get her point across. 'I just mean to say... thank you... For helping me, even though you don't want me to be a part of this...'

She didn't expect Seth's face to soften. 'I will support you, Maya... no matter what.' Maya felt the grateful smile return to her. He cared about her... and he wouldn't leave her just because she was reckless. With that, Maya was comfortable.

***

David unzipped his jacket as he entered Silver Roots and hung the coat in his arms. He scanned the booths, finding relief when he recognised Takon. As David approached Takon, it dawned on him that the Mandati Dux was not alone.

'Thank you for meeting with me,' Takon said with a slow nod. 'Come sit with us.'

Taking a deep breath, David joined them and his eyes wandered towards the stranger.

The man beside him remained silent. Unlike Takon he had short light brown hair; it had a reddish tinge as if it was giving a ruddy colour. His brown eyes watched David with a hint of wariness, but otherwise it was neutral and calm. Judging from his younger features, this kid was only in his early twenties and still following along with Takon.

The stranger's critical gaze made David feel uncomfortable, so he directed his attention on Takon.

'What did you need?' David asked, leaning into his seat. He had a feeling this would take a while.

'As you know, the key to a Forte's bloodlust is the desire for revenge,' Takon explained with a dark frown. 'Whether it's horrible or a mere simple death, the Forte filled with bloodlust won't stop until it's an endless circle of vengeance and hatred.'

'So our enemies happen to be a bunch of Fortes?'

'Tahani has informed me that the shifters responsible for all this are Charmi and Nick Forte.' As Takon shot David a look, David realised he didn't know them. It was definitely an unregistered shifter. 'However, they weren't responsible for the Jane Doe attack. They might have found the body and decided to dump it in Brodie's lawn.'

David recognised the name of Laria's friend. 'What's it got to do with him?'

'Brodie Forte killed her brother Brad, and Charmi went rogue against Lucien in order to take over the town,' Takon replied sternly. 'By killing off the people and taking out Brodie's friends, it's causing a disturbance in the S.H.O.

Which is why I brought Ruddy Ryans here.'

The ruddy haired man named Ruddy? Someone's parents clearly lacked a creative name.

The mentioned man finally spoke, 'My abilities can temporary control the bloodlust.'

'Sounds like a power of a Forte,' David confessed when he locked eyes with the man. His brown eyes seemed to lack emotion, similar to a Laurence.

'Exactly,' Ruddy returned the even tone. His blank features appeared somewhat bored as he tried to explain everything. 'To be precise, my abilities are closer to the instinct and the fact that I can awaken them.' He spared a glance at David who stiffened automatically. 'A bloodlust is only the instinct that the shape shifters possess from the rectocs. With my power, that's probably the thing that the S.H.O needs, the proof that the shifters have been trying hard to protect.'

CHAPTER 9

Laria sighed as she collected her history books from her locker and felt her mind wander. In fact her mind was still reeling from the recent events from the past few days. Everything was changing.

She had no idea what to do at the moment. All her hope faded when she discovered Haroni's departure. He said nothing and left without so much as a warning. It wasn't like Tahani was any better with his disappearance – but it looked like it was for different reasons. Yet the big question remained, why didn't Haroni tell her until now?

She should've been happy that he was gone. Haroni was the last person that she wanted to live with three months ago. But then Laria remembered the times that he helped her; he rescued her from Edward when her bloodlust revealed itself, he gave her a home, he took her to see her brother even though he didn't have to, he believed in her and he loved her. Laria was annoyed with herself that she brushed him off like he was a nuisance.

Haroni was probably the second closest thing she considered to be a father figure. Leon Forte was the first – and he was dead. It seemed that no matter what, Laria wasn't allowed to have any father figure in her life. They either died or ditched her for unknown reasons.

Everything went from bad to worse ever since Laria killed Edward. All of her friends were distant with each other, Charmi was determined to make Brodie's life a living hell, Jason was training with Tara to control his bloodlust and Lux continued haunting her nightmares.

'Are you alright Laria?'

Laria recognised Heather's voice and she turned to the witch with another sigh. 'I'm not sure,' she confessed. 'Everything's just a mess.'

Heather leaned on the locker with guilt. 'How's Jason?'

That surprised Laria. 'He's just unlocked his bloodlust,' Laria replied even though she was still stunned that Heather asked about him. 'In fact, I think he's just trying to focus on control – he was devastated when I found out about you two.'

'I see,' Heather muttered quietly. 'It was just that something terrible will happen if we did continue...' She trailed off and Laria frowned. What did that mean? Immediately Heather cleared her throat. 'Are you coming to the Halloween party on Thursday?'

Honestly Laria forgot about the Halloween party. So much had happened the past week that she hadn't had much time to consider it. 'I'll consider it.'

With everything that had been happening, the group needed their break.

'Well, the theme is predators and prey,' Heather said and showed a flyer from her bag. As Laria took it, she suddenly looked up to see Jenna but there was something different about her. Then it clicked, and Laria widened her eyes.

Her hair, once shoulder-length and wavy was now cut short. Even though it was a change that Laria found... interesting, she pulled a smile of relief.

Jenna not knowing about the shifters was definitely a good thing. It meant that Laria could come to school and not worry about her problems. And Jenna's cheeriness made sure that Laria was able to make it through the rest of the day.

'Excuse me, Heather. Jenna!' Laria's voice was loud enough to catch the blonde's attention. She appeared to be walking at a quicker pace than normal and the second she heard Laria, she froze.

'Hey there – what are you doing?' The tone that Jenna had certainly wasn't normal. 'You haven't been to school for the past few days.'

'I had something come up.' She wasn't exactly lying, so Laria didn't feel as guilty. 'Are you okay? You've been acting pretty strange.' Maya's words rang back to Laria, reminding her that Jenna had not been in the right mood recently.

However, Jenna flashed another grin. 'I'm fine,' she insisted and Laria felt sceptical. 'I just realised something about the party.' She strolled into the classroom and she even avoided David's stare. As he noticed the lack of communication, the hunter shot a glance towards Laria as if she knew what was going on.

Even though she had no clue on the what, Laria knew there was something wrong.

A vibration from Laria's pocket brought her back to reality and recognised Tahani's ID. It was a message from the dux. A text from her magister; it couldn't be good.

The bear trap results are back. They are property of the S.H.O.

This day was not getting any better. Dejected, Laria returned her phone in her pocket, not bothering to come up with a reply. Dismissing the morning's events, Laria took her seat next to Jenna and she noticed the distance.

The lesson commenced and throughout the session, Laria kept eyeing Jenna with a wary frown. Whatever ran through Jenna's mind, it was damn obvious that Laria wasn't going to find out by interrogation. So maybe, Laria should try another tactic.

'So Maya wants us to come over to her house just for a chill,' Laria whispered to her casually, noticing that Jenna remained stiff. 'I might not be able to make it because I need to help out Jason with some errands – but I promised Maya I would tell you about it.'

Jenna still remained stiff as she turned back to face Laria. 'I can't.'

Laria tilted her head. 'Why?'

'Because I have things to do,' Jenna said briskly. She turned away, focusing her attention away from Laria.

In response, Laria shook her head in disbelief. 'You're lying…'

Laria saw Jenna tightened the grip on her pen. 'You have no right to accuse me of lying…' Her voice was soft. '… Especially since that's all you seem to do for the past three months.'

Laria was stunned into silence. Just what happened to Jenna? With Maya's previous warning about Jenna asking questions, it seemed possible. But how could Laria prove it? Her dad was a hunter, he could've mentioned it to her but then again, why would Clark tell Jenna after keeping it away from her for so long?

Laria immediately stood up; the class were filling out notes from their textbook while David sat on his seat with paperwork. She made her way to her history teacher and he curiously raised an eyebrow. 'Is there a reason why you're up?'

'I think Jenna knows…' Laria glanced back at Jenna, who didn't return the stare.

***

Jenna parked her car at the front of her house. Taro told her everything that Nick hadn't – that the world wasn't so simple as she was led to believe.

Laria was a shifter, it was why she had been pulling herself away since her mother died. It wasn't just Laria though; Brodie, Seth and even Maya! But all this time, they were filled with the urge to kill innocents.

Then Taro told her something that shook her to the core. He was a part of a hunting organisation, known as the S.H.O. Why he would be willing to sign up to be a part of the group was beyond her. But Taro added that someone she knew was a shifter hunter as well.

Her dad, Clark Sommers.

Jenna didn't want to believe it. Her father, a hunter? He was a man that didn't even believe that guns were allowed in the house. How could he be a hunter?

I have to find out the truth. Jenna told herself, finally bringing herself out of the car. It took her longer than she expected to reach for her front door. Her dad claimed that he was 'working' throughout the weekend and Jenna hardly had the chance to speak with him.

Now it was her chance.

She entered her house cautiously and dread filled her. What if her mum was home as well? Jenna remembered her mother saying that she was taking her baby sister to the doctor, but Jenna didn't want to risk it. Her current business was with her father, not her mother.

'Are you home mum?' Jenna asked into the empty space.

'It's just me!' Clark replied and Jenna let out a sigh of relief. Jenna followed her dad's voice into the garage where she stumbled upon him working on his car. He flashed a grin. 'How was school?'

Surely Taro was lying… Jenna thought to herself. 'School was fine.' They had matching tattoos. When Jenna asked about the origin of the tattoos, her dad said it was a part of a club in his college years. Yet Taro claimed it was the mark of a hunter. 'Dad… I need to ask you something…'

Clark paused in his work with a curious frown and he reached for a towel to wipe his grease stained hands. 'What's wrong?'

Jenna clenched her fist and dug her nails into her palm. It stung, but it gave her the spike of adrenaline that she needed. 'Are shape shifters real?' If he answered this correctly, then Jenna would confirm Taro's story.

Her question caused him to freeze on the spot and his face paled. 'What's going on, Jennavieve?' Jenna refused to flinch at the sound of her full name. When she was younger, her parents called her by the full name when she was in trouble. She somehow convinced her teachers and friends not to call her that. But hearing her dad call her that now… it meant that he knew more than he let on.

'Taro told me everything,' Jenna answered without

hesitation. Clark muttered a curse under his breath. 'Dad… does that mean that my friends… they hurt people?'

'I'm trying to do everything in my power to save them from themselves,' Clark answered the question. 'Please, Jenna, you have to stay away from the shifters. They are a dangerous bunch – recently they have been acting out.'

'Why?' Jenna gritted her teeth and shook her head firmly. It turned out that just about everyone had lied to her. After the days of suspenseful build-up, Jenna knew she needed to leave. Anywhere.

Without thinking, Jenna fled. She could hear Clark stumbling behind as he tried calling out for her as she headed out of the house. The adrenaline flooded through her as she ran past her car and didn't focus on where she was going.

She just needed to be away from her lying father.

***

Laria grabbed a branch and cautiously walked through the forest. After finding out that the bear traps belonged to the S.H.O, Laria thought it would be better to search for the traps to avoid conflict.

It was a horrible thought, Laria loved to enter the forests. To think the hunters placed something in a place where humans and innocent creatures could roam that put them in danger. Laria only hoped that the forest creatures stayed away.

A sound in the echoed within the forest and alerted Laria of someone's presence close by. Laria immediately darted behind the bushes. Whoever was close by meant that Laria could be in danger.

Was it Charmi? A hunter? Laria would've preferred the latter.

However much to Laria's surprise, Jenna was the one who appeared through the trees as she gasped for air. The blonde reached for a tree beside her as she coughed in distress.

As she recognised her friend, Laria pulled herself away from her hidden position. The rustle of bushes caused Jenna to stand upright with a yelp. 'Jenna – what are you doing here?'

It didn't make sense for Jenna to be around. Jenna was never a fan of going through the forests since bugs seemed to follow her. Yet when Jenna stood against Laria with a glare, it was when Laria's theory was confirmed.

'Why Laria?' Jenna whispered back heatedly, her brown eyes flashing with boldness. 'Why didn't you ever tell me about what you are?'

'I'm sorry,' Laria said to her. Jenna shook her head, with tears glistening in her dark eyes. 'We didn't want you to find out this way.'

'You didn't want me to find out at all!' Jenna cried, halting Laria completely.

Laria didn't want to scare Jenna away. It was the reason why Laria didn't want to tell her in the first place. Fear always caused others to lash out and Laria had to do her best to defuse the situation. 'Who told you? Your dad?'

'It doesn't matter who told me,' Jenna responded and Laria cursed softly. In this state, Jenna wasn't going to calmly discuss this. She was angry at them and Laria didn't blame her. Hopefully she listened. 'I just want the truth. Did you kill anyone?'

Laria hesitated in the question. She wanted the truth? As the question bounced in Laria's mind, her thoughts went back to Edward. Her reason of killing him happened because she lost control. Lux took control when Laria was at her weakest point.

But the truth was needed. Laria's brow furrowed and she locked eyes with Jenna. 'I did. I killed the man who–'

Laria heard the sound of gunpower before a hot pain flared through her shoulder. The force knocked Laria off her feet and she slammed into the ground with a whimper.

'Laria!' Jenna cried out.

'Stay back Jen!' Laria barked, causing the blonde to halt. With a groan, Laria managed to pick herself up and glared through the trees. Someone was there; a hunter.

'Did someone follow me?' Jenna asked, but Laria focused her attention on pain. This wasn't her first time being shot, but it still hurt like the first.

This hurts… Laria gritted her teeth, holding the bloodied wound. It was as if flames were burning through her shoulder and her arm was suddenly numb. *How could I let this happen?* Anger filled her and Laria's eyes wandered over to Jenna who still seemed to be talking in the background. *Did she do this to me? Why would she?*

Why would she indeed? Lux's voice echoed in a mocking tone. *Face it – she's your enemy now…*

No… She's not… Laria shook her head to dismiss the voice. Jenna wouldn't betray her – Jenna was her friend and Laria wasn't going to let the bloodlust convince her otherwise. *I won't…*

Laria trembled in protest, but the discovery came upon her. Lux's cage was weakening and Laria didn't have the strength to fight back. The pain was the only thing Laria could feel.

No… Lux… don't…

'Laria…?' Jenna approached her cautiously. 'I'm going to call 911.'

In that moment, Laria knew she was no longer in control. The pain faded as Lux took in the reigns and suddenly Laria was the one trapped watching from afar. It was like watching through a film, unable to interact with the other side.

'Don't bother,' Lux muttered and stood back up.

Jenna's eyes grew wide. 'Your eyes… It's like Nick's.'

Lux raised an eyebrow and Laria could feel the curiosity from the bloodlust. 'Nick? I wonder if we met before…'

Of course you have! Laria thought furiously. *You broke his wrist! He hates us because the torture you caused him!*

Whether Lux could hear her was unknown. Instead the bloodlust scoffed and flashed a menacing smile. 'I would have to thank that little hunter for bringing me out. Right after I kill you!'

The panic came flooding back. *Lux!*

'Laria!' Jenna tried to back away, but the bloodlust was faster. With a snake-like grip, Lux held Jenna's throat and chuckled. 'Laria… why?'

'You naive brat,' Lux sneered with a snide tone. 'A human such as yourself shouldn't dare to stand in my way.'

'Laria... please don't...' Jenna begged as Lux chuckled. Laria heard the gunshot again and judging by the way Lux cringed it meant that the bloodlust was hit. However Laria still couldn't feel the pain. Maybe the adrenaline was shielding her.

'I must admit, I feel pleasure at killing the old-fashioned way but I have to send a message.' Lux pinned Jenna to the ground. 'Right after I drain your essence, I'm going to kill the one that shot me.'

No. Anger flooded in Laria's chest. *I won't let you hurt my friends anymore!*

Laria forced herself to break free from the binds that trapped her to her mind. The pain began to return to her as she mentally fought against the bloodlust. Slowly, Laria regained movement in her limbs and she forced Lux back into the cage.

You fool! You've doomed us, I was trying to save you!

Shut up. Laria thought, ignoring the cries of outrage in the back of her mind. As soon as Laria had the strength, she immediately yanked her hand away from Jenna before a wave of dizziness.

What was going on?

But Laria didn't have time to question it, Jenna was immediately crawling backwards with a choked sob. She reached for her neck tenderly as she kept her back against the tree.

Laria shook her head. 'Jen… that was not me.'

'We're not friends anymore,' Jenna said firmly. 'Tell that to Brodie and Maya too, since they are just like you.'

The dizziness blurred her vision and Laria lost the strength to remain in her position. As she hit the forest floor, she could make out the shape of Jenna recovering from Lux's attack. As Jenna disappeared in her vision, Laria clawed the dirt and ignored the heat flooding her face.

Laria wasn't sure how much time had passed, but it felt like an eternity. With pain flaring through her body, Laria felt her chest twist with guilt.

Why wasn't I strong enough? Laria asked herself. *I'm losing consciousness…*

As her world darkened, Laria felt a glimmer of hope when she sensed a warm presence hold her.

CHAPTER 10

'So,' David muttered and went through the forest. Next to him was Ruddy, who was silently strolling. 'How long have you been under the Mandati Dux's wing?'

'I hope that this isn't your lame attempt at small talk,' Ruddy replied dryly and confused David. 'But to answer your question, I have been training with my magister for several years. Takon believes that I'm capable of taking over his position if anything were to happen to him.' The shifter pushed away a branch, easily snapping the twigs without remorse.

David really did have a strange feeling about the apprentice. 'And do you believe that?'

'I won't deny it.'

'You're a tough nut to crack,' David admitted with a low chuckle.

Ruddy paused when he noticed David's curious nature. 'But I say that I could handle the Mandati Dux position, because I am Takon's son.'

Ruddy's comment made David falter in his step. 'You're what?'

'My mother was a Forte, Kira Ryans... and my father was bit of a rebellious shifter back in the day. It's not exactly safe when you're the son of the Mandati Dux and everyone knows it,' Ruddy explained bluntly and continued walking. 'Takon's a member of the Laurence family, and he was responsible for assisting the seal of the rectocs. When a shifter is born from two separate families, there is always a more dominant side and mine happened to be Forte.'

'Wasn't expecting that,' David announced boldly and Ruddy ignored him. 'Anything else that I should need to know about the Mandati Dux just in case I trip again?'

Again, Ruddy halted in his tracks and raised his hand to keep David quiet. He seemed to be in concentration, as if he was searching and suddenly he scowled. 'There's someone else here.'

Were the hunters here? No one informed him that they were meant to be around. For a moment, everything was still. David's body froze along with Ruddy's words and finally, the sound of a gunshot echoed within the trees. Without hesitation, David and Ruddy spared each other a knowing glance and they raced through the forest. Ruddy was faster, but David knew this forest like it was the back of his hand. The second gunshot made David pick up the pace.

He rushed forward, cursing when he recognised Laria on the ground. Yet she wasn't alone.

'Laria!' David yelled, running towards his student and ignoring the other male figure. Laria had two gunshot wounds; one was on her shoulder and the other was in her thigh. Her bloodied clothes were torn by the bullet wounds.

Without warning, Laria shot up from her position and looked around with alarm. Her breathing was shallow and her face was flushed.

'I'll see if there's any hunters nearby,' Ruddy mentioned and David found himself sighing in relief. As he darted out of the trees, David returned his attention back on Laria. If it were the hunters that were indeed around, then why didn't they inform David? It didn't make sense.

'Laria, you have to stay down. You've lost a fair bit of blood,' the man holding Laria instructed as she met his gaze.

Judging from the soft look in her eyes, David then knew that they knew each other well. 'Chris... you're here...' Laria went into a coughing fit and reached up to cover her face. Chris looked back at Laria in panic when she threw up; it was a disturbing sight, but David's heart seemed to stop the second he noticed traces of red in her system.

Laria passed out in Chris's arms. David started to freak out. Her body was trembling and David saw the goosebumps rise on Laria's skin. David knew what was going on. The S.H.O knew how shifters could tend to their own bullet wounds... but if it was poisoned...

'These bullet wounds have foxglove in them,' a woman spoke up suddenly. David hadn't noticed her until then. 'We need to get her out of here!'

'Hold on Laria!' Chris begged desperately, raising a hand over her chest. David heard the desperate voice. 'Ponite...'

This guy was a warlock.

With his hand hovered over Laria, her tremors stopped just as Ruddy returned to the scene with a scowl across his face. He paused when he saw the stranger duo and recognition flashed in his eyes.

'The poison's slowed down,' Chris announced with a huff of relief. The woman beside Chris showed her gratitude and let a breath of air escape of her lips. 'I slowed down her heart rate so that we can get her out of here on time.'

'Whoever shot this girl is no longer around,' Ruddy pointed out. 'I did see a blonde human here however – she seemed frightened.'

Could it be Jenna? The thought of it seemed to be a possibility for David, but he knew if she was frightened, then chasing after her wasn't a good idea. He just had to hope that if it was Jenna, then she was alright.

'Let's leave her be for now,' David decided before turning to the pair. 'What's going on here?'

'My name is Liza and this is Chris,' the woman introduced herself with a frown of concern. 'Haroni Ladas sent us here, so we decided to track down Laria – only to find her here.'

'How do you two know Laria?' David questioned, pushing himself to his feet and took a closer look at his student. She was still pale and the rash wasn't getting any better, but at least they still had a chance to save her.

Now it was Chris's turn to scowl. 'I'm her damn brother –

and I'm going to find out who's responsible for this after I get Laria to safety.' Before David could comment, Chris ran with Laria in his arms and didn't bother looking back.

Liza looked on and turned against David. He felt her gaze on him and fidgeted uncomfortably. 'Could you perhaps tell us what is going on?'

Ruddy was the one to explain, 'Hunters have been attacking the shifters for stupid reasons.'

'Hey,' David warned and shot a glare towards Takon's son. 'Those hunters are my friends that you're talking about. They aren't stupid – they're just fighting back the wrong way.'

Immediately Ruddy turned back to Liza. 'So they're hunting shifters for stupid reasons that don't make sense.'

This guy was really Takon's son? How on Earth would David learn to co-operate with him if Ruddy kept brushing his comments off? He wasn't really the clone of the Mandati Dux. Takon was patient, calm and mostly everything that this guy was not.

Whatever Ruddy said to Liza, she seemed to agree with a frown.

'I don't blame the hunters for what they're doing,' Liza confessed softly. David raised his head and he was curious to why she had the point. 'In Cheyenne, there has been a growth in shifter population. Fights are starting, the witches are getting concerned. It might even be a point when the witches finally have enough.'

'Do you think they will attack the shifters?' David asked and Liza shook her head.

'I wish I knew – I don't have a high enough position among the coven to be disclosed with such information.' Liza looked back at the direction of where Chris and Laria disappeared to. 'I just know we can't let a civil war break out; it could be deadly for everyone.

'How do we stop it?' David questioned, watching as Liza look back at him with uncertainty in her eyes.

'I don't know...'

***

The door in front of Jason's face opened, revealing Brodie's annoyed expression. Jason kept his glare in return since he was in no mood to deal with his grumpy twin. Brodie's eyes remained hard and blocked the doorway, much to Jason's annoyance.

Brodie kept stern and leaned on the frame of his door. 'Jason.'

In response, Jason returned the flat tone. 'Brodie.'

They kept their silent stare contest between themselves. Eventually Brodie stood back and allowed Jason to enter, as if he knew the reason of his arrival.

Jason recognised Tara the second that he stepped into the estate. At first glance, he flinched upon seeing the scar that crossed over her right eye. Even when Jason knew that it was there, it still brought questions up to the reasons of her scars. Her dirty blonde hair was tied back into a low ponytail.

Her lips twitched into a smile. 'It is nice to see you Jason,' she said while nodding.

Despite knowing her as the sister of his deceased father, Jason still found it strange that he had a family. Before moving to Golden Cliff, Jason never thought he would meet his family – and that included Brodie.

But Jason didn't voice it out loud. He didn't want to seem ungrateful to the woman, despite the kindness she has shown him. Maybe in time he would be able to connect with her and Brodie.

'So what did you want to meet me for?' Jason asked, straightening his posture and folding his arms.

Tara's smile tightened, but she seemed confident. 'Ever since Leon died, I've been training with Brodie in Krav Maga. Training also helps me with my vision.' She referred to her scarred face and Jason forced himself to keep the curiosity down. He wasn't ready to hear the reasons of her injuries. 'And I know that you've been training with Brodie as well.'

Jason eyed his brother and much to Jason's surprise, he remained silent. Brodie was leaning on the wall with narrowed eyes, almost as if he was calculating everything that Jason was doing.

'Why do you want to train me?' Jason asked Tara, glancing back at her with hesitation. 'Surely Brodie told you that Ultio hasn't really bothered me.'

'Regardless of how you feel, I think it would be a great way for us to bond. You need to learn how to protect yourself – without the bloodlust.' Tara then stepped forward. 'I take it that Mae didn't teach you to fight.'

With the mention of his deceased mother, Jason clenched his fist. 'No,' he said coldly and avoided Tara's stare. 'She scolded me whenever I picked fights, one day I got into a fight and bit off more than I could chew. Since then, I didn't fight.' He remembered the days when he was sent to the principal's office with bumps and bruises. 'Brodie's training has been the only exception.'

And the mercenary that his bloodlust killed.

'I'll show you an example of what I will teach you,' Tara told him and gestured for Jason to come forward. 'Try to hit me.'

Her comment caught Jason off guard. The moment passed and Jason shook his head with a heavy breath. 'I know this isn't going to end well.' How did Tara not see the disadvantage? She was a trained professional and literally claimed she trained in order to help with her missing eye.

'Don't worry,' Tara told him with a smile. 'I'll go easy on your first lesson.' In the corner of his eyes, Jason spotted Brodie flashing a grin.

'I don't think he's going to do it Aunt Tara,' Brodie confessed dryly. 'He just thinks his bloodlust is going to save his hide every time.' Great, now his own brother was mocking him.

Prove them wrong.

Jason froze. *Ultio.* His bloodlust rumbled from the back of Jason's mind, but Ultio made no further action to take over Jason's movements.

'Fine,' Jason muttered to convince himself. Brodie watched with a glint of amusement in his eyes. 'I'm not going to back down.' Relying on his previous training with Brodie,

Jason tried to find a weak spot on Tara. From head to toe, it looked like that Tara didn't have an unguarded position.

With the hazel eyes scanning Jason, the look unnerved him. Yet the stare from her eye only brought back his confidence. She wanted him to try and Jason wasn't going to let her down.

Jason attacked with a palm strike first without a sound, but Tara moved her head to slip past his movement. She stepped backwards and Jason gritted his teeth as he saw the playful expression grow.

'Come on,' she taunted lightly. 'Move faster.'

Easy for her to say.

Keeping his cool, Jason tried again to aim for her sternum only for her grab his wrist before he could make the hit.

'Brodie seems to have taught you techniques,' Tara said to Jason. 'Unfortunately that's the second time I could've countered these attacks.'

'Like how?' Jason demanded, ignoring the snicker from Brodie in the background. It only took a second for Tara to back up her words. Jason's world was spinning in an instant as Tara flipped Jason to the ground. Hitting the floorboards, Jason felt the sting from his back and he let out a wounded groan.

Tara hovered over him, her smile fading. 'Not bad – you still have a long way to go if you want to be able to keep up with Brodie, let alone me.' She backed up and rested her hands on her hips. 'Get up, I'll let you know when we're finished.'

His body still hurt. Whatever Tara's intentions were, he had to trust that she was going to make him a fighter.

With a shaky breath, Jason picked himself off the floor and tensed his body. He wasn't sure how long this training session would be, but it was still experience that he needed.

***

Brodie sat on the couch of his living room, observing an empty glass. Jason was long gone; Tara went to make some important calls and Brodie was alone. Since it was a quiet moment, the Forte heir only could sit back to watch the flames of his fireplace. Unlike Laria, the sight of fire settled him whenever he looked at it.

'I dare you to look me in the eyes and say you're still not tempted to kill her in order to stop her father's plans.'

Again Charmi's words haunted him. Brodie tightened the hold on his glass. Was Brodie the fire that Laria feared? She had nothing to do with Leon's death – yet somehow, when alcohol was involved, Brodie wanted nothing more to see her killed to quench his thirst for vengeance against Lucien.

Leon's ghost appeared behind Brodie; he didn't have to turn to recognise his father's presence. The visits from Leon were a clear sign that Brodie was starting to lose his touch with his old self and his father could only watch.

'Brodie,' Leon spoke coolly, and Brodie stiffened once his father took a step towards him. 'Your inner beast is beginning to manipulate you – you have to fight it.'

Brodie immediately snorted at Leon's comment. 'Fight it...' Leon's expression remained neutral, as the younger Forte glared back. 'I can't fight Orgul anymore... the bloodlust has won. I need him in order to fight off Charmi – if losing my friends is the price for defeating Lucien like I swore, then that's what I'm going to do.'

'Don't you see, Brodie? I know you, and this is not you,' Leon growled with a hint of annoyance, the first emotion that Brodie saw from his father in a long time. 'Your bloodlust is doing this to you. You're not a monster – you are my son. Jason is my son too. You both are of the Forte bloodline that has to keep fighting.'

For the first time in his life, Brodie felt anger towards his father. How dare Leon talk to him like this? 'No, that's where you're wrong,' he snapped. 'You died and left me alone to find out that everything you said was a lie.' He moved his gaze away from his father, ignoring the stunned look from Leon. 'You didn't think of the consequences of your actions, *Dad.* I do things my way now.'

With those words, Brodie's eyes fluttered opened. When

Brodie knew about his father's visits, Brodie naturally felt exhausted from making contact with the dead. He probably needed to get away from Rel.

'How was your conversation with Leon?' Tara asked, from the other side of the living room on a separate armchair. She made herself comfortable, twirling a glass of bourbon with a bored look. 'I could sense Leon's presence... but he's been talking to you more frequently than you told me.'

At first Brodie said nothing. His hazel eyes went over to the fireplace. Unlike his dreams, the fireplace held no flames and glow – just like it had been before Brodie fell asleep. 'Tara... I want to tell you a secret.' Tara's frown deepened and Brodie brushed his hair back. 'I've been having these thoughts; that I need to kill Laria for my vengeance... why is that?'

'I should've predicted this,' Tara sighed and shot down her drink. 'A Forte's vengeance is a powerful weapon. It's their representative of killing. The rectoc that gave us this power – Vindi was dedicated to having the last word.'

Brodie recognised the name Vindi; he even flinched when he thought of the name. It was a name that he feared. While he never met the Forte rectoc, he knew of her well. He heard the story about her countless times, and it still put shivers down his spine.

'The one thing that we are good at... is holding grudges,' she explained and clenched her fist in a tight ball. 'Vengeance doesn't have to be one person – as you're witnessing with Charmi. You can pass it on to friends, descendants and family... My theory is that you want Lucien to suffer the same way that you did... and take it out on Laria.'

'I can't do that,' Brodie snapped and he slammed his fist on the table beside him. Tara didn't show any reaction to Brodie's outburst. 'Aunt Tara – you know how to control your bloodlust, tell me there's another way.'

'And there is,' the auntie replied calmly. 'You have to tame Orgul – because he's the one that has been filling your head with ideas that killing Laria would quench your thirst. Before your father's death – Orgul was the last problem on your mind... so why should he bother you now?'

'There's this sensation that I get whenever I see Laria,' Brodie explained curtly. 'I feel like Lucien's plans will fail if she dies, and that's why I have satisfaction for the thoughts of her death. But I've been thinking... Seth was right – I would never want to hurt Laria. Not now. Not ever. I need to control this bastard.'

'Glad you see it my way,' Tara admitted plainly. 'Soon, we will find the root of your bloodlust and lock Orgul up.'

CHAPTER 11

Laria immediately felt her body fly up with a hacking fit due to lack of air. Pain shot through her body as soon as she woke up and the coughing slowly settled down.

For a moment she panicked when she couldn't see the forest surroundings. It took her a moment to settle and Laria realised that she was in her room with bandages over her injured limbs.

Laria would've sworn that she recalled her brother clutching her close, but she was alone now. Perhaps she'd imagined him. Instinctively, Laria reached up for her shoulder and winced at the pain.

Then there was Jenna. Laria's heart sank when she recalled the fear in Jenna's eyes as Lux took control of her body. Jenna had been one of her best friends since they were kids, and now she didn't have trust in Laria.

Laria growled under her breath, swearing to herself that Lux would not gain possession again. The reason Jenna was afraid of them was because she hadn't fought hard enough when Lux took over. Now Laria made this mess, it was up to her to clean it up again and prove to Jenna that shifters were desperately protecting the humans.

The sound of footsteps rushed into the room and the door slammed open, revealing Chris. Laria felt her eyes grow wide with a mixture of relief and alarm, recognising the shocked features of her older brother.

Chris moved, walking up to Laria in a few strides to embrace her tightly. His arms wrapped around her tightly and

Laria felt tears sting her eyes as she returned the hug. With everything that happened for the past week, Laria finally felt the walls crumble with her brother's contact.

'I'm here Laria,' Chris promised and tightened his hold. 'I'm sorry for leaving you alone in this.'

When Chris did let go, he explained to her that she had traces of foxglove in her system and she had been out of action for a few days. Chris also said that Liza was in town, staying with Heather.

'Chris...' Laria's voice was quiet and the elder brother frowned in her direction. 'I was wondering if you could tell me about Lucien... well, when he was known as our Dad...'

He was quiet at first, but he cleared his throat awkwardly. 'So you know...'

'I do.'

The surprise was obvious in Chris, but he seemed to nod to himself in agreement. 'Alright then.' Chris took a seat by the foot of Laria's bed. 'Where would you like me to start?'

'How did our parents meet?' Laria asked curiously and Chris blinked in surprise. She didn't see why he was surprised. Like all kids, she wanted to know the story of their parents.

'Well – according to dad it was shortly after Takon became the Mandati Dux twenty-six years ago,' Chris explained and scratched behind his ear. 'As a dux, they have to swear an oath with the witches, hunters and the shifters as witnesses. Dad, Zanobi and Takon were close friends, so he was strung along. Our mum, she came from a town that is east from here and looking for information about shifters. Dad pissed her off.'

Laria snorted with disbelief. 'No way.'

Chris laughed in Laria's response. 'It's true. Something about red wine and tripping over himself. You know how that usually ends.'

Again, Laria felt a snort escape her. Who knew that her dad could be a dork?

'She was fuming, and Dad promised to make it up to her.' Chris was still smiling. 'He paid for her dress and took her out to dinner – then their tale of denial and love took years to develop.'

The next question left a bitter taste in her mouth. 'Do you know what made him become Lucien?'

His expression turned serious. 'Honestly no,' Chris muttered. 'But it was after the day of my sixth birthday – a group of outside shifters tried to kill Mum in order to get me to snap. Dad fought back viciously, but it was when Edward attacked.'

Laria recognised his name.

'He trapped you in flames. It didn't do anything to me, but it did something to Dad. He was frightened for your life. You were two – it wasn't uncommon for shifters to be young when their powers blossom, but it was enough for you to show signs of a shifter's power. The outsiders retreated and we feared the worst from you because you were so terrified. You had burns all over your body, and you flinched at anything that moved so we – our parents did what was necessary.'

Laria finally realised what Chris was implying. 'Mum sealed up Lux...'

'Aye,' Chris responded guiltily. 'They got Hugh to heal your wounds and with the help of a Laurence, they managed to make you happy again. But... unfortunately, Dad had other plans. He swore that he would make them pay, took Viri and never came back.'

'That's when he lost himself.' Laria found herself frowning. Not only that but Zanobi had always been loyal to her father, there had to be more to the story.

'Look, I promise I will stay with you until you finish school,' Chris swore, clearing his throat for the second time. 'I will help you train your bloodlust, since it's my responsibility as your older brother.' He offered a smile to Laria. 'Speaking of responsibilities, where is your magister?'

Tahani had been missing since Haroni's departure. 'Honestly, I have no clue.'

***

Tahani dodged a flying fist and sneered in satisfaction as the opponent grunted in annoyance. Around her, the crowd around the cage let out violent cheers. The dux slammed her fist against the ribs of the opponent and she scoffed.

Ever since Tahani left the mansion, she went back to spending her nights at the pits. It was better for her, especially when she could take out her frustration on recently matured shifters.

As the shifter pulled herself back up, Tahani found herself staring deep into the olive-green eyes. Tahani prepared for a strike, but her strength dissolved along with her courage to fight. Her arm dropped to the side, and she was no longer standing within the ring.

Again, Tahani was watching Zanobi leave. The seconds drew on as the distance widened between them, causing Tahani to shake on the spot. Watching the scene before her felt like her heart was being ripped out of her chest.

'Why are ya leaving?' She demanded, voice trembling. It wasn't the first time she was betrayed, but losing her best friend made the difference. Tahani could handle losing her parents, her sister, Haroni but Zanobi… Tahani couldn't bear it. 'Zanobi-!'

A force connected Tahani's face, knocking her off her feet as her head hit first on the cold concrete ground.

Tahani blinked herself into awareness, realising that she was no longer in the forest and back within the pits. Around her, the cheers were mixed with booing towards her. In front of her, Tahani saw the shifter stand tall.

Within that moment, Tahani could only hear her pounding heart. As she lifted herself from the floor, her head felt like it was spinning. The shifter got her good, Tahani had to admit that.

However, a gunshot echoed within the pits and Tahani froze again. Her chest felt like it was bleeding again, but as Tahani touched the scar she noticed there were no signs of blood.

Stop imagining it… Tahani protested and she tried to block out the noise. The gunfire was fake. *It's not real. It's not real. It. Is. Not. Real!*

Again, Tahani felt something hit her but this time is was in direct contact with her chest. The pain exploded as Tahani let out a short gasp with a stagger. In return, Tahani's eyes glowed and she clenched her jaw.

'Ya shouldn't have done that!' Tahani snapped, and tackled the other shifter into the ground. She kept the shifter pinned and with a yell, Tahani slammed her fist against the shifter's face.

'I forfeit!' The shifter cried out, but they were drowned by Tahani's yells. Again, Tahani punched the shifter, breaking skin as she made contact. 'I said forfeit!' Tahani ignored the pleas, she just wanted to stop hearing the gunfire.

Before she could make contact again, Tahani felt someone grab her arm and pulled her away from the other shifter. As Tahani was pulled back into reality, she realised that the gunfire was gone and Tahani wasn't shot.

'That's enough Rosa!' said a familiar voice.

Tahani looked back at the shifter that held her with wide eyes. 'Nadia…'

'It's Sheriff Cyler to you,' Nadia whispered harshly and Tahani looked back at shifter she injured. It appeared as if a bunch of medical professionals had gotten to her. 'You have a lot of nerve to do what you just did. You're coming with me.'

As Nadia pulled Tahani to her feet, Tahani managed to catch a familiar face in the corner of her eye. Within the panicked crowd, Charmi watched them with a soft smile. With her appearance, she stuck out like a sore thumb.

But Tahani didn't get a chance to call her out. Nadia wordlessly took her out of the pits, keeping her in a secure hold. Tahani didn't protest to the idea, but as soon as they were away from any onlookers, Nadia released Tahani.

'What were you thinking?' Nadia demanded and Tahani didn't face her. 'I didn't allow you to be released without parole just so you could go around to break more rules!'

'What were ya doing there in the first place?' Tahani responded, finally looking at her. 'I thought we were allowed to do our business there.'

'I was undercover,' Nadia answered coldly and Tahani frowned. 'I was looking for information regarding Zanobi… but you ruined it by trying to kill that poor girl.'

Tahani blocked out the memories, and shrugged. 'It happens sometimes, no one died or anything.'

Nadia gritted her teeth and got in Tahani's face. 'Listen here Rosa, you may have been innocent from The Beast murders, however the public does not see it that way. Clean up your act, or else the people you care about will get hurt.' The sheriff turned in the opposite direction and began to walk away.

'So I just go back to hiding huh?' Tahani shouted, but Nadia kept walking. 'I think yer the one who needs to stop hiding from the truth!' Immediately the sheriff stopped in her tracks. It seemed that it was the first time that Nadia Cyler actually heard her.

A moment passed when Nadia kept walking, leaving Tahani alone in the dark streets.

***

Charmi's night had been rather eventful. Watching Tahani breakdown once more was quite amusing. After the issue within the pits, Charmi made her way back to her secret location, deep within the forest. It was the same one where they played as children and luckily nothing changed.

She looked at the paper she found on the dirty street, before entering her cabin. As she stepped inside, she saw Nick occupying himself with a dartboard. Charmi rolled her eyes – he always seemed so invested in human trinkets for someone who hated them.

Nick didn't bother looking in her direction as he threw a dart. 'I hope you had a good evening, sister.'

'It was,' Charmi confessed, 'I have something to show you.'

It got his attention. Nick raised an eyebrow and approached Charmi as she showed him the dirty flyer.

He read it and scoffed. 'A Halloween party at the school?' the brother demanded flatly. 'Do I look like a whiny teenager to you? Sounds boring.'

'Read it then,' Charmi hissed and Nick looked down at the flyer again. His eyes stopped on a particular set of words. As she saw a small smile cross his face, Charmi knew that it got his attention.

'Humans are prey?' Nick read out loud and he met his gaze with Charmi. 'Now it sounds interesting. I take it you want me to be a real predator?'

'Of course,' Charmi replied with a snide smile. Brodie's sorry lot would have a harder time protecting drunken teenagers, especially at night. 'You get your prey and in the meantime, I will find more of those bear traps that Tahani Rosa found.'

'That sounds like an excellent idea,' Nick decided with a sneer of satisfaction. 'So when is it?'

'Tomorrow night, at the school grounds.'

'I'll be there,' Nick replied with a grin. He stood to his feet and put on his leather coat as Charmi questioned his intentions. 'Just so you know...' His eyes flashed gold and Charmi met the look. 'Jenna Sommers is my prey... you do not harm her – or else you will suffer repercussions.' And with that, Nick left the cabin.

CHAPTER 12

Maya leaned on her locker while she waited for Jason to take out his things. He acknowledged her existence with a nod and Maya silently returned the greeting. Life had been hectic for everyone for the past week.

First a Jane Doe died in Brodie's front yard. Jason was still working on his control of the bloodlust – so far, he seemed to be doing well – while Brodie was training and missing school. Laria was poisoned with foxglove. Seth had been helping Maya with her search of Azu, meaning that he was going through the past records on the Rosa stone, and Jenna had discovered the existence of shape shifters but she believed them to be bad people.

'So are you still going to the Halloween thing tonight?' Maya asked quietly, trying to distract herself from all that.

In response Jason closed the door of his locker and sighed. 'I completely forgot about that. So much has happened since my – I mean, Brodie's birthday.'

'You know that you can say it's your birthday too. There are only three hundred and sixty-six birthdays to go around. People would just say it was a coincidence rather than assume that he's your long-lost twin,' Maya said flatly and raised an eyebrow when Jason shook his head. 'But I agree – when did our lives become such a pain?' Suddenly Maya paused when she recognised Jenna's new haircut from the end of the hallway.

Jenna was standing next to Taro; the latter glared in Maya's direction. While Jason didn't seem bothered by Taro's look, Maya returned the glare and puffed up her chest. She held no trust for Taro and she couldn't stand that her friend was standing with him.

'Why are you glaring at Taro?'

Recognising Seth's voice, Maya turned to see him approaching them with Takon Falls. The school councillor softly smiled towards Maya but said nothing. Truth be told, Maya wasn't sure what to make of him. Takon Falls was a man of mystery, like Seth in a way. He always presented a smile and kindness, but his eyes showed pain.

Finally Takon looked down at Seth with a serious frown. 'Remember what I told you, Seth.'

He nodded. 'Understood.' His response struck Maya as odd. Maya noticed the strangest glint in his dark eyes. Was it admiration? No – it was deeper than that. It occurred to Maya that even though she was friends with Seth, she was still clueless about him.

After pushing his glasses against his amber eyes, Takon bowed his head and headed back in the direction he came from.

Despite understanding that Takon was a shifter as well, Maya didn't know that Seth hung out with him.

'He was informing me of the hunter movements.' Seth went to his locker with the confused pair following him. 'So far we don't know their final motive, however we have short term goals. After the Jane Doe incident, they want to make sure that there isn't another so chances are they will be tracking us during the party.'

'Us?' Maya realised what Seth implied and she looked surprised. 'You're coming too?'

It looked as if Seth was suddenly annoyed – any signs of the strange look towards Takon were gone. 'Don't think it's because I want to.' He grunted impatiently and avoided their stare. 'I was told to watch out for hunters while Mister Embers tries to lead them in a different direction. We tried contacting the Ungue Dux, but she has been missing for quite some time so Laria is going to take her place by going.'

'Wow,' Jason muttered under his breath. 'You've been pretty busy the past week.'

'So have you two.' Seth noticed and looked back at them with the passive expression.

Checking the time, and Seth's eyes narrowed. 'I've got to go to class,' Seth reminded before giving a pointed look towards Maya. 'I know you have Math with Launten so don't start anything – especially if he believes you're one of us.'

Don't be yourself.

Maya may not know Seth well, but she could translate his blunt words. The last thing he needed to worry about was babying her – Maya could take care of herself. It was something she had been doing for as long as she could remember.

'I've got to go to my class,' Jason realised and scratched the back of his head. Seth nodded stoically and went in his own direction to class. 'Do you happen to know if Laria is coming today?'

'Well she was still recovering from the poison last time I checked,' Maya said uneasily. She was shocked when she got a call from Chris saying that Laria was attacked by hunters. It was before Chris mentioned that Jenna was with them, and Maya was sure she'd heard everything. 'But I will text her about tonight.'

Maya doubted that Laria wanted to go to the Halloween party, especially with the poisoning incident. A surge of annoyance was directed at Tahani. Wasn't the woman meant to guide Laria? Slowly, Maya was assessing that Tahani wasn't the best teacher.

'I'm sure she'll be alright,' Jason said with a smirk as he turned away from Maya. It was strange to hear him so confident about Laria. After all, Jason was the overprotective one if Maya was being honest. As if Jason heard her thoughts, he added, 'Laria has us after all.'

She offered a small smile in return and silently agreed. 'See you after class Jason.' As Maya turned away from him, she regained her confidence and headed to class. Maya stepped in the class with a few groups but took her usual spot and it was then when Jenna entered the class with Taro.

Maya's eyes met Jenna's. It was strange to see the look of hurt in Jenna's eyes. What happened to her? While Maya knew that Jenna discovered the existence of shape shifters, she didn't know what caused Jenna to be so stiff around them. If only Laria was around to tell her.

Taro ignored Maya, going to his seat away from the girls as Jenna approached. As Jenna came closer to Maya, she didn't seem to be pleased that she had to take her spot next to Maya.

Even the rest of the class was stunned by the look between the girls. It was their first time seeing a negative reaction from Jenna after all. Jenna stiffened her posture as Maya stood back to her feet and looked at her companion.

'Maya.'

Don't start anything. Seth's earlier warning echoed in Maya's head as she flashed a small smile to comfort Jenna. 'What's up?'

'Don't act like you're so innocent. I thought we were friends,' Jenna replied hastily before she placed her things on the table. 'You're just like Laria. A liar.' The last part was a mutter for only Maya's ears. Anger bubbled up in Maya's chest as she tried to protest but the teacher came in.

The classmates broke into loud whispers, curious about what went on with the two friends. Maya settled in her seat after the teacher began the lesson, occasionally glancing in Jenna's direction.

Now Maya knew that she had to go to the party. Just because she was human, it didn't mean that she would bother sitting in the sidelines. Only cowards sat back while everyone else did the work.

This wasn't about her pride though – it was about her friends and it gave her a chance to prove that she wasn't useless. With people like Taro, Maya wasn't even sure if she was safe from them.

***

Laria cursed as she pulled away the bokken, dodging Chris's practise sword. The wood met with a loud clank and her brother was superior when it came to sword fight. And fencing. And pretty much any sort of fighting.

Yet Chris looked like a child on Christmas. He had a grin on his face as he fought against Laria and challenged her every movement. It frustrated her that Chris overpowered every effort she made to stop him. His attacks shoved her in a corner and stopped her from countering anything.

'Come on little 'Ria,' Chris teased and took the advantage of Laria's misstep. He easily whacked the wood out of her hands. The force of the hit stung her palms and she cried out as the fake sword left her hands.

'Ow,' Laria whimpered shaking her hands. A grimace appeared as Laria shot Chris a cold look. 'That really hurt!'

'Now you're dead,' he sang, lowering the weapon to meet Laria's throat as if it had been a real sword.

A huff of air escaped Laria and she swatted the weapon angrily. 'I get it... I can't use a sword to save my own life.' She reached down for the weapon and nursed her hand. 'Besides, I still don't see the connection between training to hit people with a sharp object and my bloodlust.'

It was then when Chris turned serious. 'From what you've said, your bloodlust is most active when you're fighting. Either it can see your hesitation, or it's acting on its instincts to protect itself. Possibly both.'

'Then maybe I shouldn't fight anymore,' Laria muttered as she returned the weapon back into the barrel of practise swords. 'If I never fight, then the bloodlust will never come back out.'

'You've never really liked fighting... have you?' Chris asked and Laria didn't deny his comment. Sure, as a kid she got into fights with Sara but those were different. At the time, Laria was never afraid of losing herself to her inner shifter. Even then, she didn't want to resort to violence and only did so when Sara pushed her buttons.

'I've just been lucky so far,' Laria confessed and looked at her hands. Ever since Edward's death, Laria occasionally saw them for what they were – weapons. They were the weapons that snapped Nick's wrist and tore out Edward's heart. 'I just want it to be over.'

'I understand,' Chris said, patting her on the back. 'But if you stop now, will it solve the problem? The bloodlust is still there, and you have to deal with it even when you aren't fighting.'

'So what, you want me to unleash the bloodlust right now?' Laria questioned dryly, referring to the access of weapons around her. 'Isn't that a bit reckless to do especially in a room full of swords?'

Chris smirked lightly at her attempt of a jab. 'No. Your hesitance is making you open to the bloodlust and refusing to fight only encourages it. Shifters have to live with it, to co-exist like the natural world does.'

Laria suddenly felt uneasy. 'So if I accept that Lux is a part of me, would the voices stop? What if the bloodlust wants more than I do?' She hated the thoughts of killing Edward; the guilt of his death haunted her nights. The worst part was that she wanted him dead. She didn't want to feel like that for anyone. Was that the bloodlust talking? Or was it herself? 'I won't do it again.'

'It's terrifying. I know,' Chris said and took a step closer to her. They were at arm's length and Laria raised her head to meet his eyes. 'But you need to forgive yourself and understand that what you did was a last resort. These hunters are your enemies. They don't care that you are trying, they want you dead. Being guilty will distract you – you need to connect with Lux in order to control that bloodlust.'

Laria felt herself frown. 'I don't think it's a good idea Chris. This isn't me – I won't kill another life and you know it, Chris.' She didn't want to have this argument again.

'Why do you think that you lose yourself all the time?' Chris's expression turned serious and Laria paused to look back at him. 'It's because you bottle everything up – you're worried about killing so much that it haunts you.' He finally returned his weapon back in the barrel with Laria's. 'You have to be willing to step into the dark boundaries in order to tame the darkness.'

Recognising the words, Laria formed a small smile. 'Liza said those words to me once.'

'It's not like I'm telling you to kill recklessly,' Chris continued after his own smile. 'Work together. Your bloodlust will not let you die, and by accepting it will be the time that you can fight with it without fear.'

Laria felt uncomfortable that Chris was encouraging her to attack. But was he right? Was the bloodlust attacking her head and her friends because Laria refused to use Lux?

'Sorry that I had to drop that bombshell on you,' Chris said, placing a hand on her shoulder. Laria felt the familiar comfort. It seemed strange though, Laria wasn't sure where the comfort was coming from, or if it was the fact it was just Chris. 'It's just our dad was a lot like you. He resisted for a long time before it claimed him.'

A look of understanding dawned on Laria and she offered him another smile. 'It's alright,' she replied and accepted his tenderness. 'But... for you I will try to do it. If that was one of the reasons why Lucien is the way he is now then I will do everything in my power to not become Lux.'

With that, Laria felt extremely content with her promise. Lux wasn't going to get a hold of her anymore; it was time to start accepting every part of Laria's cursed life. Even if she didn't like Lux, Laria wasn't going to let Lux hurt her friends again. No matter the price.

'Now – we can get to the fun stuff.' Chris let out a huff of air and offered a grin. 'What are you doing for tonight?'

'Isn't that obvious?' Laria asked slowly and crossed her arms over her chest. 'I'm stuck at a party that's filled with lunatics that are bent on trying to kill me.' And Jenna.

'I should come with you,' Chris stated and he crossed his arms over his chest. 'If I do, then I won't have to worry about those hunters.'

'Don't worry so much Chris,' Liza's voice announced and the siblings turned to the woman she entered the room. 'Heather's going to the party.' It still came to a shock that Heather had a sister. Now that Laria thought about it, Heather didn't talk about her family life.

'And some of my friends are coming as well,' Laria added when she recalled Maya's earlier text. So far, Seth, Maya and Jason were going. She wasn't sure about Brodie yet.

'Fine,' Chris relented before ruffling Laria's hair. She grumbled under her breath once Chris moved his hand away so that she could fix her hair. 'But let's not forget that if you get caught, it will be the same as our ancestors in Salem.'

Suddenly, Laria looked at her brother with wide eyes. 'You mean that stuff is real?'

'I forget that you don't know much about the witch history,' Chris confessed sheepishly and scratched the back of his head. 'We have an uncle that would have a field day with you.'

'I haven't seen him around,' Laria said with a wary tone. 'Why hasn't he been here for anything?' The last part included Lesley's funeral. If it was one thing that Laria was curious about, it was about her witch heritage. Lesley never said much about her family, but apparently, she and her brother had the occasional chat.

'He only knew what I told him,' Chris answered reassuringly. 'He has a daughter as well – a bit younger than you but apparently she's pretty good. They both have their issues back at home as well.' The thought didn't please Laria.

So, she changed the subject. 'So, what happened with the Salem witch trials?'

'Anything that was different from humanity was hung; witches, werewolves, vampires-'

'Werewolves and vampires are real too?' Laria asked with disbelief. Her life seemed like a lie at the moment. 'I can't believe it.'

'Really, you can believe in shape shifters, rectocs, witches and even angels... but the second the most common supernatural creatures are mentioned, you flip out?' Chris asked and sighed quietly. 'Thank goodness I didn't list the other supernaturals and their location.'

Shooting her brother another look, Laria felt like the bomb was dropped again. Halloween wasn't the best time to be realising that the world wasn't just filled with shifters. 'Other supernaturals?!'

'Let's just get you a costume.'

***

'Pfft.'

'It's not funny.'

'I'm laughing.'

'I hate you.'

Laria was dressed in a costume that was too short for her liking. How on Earth did Chris — her overprotective older brother who didn't like Brodie just for being a male teenager — think that wearing this costume was a good idea? On second thought Laria didn't want to know why. Her brother was insane.

'It would be good to embrace your other side of the family,' Chris had said.

Finally, Laria gave in and wore the black dress. If it hadn't been for the jumper she borrowed from Chris, she would've been frozen solid. A pointy hat was placed on top of her head harmlessly and she held a mini broomstick. Finally, Laria glared at the teasing smile from Jason who wore a tuxedo with make-up.

'Hey, I prepared my costume,' Jason insisted as he referred to his face. 'It took hours to get someone to help me; Seth refused so I convinced Aunt Tara.'

Suddenly Laria paused at Jason and she offered a smile. 'You called her aunt.'

If the dead groom Jason could blush, he probably would've by now. 'Yeah. Actually it just came naturally... I wasn't thinking.'

'It's not a bad thing to accept that you have your family,

Jason,' Laria confessed and reached for his hand. As she held his hand within hers, Laria noticed that Jason looked at her with astonishment. 'It will be okay.' Her voice was soft as she spoke, yet Jason kept staring as if she yelled it at him.

Finally, Laria noticed Seth was approaching them with a serious expression and Laria let go of Jason's hand. It was weird seeing Seth out of his normal clothes and in a costume of all things. He had a doctor's uniform with fake blood sprayed over him.

'So far there's nothing out of the ordinary,' Seth confessed and looked at the countless people around him. 'I don't know why I agree to these foolish events. There are too many people here for me to concentrate.'

'I'm sure you will be fine, drama queen,' Laria teased.

The look he gave to Laria sent chills down her spine. 'I'm going after Maya,' Seth declared after turning away from Laria. As he strolled away from the pair, Laria frowned in confusion.

'What is with him?' Laria asked Jason who shrugged.

'You know, Seth's not exactly a social butterfly,' Jason replied as if it was an obvious fact. 'He's probably got a headache from his power.'

This was new – no one had this conversation with her before. 'Which is?'

Suddenly, the expression on Jason's face surprised Laria. He was acting like a kid caught in a cookie jar. 'Well – it's no use hiding it now. Seth's a telepath.'

Laria's eyes widened as she processed this information. 'He is?'

'Yeah,' Jason replied with a chuckle when he noticed her shocked features. All this time, Laria never expected Seth to be a telepath. 'Imagine reading the thoughts of everyone in this party including ours – it can't be easy.'

'Wow,' Laria muttered and played with her broom. 'Now I feel bad.'

'Yeah – that feeling is normal.' A smirk formed on Jason's face, and Laria smiled in return. Immediately Jason's smirk dropped as he eyed behind her and Laria turned to see what he was staring at.

Brodie was walking towards them with a serious glare. The costume he wore was based on a traditional skin walker. His arms were coated with dabs of paint and he wore tan trousers. A fake pelt hung over his shoulders, shielding most of his exposed body. but he had a pelt hanging over his shoulders.

'I promised Jenna that I would come as a skin walker,' Brodie announced, glaring at Jason. His brother glared back, but their glares dissolved when Laria stepped in between the pair. Right now they couldn't afford to hate each other. 'So we're going to do this?'

Laria nodded slowly. 'Yeah,' she muttered and frowned once she recognised Taro in the distance. He was in a police officer costume, and Laria wondered uneasily if she should confront him about Jenna. Thinking back to Jenna's frightened expression, Laria decided against it.

CHAPTER 13

'So what's the plan?' Jason asked, looking towards Laria and Brodie. With the hunters at large, Jason knew that he had to tread lightly – especially if they didn't know about his shifter side.

'There are a few hunters that are circling the school,' Brodie muttered as he pointed out a few of the costumed guests.

'Then we stay in the crowd,' Laria suggested. For the first time, Jason realised that he wasn't seeing Laria, but a leader. 'Brodie, you can go inside and blend into the party. If you find anything, make sure you tell us immediately.'

'I know.' And with that, Brodie went into the school building as he put the pelt over his head to conceal his features. Once he did, Jason realised that he couldn't locate Brodie's scent even if he wanted to.

'In the times of the massacre, shifters used to use the pelts of animals to hide their trails,' Laria reminded as she watched Brodie leave. 'Even with sensors, they won't be able find him.'

'I'm not surprised that Forte has the skin of a dead animal on him,' Jason confessed and paused when he noticed that she was glaring at him. 'Look. I'm not going to change my feelings for Brodie anytime soon – he would probably say the same thing.'

Laria sighed irritably. 'I'm not asking you to be friends with him.'

'Then what are you asking for?' Jason demanded, surprising himself for the outburst. 'You heard him that day

Laria – he doesn't care about me. We may be blood, but we are not family. I feel nothing towards him and it surprises me that you do.'

For a moment, Jason saw that Laria was startled by his comment. She lacked a response to him, but Laria's desperate expression told him everything.

But finally, Laria spoke. 'I'm going to find Jenna.' Her voice was cold and she pulled herself away from Jason's gaze. In a split second, Jason knew that he should've held his tongue. Guilt came back to him.

Jason reached out for her. 'Laria-'

'Keep Taro at bay,' Laria ordered sternly and Jason felt like he was punched in the gut. Great, she was annoyed with him. 'He has been a part of this hunting business for too long – who knows how much information he's got on us.' Laria stiffly turned away from Jason and went in another direction.

He had to do something. Jason walked up to her and grabbed her arm, forcing her to halt. 'Laria wait, we have to talk!'

'What do you want me to say?' Laria snapped, eyes flashing amber with the infamous glare. 'We don't have time to talk – and you're making it clear that you can't get along with Brodie for five minutes.' She angrily yanked her arm from his hold. 'Go distract Taro because I have to make sure Jenna is fine.'

As Laria stormed off, Jason ran his fingers through his dark hair. It wasn't like him to snap at her like he just did. Now would've been a good time to have Seth with him.

Spotting the quarterback with a group of people, Jason made his way towards him in silence. Ever since their first meeting, Jason avoided Taro like the plague. He recalled that Laria first lost control in front of him and that most likely gave the young hunter motivation to go after her.

And Laria was another issue.

At the end of the day, you still hate him, a voice insisted and Jason clenched his fist to contain his annoyance.

'Hey, Taro,' Jason spoke up, gaining the quarterback's attention.

The hunter scowled as he recognised Jason. His

recognition wasn't a look of positivity. It took Taro a moment to halt the conversation between the other students before gesturing Jason to follow him. Jason went along with Taro's wishes, following the quarterback into one of the classrooms.

When they were alone, Taro whirled around to face Jason with his arms crossed. 'What the hell do you want?'

'I don't know what you've said to Jenna, but we don't appreciate it,' Jason replied, ignoring the harsh tone directed at him.

'What does it matter to you?' Taro responded back. 'I just told Jenna the truth – about what Laria and the rest of her friends are.'

'When did you know?' Jason asked calmly. The last thing he wanted was to bring attention to them. If any other hunters saw them, they could take it the wrong way. 'Better yet, when did you become a hunter?'

'The day of the bonfire,' Taro answered and Jason recalled the event. It seemed like a lifetime ago, Jason realised. Edward decided to attack them and used Sara as bait. Jason remembered that Seth nearly lost himself when Maya was being threatened. 'I saw you trying to help them. I didn't expect for you to be a shifter at the time.'

'Well I didn't expect you to be this much of an ass, but look where we are?'

Taro's lip pulled back with a snarl. 'Is it true that you are a shifter?'

Jason was surprised with himself when he didn't react. But he had to get himself out of this mess. 'I am – but I promise you that we're not your enemy.'

'Then why is everyone telling me otherwise?' Taro demanded stepping into Jason's personal space. In an attempt to distance himself, Jason moved away from Taro. 'Why was there a Jane Doe at Brodie's place?'

Remembering the girl back at the party, Jason avoided Taro's cold stare. 'I don't know…' His confession was enough for Taro to step backwards. 'I didn't see who did it, the only thing we have is that it wasn't a shifter.'

'Not a shifter…' Taro muttered thoughtfully and Jason looked back up to see Taro appeared convinced about Jason's words. 'I'll believe you for now, but I swear that if any of you hurt any innocent people in this town, you'll regret it.'

Jason knew he had nothing to worry about. 'I'll only protect my friends and myself,' he promised. In the background, Jason heard the crowd of students cheer. 'You should probably go around and see if anything suspicious happens.'

Taro's frown deepened. 'I mean what I've said,' Taro said before he walked around Jason. 'Stay away from Jenna as well, if you want what's best for her.' Before Jason could retort, Taro was already shutting the door behind him, leaving Jason in the classroom.

***

'Nice costume.'

Maya turned to see a masked male comment on her basketball uniform. Her curly raven hair was tied into a low ponytail, to give more of a male style despite her feminine figure. She knew that it wasn't exactly the theme that most people would choose when coming to a Halloween party but she had opted to dress up like her favourite team, the Wyoming Cowboys. It wasn't a creative costume – but a costume, nevertheless.

Pride swelled in Maya's chest. 'Thanks,' she replied, looking at her clothes. 'I'm missing tonight's game just to go to this party – I hope they win.'

'I'm pretty sure they will,' the masked stranger insisted and raised a hand. A grin stretched on Maya's face as she returned the gesture as a high five. 'Well, Miss Cowboy, I'm going to go back to my party.'

As the stranger went into the crowds, Maya scoffed to herself. She couldn't believe that she was at this party at all.

As a child, Maya had joined parties and attempted to decorate her house with Adelle when kids came around in costumes. Now she was eighteen and trying to figure out a clue to unlock her bloodlust – times changing too quickly for her liking.

Just as she heard her phone ring, Maya reached down for her pocket to answer it but a gloved hand grabbed her mouth. Alarm bells rang in the back of Maya's head as she struggled against the iron hold that the figure had on her.

Who was holding her? She tried to see their face but it was another masked face. Halloween was made for those people underneath masks that were too cowardly to show themselves.

'You better be careful - Shifter,' a muffled voice said and Maya growled in annoyance. If one more person referred her to as something that she wasn't then she was going to lose her mind. 'I'll kill you faster than you can call your friends.'

I was given one job and I can't even do that right, Maya thought, spotting the hunter's tattoo on his wrist. The hunter dragged her along the crowds and the rest of the audience assumed that this was part of the 'Predator and Prey' act. Now Maya regretted offering Jenna the theme.

Just as she went into one of the storage rooms, Maya used this chance to bite into the fingers that were stopping her yells. He screamed in agony and used his free hand to whack Maya in response. She felt the pain on her face as the force knocked her into the shelves.

'You little bitch,' the hunter spat as he advanced on her, his hands curling viciously. Maya returned the fierce glare and refused to cower. 'I'll make sure that you beg for mercy before I string you up for being a part of their disgusting kind.'

The door swung open, revealing Seth.

Maya could only stare as Seth's rage flashed in his eyes, reeling his fist back and connecting with the hunter's face. She didn't flinch from his grunt, recognising the scene from almost a month ago at the bonfire. His mask flew off his face and clattered uselessly in front of Maya.

Before the hunter could collapse, Seth grabbed his shirt and pulled him to his feet. Seth slammed the hunter against the shelf and held him with an animalistic snarl. He had one arm pinned against the hunter's throat was his hand was still constricting the shirt.

'If you lay a finger on her again,' Seth threatened quietly and added pressure to the man's throat, 'you will experience a Laurence's bloodlust.' Finally, Seth dropped the man and he coughed as he nursed his throat. Seth's golden eyes went to Maya and she stared at his gaze with alarm.

'How did you find me?' Maya asked, looking at the man that tried to kill her.

'I saw you get dragged in,' Seth answered as he offered a hand to help. His eyes returned to their chocolate colour and Maya took his hand. She stood up and winced when the pain pierced her skull. 'I apologise.'

'Don't do that,' Maya cut him off with a scowl. 'It wasn't your fault that *I* got dragged away and it wasn't your fault that I bit the guy's hand. Stop blaming yourself and I'm gonna make sure that this doesn't happen again. Don't follow me.'

'If you wish. I will have to call the sheriff about this hunter anyways.' His voice went to the back of Maya's mind as she left him, sensing his dark eyes studying her like he could see through her.

Maya tried her best to ignore him as she battled the internal guilt.

***

Still nothing.

Laria went through the crowds, depending on her sense of smell to find Jenna but the perky girl was nowhere to be located. To make things worse, she had some pent-up frustration about everything that was going on currently and that included Jason.

She should've known that Jason wouldn't listen to her about Brodie, but she couldn't help it. If they were going to work together then the brothers had to settle their differences.

Laria just wanted it to be over.

'Laria!'

Suddenly, she stopped at the sound of her name and she turned to see David as Count Dracula. 'Really, Mister Embers, you're going as Dracula?'

'I need to blend in,' David replied with a grin, before rubbing his hands together. 'And this is coming from the witch.'

'I need good news,' Laria said and ignored David's comment on her costume.

'Well, Seth took someone out,' David explained with a smile. 'They're in the storage room unconscious and Maya's with him. I saw Brodie knocking back at few hunters that were surrounding the campus and he unwired all the vans.'

'The vans?' Laria wondered, tilting her head in confusion.

'I'm just as clueless as you are,' David insisted. 'Recently the Mayor has been acting rather distant with me. She's been like this since announcing the "let's kill shifters" plan.'

'What about Jenna?' Laria wondered, turning to see that David stiffened. He had a look of shame and guilt as they exchanged glances but David tried to avoid her look. 'Mister Embers.'

'I haven't seen her yet,' David muttered and he scanned the area around him. 'I don't know where she is.'

'I've got to go find her,' Laria suddenly said and she ditched David without a goodbye. From the sidelines, random puppets tried to jump at her and Laria flinched when she heard the fake screams. She had to convince herself that they weren't real screams.

As she got deeper into the building, Laria halted in her tracks when a scent drifted past her. It was the same smell she got when she witnessed the dead girl at Brodie's party.

Nick.

He was here. But the question was, why? Hiding the panic, Laria followed the trail into an empty hallway. It seemed to be an out of bounds area, so unless a human was sneaking around then Laria had no need to worry about people.

The trail ended in front of one of the science rooms and Laria gritted her teeth. Was she ready to do this? If Lux came out again –

I have to stop Nick. Laria thought, ignoring her fear and

entering the classroom.

Laria would've sworn that he was nearby.

A blur knocked her into the ground with a hand constricting around her throat. As Laria regained her awareness, her eyes met with the pair of gold.

'It is about time you came around, love. I thought I would've had to bring in Amarel to get your attention again.'

Laria heard Nick's unforgettable voice and it shot tremors throughout her skeleton. He held her down without effort, and Laria tried to push him off. 'What do you want?' She demanded through a hoarse voice.

'Let's just say I'm bored,' the enemy replied snidely. A sneer of satisfaction formed when he tightened his hold around Laria's throat. Her throat burned. 'Do you remember what you did to me when we last met?'

Oh Laria remembered was Lux did to him. The memories of the bloodlust snapping Nick's wrist was still fresh on her mind. It had only been a few months ago, but it still felt like yesterday.

Nick's smile widened with delight. 'I want you to die... painfully. Then I will go back to my hunt.'

His hunt? That didn't sound good. It meant he was targeting someone asides from her.

Suddenly, Laria heard the doors slam open once more. She couldn't see who came in, but Laria took the opening of Nick's distraction and used her claws to dig into his arm. He cursed and loosened his grip, allowing Laria to push him back with a kick.

Her foot connected with his abdomen and it lifted the pressure. Immediately, Laria turned to her rescuer and relief pooled in Laria's chest.

Laria coughed and nursed her neck as she pulled herself to her feet. 'You have no idea how glad I am to see you Heather...'

'Are you alright Laria?' Heather asked, eyes softening. 'I saw you come into this room; I wasn't expecting a shifter to attack.'

With a groan, Nick recovered from the attack and snarled. 'I wasn't going to just attack,' he confessed and his eyes glowed. 'I was going to strangle her until she was blue in the face, and now I'll do it to you as well.'

'The fact that monsters like you exist sickens me.' Her voice was soft, catching Laria off guard. Heather at the moment didn't look like the shy girl that occasionally hung out with them. Seeing the confidence in her eyes was a rare thing.

'Good,' Nick said and with a yell, he tried to run at them. In response, Heather shook her head with a deep sigh.

'Such a shame...' With a flick of her hand, Laria felt a strange tingle in the air. As soon as Nick came close enough, he froze with his claws inches from Heather's unflinching face.

'What the bloody hell?' Nick demanded and tried to lunge at Laria. She cringed, but didn't feel him touch her. Laria realised that Nick's claws hadn't gotten to her. 'What the hell did you do?'

'My name is Heather Verdas, a witch from Cheyenne,' Heather introduced herself as Nick gritted his teeth and snarled at her. 'My family specialises in barrier magic, so while I draw breath you won't be able to lay a finger on me.'

With a grumble, Nick paced in front of the pair like a wild animal. 'I may not be able to touch you, but it doesn't mean that you're immune to death-'

Heather flung out her hands with a yell and in the next moment, Nick was flying off his feet. Laria watched with a dropped jaw as the enemy shifter smashed through the glass window.

'Heather?' Laria regained her vocal cords and shook herself out of the daze. The witch raised an eyebrow and deeply exhaled. In that instant, the strange tingle was gone and Laria looked at her hands in confusion. She didn't know that Heather was gifted. 'I couldn't thank you enough for saving me...'

'I'll protect you Laria,' Heather promised as she smiled softly. 'I'll do anything to protect my friends and the people in this town, just as long you keep doing the same.'

The realisation dawned on Laria and she cursed. Without thinking, Laria went to the broken window, only to find no sign of Nick.

'He's gone!' Laria slammed a fist on the wall. 'I still don't know his plans, or who he was after... aside from me...'

Heather's presence was warm as the witch brushed Laria's arm with a soft hand. 'It will be okay,' she promised softly. 'He couldn't be too far—' The door creaked open from behind, and Laria whirled around with a raised guard.

However the guarded nature dissolved into a shock. 'Jenna...' Laria was back to being speechless. The last time they encountered, Lux took over and it didn't end well.

The fear was obvious on Jenna's face as she looked at Laria. 'What did you do Laria?' Before Laria could answer, Jenna turned tail and fled.

Knowing that Nick was close by, Laria couldn't let her friend run away. In a panic, Laria shouted, 'wait Jenna don't leave the school!' Heather cut Laria off by grabbing her arm. 'Heather, don't you get it? Jenna knows about the shifters; she doesn't trust us...'

'It's better to let her go,' Heather told her, 'Liza told me what happened. She's not going to appreciate being followed and it's not safe to do so with the hunters around.' Laria's shoulders slumped and guilt returned as Heather dropped her arm. 'I know it's hard...'

Laria didn't have the strength to respond. Instead she glanced back to the outside world and narrowed her eyes. 'I just hope she isn't the one that Nick is targeting...'

CHAPTER 14

Jenna's mind was buzzing from two days ago at the Halloween party. She didn't tell anyone of what she saw. Not her dad, not even Taro. The last thing she needed was for her father to hide her just because she saw Laria.

Her dad didn't need to know that Laria attacked her in the first place. Jenna didn't know the identity of Laria's shooter, nor did she have any intentions on finding out. If someone could be so heartless to shoot her friend, who knew what that shooter could do to her.

And now Heather was mixed up in their business. Were any of her friends normal? Oblivious to this new world?

It wasn't a new world… Jenna thought to herself. Huddling herself into a foetal position on her bed, Jenna knew that she was lying to herself. *This has been the truth for so long… how could we keep a secret like this?*

A sudden beep alarmed Jenna when it broke the silence, and Jenna did her best to not look at the number. Just like the previous messages, it was most likely from Laria. Whatever Laria's game was, Jenna wanted no part of it.

She just needed to get away from the house. The longer she stayed, the crazier she felt. Trapped inside her house with no one to talk to felt isolating. Ever since her dad told her the truth, Jenna hadn't felt the courage to talk to him. Taro was no better – he lied to her. She only had him around so that she could have at least one friend.

That was what she needed. A friend.

Before she knew it, Jenna was driving her car without hesitation towards the Silver Roots. Even though it was public place, Jenna craved the attention of socialising. If it was a waitress, or a random customer she didn't care.

Jenna parked her car and entered the diner. It seemed to be a quiet day, however there was one person that Jenna recognised within the few people. Shyly, Jenna made her way to the booth and cleared her throat.

At the attention, Nick turned from his spot with a glass of cola in his hand. His eyes grew wide at first, before he settled and chuckled into his seat.

'What's the matter, darling?' Nick asked, flashing a wide grin. 'Did you come to seek me out?'

'What? No!' Jenna denied immediately. With a scowl, she sat across from him in the booth. He seemed like he was injured, covered in healing cuts. What could've happened to him? She observed him from her spot, hardening her eyes when Nick shifted uncomfortably in his seat. 'Don't call me darling – my name is Jenna.'

'My mistake,' Nick mocked an apology and Jenna was almost tempted to leave at his intolerance. 'Now I ask again, what is the matter?'

'Why did you tell me about the shifters?' Jenna asked in a hushed tone, but her question didn't startle him. Much to her surprise, he appeared amused. 'Why would you expose yourself to me? A mere stranger?'

'Would you believe me if I had told you I was sick of everyone lying to me?' Nick wondered and his response caused Jenna to sharply inhale. She wouldn't believe it if she hadn't been just lied to all the time. Nick took a drink and glared out the window. 'I believe I know a companion of yours… Laria Alfero…'

Jenna's face dropped and she clenched her fist. Why did he have to know the one person that she was trying to avoid? 'Is that why you got to me?' Jenna hissed and finally, it took Nick by surprise. 'Listen, whatever deal you have with her – I'm not interested. I'm not her friend anymore.'

So much for being relaxed in this place. Jenna got up from her seat and Nick tilted his head with a frown. 'What did I say wrong, love?'

Hearing Nick caused Jenna to shoot a cold glare towards him. 'I don't know what your game is – but I'm not playing. I'm done being a victim of everyone's secrets and lies. So I don't think I'll be seeing you after this.'

'Stop.'

His firm voice was enough for Jenna to listen to him. Despite her thoughts were telling her to move, Jenna's body wouldn't obey. Her hands couldn't even twitch. To the view observers of the Silver Roots, she probably looked like she was letting Nick talk.

'What's going on?' Jenna whispered frantically.

'I don't want to force you, love,' Nick told her and the horror dawned on Jenna. Did shifters have the power to control actions? This wasn't something she expected. 'But I do want you to listen to me right now, so if I must, I will force you to stay. Turn around.'

Jenna's theory was confirmed when she slowly faced him. She frantically tried to break out of the control but it was pointless. Whatever he did, he held her in a vice-grip and he wasn't letting go.

Nick reached out for her hand, unfortunately Jenna still couldn't move to whack his away. 'We live in a cruel world – I simply want to tell you my side of the story. Humanity is just as cruel as the monsters you can't stand.'

Jenna bit her lip nervously. 'Why me then?'

Nick flashed a smile again. 'Why not? Would you rather be oblivious – I'm sure there is a shifter out there that can arrange to have your memories wiped–'

'No!' Jenna cut him off. 'I want to know, if that means I have to listen to you then I will.'

'Fantastic.' Nick slid a business card towards her. 'You can take my card, call me if you ever want to talk.'

Suddenly, Jenna regained her movement and took the card cautiously. She read the details and she suddenly realised what his full name was. 'Nick Forte?' One of Brodie's cousins. No wonder he knew Laria. Even if she wanted to, Jenna couldn't run from him. He found her once, there wasn't anything that could stop him from finding her again.

'My name may be Forte, but I'm adopted.' Nick winked at her and Jenna was surprised to hear the confession. Not many people would be so opened about being adopted or fostered. 'A story that will be for another time. I have errands to run.'

He pulled himself to his feet and left Jenna in the Silver Roots. As she found herself alone, she let out a shaky breath.

Maybe she should've stayed home. It would've saved her from the trouble of Nick Forte – he was strange and Jenna wasn't sure if that was a good sign.

***

'You've been quiet, Maya,' Adelle spoke up when Maya flicked the different channels on the television with a bored expression. The Wyoming Cowboys won their match, but her mood wasn't interested in sports. Her mind was going back to the night of the Halloween party – the reminder of her weakness.

'Well... It turns out that your son might be one of the reasons why Azu is missing in the first place and I can't help but dread it,' Maya huffed in annoyance.

If only she had more clues to work with, it wasn't like she was a wizard and knew where her bastard of a dad was. He ditched her; maybe it was for a good reason, or maybe it wasn't but Maya hated going down that road. She gave up on those things after her mother died.

'Well, if you want to consider meeting Jeffery... try finding him here.' She patted an old journal for Maya on the table and left her to ponder on her thoughts.

Maya let out a sigh and grumbled to herself. This was her task; she didn't need to worry about her friends. She wasn't a damsel in distress that needed to be protected by everyone. In fact, Maya was sick and tired of hiding behind the walls that were protecting her. There had to be a reason why her bloodlust hadn't activated and Maya was going to find out.

Maya shut the book and placed it back on the table. Where could her father have run off to? This world was big enough to hide in without getting caught by a bunch of killer shape shifters. She would've asked Seth, but she didn't want him to drop everything he was doing because of her. Brodie, Jason and Laria were out of the question.

It only left one shifter.

The one thing Maya hoped was that Tahani was in a decent mood. She pulled on her hooded jacket as she considered the woman's location.

If she couldn't find Tahani, then Maya had to find someone who could. She unlocked her car and hopped inside, ignoring the strange tingle in her gut. Honestly, Maya didn't really think about where she was going, pulling the car into a drive. Even though she was braking when she needed to, turning at random times, Maya felt her mind focused on the journal.

Suddenly Maya found herself in an unfamiliar street where children seemed to roam. Despite their young age, they rode their bikes and seemed like they were having a good time, with their parents watching them like hawks. The houses seemed tiny for an urban setting and Maya wondered how she ended up in an unusual place.

After pulling her car, Maya huffed and rested her head on the steering wheel.

'Damn it,' the tomboy cussed and pulled out her GPS. Just as she was about to get the GPS working, she looked over in the direction of the forest of trees at the end of the street. There was something about them that called her – how strange.

Placing the device back into the glove box, Maya stepped

out of the car. The cold breeze came in, forcing Maya to zip up her jacket. Crossing her arms over her chest, Maya approached the forest and observed the area around her.

In the forest, she could hear the birds chirping and the sound of scurrying feet. They were running from something – maybe it was her. Maya ignored the background noise, approaching a thin creek several metres in front of her.

As Maya came closer, she realised that it was connected to the body of water that was close to Seth's place. The water was surprisingly clear, with little to no trash. Small fish were in her line of sight, nibbling at the algae around them.

The environment around them seemed… *Peaceful*… The word came to Maya's mind and a pang of sadness overcame her. If she couldn't figure out how to become a shifter, she would continue to feel like an outcast in this world. She was meant to be a shifter, every fibre in her body felt like it was meant to become a shifter.

Even before she knew she was a shifter, Maya always felt like she was lost. Something was missing from her. Once she became a shifter, it would be over.

'What am I doing here?' Maya asked herself, watching her reflection. With a deep breath, she leaned back to look at the sky within the gaps of the trees. 'I feel like an idiot, Tahani isn't here.'

A chuff responded to Maya and immediately she felt alarm prick her. What on earth was that? Squinting her eyes while observing and spotting a white figure behind the bushes, Maya froze. Was it a wolf?

Wolves don't get that big… Maya realised and the horror came to her as the creature revealed itself. If the giant white cat didn't make itself obvious, then the black jagged stripes did. 'Holy crap…'

The white tiger approached Maya, an emotion impossible to read in its icy eyes. With heavy paws, Maya was surprised that she didn't realise that there was a giant cat with her sooner. She couldn't move, even when it came close enough to touch her. It let out another chuff, a low rumble left its throat and Maya knew in that instant it was a shifter.

If it was a friend or not was the real test.

'Is that you… Tahani?' Maya whispered, her heart pounded through her chest. All it took was the wrong movement and it could end badly. The tiger let out another quiet rumble before slowly nodding its head.

Relief came back to Maya and she let out a breath she didn't realise she was holding. It wasn't the first time she felt like she was facing death in the eye, but it was the time she felt terror.

However, it looked like Tahani seemed amused and rather curious.

Maya slowly recovered from her scare and stood back to her feet. 'I don't know how I managed to find you. But I'm glad. We need to find someone.'

Tahani didn't make a sound, but tilted her head. It was weird to see a tiger move almost in such a human like manner. However, she gestured for Maya to follow and led the tomboy towards a heavy bush area. Pushing away the spiderwebs, Maya grunted about the insects but continued until there was a sudden clearing.

Within a clearing, a treehouse stood in the centre of it. Maya had to take the moment for the image to process in her mind. Tahani chuffed at Maya's moment, before climbing the tree with quiet grunts.

When she disappeared within the house, Maya realised there was something familiar about the place. Had she been here before? No, Maya would've remembered it. Maya never entered these parts before and surely, she would recognise the treehouse.

'So who are ya looking for?' Tahani's voice echoed from the treehouse and Maya snapped out of her thoughts to see the woman fixing her clothes. Her hoodie looked like it was covered in mud and trousers looked torn. Since her arrest, Maya didn't often see Tahani. This was the first time Maya was willing to talk.

Here went nothing. 'His name is Jeffery Cadmen — he

might have a clue about Azu. You were looking for Azu too, weren't you?'

Tahani's face darkened and she crossed her arms over her chest. 'Why are ya looking for ya father?'

'Do you know him?' Maya wondered curiously.

'Never met 'im before,' Tahani muttered bluntly. 'Probably a good thing as well – he was the reason Kaeylin and I went separate ways.'

'So you guys were close,' Maya realised and ignored the glare. Was that all Tahani was capable of?

However, it surprised Maya when Tahani relaxed with slumped shoulders. 'This was her treehouse, one thing that we shared as a Rosa was the ability to get our hands dirty. Kaeylin loved her woodwork.'

Now that's why it seemed familiar! Going through the journals, Kaeylin mentioned that she built a treehouse that she spent time in. There was even a faded photo that bookmarked her page.

Not that it mattered at the moment, Maya didn't look away from Tahani. 'So will you help me?

'How on Earth are we gonna find a man that hasn't been seen for fifteen bloody years?'

'I have a starting point,' Maya replied simply and spared a glance back at her car with the journals. 'I was reading through my mum's journals and I noticed that she mentioned Maine a lot. It got me curious – what happens if my dad somehow went to Maine and kept in contact with her in secrecy? It's not really accurate since the evidence I have are a bunch of old books but it's the best shot.'

'Ya want me to come with ya to Maine?' Tahani realised, raising an eyebrow in suspicion when Maya nodded softly. 'Ya might be disappointed in the results kiddo – in fact, there could be a chance that we don't find anything at all.'

'I want you to come with me, Tahani.' Maya was surprised with how sincere she sounded. 'Because believe it or not... I think that you have the best chance at finding this man. Besides, I'm willing to take the chance.'

Finally, Tahani shook her head with a chuckle. 'Fine then,' the dux decided and brushed her hair back with the stretch of her muscles. 'But I'm warning ya kiddo. If ya find something ya don't wanna know... just don't forget that ya putting yourself in a situation.'

Maya's eyes flashed with determination. Of course Tahani would be willing to warn her of the risks. 'I'm aware of that, but it's not just me who's looking for the stone. Our lives depend on this search, Tahani, so that's why I'm taking a chance.'

Tahani scoffed lightly and closed the door behind her. 'Very well, little Rosa. I must say though – ya have Kaeylin's eyes. It's rather admirable.'

Maya blinked in confusion. 'Thank you?'

'Now, ya said Maine, right?' The dux tied her hair back as Maya nodded. 'Son of a bitch.' She let out a sigh just as Maya tilted her head. 'I might know where in Maine – but there are people over there that ain't happy with us – hell, even Kaeylin couldn't calm them down.'

'Who are these people?'

Tahani's eyes hardened. 'They're the Rosa family.'

Maya's blood turned cold upon the news. The family she barely saw when she was growing up were possibly the only link to her finding Azu. In a way, Maya understood why her mother wanted to hide the powerful stone.

'Well then,' Maya said with a small huff. She noticed that Tahani was mildly surprised by her reaction. 'This isn't going to be easy – we might as well get it over with.' As Maya sat in the driver's seat of the car, she ignored her annoyance. No matter what happened, Maya was doomed to meet her unhappy family.

Tahani took her seat in the passenger side and smirked coyly. 'So we're going to Maine?'

Maya returned the smirk, pushing it aside. It seemed that Maya wasn't the only one that hated her family. 'We're going to Maine. I guess it's also time for me to pack.'

***

Laria began her transformation as a run and her body did the rest. Her bones snapped into place on their own, morphing into her grey form and ran within the trees. Before Laria knew it, the sharp agony faded and Laria was running on four legs instead of two.

The bag strapped around her canine body, Laria relied on her instincts and memory to locate Brodie's house.

It was night when Laria recognised the scent of Brodie's home. She halted within the trees and shifted back to her human form. Turning human was harder than wolf, but it wasn't as painful as her fur shrank back into her skin. Her legs and arms formed back to their original state, ignoring the cracks of her joints mending.

Her body shuddered against the cold, the comfort of her bag reminding her that she still had clothes in them. Once her senses dulled down to her above-average senses, Laria knew that her transformation was complete. She picked her clothes from her bag to put them on, ignoring the nervous feeling in her chest.

Laria didn't question her nervous tick but the second she pulled her jeans on, Laria considered backing out. In annoyance with herself, she walked up to the front door.

Brodie opened the door before Laria knocked. It wouldn't surprise Laria if he heard her from inside the estate. 'What's going on?' he asked in a heavy voice, as if he had just awoken from a deep slumber.

'Can I come in?' Again, Brodie gave her a suspicious look but allowed her to enter the house. She grinned and went into the estate without any words and sighed in relief at the warmth. However the smile slowly faded the second that she saw a fire burning within its home of a fireplace.

'I wasn't expecting guests,' Brodie muttered and took two glasses of whisky. He offered the glass to Laria who was first reluctant at the idea of drinking it. She knew what it did to Brodie, Brodie became a dark person because of the influence of alcohol, but then she decided that she needed a drink.

'Thanks,' Laria said, offering another grin and winced when she took down the drink.

'I didn't want Jenna to know – it's far too dangerous.' Brodie started the conversation and turned back to face Laria. She watched him take a drink and Laria reached up for the wounds she received recently.

'Neither did I,' Laria agreed, taking another mouthful. 'But the hunters got to her first – it pains me to think that she doesn't know the shifter side to the story.' Something Laria hadn't realised was that Brodie kept walking up to her until he stepped into her personal space.

His hazel eyes were searching for something. 'Why are you here Laria?'

'I beg your pardon?' Laria shot back, her frown formed on her face.

'You pop up just out of the blue,' Brodie explained curtly and the grip on his glass tightened as if to contain something. For a moment, Laria considered stepping away from him but she stopped herself from moving.

'On the day Jenna found out about us, it was my fault.' Laria began explaining and she eyed Brodie drinking from his glass. 'A hunter shot me, but by then it was too late – Lux took over.'

Brodie's eyes darkened. 'You *what?*'

'Believe me,' Laria returned with a scowl. 'I didn't mean for to happen – it only took a shot, a simple bullet to bring my bloodlust out-' Her voice was silenced by a smashing glass.

Brodie took his anger out on the glass by pegging it at fireplace. The flames brightened with hunger and Laria immediately jumped back. Whether it was from Brodie or the fire, she honestly didn't know.

Why would you do that?' Brodie demanded, and his eyes changed colour. 'Jenna was our friend, your friend! No wonder she doesn't trust us.'

'You don't think I don't know that?' Laria stepped up, annoyance flashing her features. This wasn't what she expected from Brodie. 'I made a mistake; I should've been more careful when looking for those beartraps.'

'You don't think I don't know that?' Laria stepped up, annoyance flashing her features. This wasn't what she expected from him. 'I know it's dangerous – but I believe that the hunters will keep her safe.'

'If anything happens to Jenna, then it's on you Laria!' The snarl on Brodie's face looked almost life threatening to Laria. 'It doesn't change the fact that you screwed up big time!'

'What, like you did with your father when you chose to treat Jason like dirt?' Laria retorted but she suddenly realised what she had said. His body froze as Laria felt her body quiver in horror. 'Brodie, I-'

'What Jason and I go through is none of your business,' Brodie muttered darkly and turned away from her. Just as Laria tried to speak again, Brodie cut her off with a harsh tone. 'Get out of here, you're no better than your bastard of a father.' He started to walk away from her, but Laria didn't move a muscle.

'Why can't you two get along?' Laria snapped, halting Brodie's movements. 'Brodie, you have to open up to me and tell me how to fix this... If we can't work together... then we don't deserve each other at all.' His back faced her and Laria saw his fists clenched to contain himself.

However Brodie turned around to face Laria, his eyes filled with fury. 'I will tell you my problem, Laria.' He stormed up to her in a few strides and Laria refused to move. 'My dad died in my arms and I couldn't do anything about it. I want to kill you – just so I can avenge my father. I want revenge for what Lucien did to me.'

This had to do with Lucien? Laria hid the horror and she scowled. 'You think killing me would do something to deter the man that abandoned us? Can you hear yourself?'

'I can,' Brodie answered hoarsely and Laria felt the alarm come back to her. 'For the first time, I can hear the voice clearly.' This was his bloodlust talking. It had to be – and Laria had to stop him.

Before Laria could react, she felt him shove her to the wall.

The force took the breath out of her lungs.

Her chest tightened as Brodie locked eyes with her. In that moment she felt like she was staring at an angry animal. 'Brodie please-!' She needed her friend to see her. The bloodlust was getting too strong for Brodie to fight alone. 'This is not you... I know you, Brodie Forte, and you wouldn't hurt me.'

'It doesn't matter, does it?' The bloodlust from Brodie taunted with a wide sneer. 'Brodie has been weak ever since his father died. It was easy to step into his boundaries to kill.' With ease, Laria felt herself flying and she crashed into a cabinet. Glass shattered around her form and she winced when her body hit the floor.

'Brodie...' Laria tried pushing herself up, but all her wounds stung. With fresh cuts, Laria felt the stickiness throughout her body. 'Please see me... I know it hurts...'

'It is true though,' the bloodlust announced, grabbing a gun from the sofa chair. He stepped towards Laria and with a whimper, she tried pushing herself back up. 'Brodie cares about you; he wanted to fight me off in order to return to himself. I gave him ideas, thoughts and even the pleasure of feeling this vengeance. He now can't even tell what his real thoughts are anymore.'

'Screw you,' Laria spat out blood when she glared at the gun. 'Brodie is in there and I will save him from you.'

A chuckle escaped from the bloodlust. 'I highly doubt it... since you'll be dead.' Laria expected to be shot between her eyes, but the sound of the door slamming open stopped everything. The bloodlust looked over towards Jason who had anger in his eyes.

'Leave her alone, Brodie.' Jason's voice was so quiet, Laria would've sworn that he didn't say anything. But the words were clear in his expression.

'Sorry, *brother.*' The bloodlust lifted the gun to point it towards Jason and held a mocking tone. Jason didn't move. 'No can do.' It was Jason who reacted first; letting out a yell of anger and tackling Brodie into the ground.

Jason's bloodlust was kicking in; Laria could see the desire to end Brodie there. He made the first hit and made another when Brodie was on the ground.

No… this can't happen. Laria tried to push herself up but groaned in agony. There was still glass in her arm and she couldn't fight back in this condition. 'Stop it Jason!' She could only imagine how insane she sounded for defending the man who just threw her into a glass cabinet.

Jason ignored her and he slammed Brodie into the floor. 'Is this how you treat your friends now?' he snapped, punching Brodie with a yell. 'This is low. Even for you.'

'You're just as bad, if not worse,' the bloodlust said in retaliation. Brodie used the gun to hit Jason. The force knocked him into the ground, then Brodie was holding the gun towards Jason.

Laria's stomach tightened as everyone stopped moving. For a beat, she thought they hesitated, but it seemed that they were taking the moment.

After seconds of silence, Jason was the first to speak. 'Do it.' Jason's eyes remained on Brodie. 'Prove to me that you're not the saint that everyone praises you to be!'

What on Earth is he doing? Laria thought desperately. Was he not aware that this wasn't Brodie? She needed to stop them from making things worse. Looking around, Laria noticed a small jewellery box from the shattered cabinet. She instinctively grabbed the box and looked at the form of Brodie.

Laria wouldn't let Jason get killed for her. With another whimper, Laria forced herself to stand and stumble into Brodie's way. She was only glad that they were close enough for Laria to get to them on time.

'Brodie.' Her voice caught the bloodlust's attention, turning towards her with a glare but Laria swung the box and knocked Brodie out.

Laria tried not to wince as he fell beside them. Recognising the gun still within his reach, Laria kicked the gun and it slid under the couch.

A moment passed and Laria dropped to her knees from where she stood. She felt Jason's presence beside her as he called out her name.

He grabbed her and Laria finally looked towards him with hesitance. 'You shouldn't have pushed yourself to stand up.'

'I needed to save you,' Laria answered back with a scowl. 'I will always risk my life for the people I care about.' She winced again when Jason brushed the bloodied skin on her arm.

Instead of arguing, Jason's eyes softened. 'Can you walk?'

'I just need help getting back up.' Laria shot a look towards the Amarel. 'You expected him to kill you.'

'No, I didn't.' He wrapped his arm around her shoulder. 'I just needed to distract him. I'm not going to leave you — especially not now.' With his help, Laria found herself on her feet and he moved away to let her stand on her own.

Laria firmly took in a deep breath, trying to ignore his stare. She didn't want him to disappear, the thought of losing her friend tore at her chest. Why did he have to say that?

Instead, she forced herself to ignore the lingering fear and Laria's lips twitched into a smile. 'I know.' Immediately, she returned her attention onto herself. With a stumble, Laria felt pain shoot through her body.

'Laria!' He reached out for her, stopping her fall. She grasped him as he rebalanced her. 'I think you need help.'

Laria scoffed in embarrassment. The last thing she wanted was to seem like she was always a mess — but it seemed hard to hide her weaknesses in front of him. 'I guess I need your help after all.'

'I'll take you to the hospital,' Jason suggested and the idea of going to the hospital didn't sit well for Laria.

'No hospital,' Laria told Jason, squeezing his arm. She didn't want the explain what happened to her and she didn't want Chris to worry about her. 'Please Jason, it's just glass.'

In his grip, Laria could feel his body tense up. As she looked back at him, she could see the confliction in his eyes.

Then he relaxed. 'Fine, we can head to Seth's,' Jason

decided. He assisted Laria by leading her to Seth's car with a limp. They didn't speak and Laria assumed it was because Jason wanted to give her some space. As Laria sat in the passenger side of the car, she looked at Brodie's estate with a heavy heart.

CHAPTER 15

Pain shot through Brodie's skull as he regained consciousness. His arms regained the strength to lift himself up. His bloodlust was beginning to take over his life. Occasionally he slipped in whenever Brodie was vulnerable, or putting himself through enough pressure.

As Brodie stumbled onto his feet, his head spun. His body collapsed onto the couch before he could regain himself and anger got the best of him.

'Damn it!' He slammed his fist against the cushions. He was confident that he had lost Laria's trust and Jason got to look like the good guy. Why was he so weak?

Don't act like I've done something wrong, Orgul commented in the back of Brodie's mind. *You're weak Brodie — you let them walk away when they deserve our wrath.*

'Shut up.' A hiss escaped Brodie's lips and instinct made him grab the nearest glass to pour himself a drink of whisky. When Brodie pulled the drink over his lips, he couldn't even taste the contents of his beverage.

Without taking the drink like he planned to, Brodie placed it back down on the nightstand before he could smash the glass and his eyelids grew heavy with exhaustion.

An urgent knock from the front of his door snapped him out of his state. Brodie frowned and pushed himself off his couch with a stagger. His movements still felt out of place, but the second he opened the door, Brodie recognised Tara's stern face. Brodie should've anticipated Tara's arrival.

'Jason called me and told me what happened,' Tara told him bluntly and she entered the house, instantly frowning. 'What were you thinking?'

'I wasn't,' Brodie replied hoarsely and noticed Tara's disappointment in her single eye. 'I haven't been in control – you know that.'

'Old Brodie was always in control,' Tara stated and Brodie felt irritated. What would she know? She knew nothing of the suffering that he was going through. 'I know that you're giving yourself up to your bloodlust on purpose.'

Brodie snarled. 'How dare you, Tara?' Tara's eye narrowed as he voiced his thoughts to her. 'Are you really going to believe that I would hurt Laria on purpose?'

Yes.

The words didn't need to be said, because Brodie knew he was lying. It was because it was the only way to get rid of his pain.

'We both know the answer to that,' Tara muttered in response, sparing a look at the mess. 'You really have fallen into the deep end Brodie. I can help you get through it but you have to start accepting reality. This bloodlust is exactly what the enemies want you to experience.'

You let this woman talk down to you like you're a mere child that disobeyed his parents, Orgul taunted in the back of Brodie's mind. *Maybe you can show her how you really feel about your brother... or show her how you want to tear out your friend's throat.*

'I've got it under control,' Brodie replied quickly to dismiss Orgul. She stared back at him with the calculating gaze of hers before she brought her fists up. 'What are you doing?'

'Let's prove it, Brodie,' Tara demanded. She looked like she was ready for a fight. 'For your next task, you will go against me and win. If you have it under control then it means that you are at your full strength – I know that you won't hesitate when it comes to hitting me.'

Brodie knew how his auntie fought; the dux was a skilled fighter on par with Tahani. There was no way that Brodie could win a fight against Tara. Yet for some reason, Brodie considered that there was a deeper reason. Perhaps Tara knew Brodie was stronger than her – unfortunately there was only one way to prove it.

'Alright then.' Brodie lifted his fist. Tara's single eye glared down at Brodie and he was the first one to strike. His fist connected with her blocked arm and left Brodie open. Just as she struck out her counter, Brodie moved out of the way.

For a moment, Brodie felt Orgul trying to possess him. In annoyance, Brodie put more force into the mental barrier that kept his bloodlust trapped.

'Don't focus your attention elsewhere,' Tara warned and she slammed a fist into Brodie. The air felt as if it was ripped from his lungs. Just as Brodie tried to regain himself, he felt Tara's foot plant into his chest and sent him flying into the same cabinet that Brodie previously threw Laria into.

Brodie winced when his body dropped to the ground, ignoring the glass puncturing his skin. He prepared himself to pull himself up to fight again, but Tara already stood in front of him.

'That's enough,' the dux ordered coldly. 'You lost this Brodie – and it's clear that your bloodlust has been affecting you far more than I realised. The next time I come, I will bring a witch with me to block the bloodlust until we figure out what we can do to tame that inner beast of yours.'

Without warning, Brodie pushed himself to his feet and shot a glare back at his auntie. 'How is that fair?' he snapped, losing composure of himself once more. 'I keep telling you that I can handle it and I will.'

'Don't try it,' Tara challenged. 'I've told you Brodie, of how I got this scar?'

Settling his anger, Brodie nodded. 'Dad did it to you… because you two never got along growing up.'

'And he regretted it ever since,' Tara added firmly. 'Your father and I were at each other's throats until one day he went too far. If you keep acting like this to your brother, the same thing is going to happen – if it isn't a missing eye, then it could be something else and you'll regret it forever.'

Pinching the bridge of his nose, Brodie decided to go along with it. 'I understand,' he muttered blandly, watching Tara's body move from her spot and to the door. She reached out for the door and paused for a moment.

'Clean up the mess,' Tara added and left the house. As soon as the door closed, Brodie felt the anger stir in the pit of his stomach. His anger spread to everyone in his life, but it was mostly directed at his brother.

CHAPTER 16

As Jason hung up on the phone to Tara, he spared a glance towards Laria. She fell asleep within the first minute in the car and her head was on the window.

When he rescued her from Brodie, Jason would've sworn that something in him broke. He had no clue to why Brodie would hurt Laria. Brodie's intentions with Laria weren't clear, but considering that he nearly killed her, Jason knew they weren't good.

Finding Seth's driveway, Jason parked the car and pressed his foot on the brakes. For a silent second, Jason let himself stare at his hands. They were swelling up from attacking Brodie and Jason wondered if his hands would ever be pain-free again.

He pulled himself out of the car, ignoring his sore fists as he made his way to Laria's side. The car door creaked and he went to undo her seatbelt. Now that he got the easy part out of the way, he had to do the next part with a bit more caution. He let out a huff of air and went to grab her, but the second he touched her, Laria jolted awake.

'Hey, calm down,' Jason whispered, grabbing her arms as she squirmed frantically. Instantly, her chestnut eyes met his and she settled. 'How are you feeling?'

'Feels like I've been thrown into a glass cabinet,' Laria tried to joke but Jason couldn't smile to that. The image burned in the back of his mind.

'Okay,' Jason muttered softly. 'Come on, you need to get those cuts cleaned up before they get infected.' Laria looked down at her wounds and nodded in agreement, pulling herself out of the vehicle with a wince.

For a moment, Jason was worried she would fall over and tried reaching for her, when he felt her hand on him. He allowed her to proceed. Laria wasn't someone who needed rescuing all the time; she was a tough girl.

Jason let Laria follow him into the house, swinging the door open with a sigh. 'Go make yourself comfortable.' He motioned to the couch in the living room. 'I'll get the first aid kit and some blankets for tonight.'

As he headed into the bathroom, Jason hesitated as he passed Seth's room. While Jason was still not used to the enhanced senses, he could still recognise his friend's scent. Seth stepped out of his room, crossing his arms and frowning.

'Why would Brodie attack out of the blue?' Seth asked, instantly aware of the situation.

'Don't know, don't care,' Jason replied impatiently. 'Honestly, I was annoyed with myself that I didn't kill Brodie for hurting Laria.' Much to Jason's surprise, Seth didn't show a response to Jason's confession. 'And the last thing she probably wants is to come home to Tracy Ladas with glass all over her body.'

Seth studied Jason's expression. There was no emotion betraying his dark eyes. 'You seem... off today – ever since the party...'

'I'll be fine,' he said and went to collect the promised items. Once he got the blankets, pillows and first aid kit, he went back into the lounge room. He slowed down to a stop to watch Laria.

Her attention wasn't on him, but rather plucking out the glass with a pair of tweezers. Every time she failed to pull the glass out, Jason heard a curse along with a hiss escaping her lips.

She was in such deep concentration that she didn't even notice that Jason was watching her. It was strange; Jason had seen her treat her own wounds countless times, but this time felt different.

'Would you like help with that?' Jason asked quietly and Laria jumped from her seat. As she bumped her sore arm, Jason winced at the sound of another curse. 'Sorry about that. I thought you were too quiet and I was worried that you passed out again.'

Laria looked back at him with a faint smile. 'Thanks for the concern Newbie... but I'm good.'

She went back to her wounds with a focused eye on the glass. Jason chuckled lightly at the name. 'And we're back to that.'

'Newbie suits you. Besides, you're the newest in the shifter squad,' Laria replied honestly, not taking her eyes off her wounds as Jason raised an eyebrow. The shifter squad? 'But to answer your first question, I'm alright. If I can get this last bit out of my – damn it!' The last piece of glass was yanked out. It was larger than the rest.

Next to Laria, Jason noticed the shards in a white bowl. All of them were coated with a scarlet that made his stomach coil. The sight of the blood was more disturbing than Jason wanted it to be.

'Here.' Jason offered the first aid kit to Laria who took it greedily. As he placed the bedding materials next to Laria, he noticed that she barely paid any attention to him. He sat on one of the armchairs and watched with a curious gaze as Laria began to wrap her own wounds.

Jason almost smiled at the déjà vu when he realised that she missed a scratch on her forehead. It seemed that he needed to get a mirror every time Laria was around. Just like the time of the bonfire, there was an obvious scratch on her forehead. It was the same results, but different beginnings. Without a word, he picked up a plaster and ripped the plastic off, gaining her attention.

'Stay still for a sec – you forgot to clean up this scratch,' he said familiar words and Laria let out a scoff as Jason placed the plaster over her forehead. 'There.' Jason flashed a boyish grin. He stepped away from her. 'All better.'

Laria laughed, her eyes flashed with recognition. 'You

really are a dork... you realise that, right?'

'Hey,' Jason muttered mockingly as if he was scolding a child. 'You have got to stop insulting on the guy who's been nothing but kind to you.' This time, she rolled her eyes, but she didn't respond out loud, as if she had been consumed with different thoughts.

'Thanks for this,' she whispered, closing the box and grabbing a pillow. Jason noticed that she looked upset and he felt angry at Brodie once again. 'I'm sure that Seth's probably bothered that I'm sleeping over here again.'

'It's nothing. Seth's just being Seth.' Jason dismissed her gratitude and offered a smile. 'About the Halloween Party... I'm sorry I snapped at you.'

'Don't mention it,' Laria replied softly. 'I'm sorry that I acted how I did as well. I didn't know what I was angry about to be honest.'

He smirked at her and finally managed to crack a joke. 'If I recall, you were angry about me hating my twin brother.' Slowly his features turned serious. 'I can't forgive him now... so please don't try to make me get along.'

Laria nodded in agreement, but didn't say anything. They were together in a strange silence. He wasn't sure what was meant to happen, but he discharged his thought with the clearing of his own throat.

'Well, I'm heading to bed... get some rest,' Jason said and waved as he went back to his room. Seth's door to his room was closed and Jason knew that he overhead the conversation. 'Night Seth.'

The cool weather was beginning to get to him. He changed out of his current clothes into a pair of boxers and a singlet. As soon as he dumped the clothes, Jason got himself comfortable on the pile of blankets with an irritation huff. His mind was buzzing from the night.

Jason occasionally glanced back at his glowing alarm clock as he waited in the dark silence for his sleep to consume him. Time kept moving onwards, and the exhaustion had yet to hit him.

Again, Jason looked at his clock as it reached midnight. His annoyance was mostly covered by a sigh to himself but he gave up. He pulled himself out of bed and went to the door but he didn't expect Laria to be at the other side.

'Laria,' Jason breathed as if he was in the dreamland.

She stood with an awkward wave and a lazy smile. 'Hey… I was wondering if you just want to…' She seemed hesitant at the next part. 'Wanted to talk.'

Without another word, Jason let Laria enter the room. He moved out of the way and shivered when her arm brushed his and she went to sit on Jason's bed. The only source of light was the glowing alarm clock.

'So what do you want to talk about?' Jason whispered, joining her on the bed.

Laria seemed content with sitting. 'Nothing really… I've been trying to sleep but I honestly give up on it. Can we… can we talk about normal stuff? I feel like we never do that, and I… don't want to talk about all our problems, just this once.'

Throughout the night, Jason learned that Laria's brother Chris was staying at the Ladas mansion with his girlfriend. The siblings were beginning their own training, learning to control Laria's bloodlust.

Jason told Laria about his training with Tara. While Tara wasn't as outgoing as Tahani, it seemed that her training was just as effective. While they spoke, Jason learned that Laria's favourite film was The Princess Bride.

In return, Jason told her his favourite childhood movie was The Adventures of Robin Hood. Laria snorted at this new information, and she admitted that she just tried imagining him dressed up as the popular thief.

'Can I ask you a question?' Laria's soft voice got his attention but Jason smirked.

'You already did,' he chuckled but his voice hesitated when Laria laid next to him. Her face was close enough for him to feel her breath.

'How come you went to Brodie's in the first place?'

'I wanted to try for you,' Jason confessed. In the shadows,

he noticed that Laria shifted closer to him. 'I felt like we need to get along for the future, but seeing him there with you... couldn't allow it to happen.'

'Thank you,' Laria replied gently. 'What Brodie is experiencing, I get it. Despite his current actions, Brodie is loyal and brave. Even though it won't be now – I know that you two will get past your differences.' Her voice quietened and Jason noticed that her breathing pattern evened out in her sleeping state.

'Goodnight Laria,' Jason whispered and strangely enough, he was able to fall asleep.

***

Tahani hated flights. After leaving so early in the morning from Boston, she wasn't prepared for the eight-hour flight. There was nothing worse than being forced to sit still throughout a flight with screaming children and snoring adults while be forced to stare out the windows.

However Tahani looked fine compared to Maya. While Tahani could nap in the middle of an earthquake, apparently Maya wasn't so lucky in the flight. Maya's eyelids looked somewhat like a bloodhound, drooping occasionally as she lagged along the semi crowded airport.

It was strange – Tahani realised as she found herself looking towards Maya. Each time Tahani saw something new with Maya, it astounded her of how much she looked like her mother. Back when they were kids, Kaeylin shared the same bloodhound look as Maya did at the moment.

It's almost as if Kaeylin never left. Tahani thought to herself, flashing a smile.

'Chop, chop kiddo,' Tahani teased her niece who grumbled in annoyance. 'Our cursed rock ain't gonna find itself – and ya *papa* is the only way we're gonna find the damn thing.'

'I swear if I find my dad then I'm gonna kick his ass,' Maya hissed in annoyance and followed Tahani's lead. 'First the bastard had the nerve to take off. I will hit him if his reason for leaving is something stupid.'

They stopped by the main boards and Tahani noticed that the staff members were checking tickets. Now that got Tahani's interest. Honestly, Tahani couldn't remember much of the airport; it had been a long time since she had left Golden Cliff, let alone been in a strange airport.

'Yer speaking like a true Rosa,' Tahani replied with a mocking tone. 'Let's go rent a car since I can't trust a damn taxi – last time I took a taxi, I fell asleep and the bastard robbed me dry.'

As they reached at the end of the line, Tahani passed her and Maya's tickets to the security and they studied the name. The guard that was responsible for their tickets whispered in another's ears, and they both shot a look at the Rosa pair.

A third security guard approached them and Tahani's muscles locked up when they tapped her on the shoulder. Something was wrong. 'You need to come with us.' Before Maya could protest, the guard added, 'The both of you.'

Slowly, Tahani nodded and followed the trio of guards. She shot a silent look at Maya to tell her to shut up and play along.

Once they were locked in a sealed room, they were offered to sit down by the desk. Since Tahani wasn't sure of how long they would be, she took a seat comfortably and noticed that Maya remained standing.

It was Maya who spoke up first, 'So what the heck's going on? We haven't done anything wrong.'

'Seems suspicious, don't you think?' One of the men leaned towards Tahani and she read the nametag with a curious gaze. 'Why did you come to Maine?'

'Now that's none of yer bloody business – Earl,' Tahani spat back, but she had a mocking smirk in her features. 'My sister and I are here to go see some old friends of mine.'

'That's what all criminals say,' the man closest to Maya admitted and Maya's eyes narrowed from her spot. 'They're innocent, that they aren't going after Azu, the lost stone of the Corvena.' Not really security guards after all. Of course they were hunting after Azu. Tahani felt the claws form underneath her palm. 'So we ask again... what are you two really doing in Maine?'

A scoff escaped Tahani's lips. 'Yer idiots – guts, ya may have but incredibly stupid. Especially when ya picking a fight with the Ungue Dux!' She stretched out her hand and ice shot from her palm to separate Maya from the attacker. Both parties jumped away in surprise from the ice wall that materialised between them.

Just as Earl shot a hand to attack her, Tahani grabbed his wrist with a twist and slammed his hand into the table. He yelped at the sudden movement, and the dux felt her fist connect with his face as he jerked back from the impact.

Tahani released him and dodged an incoming attack from the third guy behind her. She used the chance to elbow the attacker across the jaw and she faced him to plant her foot in his chest. The force of her attack sent him crashing against the wall, knocking him out instantly.

'Get the hell off me, bastard!' Maya snarled and Tahani shot her head up to see her niece held in a headlock.

'Maya!' Tahani's protective instincts kicked in, but the dux halted when Earl stood in Tahani's way. A snarl that must have appeared more animal than human grew on Tahani's face. 'Yer gonna let her go or else I'll let Sangri play for a bit!'

'Now you're going to tell us everything you know,' Earl instructed with a hint of blood trailing down his lip. Angrily, Tahani spared a glance at the annoyed Maya, and she shot her head up to glare back at the shifter in front of her. 'We will find Azu – then we will give it back to Lucien so we can proceed with our plans.'

'Sure,' Tahani replied and it surprised the two remaining men. Instantly, Maya dropped her body like she was a rag doll and the man was caught off guard by her actions. Just as Earl turned to face the pair, Tahani acted first. She slammed her fist against Earl's face again and he fell to the ground unconscious, meanwhile Maya used her low position as an advantage.

With a grunt, Maya kicked out both of her legs and pushed

the attacker away. Just as he flew back, she picked herself off the ground with a wobble. As the attacker tried to go for Maya again, Tahani stepped in and grabbed his wrist.

'That's enough,' Tahani told the attacker. 'Now what did Zanobi tell ya?'

The man said nothing, gritting his teeth and avoiding her gaze.

In response, Tahani narrowed her eyes. 'Suit yerself.' Like a snake, she wrapped her other arm around his neck. She dropped his wrist in order to reinforce the hold, feeling his body struggle in protest.

To prevent an escape, Tahani added pressure with her hold and kept still. Using the sleeper hold wasn't something she did often, but she wasn't willing to let anyone hurt Maya.

Slowly, his body went limp and Tahani kept the hold for another few seconds before she let him down. As soon as she released him, she gestured for Maya to leave the room with her.

'How long is he going to be like that?' Maya asked as soon as they got out. She frowned as she sparred another look behind them. 'I thought it lasts only a few seconds.'

'It can,' Tahani replied with a shrug. 'Really depends, it was the reason why I held him a bit longer.'

'So what are we going to do?' Maya asked, fixing her hair. 'If there are guys after us, then surely they know we're after Azu.'

'The only thing we can do,' Tahani pointed out. 'We need to find the Rosa family as soon as possible and hope they have Azu.'

The look in Maya's eyes indicated she wasn't happy about it. Tahani wondered why she wasn't a big fan of the Rosa family. Truth be told, neither was Tahani – but at least she had an actual reason.

For now, we just need to focus on getting there. Tahani thought to herself.

CHAPTER 17

The first thing Laria felt was a glare of light upon her. She scrunched her face, cursing the morning sun in silence. Laria would've sworn that the sunlight wasn't like this at the mansion. That was when it occurred to her that she wasn't in her room. She opened one lazy eye but both went wide open when she recognised Jason's sleeping form in front of her.

Sparing a glance at Jason, Laria noticed his passive features. The bed provided them with plenty of space, but Jason was trying to keep his distance from her.

Slipping out of the bed, Laria winced when she tried stretching her arms. Her recent injuries were as fresh as her memories. By the time she reached the door, Jason was still in his unconscious state and Laria was thankful.

As soon as she opened the door, Laria flinched at the sight of Seth standing at the opposite end of the hall. While he looked like he was in a mess, Seth's suspicious expression towards Laria made her realise that he could be thinking that something happened between her and Jason.

But then again, she knew about his telepathy; Jason told her about it. And he most likely knew that she knew – even though it was most likely a secret because it was Seth that she was thinking about–

'Please stop having an overreaction,' Seth finally said, irritation colouring his tone. Heat flooded her cheeks. 'Yes, I am a mind reader, get over it – Jason told me about his confession the other day.'

'That means you know a bunch of other secrets, right?'

Laria realised. How devious would it have been that Seth knew all opinions from other people at school? No wonder he was so distant with everybody, he knew exactly what they would've thought of him. She didn't have to ask these things out loud. 'Does Maya know about this?'

'No,' Seth answered coldly. 'And you do your best to not tell her – I will tell her myself.'

'So can you read minds of everything?' The realisation overcame Laria and her eyes grew wide. What a gift.

'More like a curse,' Seth replied and Laria sheepishly shied away from Seth's watchful stare. He groaned softly. 'I cannot read everyone's mind, foreigners who don't speak English are an example. Perhaps I can, but I never try to. Sometimes I can't read thoughts that people want to block out, it takes a trained mind to hide the thoughts however. Animals are different as well – the closest I get to reading their minds is sensing their intentions.'

After Seth's explanation, they stood in silence for another few seconds and Laria found herself nodding awkwardly. They shared their chemistry class and all this time he knew about her strange feeling with him. Even now, she couldn't even keep the realisation out of her head.

He was reading her mind as she was thinking-

'I said stop.'

'I think I need to tell Chris about something.' Laria silently thanked her brother for being back at the mansion. 'It was... nice thinking... I mean talking with you.' Without another word, Laria moved out of Seth's way and cleaned up the mess from the night before. She went over to grab the phone from the bench and read the message.

Tahani and I are going to Maine to find leads for Azu. I'll keep you updated.

Laria wrote a swift reply to her friend and read through Chris's messages. She scrolled through the phone and read the constant worried messages from her brother.

'Maya has gone to find Azu?' Seth's voice echoed through the other room and Laria turned back to see the brunette. 'At least she's with the Ungue Dux... I trust her to keep her safe.'

'Wait a minute,' Laria realised and she frowned at Seth. 'You would've known that Maya is Tahani's niece. That means you know about most of the issues we had with Edward. Do you know why she has no powers?'

Seth's eyes narrowed as if he silently confirmed Maya's heritage. 'I'm a telepath, not a wizard. I tried asking my uncle if he knew why Maya was powerless, but he refused to tell me.'

'Your uncle? Who's he?' Why would someone want to hide Maya's origin? The look Seth gave her made Laria focus her attention on the floor. She really had to stop thinking around him. 'I'm going to go now.'

She left the house and closed the door behind her. As soon as she did, Laria leaned back on the wooden door with a heavy sigh. Learning about Seth's true face really changed her outlook on everything – especially now that she knew.

From now on, Laria had to be careful about thinking in Seth's presence.

'I can still hear you.'

Suddenly jumping at the sound of his irritated tone, Laria quickly stood to her feet and left the front porch. Definitely had to be careful from now on.

***

I'm an idiot. Jenna thought to herself, standing next to her car by the Silver Roots. It took hours of considering before she decided to send a message to Nick. His cryptic reply only told her that she had to meet him at the Silver Roots.

So she came, shivering in a thick jumper, trousers and ugg boots. It seemed strange but fall seemed colder than usual. No doubt snow would be coming soon, but it wasn't a bad thing. Snow was a natural beauty and it had many meanings behind it.

She might not have any friends at the moment, but she could still have fun. Maybe after Nick left her alone, Jenna could hang out with her mother and baby sister. It would be a good time to let her hair down.

'I'm surprised you're here.' About time.

Jenna spun behind to see Nick smiling down at her, flashing his dimples. Watching the blonde shifter, it took Jenna an instant to realise that he wasn't as tall as he first appeared.

It was like he was just like the rest of them. In her mind, Jenna tried to imagine younger Nick puffing his chest to appear bigger than his actual size.

She almost giggled at the image. 'You wanted me to listen,' Jenna told him as she forced the smile away. Instead she kept her attention on the cold and kept her arms crossed. 'So I am.'

'Are you cold?' Nick asked, raising an eyebrow with a chuckle. Now that he mentioned it, his clothes were certainly not something worn in colder weather. It was as if he was in the springtime. 'You humans… I can't help but wonder if I should pity you or not.'

'Yet you're willing to listen to me,' Jenna told him hotly. 'There's clearly a reason why you wanted to talk to me – of all humans.'

'I have my intentions,' Nick told her and Jenna's gut churned uneasily. Her senses told her that she shouldn't be near this man. Everything about him screamed danger. Yet despite everything, there was something about him that caused her to stop.

Jenna sighed quietly. *I really am an idiot.* Instead, she straightened her posture and ignored his wolfish grin. 'So do you plan to talk to me out in this cold? I would rather be inside for a coffee.'

'Not here,' Nick said to her. With a simple gesture from his head, Jenna found herself following him without hesitation. It wasn't his power that was speaking to her, she was literally going along with his directions.

Jenna didn't try to speak up within the time they were talking. Her eyes remained trained behind his head, trying to understand his intentions. Perhaps he will open up to her –

many people did that with Jenna, surely he was no different.

'Stop staring at me like that,' Nick scolded her, without turning his back. In embarrassment, Jenna squeaked and directed her attention on the footpath. 'You will see the place soon. Just be patient.'

Jenna's cheeks felt warm, which felt better than the constant cold. 'Sorry…' Now she felt like a child that just got caught something they weren't meant to be doing.

Finally Jenna stopped when she spotted a looming forest in her path. A scowl appeared on Jenna's face as she observed the area. Why was it always a forest?

Nick paused in his step into the darkness and tilted his head back at her. 'Is there something wrong, love?'

Memories of Laria came back to her mind. They were still fresh on her mind. With a shaky breath, Jenna took a step away from Nick.

'I can't…' Jenna told him apologetically. The look that came from Nick was one of surprise. 'It has to be here Nick, I don't want to go in.'

'You have nothing to be afraid of,' Nick promised her and tried to approach her. As he stepped closer, Jenna shook her head. He didn't understand – he couldn't understand what it was like. She shook her head to dismiss him and Nick let out a sigh. 'Well this is rather disappointing… this is no secret location…'

Jenna clenched her fists to force herself to move, but nothing was happening. Then, an idea came to mind. 'Use your power…'

Nick raised a brow. 'Power?'

'The mind control,' Jenna told him as she gestured to his hands. 'The other day, you stopped me from moving. Maybe this time, you can help me get to this place by controlling my mind.'

When Jenna suggested her idea, she wasn't expecting Nick to laugh. His laugh sounded rather normal – like a regular man from England. Instead of amusement however, Jenna's blood began to boil.

'Are you making fun of me?' She placed her hands on her hips. 'I'm being serious! Use your mind control.'

'I have been alive for decades,' Nick told her as his laugh settled. 'Never has a human willingly used themselves as a guinea pig in order to brave a tiny forest. Your idea is bizarre!'

'I trust you…' Jenna told him. 'I would rather trust you than myself.' *What am I thinking?* Better yet, how would her dad react? Or Taro?

That caught Nick by surprise once again. 'You trust me?' As he stepped towards Jenna, she didn't budge this time but she still felt startled. 'You don't even know me, for all you know I could be a big bad wolf.'

Jenna tried to respond back to him, but he had a point. He was leading her into a dark forest that could end badly. Why was she trusting towards him? Was it because he told her secrets that normal shifters wouldn't tell her?

Just like that, Nick shook his head and flashed a grin. 'You are something. Like a lamb – curious, innocent and trusting. Let's just hope no wolves get to you.' Nick began to descend back into the forest and it took Jenna a moment to realise he hadn't mind controlled her.

'Wait…' Jenna got his attention. 'I thought you wanted me to listen…'

Nick shrugged. 'You don't seem to be ready for the answers little lamb. When you're ready to come here, let me know but don't claim that you're ready to learn about the world when you can hardly step into a forest.'

Jenna lost the confidence to reply to him as he disappeared in the shadows. He didn't return like she expected. Nothing was to stop her from following after him.

Except myself… she thought to herself. He was right. If she wasn't ready to walk through the forest, how could she bear the knowledge of the shape shifters? With the shake of her head, Jenna felt disappointment as she walked back in the direction she came from.

***

The drive to their destination felt long, so Maya used that chance to tell everyone of her trip. It took Maya a few minutes to text her friends, but at least 15 minutes to explain to her grandmother of why she was skipping town briefly. Of course her grandmother was the one who showed the most concern, but after Maya explained that Tahani was the only one that could help her, Adelle understood.

Her blue eyes went out to the window, watching the trees and buildings zoom past her line of sight with a look of boredom. Tahani kept her attention on the road, trying to pinpoint a certain location with their rental car.

The music radio that they had been listening to lost its signal and Tahani let out a huff of irritation and turned the blasted thing off. Once the world went silent, Tahani returned her eyes to the road and scowled.

'Bloody humans can't do anything right,' Tahani muttered under her breath and Maya frowned.

Maya was bored and she didn't want to put up with silence for the rest of the drive. 'Could you tell me about my mum?' It had been something that Maya didn't expect to slip out. Tahani froze and tightened her grip on the wheel.

Before Maya could take back her words, Tahani said, 'Sure thing kiddo... what do yer wanna know 'bout her?'

'I know I'm not really interested in meeting my other family...' Maya said sheepishly and ran her fingers through her curls. 'But I was wondering if my mother had siblings.'

'That she did,' Tahani replied bluntly. 'An older sister.' Maya's eyes went wide. All this time she had an auntie and no one told her about it?

'Do you know her?' Maya wondered curiously and Tahani uncharacteristically tightened the grip on the steering wheel once again.

'I didn't know of her,' Tahani said and didn't look back at Maya. 'Back as a kid, Kaeylin lost her parents in the shifter massacre. Since shifters were considered monsters, humans believed that they needed to be exterminated and when she saw them...'

Tahani squeezed her eyes shut and she pulled over unexpectedly. Maya almost wailed at the sudden jerk of the car and it screeched out in protest. The car halted to the side of the road and Tahani held her head as if she gained a migraine.

Maya tried to touch Tahani's shoulder. The second that Maya made contact, an image floated in Maya's mind. It was distorted, and gone as quickly as it appeared. Looking back at Tahani, she saw that the dux looked startled and conflicted. Did she see something too?

But Maya didn't say anything about it. Instead she said, 'If it's too personal, then I won't push you. I'll change the subject…'

The dux seemed to take that as an answer, slowly nodding to recover. 'Alright then.' A shaky breath escaped the dux and she massaged her temples. 'How 'bout this? I answer a question 'bout Kaeylin and I learn something 'bout ya.'

'Why?' Maya asked with a raised eyebrow.

'Do ya want ya answers?' Tahani shot back with a similar action to Maya. Almost immediately Maya nodded in agreement. 'Good – now let's get cracking with the Q and A time of our bonus road trip.' She began to drive once again and Maya frowned to herself.

Maybe there were some harmless things she could learn about her mother. 'Favourite food?'

Instantly Tahani smirked as if she recalled a distant memory. 'Cherries.' Maya slowly smiled at the thoughts of cherries. She enjoyed cherries as well. 'I'm actually allergic to them, so she pretty much devoured anything that looked like a cherry. Now… what about yer favourite sport?'

Maya lit up in response. 'Basketball – one time I gave Seth some pointers to knock out Taro but the idiot didn't do anything. He said and I quote *'I wouldn't waste my breath on an idiot like him'* – I forgave Seth since he made an amusing comment. But the Wyoming Cowboys are my favourite team.'

'Kaeylin preferred tennis,' Tahani admitted and a snicker escaped her lips. 'I remember that she got cross when I said that it was a boring sport.'

'Really?' The tomboy gave another disbelieving look to the dux. 'Tennis *is* boring – I mean... come on, it's running side to side like a chicken lost its head just to hit a tennis ball and you can't rely on teammates to back you up.'

'I know right?' Tahani exclaimed and Maya didn't realise that she was laughing with Tahani until she snorted in amusement. 'Watch out Maya... yer getting attached to me.'

'Shut up,' Maya muttered playfully. 'And I believe that it's my turn so don't change the subject. What was she like?'

Tahani's grin fell and she kept her eyes on the road in a different way. Unlike last time, her gaze wasn't distant with the world but she was in a pensive mood. 'Kaeylin was different from a majority of the Rosa family – strangely enough, she didn't have bloodlust and didn't like violence or being sporty for that matter. But she was stubborn to the bone, she was the reason why there was a treaty in the first place and ya've inherited a bunch of things from her. One of 'em was the one where ya didn't want to be protected by anyone.'

Slowly Maya felt a smile crawl on her face once again. 'She sounds... amazing...' It felt nice to know about the mother she never really got a chance to know about.

'How about this,' Tahani said while using one hand to stroke her chin. 'Cats or dogs?'

The question aroused some suspicion in Maya. 'I'm not gonna say cats just because you're a giant cat.' After Tahani spared her a look, Maya rolled her eyes. 'I don't mind either – I'm more of an owl person anyways.'

'Fair enough,' Tahani muttered and focused on the road. 'Yer mum was the same though to be fair, owls are pretty badass. Not as awesome as tigers though.'

'I still have a question by the way,' Maya reminded and Tahani didn't back at her this time. 'What's with the accent? No one else really has that accent.'

Finally, Tahani looked towards Maya and squinted her eyes. 'Not about Kaeylin this time?'

'Just answer the question,' Maya told her. 'I'm actually curious about it. I don't remember my mother having an accent like that and it sounds a bit more Southern.'

It took Tahani a moment to compose herself. 'It's fake.' The answer wasn't what Maya was expecting. Before Maya could ask for more information, Tahani continued, 'I just call it my bad habit, but I can speak normally like this if you want.'

'No it's fine…' Maya was a little confused, but the idea of Tahani having a different tone was strange. Behind the voice, there was less arrogance, but it felt… sorrow…

'My turn!' Tahani piped up, accent returning and her smirk turned lewd. 'I noticed this before... but what's going on with Seth?'

That wasn't something Maya was expecting. Her frown deepened. 'What about Seth?'

'Well he would've known right away if ya had feelings for him,' Tahani said more to herself than she had with Maya. Now Maya understood and her eyes narrowed. 'Now if only we could read the mind of the grand telepath himself.'

Wait – 'What?' Maya shot back immediately, shooting a glare for answers.

Tahani's face dropped when she realised. 'Yer didn't know that Seth could read minds of those around him?' Maya's eyes went wide with disbelief and it finally dawned on her. 'Oops... There was probably a reason for that secret...'

'I can't believe it.' Maya heaved.

'Well I've made things awkward,' Tahani said and her eyes went to side of the road. 'I need to get some gas for this car – are ya hungry kiddo?'

'I might need a lot more than food...' Maya seethed, clenching her fists to her side. 'I need some sort of way to teleport back to Golden Cliff and kick Seth's ass.' A snort escaped Tahani and Maya shot a look towards the dux. 'How can you find this funny?'

'The way ya acting all defensive 'bout it – it's cute,' Tahani snickered with delight as Maya's eyes narrowed. She was *so* glad that Tahani was having the time of her life.

Not.

'You need to cut it out,' Maya muttered and her previous fear with Tahani felt like it faded throughout their trip.

'Okay – snacks and drinks it is.' Tahani pulled over into the gas station and went to fill up the car.

By the time Tahani walked into the building to pay, Maya let herself cool down. Yes, she was annoyed that Seth had this information and didn't bother to tell her. How dare he think that he could keep something like that from her? What Maya really needed was to take a break from this damn car.

Maya got out of the car and went into the bathroom. The door creaked open as she stepped into the room and washed her face from the tap. With a splash of her face, Maya looked back at her reflection only to see that she wasn't alone. Her body froze as soon as she heard the click of a gun.

Slowly she turned with her hands raised and met the guy in the eyes. She couldn't tell if he was a shifter or a human, but she couldn't afford the wait. He was ready to fire through her head when a distant gunshot interrupted them. This caused them to jump, but Maya quickly recovered and grabbed the guy's wrist.

The man cursed as Maya shoved automatically downwards and forced him to shoot his own foot. She let him drop to the floor with yells as she collected the gun to warn Tahani that someone was trying to kill them, once again.

Apparently Maya didn't have to say anything. Tahani was wrestling with someone already with extra two bodies on the ground.

'Hey kiddo we're being hunted!' Tahani called out and Maya stiffened. Why did she sound so excited over that? The dux flipped the man over her with ease, knocking him out instantly with a palm strike to the chin.

Maya hesitantly took a step towards Tahani. 'Did they get you anywhere?'

'Nope – it wasn't anything that I couldn't handle.' A scoff of amusement escaped Tahani's lips. 'Geez... that backfired for them.' Tahani turned to face Maya and her smirk turned into a look of horror. 'Maya!'

It felt like time slowed down, Maya turned to see the man that she shot in the foot was still standing and not happy. He snarled and tackled Maya into the ground with his hands around her throat.

Her throat felt like it was being tightened and Maya wheezed for air. This man easily overpowered her and she had no strength to fight back. She needed to do something.

In a desperate attempt, Maya tried reaching for the gun nearest to her. If she didn't defend herself then she was going to die and Maya was not ready to die in the middle of nowhere. As soon as her hands touched the cool metal, she firmly gripped the gun and used it to whack the man against his face.

The attack caught him off guard, sending him into the ground and Maya immediately pointed the gun at him.

With a grunt, the man tried to pull himself up but hesitated at the sign of the gun and suddenly, Maya felt her confidence waver.

This is wrong, she told herself, gritting her teeth as her arm shook. *I can't kill this man, because I would be no better than him.* Finally, Maya lowered the gun and clenched her free fist. It was time to stop this violence. Maya threw the gun in Tahani's direction, avoiding the other woman's intense stare.

In the corner of her eyes, Maya saw the glow from the man's eyes and her alarm came back to her. He got to his feet and stalked his way to Maya without the hesitation that she had.

However it was over before it began.

The sound exploded in Maya's ears and she saw the blood in the air like it was a simple movie. It seemed so easy for someone to die – it was horrifying. As the man dropped in front of her, Maya immediately turned to see Tahani with the gun in her hands.

Tahani seemed to unfreeze from her halted position. Her eyes weren't filled with sternness like they were a second ago, but she had a concerned look in her eyes. It had been like she was a different person while she held the gun.

'You killed him,' Maya said the obvious. Her thoughts came back to her and she felt sick again. 'How?' She couldn't find the strength to form the words. Maybe she was going into shock – it was the only thing that made sense, why she seemed to freeze.

'He was gonna kill ya,' Tahani said calmly and she reached Maya's side. 'I just did something that yer couldn't do.'

She swallowed the lump in her throat and looked towards the other woman. 'Why do you find that normal?' *Didn't it affect her that she managed to kill others without blinking?*

'I've been doing this for a long time,' Tahani answered and she avoided Maya's stare. 'I would do it all again in a heartbeat as long as it…' She trailed and hesitated.

'Was it to protect my mum?'

Tahani seemed surprised at Maya's observation. It was strange – Maya had no idea what their relationship was, but something changed. She couldn't tell if Tahani was ready to open up yet.

'We need to go,' Tahani muttered and took the newly acquired gun. 'The sooner we find yer father, the sooner we can get that stone.' Tahani headed towards the car, leaving Maya to stare at the bodies.

Couldn't they at least do something?

Finding a phone by the deceased clerk, Maya made an emergency call and made the report. After stating the location, Maya turned off the phone and shoved it in her pocket before she followed Tahani.

Her appetite was gone unfortunately.

CHAPTER 18

Brodie uneasily eyed the half-eaten hamburger in front of him. He was thankful that Silver Roots was quiet, simply for the peace. A week passed since Brodie last saw Tara. He was surprised that his auntie allowed him to be on his own even after what happened with Orgul.

Jason's harsh words over a week ago, burned the back of Brodie's skull and Brodie huffed in irritation. Jason's words were coming back to him and it bothered him more than it should've.

A familiar presence approached him. 'I thought you would be here,' Jason told Brodie as he took a seat on the opposite end of the booth.

Brodie's eyes narrowed and he let out a sigh as he pushed away his burger. His appetite disappeared. 'What do you want?' His venomous tone caused Jason lean back in his seat with his arms crossed.

'I want to talk to you about Laria,' Jason admitted and Brodie scoffed dryly. Of course he was going to talk about the previous week. 'She's concerned for you. You can at least talk to her.'

'Did she put you up to this?' Brodie responded, meeting his stare.

Jason was silent at first, eyes refusing to look away. While Jason stared at Brodie from his high horse, Brodie couldn't help but recognise the feeling of impression. It wasn't too long ago when Jason cowered behind Seth, and now he was staring at Brodie without hesitation. 'She doesn't know I'm here.'

'Just like a dog,' Brodie told him while scoffing. In the

corner of Brodie's eyes, he noticed Jason's clenched fist. 'Just so you know, that loyalty is one-sided. She only cares about what benefits her.'

'Rather be a dog than a bastard,' Jason shot back without hesitation. Brodie's scowl deepened and he straightened his posture.

Are you going to let your puny brother speak to you like that?' Orgul's voice echoed in the back of Brodie's mind. The bloodlust's voice was hoarse – it sounded as if he had been parched yet it didn't make sense. Why would his bloodlust sound like it needed a drink? *It's not water I need...*

Gritting his teeth, Brodie pushed the thoughts away. Shaking his head to discharge the desire for revenge from the other night, Brodie told him, 'you wouldn't get it.'

Suddenly slamming his fist on the table, Jason got up. The sudden movement caused Brodie to raise an eyebrow. 'How can I not understand?' Jason snapped, picking up the attention of the few people around them. When the eyes went on him, Jason settled and clenched his fist. 'I don't even know why I try.' He shook his head with a scoff. 'No matter what happens, I'm always going to feel like you're a part of my life – as much as I hate it.'

Before Brodie could ask, Jason was already walking away. However Brodie's hand snapped out to grip Jason's wrist before he could leave.

'Let go of me,' Jason demanded and his eyes flashed brown.

'Do you really think you can take me?' Brodie challenged with a cold smirk. 'It didn't end well for you last time.'

'Are we interrupting something?' spoke a cold voice.

Brodie froze, glancing behind Jason's shoulder to recognise Mister Embers and Ruddy Ryans. This was Brodie's first meeting with the son of Takon, but he heard stories of him. He mostly remained in hiding and only revealed himself when someone or something was at risk.

Judging by Jason's expression, he didn't know Ruddy. Being caught off guard by Ruddy, Jason yanked his arm free. 'I was just leaving.' Shooting a glare towards Brodie, Jason began to walk away.

'Give my regards to Seth,' Ruddy muttered and Brodie frowned. Seth knew this guy?

Jason didn't say anything and he disappeared behind the doors. Once he was gone, Brodie realised that Mister Embers had been watching him with sympathy. Why did everyone have to pity him?

Brodie avoided the history teacher's stare. 'Sir, aren't you meant to be stopping those hunters from finding out our identities?'

'We should be,' Mister Embers answered honestly. 'But how can we focus when you're threatening to fight in public? You realise had we not been around, then you and Jason both get sent to the sheriff?'

Of course that was why they got involved. As always, someone was sticking their nose in business where it didn't belong. 'I'm glad you care,' Brodie muttered dryly. He pushed himself from the booth with a shake of his head. 'But I can take care of myself.'

'Until you can't,' Ruddy added and Brodie's body froze. Now Brodie knew that Ruddy was referring to Orgul. 'If that happens, then it doesn't matter who your father was. I will put you down if it ever comes down to it.' The comment wasn't a bluff, Brodie discovered. Ruddy was completely serious – the stories were true that the man didn't hold back on his threats.

'There will be nothing for you to worry about,' Brodie finally answered, without looking back at the other shifter. 'I have my thoughts under control.'

If only there was a way to stop him from threatening you like that. Make that stranger pay for threatening you. Orgul taunted, but with an effort to prove everyone wrong, Brodie kept walking. The voices of Orgul kept whispering to him, but Brodie knew that he had to fight it.

I have to… Brodie cut off his thought with a clenched jaw. Were these dark thoughts really coming from Orgul? Or was it his own thoughts?

***

'Wat'cha reading there, little lamb?'

Jenna raised a suspicious eyebrow when she heard Nick's voice. Her mind had been occupied within an old leathery armchair that she didn't even realise he was in front of her until he spoke. She didn't expect to see him within the public library. Being a shifter, he probably didn't care much about literature in the first place.

'What are you doing here?' she asked him, placing the book on her lap.

'Nah, ah.' Nick raised a scolding finger. 'I believe I asked first, you shouldn't be dodging my question.' When Jenna didn't answer, he added, 'I promise I won't laugh.'

He wasn't using his mind control, but Jenna knew he wouldn't leave her alone. It was something she realised while he spoke to her – he was persistent. Jenna had to admit that she admired that – whether they were human or shifter.

'I'm reading up on the novel of Mice and Men,' Jenna told him. She saw the edge of his lips twitch with a smile and she tried to ignore it. 'With everything going on, I still need to study. I want to get into psychology, and it means I have to read the boring books.'

'It doesn't sound boring to me,' Nick confessed with a shrug.

This caused Jenna to doubletake on the shifter. 'It doesn't?' Why did this man surprise her every time she saw him?

His grin widened. 'Of course not,' he took a seat next to her. 'To be honest, I prefer poetry. I grew up on it – Invictus, Fire and Ice, The Alchemist, you name it. But my personal favourite, A Poisoned Tree.'

'I didn't take you to be a fan of poetry.' It probably explained why he was here in the first place. Jenna was only aware of the Fire and Ice poem from a movie that she loved when she was younger. The other poems sounded like some strange gibberish that she probably wouldn't understand.

'Why do you sound so unconvinced, lamb?' Nick looked mildly upset and it was a strange expression from him. This was pretty important to him. 'Poetry reflects the soul, and in dark times… Let's just say it was a light that kept me guided.'

The way he spoke was rather gentle. Jenna found herself rather surprised about the observation. It wasn't like he was rough – but he gave the impression that he was a loner and despite being open, he seemed secretive about himself. It was strange, Jenna couldn't explain how she knew it.

'Lamb? Why are you staring at me like that?'

Jenna blinked, breaking out her trance. Her eyes remained focused on Nick's and she realised that they weren't as clear as Taro's were. *What am I thinking?* She shook her head and avoided his stare. 'So my nickname is lamb now?'

'Would you prefer love?' Nick asked, scoffing when Jenna shot him a cold look.

'I would prefer Jenna.'

'Does it bother you?' Nick asked her. If she was being honest with herself, Jenna didn't know why it was bothering her. Nick's names for her were certainly better than Jennavieve. He didn't need to know that was her real name.

'Forget it,' Jenna huffed, 'I just want to know something from you.' Nick raised an eyebrow and he tilted his head. 'Why me?'

'I told you, lamb,' Nick whispered and Jenna found herself staring at his eyes again. It was hard to focus with him being so close to her. 'Why not?' It wasn't the answer that Jenna wanted.

'I mean, why are you determined to get me to listen to you?' Jenna tried to rephrase her question. 'You told me everything about the shifters, but you still want someone to listen to you. Are you okay?'

Nick's eyes grew wide and he leaned back. 'Am I okay?'

'When someone's hurting, they seek out help,' Jenna explained and Nick's confusion remained. 'Surely you have goals and other things to do, but you keep finding me just so you could talk.'

His silence only confirmed Jenna's suspicions. He needed to talk to someone. She wanted to know why he only spoke to her – or if he tried to speak to others. There was something important that he was hiding from her.

Then Jenna heard a quiet buzz between them. Recognising that it was her phone, Jenna flashed Nick an apologetic smile and went through her bag to find it. She frowned as the caller flashed on her screen.

But she answered, 'Taro.'

'Jen,' Taro's voice sounded rather winded. Maybe he was playing sports? *'I know with everything happening, we've hardly been able to be ourselves…'*

'Yeah,' Jenna muttered and she saw that Nick was now avoiding her stare. She hoped that he hadn't shut down on her. The last thing she wanted was to lose her… friend? No, that didn't sound right. They had something between them, but Jenna couldn't tell if it was friendship. At least, not yet.

'I just thought… if you would like to go to the Acer Opacare with me?'

Jenna's heart began to race. Her favourite time of year because it was changing from fall to winter. It wasn't too long now. The previous years, Jenna always convinced her friends to come – this year would be different.

'After everything…' Jenna's voice trailed off and she spared a glance to Nick. He was still avoiding her stare. Guilt came to her, and Jenna scolded herself. 'I will have to think about it…'

'I understand,' Taro replied, but his voice was laced with disappointment. *'I have to go, my break's over.'* Before Jenna could bid him a farewell, Taro hung up to continue whatever activity he was doing. When Jenna put the phone away, she still was in shock. Why didn't she say yes? A few months ago, she would've been ecstatic to say yes.

'Your boyfriend?' Nick asked, and Jenna was caught off guard with how casual he sounded.

'I told you that he isn't my boyfriend,' Jenna told him with a huff. Nick's chuckle kept her uneasy. 'It's complicated. We had something, but that was before I found out about shifters.'

His casual expression morphed into one of confusion.

'What's stopping you?'

'Well…' Jenna bit her lip and looked into Nick's eyes. 'You…' Her answer caused his jaw to drop slightly. It wasn't enough to keep his mouth wide open, but Jenna saw his body tense up.

'Me?' He frowned again. 'Why?'

'You're a shifter,' Jenna explained to him. 'He's apparently a shifter hunter – he could kill you if he found out about you. I don't want to lose my only companion – I've lost too many people already.'

His frown morphed into a look of concern. After a moment of silence, he reached out and brushed her arm with rough fingers. 'You won't lose me, lamb,' Nick promised Jenna, gently squeezing her as reassurance.

In that moment, Jenna felt her nerves settle. With peace on her mind, Jenna awkwardly flashed him a smile. 'Thank you, Nick…' Realising that Nick wasn't going to leave, Jenna found herself finding comfort in spending time with the shifter. *Maybe not all shifters are bad.*

***

'So any news on the S.H.O?' Laria asked Takon once she entered the dux meeting room. She didn't come here often – in fact the last time she went into the room was when she introduced herself to the duxes. How things had changed in such a short time.

Ever since the hunters began their attack, Laria was advised by Takon to use this space as refuge. Since the hunters still had no idea about the secret rooms of the haunted house, they wouldn't try to search. For once, Laria was glad that they had the secrets from the rest of the town.

The remainder of the duxes watched Laria as if they expected her to jump at them. Hugh was the only one who showed a frown, as if he was worried. But Laria also noticed that he kept eyeing her injuries. It was nice to have someone look out for her that didn't have some strange intentions.

'No new information,' Takon told Laria. 'Most likely they

are beginning to take cautions since the Halloween Party, thanks to that one hunter who assaulted Maya. Maybe they discovered that Maya was human.'

Maybe now, they would leave her alone. Relief pooled Laria's gut. 'Besides the party, I haven't really seen much from them myself.'

'It seems that every time I see you, you end up with another injury. Rosa hasn't been doing her job as a magister to teach you how to watch for yourself.' Nadia sternly eyed the bandages around the younger shifter's arms.

Brodie's face flashed in Laria's mind. She still hadn't mentioned to the duxes about his attack, but apparently Tara knew. In fact, that was most likely why she hadn't shown up.

'Tahani has nothing to do with it,' Laria shot back heatedly. 'I've been training with Chris since Tahani left for Maine with Maya. I'm a little reckless when I'm training, and I forget that my brother doesn't go easy on me.' It was a smooth lie, and Laria wanted to protect Brodie from the duxes. She didn't know what they would do if they found out that he was losing control of himself.

'What would the Ungue Dux be doing in Maine with Kaeylin's human daughter?' Hugh asked kindly, reminding Laria that she wasn't alone with Nadia.

'They found a clue about Azu.' Laria answered and noticed how the remainder of the duxes went deadly silent. 'So they're hoping that they find out something once they get there.'

'Seems farfetched,' Jyle, the Scientia Dux commented flatly and the remainder of the duxes stared at him. 'I mean – if I wanted to hide the Corvena – even part of it, I would throw clues everywhere just to throw my enemies off then have it in a different spot entirely. That's exactly how I taught Kaeylin Rosa when she was my second hand.'

Apparently this day was filled with surprises. Laria couldn't imagine anyone who would want to work with Jyle since he was supposedly a madman. And to boot, Tahani hated Jyle's guts because the way he acted in front of everyone. It was Takon who cleared his throat and broke the silence awkwardly, gaining the attention once again.

'To sum it up, we have to start looking out for these hunters. Those bear traps that we found a couple weeks ago belonged to Clark Sommers,' Takon explained and spared a glance to each of the duxes and Laria. 'You are very welcome to hide within these rooms if you're no longer safe within the Ladas mansion.'

'Of course.' Laria nodded obediently.

The Mandati Dux looked away from Laria and turned his attention to the remainder of the duxes. 'Our goals at the moment would be to look out for Charmi or Nick Forte. Only Nick showed himself, but we could see if Charmi pops out soon enough.'

'*Yes, Mandati Dux,*' the three duxes replied stonily.

With the wave of his hand, Takon dismissed everybody and Laria used this chance to walk away. She felt like she was intruding. Just as she was about to move up the stairs, she felt something grab her arm.

Instinctively, Laria turned around with a scowl and prepared to slap the hand away, only to hesitate. Hugh loosened his grip on her arm. 'Miss Alfero – do you wish for me to tend to your wounds?'

'I guess it wouldn't hurt to have them checked up on.' She knew that the wounds from Brodie were recent enough to get his attention. Takon was the last to leave, bidding his farewell with a simple nod and he followed the stairs out of the room.

As the pair were left alone, Hugh unwrapped the bandages and revealed the scabbed cuts throughout her arms. 'Was it really your brother who caused these wounds? I wouldn't expect him to be rough with training.'

It was almost as if he saw right through her. Laria avoided his dark eyes and focused the attention on the wounds. 'I was reckless,' Laria told the truth. 'I consider this to be a lesson well learned.'

Hugh held no judgement, but he placed the bandages on the table. 'I apologise for the Venatione Dux's behaviour.' He changed the subject and Laria felt relieved that he did. 'She had no right to accuse the Ungue Dux for neglecting her duties as a magister.' Raising his hand next to her wounds, Laria knew Hugh had the gift of healing – it was still hard to understand why he was a healer. It wasn't a power that connected with the four families.

Honestly, Laria didn't want to tell him that Tahani had been avoiding Laria before she left for Maine. 'It wasn't your fault,' Laria replied and her arms clenched when the healing began. It felt as if she was in the glass once more. 'Why would you apologise for her?'

'Because as my ex-wife... I still feel responsible for her.'

Now if Laria had a drink, she knew that the dux in front of her would've worn it. Laria was surprised more than she was with the information about Kaeylin and Jyle working together. It was hard to imagine anyone loving the cold sheriff of the town.

'Why did you guys... split up?' It was awkward question, and one she wasn't sure it was okay to ask, but Laria was trying to get over the fact that Nadia was once a normal, living organism.

For a moment, Hugh looked like he was in a conflict with himself. 'We split up twenty years ago after we lost our children.' Laria's heart broke on the inside when he explained his story. 'Our daughter was the five and our son was three.'

Wow, Nadia had kids and with Hugh. Currently they were polar opposites and they had kids together like a normal happy couple.

'And then they were stolen from us – they were never found and we couldn't bear to look at each other. Every time I see her, I get the reminder that I failed as a father. I was never able to save them... so now I do everything in my power to save the ones within my reach. I suppose Nadia made the same choice, but I bet she spends her spare time searching for them. We both struggle to move on – even now it's hard to look her in the eyes.' Hugh went to work on the other arm. Laria's healed arm didn't even have a scratch on it. 'But in the end, we only hope that they're living happily. That should do you for now.'

With the injuries gone, Laria forced a smile. 'Thanks as always Medicinae Dux.' Laria finally made her way out of the room, pondering on the new information. Finally reaching the exit, she paused. 'I'm sorry for what happened,' she said and Hugh looked surprised. At his surprise, Laria felt strangely flustered. She mustered up the courage for her next words. 'I hope that your kids are okay, too. Wherever they are.'

CHAPTER 19

'And that's all for the meeting today.' Mayor Susan Cana concluded her speech and the hunters applauded simultaneously.

With a grateful sigh, David felt his shoulders sag. The S.H.O was in discussion about crime activity dropping. So far, the mayor seemed to back off but David couldn't help but wonder why.

Everyone pulled themselves to their feet and they made their way to leave the main hall. David got a text from his wife asking about the meeting. However before David could reply, he felt a gaze on his skin and noticed that Clark was watching over him.

'Talking to the missus?' Clark wondered, offering a smile towards David. In return, David felt his body slump. Despite their different views, David still saw Clark as his friend and wanted Clark to understand that the shifters weren't the bad guys.

But David knew he had to put on a façade. It was the only way to save the good people. 'Diana's cooking tonight but she wants me to bring some wine so we could finish the night.'

'Might I have a word though?' Clark's expression turned serious.

'Sure,' David voiced his thoughts out loud and followed Clark into one of the storage rooms. There was nothing special about the storerooms, but David knew that the walls were soundproof. 'What's up?'

At first Clark was quiet and David was unsure of his mood.

Each time David saw Clark, it seemed like he had more secrets to hide. However, Clark straightened his posture and took a deep breath. 'We've been friends since you saved me from that shifter 10 years ago.'

David's face paled at the memories. Back then Clark had just been a rookie as a hunter and David happened to be around when an outsider shifter attacked. It took some violent acts but David saved Clark, but it was through Clark's determination to protect his family that he became a hunter of the S.H.O.

'I know,' David muttered and turned his head away from Clark. 'Where are you going with this?'

'I'm going to give you a warning,' Clark announced. 'If you keep messing with the shifters then it isn't going to end well for you.'

'Excuse me?' David snorted at Clark's threat. 'What kind of accusations-?'

'I'm not stupid, David,' Clark said to him firmly. 'You were against this from the beginning – and I know you've been giving away the information regarding of our whereabouts. Let's just say I don't appreciate that.'

With a dry mouth, David tried to swallow the lump in his throat. 'I couldn't just sit back-'

Clark cut him off immediately. 'I also know about that incident with Brodie Forte, and how you're working with that Ruddy Ryans who happens to be a shifter as well. I have all the information I need to kick you out of here if I want to.' Stepping back, David's body trembled in anger. How could he be careless? 'But I need a favour done.'

'I thought we were friends,' David spat darkly. 'And I never thought you would resort to blackmail.'

'I need this favour done – call it whatever you want,' Clark confirmed. 'But you were the one who betrayed us first.'

'I never betrayed you,' David protested. He was tired of the S.H.O not understanding what his intentions were. 'I'm doing what's right – if you really saw these shifters for who they are then maybe you could see how I'm willing to work with them.'

'What, you mean Jenna's friends, right?' Clark asked, noticing that David paused to himself. 'Laria and Brodie are on the brink of self-destruction. Maya hasn't done anything wrong yet, but soon she will.'

'You really think it's that simple?' David replied, still surprised with himself that he was defending the shifters. 'Bloodlust is a dark thing-'

'See that's another problem with you, David. You believe that they can change,' Clark interrupted the teacher again and he shook his head. 'You think because they seem sweet enough in your classroom that they're still children. You want to parent them, but they shouldn't be trusted.'

Despite the accusation, David refused to falter. Why was Clark so determined to hate the shape shifters? There was something David had to understand about him. 'I don't buy it for a second. Tell me, what's the point of this?'

'Susan didn't want me to tell you – but I think it only makes sense since you're so determined to help out your students.' David's frown formed again as Clark leaned on the wall at the end of the room. 'The sacred stone is capable of many grand things – it has the power to seal a godlike species, to give power to a single human and much more.'

'What do you intend on doing with the sacred stone?' David asked warily, as if he almost feared the answer that he was about to receive.

'If we can give the shifters their power, then it's painfully obvious that we can take their power.' And it instantly clicked for David; he never thought that they had such a plan. 'The reason we haven't targeted them is simple. We want to get rid of their powers permanently.'

***

'We're here,' Tahani announced and Maya let out a sigh of relief. It seemed like they had been travelling forever. Tahani finally pulled up the rental car outside a forest. They were in the middle of nowhere, but Tahani never forgot this place that haunted her young life.

'Where are we?' Maya asked, raising an eyebrow to observe the area. 'It doesn't look like much if you ask me.'

'Within this forest we're gonna enter tribal grounds of the Rosa family,' Tahani replied stonily and she was tensed. The last time she was here was when Kaeylin decided to help the humans. 'Well... I'm gonna enter...'

Maya shot the dux a look of disbelief. 'But didn't you say that they don't get along with you?'

'That I did,' Tahani confirmed and got out of the car. 'But these guys already know that I'm here and I know that they wanna see me alone. Just stay in the car and I promise I will be back.' She looked back at Maya who was hesitating in obeying Tahani. 'Look kiddo – I can knock yer out if ya don't trust me.'

Maya's annoyance was clear in her features. 'Fine...' She looked like a disappointed kid and the thought almost made Tahani chuckle. 'But I'm giving you half an hour to come back before I'm going after you.'

'Take this,' Tahani suggested and handed her the gun. When she didn't take it, Tahani let out a quiet sigh. 'I can handle myself without a little gun and I can't promise I can protect ya from whatever comes out here.'

'Will it be dangerous out here?' Maya wondered, finally accepting the gun with a wary look.

'No, it shouldn't be,' Tahani muttered back and scratched the back of her head awkwardly. 'The Rosa family may attack for the thrill, but they should know that I wouldn't come here just for a fight. Since ya with me, they shouldn't bother ya.'

'Comforting.' Her sarcastic comment made Tahani chuckle lightly. Maya looked back at Tahani with a hint of concern and she remained in the car without another word of protest. This left Tahani alone against the family that she wanted to leave behind after so long.

Tahani acted casual and she went into the forest with her hands in her pockets. She was being watched by them, she could tell. They had the perfect camouflage in this area, and if they wanted to be seen then they would've revealed themselves. Her only theory was that they didn't want Maya to see them, even if she was Kaeylin's daughter.

The dux walked until she came into a clearing that she recognised. In her mind's eye, Tahani saw a younger version of Kaeylin attempting to conjure her powers in the same clearing. It hadn't been much, but a small spark appeared between the girl's hands and Tahani smirked when she remembered her younger self hugging her sister.

However those were mere memories.

'Just like I remembered,' Tahani said to the world around her. Honestly, Tahani had to give props for their stealth skills. 'Hiding like a bunch of bloody cowards! Show yerself to me!'

A warning growl from a canine figure stopped Tahani from yelling. She froze in recognition as the coyote's icy blue eyes met Tahani's gaze and it growled. A smirk crossed Tahani's face and she let out a sigh of relief.

'*You clearly are a foolish girl.*' the coyote growled lowly and its eyes narrowed. Its voice reverberated in Tahani's head. '*I thought it would've gotten across your thick skull to never come back.*'

'Well what can I say?' Tahani shrugged lazily and in the corner of her eyes she noticed movements within the trees. People began to materialise within the trees. 'I never really listened to what other people said.'

'We didn't expect to see you back after your disgraceful sister left with a *human*,' a tall male spoke, the pelt of a bear wrapped around his body. With narrowed eyes, he growled, 'You shouldn't have returned, Tahani.'

'As much as I would *love* to have the talk of how much of a disappointment I am, I would rather get the information I came here for.' Tahani knew how these shifters were.

'We are aware.' It was an old hag of a woman that spoke next. She didn't have pelts that covered her body like the rest of the tribe, but her torn clothing was covered in mud – not that it surprised Tahani. They were never ones to care about how they presented themselves.

'Anaba.' Tahani's eyes narrowed. The elder woman

oversaw the Rosa family – she had been the one who forced most of the family to move when the massacre was going on. 'Nice to see yer still alive.'

'What do you want?' Anaba demanded with a scowl. 'Why do you bring Kaeylin's halfling daughter here?'

'Watch yer tone,' Tahani said and in response, she heard the growls from her family. She didn't flinch from them. 'Maya may be a human, but we're still gonna find out how to unlock her power.'

'You seem to really care about her,' the woman responded gruffly. Her eyes went to Tahani and she let out another grunt. 'Why else would you be with her to assist her?'

'I'm looking for Jeffery Cadman,' Tahani announced and her gaze turned serious. The people around her recognised his name instantly. 'Kaeylin wrote in her journals and we assumed that he ended up holding Azu. I know that he ended up meeting ya at one point.'

A chuckle escaped the woman and Tahani almost growled. 'That's something that surprises me... the fact that you're willing to suck up that ego of yours to meet with him. I must say that I'm impressed.'

'To find Azu. That's all,' Tahani muttered coldly. 'Our enemies are after it, and unless yer want another massacre, yer gonna tell me where to find it.' She wanted nothing to do with the bastard responsible for ruining her life. If he hadn't gotten into the picture, then Kaeylin would still be alive with a smile on her face.

'He doesn't have Azu, nor do we know where it is,' the woman admitted and Tahani felt annoyance tick in her system. So this trip of twenty questions and killer shifters had been for nothing. It didn't help that Tahani had quite a bit to pay back for the car. 'However.' Immediately Tahani raised a brow. 'There's a chance he knows where it is – he left the day that Azu disappeared.'

'Really now?' Tahani frowned and felt her mind calculating. 'Where is he now?'

'Back in Wyoming,' Anaba replied and Tahani fought

herself from groaning. So this trip *had been* a waste of their damn time and money. If Kaeylin wasn't dead, Tahani would've throttled her.

'Alright then – thanks for the info.' Tahani turned around and passed a lazy wave. None of the shifters looked happy with Tahani but she was over it. 'I've gotta go back and do things the bloody right way-'

'That's not all,' the old woman continued with a rasped voice. For a moment, Tahani froze on the spot and tried to not think about the other reason she was around. 'You're here because of the visions you've been receiving... like you are full of regret.'

'I am not,' Tahani denied hotly. 'I've been getting visions... but that's because Charmi used her stupid power on me.'

'Opening up the subconscious memories – I am aware. We keep tabs on you, Tahani.' Anaba's wasn't saying new information and Tahani refused to deny it. However the mood dropped when a shout echoed within the trees.

Tahani's eyes grew wide. *Maya!* Without thinking, she dashed from the path she came from. *How could I be careless?* She gritted her teeth, using her adrenaline to push her speed.

If anything happened to Kaeylin's daughter–

'Maya!' Tahani shouted as she escaped to forest. She came into view, seeing the gun she entrusted Maya with on the ground unfired.

'Tahani…' Maya's voice was suddenly quiet, as if she hadn't shouted however Tahani saw the reason why she had shouted. Holding Maya against the car, a strange woman wearing a motorcycle helmet finally whipped her head towards Tahani. On the other side of the road, a black triumph motorcycle remained stationed.

'Finally…' The hooded figure released Maya who remained leaning on the car helplessly. 'I found you, Tahani Rosa.' Her voice was muffled from the helmet, but Tahani managed to understand her intentions.

'So yer know who I am?' Tahani took a menacing step and she clenched her fists. It didn't look like Maya was hurt or frightened. If Tahani had the time, she would've praised her niece. However there were other matters. 'Am I gonna get the same pleasure of knowing ya?'

The woman shook her head. 'It's is true of what he said about your fake accent. It sounds like you're really exaggerating it. I mean, did you get raised by cowboys or something?'

What was she on about? How did this woman know about her forced accent? Tahani didn't move from the spot. There was something about this kid that seemed familiar – she couldn't put her finger on it. 'I can talk normally if you really want. Just tell me who you're talking about.' Every time she dropped the accent, Tahani's mask cracked.

It was a bad idea to expose herself, but Tahani knew she had to find out the hidden identity.

'It doesn't matter,' the woman replied honestly. Shrugging, she kept a casual an unguarded pose. 'I'm here just to test your strength – I've heard a lot about you.'

Tahani scoffed, her bloodlust chuckled in agreement. Unlike Laria's, Tahani got along well with her bloodlust. Sangri was just happy to be a part of the fighting, for the thrill.

'Why didn't you say so?' Tahani demanded, raising her hands in front of her face with a smirk. 'I'm more than happy to test my strength and when I win, you tell me who told you about me.' Her eyes glowed and with anticipation, the opponent got into position.

'Sure,' the woman answered.

Tahani momentarily eyed Maya in the background and relief came to her to see that Maya was fine. She seemed concerned, but she didn't seem injured or even a hostage in this scenario. Good.

Within a second, Tahani dashed towards the woman without a sound. It caught the woman off guard as Tahani swung her fist only to connect with her blocked arms. The force pushed the woman back a bit, but Tahani wasn't done.

Try to take that helmet off, Sangri said as Tahani grabbed the woman's arm with her offending fist. With a yell, Tahani lifted the woman off her feet with relative ease to flip her from above.

A curse came from the woman from the sudden force, only for Tahani to slam the other woman onto the road. Had it been any harder, Tahani could've broken bones, and it was her intention to hold back.

'I hope this is all you have?' Tahani mocked, walking around the wounded woman. On the ground, she groaned and rubbed her previously outstretched arm. Staring down at her, Tahani smirked. 'You're still young, so it makes sense.'

'I may be young, but you're cocky!' The woman replied, and Tahani wasn't expecting her to recover quickly. She felt the kick from her opponent, and with a yelp Tahani lost her footing.

As Tahani landed on her back, the cold travelled through her coat and blocked out the pain. In her line of sight, the woman began to bring herself to her feet.

'Tahani!' Maya shouted and tried to run to her.

Immediately the woman turned to face Maya. 'Stay out of this.'

'Screw you,' Maya replied without hesitation. Hearing Maya respond was a moment of pride for Tahani. While Maya was human, she definitely shared the proud Rosa blood that Tahani had. 'You don't scare me.'

Tahani used the chance to stand back up. 'I'm alright, Maya.' Her chest tightened in protest, but Tahani forced herself to stay focused. Maya's face dropped in confusion and it allowed Tahani to explain, 'it's dangerous to get in the way of two shifters. No matter what you are.'

The woman scoffed. 'I'm glad you see it my way.'

Tahani's fist clenched to the side. What was this woman's deal? There was something familiar about the way she moved. If only she had a look at her face. It seemed to be the only way to lower her guard.

Using her silence as a strategy, Tahani charged towards the woman again. Her speed caught the other woman off guard, raised her arms for another block. Yet Tahani had no intention on harming her. Instead, Tahani reached out and yanked the woman's helmet free. Surprisingly, there was no strap that held it down, slipping off instantly.

'I got ya!' Tahani's confidence dissolved and her jaw dropped upon seeing the woman before her. Dark, thick hair spilt from underneath the helmet and Tahani found herself freezing upon seeing her brown eyes. The face, the eyes—!
'Who are you?'

With a curse, the woman lashed out her claws and Tahani felt a sensation burn her arms. Tahani writhed at the short burst of pain, dropping the helmet and ignoring the cracking sound it emitted.

The woman hadn't tried to follow up with an attack. She looked as if she hadn't been caught off guard. 'You're as strong as he says,' she said proudly. 'You will be the one that will help us.'

'Who the hell are ya talking about?' Tahani's accent became clear once more with her anger. Instead of answering, the woman chuckled with a soft smile, picking up the helmet from the road.

'If you want to save him, you'll come to Cheyenne.'

Save him.

Him.

'Zanobi?' Tahani lost her voice.

Again, she didn't answer but waved her hand towards Tahani.

A strange tingling sensation went through her arm and Tahani's eyes grew wide when she realised it was around her scratches. As she looked, the wounds slowly stitched itself together until it vanished completely. If it wasn't for the dripping blood, Tahani would've assumed that the scratches were never there to begin with.

'Who the hell are ya?' Tahani asked again, narrowing her eyes. No one should be able to heal like that – except for Hugh. But even he has to have a closer examination…

'You know where to find me,' the woman told her. She turned around, taking a seat on her motorcycle as she placed the helmet on her head. 'We'll be waiting…'

'Wait!' Tahani called out, but the woman started the bike. It roared to life with a purring engine and before Tahani could move, she sped off into the distance. Tahani remained unmoving, her thoughts frozen in place.

This just got messier.

'That was awful.'

The voice of Anaba snapped Tahani out of shock. Immediately, Tahani's irritation returned as she faced the older woman. Despite being only her in sight, Tahani doubted that she was alone.

'I thought we taught you better than that,' Anaba continued to say coldly. 'It seems that we were right to disown you and Kaeylin from the beginning. You had the chance to kill her. I'm ashamed of you.'

'Screw you!' Maya shouted from the side of the car. Hearing the anger in her tone caused Tahani to raise an eyebrow.

'Watch your tongue, half-ling,' Anaba warned as her eyes changed to bright blue. 'Or else I will have it is my trophy.'

'I've faced worse than you,' Maya answered back with a scowl. She folded her arms and huffed. 'Besides, I wouldn't be afraid of a family that ran away and hides in a forest like in a Stephen King novel, while they left two innocent sisters to face the cruel world.'

The last part caused Tahani to do a doubletake. Maya knew that Kaeylin was her sister?

'You know nothing of pain, child,' Anaba told her. 'Believe me when I say that you have yet to face the worst.'

Before Maya could retort, Tahani grabbed Maya's arm. 'Don't waste your energy, kiddo.' She motioned for the car. 'It's not like they cared about us in the first place.'

Maya didn't seem to argue much for Tahani's relief. As soon as the tomboy got into the car, Tahani followed after her. She held the door when Anaba spoke once again.

'Sooner or later, Tahani, you will have to make a choice. Good for you, or good for the future. Which one will you go for?'

Tahani shot a cold look towards the elder. 'Go to hell. The choices I make will save the people I care about, no matter the price.' With the final words, Tahani got into the car and started it up.

'So I take it that we didn't get any information?' Maya asked with a huff.

'Nah we got stuff,' Tahani told her with a shrug. 'Only that yer dad is back at Wyoming.' The look in her eyes became hopeful but Tahani didn't feel right about leading her niece into the life as a shifter. Maybe there was a cause to her lack of bloodlust. For now, it wasn't an issue. 'By the way… how did you know that Kaeylin was my sister?'

Maya shot her a dry look. 'I'm not an idiot,' she said while facing the window. 'You said she had a sister – and you give me the cool aunt vibe. There was a reason why you were willing to talk to me – as you could see with that other Rosa.'

Tahani bit her lip in hesitance. 'Are yer angry that I wasn't there for ya?'

'No one's perfect,' Maya told her calmly. 'I just want to know though. What happened between you and my mum? Why weren't you around?'

So the moment of truth. Tahani's eyes focused on the road and the grip she had on the steering wheel tightened.

'Back then, I was angry.' Tahani didn't look at Maya as she spoke despite feeling Maya's stare. 'I was angry because your mother fell in love with a human… and it will be my biggest regret letting her die.'

***

'Tell me something, lamb,' Nick spoke with his eyes on the book. Jenna rolled her eyes at the sound of his voice. Was it really hard for him to stay quiet at a library? 'What is this garbage that you have expected me to read? I expected a classic, not a children's fantasy.'

'That book is not a children's fantasy,' Jenna snapped. Nick raised an eyebrow at her outburst and scoffed. 'It's not!

You just have to get past the first books and then it gets better. It's been highly regarded as a classic in this generation of authors.'

Nick let out another scoff and he finally set the book down. 'I'm sorry love but I'm not wasting my time to read this junk.'

'Suit yourself then,' Jenna muttered and kept writing down notes for her assignments, ignoring his intense stare. He had been doing that more often – simply stare at her. At first, it was unnerving, but now she could block it out. It wasn't like he would answer her if she asked anyway.

'The other day, you said I was your only companion…' Nick trailed off, causing Jenna to finally take her eyes off her notes to look back at him. He seemed curious, rather than worried. 'What happened to your other friends?'

The idea of Nick being friends with Laria and the others felt odd to her. 'Why, are you friends with them?' Jenna asked cautiously.

'Of course not.' He looked disgusted. 'Just like some humans don't get along, some of us shifters don't get along with others. I just wanted to know what caused your falling out.'

'If you must know…' Jenna hesitated, eyes flickering back to his. It had been a secret to herself for what felt like forever. She was shocked that she kept it from someone for so long. 'Laria attacked me after I confronted her, and my dad told me that the shifters were known for hunting humans.'

'It's strange of Laria Alfero of all people to attack you,' Nick confessed and he leaned back in his chair with a thoughtful frown. 'Usually she's anti-fight.'

'What does that mean?'

Much to Jenna's surprise, he answered. 'She doesn't like to fight – because when she does, her bloodlust likes to take over to have the action.'

Jenna blinked. 'That's the shifter power… isn't it?'

'It sure is,' Nick answered and now that Jenna thought about it, Laria was strange when she attacked her. 'My bloodlust is Guis, a hothead but we get along enough. It's the manifestation of a shape shifter power but when it's out of control it can be very violent.'

The idea of Nick possessing the power was frightening. 'How bad can it be?'

'Laria's bloodlust broke my wrist.' Nick showed his wrist as an emphasis and he grinned. 'As you can see, it's my reason of why I'm not a fan of her. It also reminded me that she was capable of more. If it weren't for my experience, I would most likely be buried in an unmarked grave.'

'I don't remember the details of the day she attacked me,' Jenna confessed that her mind blocked the small things out. 'I remember confronting Laria, then someone shot her – then she went crazy, in the last minute she snapped out of it and tried explaining it to me...' She felt like an idiot for not believing in her friend. 'I should've listened to her.'

'I don't blame you for your anger,' Nick said with a shrug. 'But I promise you something, lamb, out of all the shifters you have met, I am the worst.'

'What makes you say that?' Jenna wondered, tilting her head. How could Nick be the worst? He has been the one who told her everything from the beginning.

'Let's just say the humans have done terrible things to us.' Nick's smile vanished and his expression turned stony. 'Many of them hunted shifters when they were innocent – I am the way I am because of humans.'

'You can't say that,' Jenna scolded him and Nick had no reaction. While her voice was slightly louder, Jenna was grateful that the library was empty. 'It doesn't matter how someone treated you in the past. We're given choices, and no one is forcing us to do them – because of that. We make the choices and then we suffer the consequences of those choices, it's how life is.'

Nick's glare didn't falter. He stood from his seat and kept his eyes trained on her. It was the first time Jenna saw the true anger in his eyes. Is this what he meant by being the worst that she met?

'Our chats have been fun,' Nick said coldly. 'However this is the one thing you must learn – humans and shifters are on the same coin. There's a reason why the shifters hate the humans and it's the same reason why the humans hate us. I hoped with our friendship, it would change that. Apparently I was wrong.'

Jenna's scowl disappeared and she felt confused. 'Nick?'

'Stop calling me that,' he demanded softly. Jenna flinched at his voice. It seemed that he realised it was meant to be a quiet place. 'Call me what the other humans would. Monster. Bastard – take your pick, there's no shortage of them.'

'I won't call you anything else,' Jenna told him. 'Because that's who you are. It's fine if you want to believe that all humans are monsters, but I know I'm not. If I have to be stubborn and brave just to prove that to you, then I will.'

Nick didn't respond. His glare softened but he began to back away. In her confusion, Jenna wanted to reach out to stop him. Why would he suddenly act like she was the enemy? The answers were close, yet too far for her reach.

When he disappeared from her sight and out of the building, Jenna let out a shaky breath. Hiding her face in her hands, the loneliness began to crawl back. She was back to where she started.

Clueless.

CHAPTER 20

Even though it was a school day, Brodie sat in his chair with a glass of whisky in his hand. The estate was dead silent as he brooded into his drink. After everything that happened, Brodie realised that the voices in his head were quieter when he had a drink. Unfortunately, it made him unable to control his bloodlust if it did come out.

Guilt consumed him for his actions. Laria was his best friend, they knew each other since they were in diapers. Yet here he was, internally fighting Orgul who wanted her dead. It was like poison, the idea spread through his mind until it was the only thing that Brodie could think about.

Then Jason.

Brodie's blood boiled. Oh Jason.

The brother Brodie was meant to protect after learning of his identity.

At first Brodie felt distrust towards Jason, seeing him crash into Laria in the middle of Silver Roots. That night changed everything. It was the night that exposed Laria to the world of the shifters, the night that Brodie realised he couldn't protect his friends and it was all because of Jason.

The anger towards Jason only grew when Brodie discovered that he failed to keep Laria safe from Charmi, Nick and Brad. It led to Brodie killing Brad, mixed along with the rage of his dying father.

Brodie thought with one death, the voices would stop.

Orgul would feel satisfaction and leave him alone to mourn. Yet it wasn't what Brodie got. With Brad's death, Orgul became consistent. Even now, Brodie could feel the slithering presence of his bloodlust pressed against him.

Kill Laria, and you would have avenged your father.

It was wrong to think of it. His pain of his father's death would slowly fade if he went through with Orgul's words. The more Orgul spoke, the more Brodie felt they were his own thoughts. However a fear crawled in Brodie's mind.

What if Orgul's ideas become too tempting? Brodie's resistance was weakening with each day, even when he was drinking the voices away. How could Brodie look at himself for allowing such toxic ideas in his head.

'This is low. Even for you.'

Brodie straightened his posture, recalling the moment his brother tried to stop him from hurting Laria. How could Jason talk? He lost control instantly, killing another shifter in the process. Did he regret killing someone?

'Brodie is in there and I will save him from you.'

Laria's voice forced Brodie to stand up. She wanted to save him, how could she knowing that he would possibly kill her? Hiding his expression from the world, he stormed out of the estate and began to run. The adrenaline pumped through his body, forcing the aches from running vanish into the back of his mind.

'I know that you're giving yourself up to your bloodlust on purpose.'

Tara's voice. His stern but calm auntie that watched over him after Leon died. She didn't visit often, but she offered support. Yet now, all she sounded like was a broken record.

'You were far too reckless – what happens if she had killed you? Do you think that your friends would've accepted that?'

What would Seth know, having no friends and lying to the ones he had? The shadows loomed over Brodie as he made his way into the towering forest. It was the only place that he could be – the white noise of nature was comforting.

'No match for someone like me with that anger, you're better off taking out that anger out on the one you really hate.'

Immediately, Brodie halted in his tracks. Anger overcame him with the thought of Charmi. She was the reason why he was like this, demanding for him to give in to his instincts.

'SHUT UP!' he shouted to no one. His voice echoed in the forest, and the lack of response caused him to settle. The adrenaline left him and as Brodie huffed quietly, he clenched his fists once again. 'I don't want to kill her Orgul…'

Are you sure about that? The bloodlust spoke and Brodie gritted his teeth. *Because the longer that your enemies stay alive, the stronger they get-*

Why was he hesitating? Brodie cursed to himself in silence and tried to shut Orgul out once again.

Brodie felt pressure and a sharp pinch on his leg. With a yelp, he looked down to recognise a modern beartrap. The padding was stopping the metal jaws from shredding his legs, however Brodie realised that there was a syringe in his leg.

With no idea how the hunters managed to include the dart, Brodie tried to pull his leg free from the trap like a wounded animal. After a few tries, Brodie cursed his luck and a dizzy spell hit him.

'Bastards…' Brodie's voice shook. He squinted to get a better view, however his vision worsened. Along with his sight, Brodie's strength began to vanish and he lost the strength to remain standing. With a wounded groan, Brodie's numb body hit the ground with a heavy thud.

He groaned again, rolling on his back to see a shadow looming. Brodie squinted his eyes again, desperate for answers. How could he let this happen? Without the recognition of the shadow, Brodie mumbled a curse before losing consciousness on the forest floor.

***

Jason's eyes found themselves staring at the clock, blanking out on the teacher lecturing in the background. Being a shifter meant that his perception of time felt longer – or maybe it was just him.

'Seth Laurence? What are you doing here?' The teacher

demanded in a gruff voice.

Suddenly, Jason became aware of his surroundings, looking at the entrance to see Seth looking towards the teacher with an emotionless expression. Despite becoming a shifter, it was still impossible to read Seth.

'I apologise, Sir,' Seth said immediately, 'but Principal Ladas requested for me and Jason.' As soon as Jason's name was mentioned, the class immediately directed their eyes on him.

The teacher looked conflicted. 'Surely she would've told me that she was asking for you.' He checked his phone. 'Usually she's pretty strict on that.'

'Do I really need to explain myself?' Seth responded flatly. 'I'm just the messenger, I do not know what she wanted.'

After a moment of silence, the teacher finally sighed. 'You're lucky you're an honest kid. You can leave, Jason, just pack your bags. We'll be done soon anyways.'

'Sure thing…' Jason muttered with a raised eyebrow. The stares were still on him as Jason packed away his books and the teacher went back to talking. Despite knowing Seth, Jason wasn't expecting him to come to him in class. This behaviour was strange. Whatever the principal wanted, it was urgent — especially since most of his friends happened to not be at school either.

When Jason swung his bag over his shoulder, Seth was already leaving him behind without saying anything. To hide his annoyance, Jason picked up the pace and tried to call out his friend.

'Seth. Why would Tracy Ladas want us?' he asked, but immediately it dawned on him that they were going in the opposite direction. With a guarded tone Jason asked, 'what's really going on?'

'I was just texted by Ruddy Ryans,' Seth explained and Jason tilted his head. He recognised the name as the strange man back at Silver Roots, but didn't ask Seth how they knew each other. 'Some hunters were on their way here. They wanted to ambush us outside the school, so we needed to get out first.'

'Do they know about me?' Jason asked, recalling Taro's surprise when Jason showed off his bloodlust.

'I don't think they do – but I am not going to stay here to find out.' They rushed outside and Seth opened the door of his car. For a moment, Jason hesitated and Seth shot him a glare of irritation. 'We need to leave now.'

'Alright.' Jason went to the passenger side of the car.

When Seth drove, it was usually calm and collected like his personality but in a dangerous situation, it was different. Jason tightened his hold on his seat as Seth rapidly pulled the car out of reverse and recklessly drove out of the street.

But there had to be a place that they could hide.

'What about my house?' Jason voiced his thoughts and Seth sent him a surprised glance. 'I haven't been there in a few months, but no one would suspect it for a little while. While we're there we can find another place we can hide.'

'I would say the Ladas mansion,' Seth muttered and forcibly U-turned. The sudden effect lurched Jason's body to the other side of the car. 'But then I remembered that Alfero lives there and they would most likely try to hunt them down from there. So–'

Jason suddenly shot his head up when he saw movement in the corner of his eyes. 'Seth-!' Instinct forced him to brace himself for impact. It seemed that Seth heard the thoughts before Jason said anything, attempting to speed up his car.

Unfortunately it wasn't enough. The passenger side was smashed by the offending car and the pair were sent spinning out of control. Seth's curse was a mere whisper compared to the shattering glass and the screech of the vehicle.

Once the car slammed into a post, the airbags exploded in their faces. Seth was the first to recover, shaking himself out of the daze, and Jason moaned weakly. He felt sick, disoriented – it was a horrible feeling from inside and outside.

'We still have to move, Jason,' Seth muttered through agonised pants. Jason winced at the pain that shot through his shoulder when he tried to move it. It was dislocated and there were probably more pains that his adrenaline was blocking out at the moment.

'I'm alright,' Jason lied and he tried to open the door but it was crushed. Crap. 'It's stuck.'

'I know – just hold on,' Seth replied in agony and it was then Jason realised Seth was in his own suffering. Seth groaned and reached for the door, ripping off the seat belt to break out of the destroyed vehicle. Jason couldn't depend on Seth for the rest of his life. He used his uninjured foot to kick the door in desperation.

'Come on!' Jason snapped in annoyance just as his foot connected with the car door. With his motivation, the door flew open and Jason groaned as he released the belt to limp out of the car. 'Seth,' Jason wheezed and caught up to his mind-reading friend. Seth pushed himself up awkwardly and gladly accepted the help. 'It's not far, Seth... come on...'

'I don't think so, shifter.' A voice made them both freeze and the pair noticed the owner of the offending car step out. Immediately Jason felt alarm prick his senses as the unknown hunter pulled out a strange sort of rifle. Upon closing inspection, Jason realised it was a tranquiliser.

Jason's eyes turned hard as he protectively tightened his hold on Seth. 'What do you think you're doing? Do you normally ram cars to hurt other people?' *How had these people managed to get around town without arousing suspicion?*

I can stop this, Ultio whispered in Jason's mind. His bloodlust seemed rather calm despite the dangerous situation. *Just let me out.*

Not yet. Jason thought back. They needed an exit first, but with the hunter in front of them – it was hard to figure out their opening.

'It's your lucky day,' the hunter said mockingly. With the tattoo over his cheek, Jason felt his stomach flip. The hunter was quite bulky, Jason wasn't sure if he was safe using the training techniques from Tara. 'We ain't gonna kill you yet, we were told by the mayor to bring you in.'

'What makes you think we're going to go with you?' Seth

grunted, back to showing his emotionless features. 'We outnumber you and we can kill you faster than you can shoot that gun.' Jason really hoped that Seth wasn't bluffing.

The hunter scoffed in front of them. 'Fair enough.' He lowered his gun, surprising both Jason and Seth. 'So I'm going to give you the choice whether you want to come willingly, or be by force.'

What was this hunter playing at? Jason narrowed his eyes. 'We don't want to play your games, so if you're going to threaten us – at least go through with it.'

A menacing grin widened on the hunter's face. 'Very well.'

In the corner of Jason's eyes, he saw Seth turn and his face went pale. 'Jason!'

Everything moved too quickly for Jason to register. One moment he was standing, the next he was being shoved out of the way. Before Jason could hit the ground, he recovered from his fall but Seth wasn't as lucky.

'Seth!' Jason heard his groans, but he wasn't moving. Behind the unconscious Seth stood a tall male wearing classic biker's gear. It was impossible to see behind the black helmet. How did Jason not hear a motorcycle close by?

'Good thing that you were nearby,' the hunter said with a smile.

Jason's eyes darkened as he snarled. 'Get away from my friend.'

'You're really in no position to make demands boy,' the hunter told Jason. 'But we'll guarantee your safety for transport.' Everything that this hunter said to Jason made no sense. Why were they wanted?

'Touch him and you'll regret it,' Jason replied hoarsely. In his anger, Ultio began slip into action. Ultio was the only one that could save Seth and him from these enemies.

What about that exit you were whinging about? Ultio asked, the boredom colouring his tone.

Screw it. Jason responded back to his bloodlust. *Get out of here.* Slowly, Jason lost control of his movements. He was forced to watch as Ultio took over, growling like a wild animal.

'So you're not going to play along?' The hunter challenged.

'Let's let him play,' the biker replied and Jason felt curiosity from Ultio. Taking off his helmet to reveal the strawberry blonde hair, the man's dark eyes glowed yellow. 'I think this will be a good lesson.'

Jason's alarm pricked. *Why is a shifter helping the hunters?* He didn't get an answer as the shifter ran at Ultio. Without the instincts of Ultio, Jason knew he would've been screwed. Ultio dodged the shifter in silence, striking out with sharp claws only to clutch at the air.

Unfortunately, Ultio wasn't fast enough. The shifter grabbed Ultio's arm, and before Jason could register the situation, Ultio was slammed back into the ground. Jason surprisingly didn't feel any pain, but he heard the grunt from his bloodlust.

'You've got a hundred years until you can overpower me,' the shifter declared with a sinister smile. 'Now sit still, while we take the rest of you.'

Gritting his teeth Jason tried to regain control, but the last thing he saw was the shifter's closed fist connecting with his face.

***

Jenna clenched her fist to the side. This was stupid, even for her.

Why am I even doing this? she asked herself, pacing in front of the forest path. Nick made it clear that he was a horrible shifter. Even now, she was terrified of the thought of entering the forest to see the amber-eyed Laria once more.

There was something about him. She knew he was hurting, something she said struck a nerve. Was it about him being responsible for his own choices? If it were the case, then she wasn't apologising.

With her curiosity burning, Jenna knew she had to find out the truth. If it meant by going through this forest, then Jenna would brave it.

Shaking the nerves, Jenna finally stepped into the darkness

of the forest. The world around her started to lose the sounds of cars in the background, only to be replaced with crickets.

The branches brushed her arms as Jenna pushed through, ignoring the urge to cry out each time something touched her. If she managed to get through this hellhole, Jenna swore to herself that she would make the demands for a better luxury. Surely the shifter with the power to control the minds would be able to stay in a nice hotel.

Jenna found herself halting as she came into a clearing, realising that she had no idea where this cabin could be. Her eyes wandered towards the trees, before the memory of Laria's bloodlust came back to her.

'You naive brat.'

The voice was enough to cause Jenna to lock up. Her breath shook, only recognising the sound of her racing heart. She spun, cursing her lack of faith. Why did she come in here? What was she trying to prove? How could she face this if she was on her own?

I need to get out of here. Jenna thought, squeezing her eyes shut. Even with her eyes closed, she could still see Laria flashing a deadly smile. The voice slithered in her mind.

'A human such as yourself shouldn't dare to stand in my way.'

'Laria... please don't...' Jenna begged, losing the strength to stand. Her body buckled under the pressure, suppressing her urge to cry. 'Laria… please… we're friends… I was wrong to say that you weren't.'

The crunching of dead leaves brought Jenna back from her huddled position. With teary eyes, Jenna could only see someone tower over her. She whimpered, before everything went black.

Within the darkness, Jenna tried to move but her body refused to move. Even when she tried to scream, tried to flee, she found her efforts futile. Then Jenna saw Laria standing in front of her with glowing amber eyes.

Laria…

It was as if her friend read her thoughts, and a smile twitched on her face. Jenna's heart raced at recognising the claws. However, in the next moment Laria disappeared like it was a dream.

A dream.

Jenna blinked into awareness. With a groan, she held her head and questioned the dizzy vision. With the pain of a pounding skull, Jenna nestled her face onto the cushion and inhaled the strange scent of lavender.

Suddenly, Jenna realised that she wasn't asleep on the dirt of a creepy forest. In fact, she was laying on a bed that she didn't recognise. She jolted, sitting upright before cursing at the pain once more.

What happened? Jenna asked herself, observing the room around her. It appeared safe enough – homely even. On the table beside her, old books were in stacks with a laptop that appeared to be off.

It looked like the holiday house she went to before becoming a teenager. Due to funds, her dad had to sell it and since then, Jenna hadn't liked adventuring through forests.

'So you're finally awake, little lamb.'

Jenna tensed as Nick made his appearance from the door. The first thing Jenna noticed was the fact he wasn't wearing a shirt while he held a mug. Wordlessly, he approached her and offered her the mug. She cautiously watched him, still aware of their last discussion until Nick sighed.

'It's tea.' He gestured for her to take it. Reaching out, Jenna took the tea from Nick's hands and finally sipped the beverage.

She smiled. 'Thank you.' It was sweet, perhaps it was the British in him. After taking another sip she spoke again. 'What happened?'

He sat next to her, with his weight on the bed taking its toll. 'I found you, trembling in such a panic.' Nick chuckled with the shake of his head. 'I was under the impression that you were too frightened to come in.'

'I was–' Jenna immediately shook her head. '–I am. I just felt like I needed to see you, you could say I missed your company.'

'You're very lucky that my sister was not here,' Nick told her sternly. 'She is not as welcoming as I am.'

She didn't even consider that. Jenna guiltily drank her tea, seeing that Nick wasn't walking away. For some reason, she was grateful that he wasn't leaving her again. In her silence, she realised that she wasn't sure what to say to him. Was that normal?

Nick's blue eyes met with Jenna's when she eyed him again. Jenna felt alarm prick her senses and she went back to drinking the tea as if she hadn't exchanged a glance.

He scoffed and added, 'I get that I'm good looking, lamb, but could you at least try not to drool?' Of course his playful nature was back.

'Well sorry about that.' She rolled her eyes with her sarcastic tone. Her eyes went up to see the shifter smirking cockily at her expression. 'Because I totally want you.'

A glint from Nick's eyes indicated the return of his playfulness. 'Hmm, not as much of a challenge as I'd hoped. It seems that we're both each other's types.'

Now Jenna could tell the second part of his comment wasn't a joke. She raised an eyebrow back at him with annoyance. 'Excuse me?' Nick's smirk was visible in his features as Jenna placed the book down and stared at him. 'How would you know about my type?'

'You're pretty obvious, lamb,' Nick answered and pulled on his shirt. 'You are into the bad boys, the ones that rebel from authorities and even go against your own friends. That's why you're attracted to the quarterback.'

'That's not true,' Jenna replied hotly. She told herself that she shouldn't overreact to the shifter because he was wrong. 'I like Taro because he's nice under that stupid behaviour, and recently he's been showing more of his caring side.'

'Yet you're not dating him?' the shifter challenged back and Jenna had to swallow her retort. 'And also – I hadn't finished. Your types are the broken ones because you believe that they can be redeemed.'

'You know what? Forget I said anything – that's not true

and I don't like your type.'

'And now you're denying it because it's true. Like I said – open book,' Nick announced and Jenna shot him her darkest glare. 'Lamb, it's impossible to deny that we're both attractive people – though I preferred your longer hair-' Jenna was about to comment when the shifter raised his hands to stop her protests. 'But I have no intentions on courting you, you're an oddball.'

'Gross!' Jenna was glad that her tea cup was almost empty. Ignoring the fact he claimed that he liked her because she was "challenging", Jenna's cheeks flushed. 'And I'm not the weird one – you're the one who lives in a cabin in the middle of nowhere. Speaking of, why can't you have a better location? Bugs are gross, and I nearly fainted there.'

'You did faint.' Nick corrected.

Why was she friends with this ridiculous flirt? 'Not the point! My family would flip if I was dating you, being friends is risky enough!'

Nick sighed and gave a light shrug. 'It was worth a shot, I suppose the ladies from my time were much more appreciative of what was offered to them.'

'And I take it that you're like... a million years old?'

'Let's try ninety-three,' Nick suggested with a smirk and Jenna glared at him. He was older than her deceased grandparents and he still had the maturity of any idiot at her high school. 'I suppose this where my favourite poem comes in. There's a line I like to reference when I think about the old days – *I was angry with my foe: I told it not, my wrath did grow'*– and I constantly remember those days where my father ruined me.'

Jenna's face dropped at the thoughts of Nick's words. 'Your foe?'

'Father was, of course,' Nick replied darkly and Jenna noticed the change in atmosphere. 'I told you that I was adopted, life was not good. An orphan in those times were better off dead, as they were kidnapped for experiments or sold as slaves.'

'Who would do that?' Jenna asked, and judging the look in

his eyes, it dawned on her. His feelings towards humans had an origin after all.

'My *father*–' Nick said the word with such disdain – it was hard to believe he had any redeeming quality. 'The man killed my mother, then claimed me as his child. I was disgusted that a mere human would claim me as theirs. Unfortunately, the time of shifters was not a positive one.'

Now it was like he wasn't retelling the story to anyone. He lost his attention on Jenna and she noticed that she wasn't angry anymore. The only theory she had was that he used his stupid power to calm her down; if he could perform such feat.

'The man was not my real father,' Nick confessed, 'along with me he took Charmi and Brad. We were all orphans who only had each other. We lived in this very town, beaten and treated like we were animals. The best day of my life was when I finally slit his throat.'

Jenna tried to imagine it – she saw Nick's wild and angry eyes. In her mind, a faceless man tried to attack Nick but the slip up was enough for Nick to hold the knife in his hand to finish the job.

'I laughed, little lamb.' Nick's voice shook. His knuckles turned white from him clenching them. 'I laughed like a maniac – relishing in my rage and finally accepting that I am a killer.'

She heard it. In her head, his madness claimed him. The blood he spilt stained his skin and clothes. Why would he tell her this? Her mental image for him was clear as crystal. In this moment, Jenna understood why Nick claimed he was worse than the other shifters.

'To avoid the rest of the town, we fled to London and we were there for a few good decades. Truth be told, I don't know what brought us back – Brad wanted to belong, so he decided to help Lucien Alfero while taking the Forte surname after Charmi. We followed, not without realising the price of being a part of the shifters that were determined to reunite the Corvena.'

'Nick...' Jenna whispered and he didn't look back at her. 'I think... you want to trust someone... that's why you told me.'

He turned, eyebrows furrowed. 'You don't get it, little lamb, I shouldn't trust you – just as you shouldn't trust me.'

Without warning, the door slammed open. In a panic, Nick shot to his feet with his arm in front of Jenna. She froze. Was it the sister that he was warning her about? However, Jenna's blood drained from her face.

'Get down, Jenna!' Clark shouted, holding a gun directed at Nick. Behind Clark, Taro followed after them.

In her shock, Jenna refused to obey him and stood while setting the teacup down on the table. 'How did you find me?' Jenna asked, but looking down she realised her phone was still in the pocket of her trousers. 'You tracked my phone?!'

'Be glad we did,' Taro told her and Jenna shot him a look of disbelief. Did he think he was helping at the moment? 'You have no idea what this bastard has done.'

'What are you talking about?' Jenna demanded crossing her arms. They didn't have the right to tell her who she could hang out with. Not after the stunt they pulled of lying to her. 'Nick has helped me – he hasn't lied to me once.'

'Jenna, you were friends with Laria!' Clark told her firmly. 'Why else would he go after you? He was going to kill you!'

Jenna's breath became short and she tried to dismiss Clark's claims. 'Nick was sick of the lies – he wanted me to know the...' Her voice died down, looking towards the shifter in question. Not once had he defended the accusations. 'Nick?'

'You shouldn't trust me, little lamb.' Nick's voice was hoarse. He wasn't looking at her. 'I am worse than your friends, I told you that.'

Jenna shook her head. 'No.' Her answer surprised Nick. 'If you wanted me dead, you would've killed me from the first moment we met.' She stepped towards him, but he didn't move. 'You're not perfect Nick, I know that – but I know that you've been through a lot and it's only you who can change yourself.'

'Jennavieve!' Clark snapped and she flinched at the sound

of her name. He never shouted at her like that, especially with that name. 'Get away from him!'

Finally she turned to her dad. 'Then what? Lock me away? Pretend that the world is full of flowers and sunshine?' She approached him and placed her hands on her hips. 'Keep lying to me?'

'We'll talk about this later,' Clark said firmly, still holding his gun. 'Taro.'

Jenna wasn't expecting for the quarterback to grab her arm and pull her towards him. 'Taro, no! Trust me!' With a yelp, she knew that resisting his grip was pointless. Despite it, she still struggled. 'Please, Taro!'

When she heard an inhumane growl, she whirled to face the source of the sound. It seemed like a moment ago when they were talking seriously. They didn't even get a chance to talk about how Jenna managed to get into the forest. She hung her head – she really was an idiot.

'Jenna!'

Nick? It was the first time she heard him call her by her name. Despite angry, Jenna somehow felt at peace with him finally calling her by her name. Before she could respond, Taro yanked her away behind him.

'Taro!' Jenna scolded, squirming in his grasp. Whatever iron grip he had on her, Jenna knew he had no intention of letting her go until Nick was out of the way.

'You don't get to talk to her anymore,' Taro said and Jenna squirmed. How dare he tell her what to do? 'I hope you like small spaces.'

Nick chuckled dryly. 'You might want to move out of the way quarterback before I rip your throat out.' His tone indicated a threat, yet Taro merely scoffed at the 'empty' threat.

'Go ahead and try it.'

Jenna used the chance to peek over Taro's shoulders. Nick looked like an angry predator, snarling as he showed his teeth. His eyes were glowing and the images from Nick's stories came flooding back.

Nick's chuckles became darker. 'With pleasure-' He went to jump at Taro, however Clark was faster. He fired what appeared to be some sort of tranquiliser dart and Nick halted in his tracks.

The shifter pulled the dart off himself as a recovery, gritting his teeth and Jenna saw that his golden eyes went to her. At the sight of her, they changed into a blue colour before they lost focus. With a shaky hand, Nick tried to reach out and he lost the strength, falling to the ground in defeat.

As Jenna let out the breath she was holding, it dawned on her that the world around them was silent once more. All she could hear was her rapid heart and her uneven breathing as the hunters went to grab Nick.

CHAPTER 21

Laria kept her eyes focused on the ceiling of her room.

The silence within the mansion was deafening. With Haroni and Tahani gone, Laria didn't realise how isolated she felt until then. Her motivation to go outside was faint, but it overcame by Laria's exhaustion.

Even Tracy was busy. As a principal of Golden Cliff, she probably had responsibilities that required her attention. Tracy seemed distant with Laria as well, almost as she felt conflicted with being with her. Maybe it was the reason why Laria wasn't pressured to go to school.

Chris and Liza had been her only real company. They had spent most of their days training with her, Laria felt grateful that they were around. However Laria insisted that they needed a break and the pair went to Silver Roots for a few hours.

I should've gone with them… Laria regretted her choice to stay away from them despite feeling like the third wheel. She wasn't used to being so alone. A scoff left her lips at the realisation. This was probably what Seth felt like his whole life.

Probably how Jenna felt at the moment.

Laria pulled out her phone and quickly showed Jenna's number. All it took was a single tap, and Laria could be reaching out for her blonde friend. But would Jenna even answer? After what Laria did to her, Jenna shut her out and the rest of their friends.

With a deep sigh, Laria dropped the phone to the side of her. Jenna deserved better friends. She needed friends that didn't lie to her, or attack out of the blue. Maybe it was time to accept that Jenna wasn't going to forgive them.

Typical. 'Speaking of the bloodlust. Laria let out a deep sigh and found herself closing her eyes in concentration. The connection they had was stronger than it was a few months ago, but their bond was the same. Laria hated Lux, and she knew that the bloodlust felt the same way.

When Laria opened her eyes again, she was standing in the middle of the origin of her dreams. No matter how many times she came into the dream-like world, Laria still never understood it. Dreams were meant to be a representation of places she had memories of – this was a place she knew she never went to.

The land looked too perfect to be real.

Lux stood in front of her, identical to Laria from head to toe, except her eyes remained amber. It was still a strange sight to Laria – to see someone look like her, yet have a different mindset from her.

'What do you want?' Lux asked, crossing her arms. 'Come to view my prison?'

Laria wanted to ask more about the so-called prison, but thought it was better off for another time. This time, Laria wasn't going to cower around the power. 'I accept what happened to me.'

The comment caused Lux to raise an eyebrow. 'Accept?' She narrowed her amber eyes and sneered. 'Accept what?'

'You.' Laria answered calmly. 'When mum saw you, she became afraid and sealed you up with magic. I've always had the power of a shifter, but only recently was I able to unlock it. I accept you as my power.'

'What game are you playing?' Lux asked, keeping her distance. 'You weren't so willing earlier.'

'Because I know what I am,' Laria told her, 'I never used to feel alone but since realising that I have you, I haven't been able to fight my battles. You were the one who's been fighting for me, and I can't let you do that anymore.'

'I'm flattered that you care,' Lux replied sarcastically. 'Why now? Lonely much?'

Of course her bloodlust was one to project. 'Let's just say I understand what it's like to feel isolated.' Laria's answer caused Lux to frown and straighten her posture. 'You must've felt it… all those years only being able to come around in my dreams only to be shut down. I would've gone insane too.'

Lux was speechless and Laria knew that she got to her bloodlust.

Instead, Laria added, 'I'm not expecting a welcome hug or anything. I just wanted you to know that – I'm not going to reject you anymore.' Before Lux could respond, Laria brought herself back into her room.

Laria's eyes fluttered open, back to staring at the ceiling. It seemed that Lux seemed rather settled within the cage in the back of her mind. A pool of relief overcame Laria as she realised that if she could save herself, then she could also save Brodie.

Suddenly, a doorbell faintly echoed into Laria's room.

With a huff, Laria picked herself up and brushed her hair back. It was most likely going to be Chris telling her that he left his spare key and needed her to let him in. She scoffed dryly at the thought of her goofy brother as she headed down the stairs.

The doorbell rang again and Laria rolled her eyes. 'Hold on already…'

When Laria swung the door open, panic flooded in Laria's chest and she took in a sharp breath. Before Laria could slam the door, a hand snatched her collar and easily lifted her off her feet.

'Hi darling, remember me?' Charmi said with a smile. Before Laria could react, she felt Charmi throw her several metres away. Laria hit the marble floor with a cold thud, sliding back as she desperately reclaimed the air flow.

'Charmi…' Laria coughed, slowly pulling herself to her feet. The caramel-haired female smiled and her heels clicked as she made her way towards Laria. 'I won't lie, I didn't expect you to show up.'

'Neither did I,' Charmi told her with a scowl. 'But you can say I'm a desperate woman.' She tried to strike out again, but Laria was quick enough to dodge her moves. 'I know you have him. Where is he?'

The question caught Laria off guard, but she raised her arms to block a punch from Charmi. 'What are you talking about?' With a grunt, Laria pushed back Charmi and used the chance to distance herself.

'Nick!' Charmi snapped, and her eyes darkened. 'He was meant to meet me, and Nick never misses a call from me. I hope you enjoy being inside your own personal hell.'

Laria tried to defend herself, however a moment passed and she no longer standing in front of the woman but inside a new location. Her guard went up as she looked at her surroundings, but a moment passed and Laria slowly recognised the building. Pale walls, a wide window that showed the forest behind the fence and a wardrobe that was older than time itself.

'My old room…' Yet at the same time her old room was different. Instead of being the bed setting she was used to, it resembled a child's room, filled with stuffed toys and children cooking sets. Cautiously, Laria stepped towards the old wardrobe and it creaked as Laria tugged to door.

Instead of her clothes, it was clothes for a child – probably an infant.

Before Laria could make any conclusions, she heard singing outside the room. She closed the wardrobe once more and left the room. Walking through the halls of her old home was like creeping on someone. The idea of her intrusions felt disgusting, but Laria had no idea where her disgust was directed at.

The singing became clearer as Laria entered the kitchen and her eyes grew wide when she recognised a younger Lesley. Her smile seemed real, with no hidden agendas behind it. A pang of guilt overcame Laria.

Yet she couldn't interfere, despite what her heart begged to. No one seemed to notice her, not even the few faces she recognised. Takon, Tara, Leon, Zanobi and… another face she never thought she would see.

She never met him, but Laria recognised Lucien Alfero instantly. He almost looked like a middle-aged version of Chris, his short wavy brown hair, the stubble and even the body build. Yet as Laria looked at his identical chestnut eyes, she saw the things that reminded her of herself.

They sang softly while Lesley brought a cake over to the table, where a few children sat but Laria recognised the boy with the attention as Chris. Softly, Laria counted the candles and realised there were in fact six of them.

Now she understood why Charmi sent her within this strange vision.

Laria heard the door slam open and she froze when she recognised the shifter who came through the door. After all, he was the face that haunted her nightmares. His crimson eyes stood out from his pale features.

'Edward…' Laria clenched her fist and prepared herself to fight, however he walked past her as if she was a ghost. In confusion, Laria watched the scene. She couldn't make out the details, but Laria could recognise the panic.

She felt it.

Edward grabbed one of the children, an infant by the appearance and Laria's heart raced as she heard the terrified screams. Those were her screams. Laria was speechless as Edward threw her at the wall and forced flames to surround her.

'Help me…' Laria begged, tears welling in her eyes as Lucien tried to stop Edward.

'…*Ria!*'

That wasn't her mother's voice and it was too soft to be her father's.

'*Laria! Come back to me!*'

Before Laria could react, she suddenly found herself on her back, gasping for air. She sat upright in a panic, the memories of her vision coming back to her. It wasn't real, however it dawned on Laria that the dream was in fact real – it was a blocked memory. No wonder her mother wanted to hide it.

'Laria… it's okay…' Heather's voice came into Laria's awareness.

Suddenly, Laria turned to the witch beside her and she shook her head in confusion. 'I don't get it – what happened? Where's Charmi?'

Heather looked hesitant. 'Takon sent me here, saying the hunters were targeting the shifters, but I wasn't expecting…' She trailed off to look towards Charmi who was recovering from some sort of fall. 'She was about to kill you.'

Laria wasn't surprised. 'Thanks Heather.' Slowly, Laria recovered and got to her feet without looking back at Heather. 'I need to finish this – she has gone too far.' Her claws extended from her fingertips and Laria allowed Lux's power to seep into her.

'Are you going to kill her?' Heather asked, her tone seemed frightened. When Laria didn't answer, she ran in front of Laria with her arms out. 'Laria, we can't kill her – that would destroy you.'

I know. 'If I let her get away, then I pay for the price.' Laria walked around her and stared down at Charmi. The enemy shifter didn't seem to be afraid, however the anger in her eyes was clear. 'I have to protect his town; don't you want me to protect it from her?'

Heather didn't have a response much to Laria's regret. Laria knew it was wrong to kill Charmi. They could've called someone and kept her trapped, but Laria didn't want to take the risk.

'Hurry up and bloody get it done,' Charmi spat, panting heavily. 'Let's just remind you that you'll never be able to fight on your own. Not without a witch or any of your shifter friends.'

Laria prepared her claws, but suddenly an image flashed in her mind. It appeared in her mind within a flash, disappearing to the depths of her mind once more. Despite the quick image, Laria knew that she saw an image of Jason. His blue eyes remained glued to her mind, ever since the first moment she crashed into him.

There was something more important. It was like a gut feeling telling her that Charmi had to wait. Lowering her claws, Laria dropped her arms to the side. 'I'm sorry Heather… I can't do it.'

In front of her, Charmi laughed with a shake of her head. 'You're a coward,' she told Laria. 'I will remember this; I will make sure you do pay for letting me live.'

Laria tried to stop her, however Charmi's form shrunk into a form of a falcon. With a screech, Charmi slipped through her clothing and flew past Laria. Within a swift movement, Charmi glided through the opened door, causing Laria to dash outside.

When Laria reached the door, she scanned the empty skies. Laria cursed softly and she clenched her fist to the side. Beside her, Heather approached and rubbed her shoulder in sympathy.

'I'm glad you didn't go through with it,' Heather confessed and flashed a shy smile.

'I didn't do it because of a change of heart,' Laria said and she turned to the suddenly confused Heather. 'I saw Jason. You said something about the hunters… that they're coming?'

Her hazel eyes widened. 'You don't think that he was taken do you?'

'I don't know,' Laria confessed and she began to pace. She just lost Charmi and the hunters were on the way. The worst part was Chris didn't even know what going on. 'Listen, Heather – I've had enough of them. I'm going to Town Hall to stand up to the hunters, you need to make sure that our friends are okay.'

'I'm not letting you go alone,' Heather said, grabbing Laria. 'I'm coming with you, and if you refuse, I'll come anyways.'

Laria sighed hopelessly. Of course now she chose to be stubborn. Instead, Laria smiled and found herself grateful to have her around. 'Okay, message Takon and tell him we're going to Town Hall. Hopefully the mayor is there too.'

***

'It's very nice to see you here, Miss Alfero, Miss Verdas. Take a seat.'

The trip to the Hall was somewhat simple for Laria and Heather. Even the hunters that were close by allowed them to enter the building. They were even escorted to the office without any arguments or protests. Something didn't seem right to Laria – this was the first time she met up with the mayor and she seemed familiar.

'You're acting awfully casual for a group that has been laying out traps and trying to kidnap us,' Laria told Susan, refusing to sit on the chairs that were offered to them.

'Enough with the hostile nature,' Susan replied and waved her hand in front of them. 'I know what you want, and I know that you are desperate enough to do anything.' She picked up her phone and flashed Laria the screen. 'Your friends depend on your co-operation.'

Laria gritted her teeth upon seeing Seth, Brodie and Jason unconscious in some sort of dark room. So they were caught after all. The idea of them grabbing her friends didn't sit well with her. At least Tahani and Maya were safe.

'Why are you doing this?' Heather demanded, 'You know that we aren't the ones who're threatening the town.'

'I have my reasons.' Susan relaxed in her seat. 'But I know that our declaration has made a significant change – less crime, less shifters. Soon we'll live in a town where shifters will be the least of our concern.'

'The shifters aren't gone though,' Heather argued and Laria saw the frustration in her eyes. 'They've fled to other cities and it's causing people to become suspicious. If we aren't careful, the supernatural world will become exposed.' She placed her hands on her hips. 'But you already knew that… didn't you?'

When Susan had no response, Laria's caution returned. Even before the mess, the S.H.O always had to intentions to protect humanity. They were in charge of making sure they guarded the humans from the truth. It was the deal they went through with the duxes, at least that was what David told them. The hunters tracked any shifters that weren't registered in the database that the S.H.O owned and the duxes covered up any mishaps that shifters caused.

But it hit Laria – the change with the hunters happened shortly after *he* left town. 'It's because you're not really Susan,' Laria said softly.

Susan scoffed dryly in response. 'That is absurd,' she told the pair. Slowly she stood to her feet. 'How would that be possible?'

In response, Laria grabbed Heather's arm and stepped backwards. 'Because with us out of the way, you'll be able to find the remainder of the stones.' The last thing Zanobi wanted from Laria was the location of Azu, but he still needed Rel and Verm. It was unknown if Viri was within his grasp, but it was easier to grab the other stones while they were together.

Again, Susan laughed. 'I'm impressed Laria.' Her grin widened and she brushed the hair from her eyes. 'You were able to figure me out without a mind reader.'

'So you're not denying it anymore, Zanobi?' Laria challenged, clenching her fist to the side. Even the mayor was a victim of his madness. 'Where have you been hiding these past few months? Tahani has been worried sick about you.'

'I never left,' Zanobi told them with Susan's voice. Staring at the disguise, Laria had to tell herself that Susan wasn't with them at the moment. 'We found a place, a place where we can remain safe and watch you struggle. With Tahani returning with information about Azu, it's only a matter of time we can finally revive the power of the Corvena.'

'So, you're the reason…' Heather's voice became quiet. She flung her hands and pinned Zanobi to the wall with magic. It took him by surprise, slamming him with a loud thud.

'Heather?' Laria was confused. Surely this was the same girl that was against Laria killing Charmi? Heather became unrecognisable as her brow furrowed with concentration and anger.

Zanobi groaned. 'I'm surprised that you are capable of such violence, you're more like your ancestors than you thought.'

'You damned someone important to me!' Heather snapped and it caused Laria to frown on the side. Where was this coming from? 'You're ruining lives, I will forcibly pull you out of the Mayor's body-!'

In the background, Laria heard the door behind them slam open. She froze as masked hunters surrounded them in a tight circle with guns directed on them. Heather refused to falter, keeping her eyes on Zanobi without fear.

'Heather…' Laria had to grab her friend's shoulders once more. She didn't budge. 'If something happens to us, we won't be able to rescue the others. Please, you need to let the *mayor* down.' Deep down, Laria understood where Heather was coming from. If they stopped Zanobi, they finish the desperate battle.

Unfortunately it was going to come at a cost if Heather did anything.

A moment passed and Heather finally freed Zanobi from her forceful grip. He acted wounded and rubbed his throat.

'This is what I get for being a good host,' Zanobi told the hunters. 'Take them away.' Laria felt a hunter grab her by the arms, only to cuff her without fear. 'And don't try to break free, these cuffs are designed to block your spiritual energy. So no magic or bloodlust will break out of them.'

'You won't get away with this,' Heather hissed.

Instead of stopping her, Laria struggled against the hold. They lowered the guns and with her in their clutches, they probably wouldn't shoot at her. 'That's right, we won't give up our for your goal Z–!'

'Shut up!' The hunter that was holding her demanded. 'We'll gag you otherwise.'

Laria gritted her teeth but stayed silent. She needed to co-operate, especially if it would raise the chances of her being able to save her friends. Beside her, Laria sent a look of remorse to Heather. The witch didn't deserve to be in this mess.

It was up to Takon to save them now.

***

Jenna stared at the wall of her room while reading one of her schoolbooks. Unfortunately it wasn't as peaceful as it normally was, especially not with eyes on her.

'Taro,' Jenna muttered, turning around to see him leaning by her wall. 'Can't you go home? Dad already made sure that I'm here.'

'Sorry, Jenna,' he replied with a guilty tone. 'But if anything happens to you—'

Jenna groaned, throwing her arms up in defeat. 'Nothing is going to happen to me!' It was one thing to deny her of her only friend, but now they weren't going to leave her alone?

'I can't take that chance, Jenna,' Taro told her. 'I get that you feel trapped, but you had a target on your head for a while. I can't let you get hurt, especially when I have the strength to do something about it.'

She hated that she understood his situation as well. Taro probably saw the worst in shifters and he wanted to look out for her. He could deny her ability to see Nick, but Taro was no longer denying her of her friends.

Slowly, she grabbed her phone and Taro raised an eyebrow. 'Relax, I'm not planning to escape,' she informed him before writing a message to Laria. Despite everything, Jenna didn't have the strength to block her. Maybe it was wrong to do so, but it appeared as if Laria respected her space.

After the message, Jenna forwarded the message to the remainder of her friends. She placed the phone in front of her and looked at her hands.

Despite reaching out to them, Jenna wondered if they would respond. After claiming them as the enemies, it would be surprising if they forgave her. She only hoped that they at least read it.

'Taro…' Jenna felt his stare. 'I don't think I want to be your date for the Acer Opacare.' She didn't look at him for a response. It was simply she felt ever since she saw him hold her back from getting to Nick.

'Why?' Taro asked. When she didn't respond to him, Taro let out a sharp breath of air. 'I get it.' His voice was hoarse. 'I guess I don't need to be here.' That caught Jenna by surprise.

He's letting me go to find Nick?

When she finally looked up, Taro was leaving her behind. She wasn't sure how long she waited for his disappearance, but it felt like years. Yet she still didn't feel right. After everything that happened with Nick, she felt ashamed.

Since when did Nick become such an important part of her life? He was meant to be an enemy, a monster, but then Jenna heard him speak. Maybe Laria could take him and show him the good side.

His life became important to her because when she lost all of her friends, he was the one that spoke the truth. Even though it was the ugly truth, Nick admitted that he was not innocent, that the hunters weren't thinking clearly and that his backstory was the reason of who he was today. It still gave him no excuse, Jenna knew that – but he had good and anyone who had good could still be saved.

Hopefully, Jenna could receive her redemption after this stunt she was about to pull. Jenna rushed out to her car, using her phone to track the location of her father. He had to be the one who was dealing with Nick – he was discussing it with Taro after all when they grabbed Nick. Her car rumbled to life as Jenna began the quick drive. She followed the directions of the tracker until she found herself by what appeared to be an abandoned shed.

Jenna was glad that she recognised the streets that she was going towards and parked in front of the shed. If her father was around, then Jenna was going to explain that she had to let him go. If anyone else was there... then Jenna was going to distract them so that she could let the shifter out.

Jenna didn't give herself time to lock the car, rushing towards the shed and opening it with uncertainty. He really changed her. Nick was the one who showed her the discovery of shifters, he was the one who threatened Taro in front of her eyes and he was the one who taught her that not every shifter was a monster.

Jenna recognised the back of her father's head as Clark was

talking. Nick was tied up to a chair, shirtless, gagged and covered in bruises that were larger than her hands.

Jenna looked around, picking up a wood plank as she cautiously stepped up to him. At first, Clark didn't appear to hear her. Yet Jenna's foot knocked an empty can over, causing Clark to whirl around to face her.

His dark eyes grew wide, before narrowing. 'Jennavieve, what are you doing here? How did you find us?' Clark demanded.

Jenna tightened the grip on the piece of wood. 'Sorry dad, I love you.' Before her father could make a response, Jenna swung with a cry and the plank connected with Clark's head. Hearing the contact caused Jenna to cringe as her father groaned and hit the ground instantly.

As soon as Clark lost consciousness, Jenna threw the wood away. Immediately she dropped down to collect the keys that poked out of the pockets of his trousers. Judging from the cuffs that was holding Nick down, the keys were the only way to break out of them.

'Mhmm hrm hm rhmhm?'

She threw the plank away from him and focused on his cuffs. 'Don't talk until I've got these horrible cuffs off,' Jenna muttered in annoyance and unlocked the metal cuffs. They clicked in protest but Jenna pulled them off without another word. Nick went to nurse his wrists just as Jenna gently removed the gag from his mouth. 'How are you feeling?'

'Like I was hit by a bloody truck,' the shifter groaned when Jenna observed his injuries. He winced at her contact and watched her poke his bruised body. 'I have a few broken ribs; but they should be fine – I'm not as weak as you think.' Nick clenched his arms and Jenna decided to ignore the curse that left his lips.

'If you're okay to move, then we're leaving.' She didn't take in his surprise, instead she grabbed his hand and forced him to his feet.

But he stopped her in alarm. 'Whoa, lamb, what are you doing?'

'Letting you go,' Jenna decided and turned to face Nick

with a firm glare. 'I want to prove to you that not all humans are bad – I know that you wanted to kill me… but it doesn't have to be this way. I'm putting my trust in you, because I know you are capable of good.'

Nick towered over her and his eyes turned serious. 'You really have no idea of what I wanted.' He leaned towards her and Jenna stepped back. 'Your trust.'

'My trust?' Jenna questioned meekly; the fear came crawling back.

'Who do you think shot Laria back when she first attacked you?' Nick taunted, and he flashed a sinister grin. 'It was easy to steal a gun from that quarterback. He isn't as responsible as the other hunters. That led you right to me.'

After all this time he still wanted to kill her? He was right; he was the worst. He toyed with her emotions and pretended to be her friend. Ever since discovering the truth, Jenna thought he was being kind to her because he was sick of the lies. No wonder he called her a lamb – naïve and innocent.

But Jenna wasn't going to go down without disturbing his thoughts.

'So wh-what are you waiting for?' Jenna stammered and Nick raised an eyebrow. 'Do it – kill me and remind me that your endless killing is the result of bad people.' He seemed taken aback that Jenna stood up to him. 'If you want to prove to me that you can be saved then walk away and never look at me again.'

'What are you trying to do?' Nick demanded, his eyes flashing gold.

'Everyone can be read,' Jenna said and met his eyes with a trembling body. She wasn't sure if this would work. 'Just because you're a shifter, it doesn't mean that you can hide your feelings. So just get on with it or go away!'

The world fell silent and Jenna let out a shaky breath when Nick stepped forward. His expression was unreadable and Jenna flinched when she felt his hand softly brushed her face.

'I don't want to do either Jenna,' Nick whispered huskily and Jenna's eyes met with his piercing blue eyes. He called her by her name again, but this time it was different – it hadn't been filled with rage or panic but rather at peace. 'Your heart is pounding like a little hummingbird – there's nothing to worry about, love.'

And with that, he brought Jenna closer to him. His body was warm to the touch. Just as Jenna prepared to speak, she stopped to look at his eyes. She went to push herself away when his head leaned in to press his lips against hers.

It was light at first, but only at first. His lips moved against hers furiously. He used one of his hands to grasp her blonde hair while the other cupped her face. Jenna tried to keep up with him, surprised with herself when she didn't break the contact.

Finally, he pulled away from her bruised lips and Jenna caught her breath. The shifter chuckled lightly and held her face with his hands. Strangely enough, the feeling of his hands was soothing.

'Nick… I'm worried,' Jenna whispered hesitantly. What would her friends think knowing that she allowed a shifter with a dark history to kiss her?

'It's alright, love. Just follow my lead and you will be fine.' He tucked her hair back and kissed her again. His tongue brushed against her lips as if he wanted her consent. She squeaked nervously and went along with her instincts, resisting a quiet moan. Jenna felt a smirk form on his face as their lips met, but it wasn't long until Nick trapped her against the wall.

Jenna's thoughts tried to make sense of this new situation. Were they really doing this? With a moan, she reached up for his hair and combed her fingers through his blonde curls. His lips left hers to focus on her neck, which brought another shade of red to Jenna's face.

This was definitely new.

'Nick,' she moaned with a shaky breath. Jenna's senses went into overdrive but she wasn't ready for this; especially now, with Nick. Their moment was interrupted by a pained groan from Nick and Jenna stopped, having momentarily forgotten about his broken ribs.

'Sorry, lamb,' Nick muttered lightly and groaned again. 'As much as that was fun – I think we should stop before you accidentally hit something.'

'Right – you need a shirt.' Jenna huffed in embarrassment as Nick sent her a devilish smile. 'Then we need to get you to a hospital so they could help.'

'I don't think he's going anywhere with you alone.'

It wasn't Nick who gave that response. Nick froze in recognition as Jenna looked over towards a caramel haired woman standing at the base of the stairs. Her blue eyes were cold, like she was ready to kill – or in this case like she was ready to kill Jenna from where she stood. Barefooted and wearing a large trench coat, Jenna almost questioned how the woman was able to stay warm.

However, every fibre in Jenna's body screamed. The feeling she first had with Nick was bad, but it had been nothing compared to staring at the new face.

'Charmi,' Nick groaned and Jenna recognised the name. 'How did you find me?'

'By using my connections to save your hide!' Charmi hissed and her eyes shot towards Jenna threateningly. 'It looks like it wasn't completely a waste of my time; I get to finish off what I started.'

Jenna's eyes must have missed the split second in which Charmi crossed the basement, grabbed her throat and lifted her into the air. She desperately fought the grip of the female shifter but if it was anything like Nick then it would've impossible to break free.

'Let her go, Charmi,' Nick threatened. 'I told you not to harm her before – now have some honour in my request, sister.'

'It's too late for that, Nick,' Charmi spat back and Nick flinched. As she unsheathed out a sharp knife, Jenna saw the rage in Nick's gaze. He let out a yell of protest and tried to stop Charmi but her glare seemed to halt his movements. 'I never thought that you would betray me. Remember what we went through together.'

Dizzy with fear and lack of oxygen, Jenna's vision darkened but she still saw Nick collapse and heard his yells of protest. 'Nick!' Her voice slipped out as a breath and she felt Charmi's glare back on her. With desperation for Nick's sanity, Jenna had to act. 'He wants… to redeem himself! How could you… hurt him… like that?'

'Maybe he forgot his mission, but I certainly haven't.' Charmi lowered Jenna to her feet, and the blonde felt a sliver of fear as air flooded her lungs. 'You should be dead already – it was his fault.'

'You're a monster,' Jenna accused, coughing. 'What kind of sister puts their brother through so much torture just for your amusement?'

A scoff escaped the woman's lips as she confirmed, 'Oh *this* right now – is for my amusement.' Jenna winced when she felt something hit her stomach. Did the shifter just punch her? They were so quick. Suddenly, Jenna's stomach felt warm, no – sickening hot.

Jenna glanced over to Nick who seemed to look at Jenna in that moment. His eyes grew wide, and he called out her name once more.

She reached to the warm spot on her stomach, only to realise it was wet. Sticky too. How strange, there hadn't been any signs of water –

It was blood.

The pain came immediately as Jenna saw the blood, and Charmi took this chance to lean next to Jenna. 'But killing you is to honour Brad – Nick should've known better than to play with his food…'

It hurts so much… Jenna's whimpers left her lips and Charmi pulled the knife out of her body. Jenna stumbled in her step, but her strength to stand dissolved and Jenna collapsed on the spot.

'Here, you will bleed out.' Charmi's voice overcame Nick's desperate shouts. Jenna tried to force herself to glare back at Charmi as she tried to catch her breath. Everything was beginning to feel slow around her.

'He won't forgive you...' Jenna whispered, her voice too quiet to fight back the heavy feeling. All she wanted to do was sleep. Her vision was hazy. 'Neither will Laria... or Brodie... and I hope that you are punished for all the pain you've caused...' Her thoughts were cut off by the lack of air in her lungs and Jenna coughed. Something warm was in her hand and Jenna realised again that it was blood. Her blood. So surreal.

Charmi was suddenly on top of her, with a sinister smile as she held the knife over Jenna's chest. 'Let them all come – that's what I'm hoping for.'

CHAPTER 22

Maya didn't bother looking back at the dux and Tahani didn't bother to come up with a response to break the silence within the car. They were back home, but Maya felt like they had nothing to show for it. She knew she shouldn't be disappointed; Tahani warned her before they left.

A phone ringing disturbed the silence between the pair and Maya tilted her head as Tahani picked it up while driving.

'Takon, what's up?' Tahani asked on the phone, keeping her eyes focused on the road while she drove. So she was having a call with the school councillor, of course. 'Yeah, I've just gotten back to town, why?'

The change in Tahani's manner made Maya feel uneasy. What was going on from the other line? After more muffled replies, Tahani let out a sigh to colour her annoyed tone.

'That's no issue, I will be there.' Tahani hung up the phone and Maya let out a wail of apprehension when she made a sharp turn in a different direction.

'What the hell are we doing?' Maya demanded of Tahani, and she flashed a smirk.

'We're gonna go on a rescue mission kiddo,' Tahani replied snidely and Maya felt her jaw drop. What on earth did Tahani mean by rescue mission? 'Takon wants us to meet with him here so that we can rescue the sorry lot that got themselves caught.'

'Who are?' Maya asked blankly.

Tahani winked at her knowingly. 'Our sorry lot of friends.

I'll drop yer off so I can get to the hall on time.' The tomboy let the words sink in her head before she realised what Tahani said.

Their friends were in danger.

'Hell no – I'm not gonna stay out of the way this time.' Maya's protest didn't cause Tahani to react, which was strange. 'You ain't knocking me out either!'

A groan left Tahani's lips. 'You are just like your mother… fine. You can come – but you listen to what we say.'

With a relieved smile, Maya accepted the conditions. As long as they didn't kill anyone, Maya knew she would be okay. Hopefully, Maya could stop Tahani if it ever got to that point.

When they reached town hall, Maya saw Takon and David discussing something before turning their attention to their vehicle. Tahani flashed a grin as she pulled up the car and darted out before Maya could say anything.

Let's see what I can do. With a determined breath, Maya followed Tahani out of the car. She approached the history teacher and school councillor who happened to be standing behind a car filled with weapons.

Takon seemed surprised at seeing Maya approach them, but he then settled and continued speaking, 'They've been in there for too long so I can only say that things went south.' He spared a look towards David. 'David, you know this building better than we do – any advice?'

'Yep,' David muttered back in reply and loaded a dart gun. 'Any prisoner is taken to the basement for transferring. They end up being sent to abandoned buildings for interrogation or worse.'

'Worse?' Maya asked, dreading the answer.

'Let's just say we as an organisation haven't evolved much,' David confessed and he narrowed his eyes. 'I stayed silent for so long, perhaps if I mentioned something sooner…'

'We can't say for sure,' Takon reassured him. 'But let's focus on the present, we can't kill these people – especially if we want to show them our humanity.'

'Good enough for me – sucks I can't kill these guys,'

Tahani muttered and took a dart gun for her own defence. 'I can't believe this sorry lot got stuck in this bloody asylum.'

'Stop calling them that,' Maya said firmly.

'Can't help it,' Tahani replied, flashing a grin. 'They did get themselves caught, rookie mistake.'

Rolling her eyes, Maya returned her attention to the men. 'Are we really the only ones who can go in there?' Maya asked and David nodded before he rummaged through his weaponry goods. 'But that's unfair; I don't even know how to fire a gun.'

'Don't worry – we have a backup for situations like this,' David told her and offered Maya a weapon she wasn't expecting.

Maya felt herself scoff in disbelief. 'Really? You guys trust me with a taser when they apparently hurt more than bullets do?' She eyed the weapon cautiously. This wasn't the time for her to be clueless, especially since she was rescuing her friends. 'I don't even know how to use this.'

'Point and shoot,' Takon explained curtly and he loaded his dart gun. 'So in and out – Tahani, you and I will go in first since we still protect the humans.'

'Aye, aye, Mandati Dux.' Tahani saluted childishly and the shifter pair went into the building on their own. 'Stay here kiddies, we'll send ya a text as a signal when we're done with 'em.'

While Maya huffed, she noticed that David gave her a supporting glance. 'Don't worry,' he said, which made her face him with suspicion. 'Your friends will be fine, I'll make sure of it.'

Strangely enough, Maya believed him, and her suspicion faded. When David's phone alerted them of a message, the pair knew it was their cue to step in. Maya held her taser with a constricting grip as she entered the building, noticing that all of the guards were on the ground with darts injected.

'Yer done with the sightseein'?' Tahani asked sarcastically and snapped Maya out of her shocked daze. She didn't even look like she broke a sweat as she and Takon approached them while reloading their weapons. 'We don't have that much time.'

With his key card, David managed to unlock the doors that were inaccessible to the public. He led them to the elevator and pressed the basement button. With a click, the doors shut behind the group and Maya felt her stomach tighten.

Was she really doing this?

The doors opened, reveal a bright corridor however they weren't alone. Maya froze upon seeing the small group of hunters guiding Laria and Heather at the opposite end. There were at least four hunters, and they realised that they weren't alone.

'Laria! Heather!' Maya squeezed the taser in her hand. Knowing that her friends being in danger. One hunter with a red strap on his wrists made a hand motion towards his comrades, Maya couldn't understand.

Immediately, two of the hunters, including the red strapped hunter, raised their guns while the other two began to drag Laria and Heather away. The other hunter had a blue strap instead.

'This looks like fun,' Tahani said with a wide grin. 'Do yer really think we'll go down easy?'

'Don't, Tahani,' Takon ordered softly. She shot him a look of disbelief, but Takon didn't repeat himself. He dropped his gun, and raised his hands. 'David, Maya, when we give you that opening – make sure you take it and save them.'

Tahani muttered a curse. 'Would be easier if we could just kill 'em.' Dropping her gun, Tahani copied Takon's actions. With a confused frown, Maya set her weapon down along with David. They lifted their arms.

The hunters made their way towards them. They were cautious, scanning the group with their weapons. Maya kept her eyes trained on the other humans. She couldn't see their faces through the masks, but she could see their body language. These weren't normal hunters, at least not like Clark.

Immediately, Tahani dropped her face to cover a yawn. The attention of both weapons immediately went towards her with shouts.

'Keep those hands up!' The hunter with the blue strap shouted. 'We know what you're capable of!'

Tahani huffed in annoyance. 'I gotta yawn ya know? Besides it's rude to yawn without covering my face.'

The hunter didn't seem pleased about Tahani's disobedience. 'Now!'

'Fine, bloody hell…' Tahani raised her hands and shook her head. 'But just one thought – are yer sure what yer know of what I'm capable of?' Before Maya could register Tahani's words, she saw frost shoot from Tahani's palms. The frost sheeted over both guns and the hunters cursed.

That's our cue. Maya remembered Takon's words. She abandoned the taser, sprinting past the hunters without hesitation. Immediately Maya turned her head to recognise David tailing her with a reassuring nod. In the back, both Tahani and Takon used the chance to attack the two hunters.

'Come on!' David told Maya, slamming his body against the door to swing it open. By the time Maya followed through and got a clear view of the hunters, she spotted an open van. The hunters froze, holding back the protesting Heather and Laria. Maya realised the hunter that held back Heather had a yellow strap on his wrists, while the one that held Laria had a green strap.

Why were these hunters colouring themselves? Maybe it was a rank thing. Maya didn't understand the hunter's ranking system.

'Let them go now,' Maya demanded as her anger came back. 'And where's Seth?'

'Seth's in here!' Laria told Maya, before she was forcibly shoved into the van. A yelp came from the van and Heather struggled in the grip before she too, was thrown in there like a sack of potatoes.

'Traitor, how dare you side with the shifters?' Hunter Green demanded, and both of them pulled out their guns.

'This could've gone better,' David commented sheepishly.

It was a bad idea to leave her only line of defence behind.

'I'm gonna need a nice vacation after this,' Maya muttered in displeasure. However, she heard Takon and Tahani approach from behind.

Seeing the shifters in action, it was rather unique. Instead of having the guns that they held earlier, they were running at them with inhumane speed. The hunters didn't stand a chance as their guns were confiscated by the shifter pair.

'Now we're gonna save the sorry lot,' Tahani told the hunters. With a sharp punch for the stomach, hunter yellow grunted and collapsed on the spot. Takon used a quick jab to the side of the neck to knock hunter green out.

When Maya realised it was safe, she ran to the van with panic. 'Laria! Heather!' She reached the van and realised that Laria had been right, Seth was with them. He, Brodie and Jason were unconscious.

'We're pretty powerless with these cuffs,' Laria pointed out.

'I assume that these hunters have them,' David said and went to search for the keys. 'It's said that it's magic from the witches.' He found them rather quickly and went to unlock their cuffs. As they were freed, they rubbed their wrists before checking on the boys.

'Help me pull Seth out, Heather,' Maya asked. The witch silently nodded and with her help, lifted Seth safely out of the van. They rested him on the ground comfortably, and Maya immediately checked his pulse. Thankfully just unconscious.

'Wake up, Seth,' Maya begged quietly and she patted his cheek. She looked over her shoulder and realised that Tahani, David and Takon had their attention on the others. 'Come on – where's the proud Laurence when I need him?'

A soft groan escaped his throat and Maya let out a grateful sigh with her smile widening. His eyes fluttered open and he tried to regain a sense of his location. 'Maya...'

His voice was hoarse but Maya let out a sigh of relief. 'You gave me a hell of a scare, Seth – the second I saw you in their clutches I knew I had to do something.' She touched his shoulder gratefully. 'Next time I leave the state I swear that

I'm dragging your ass with me.'

'Just don't leave this time,' Seth replied and groaned again, this time with pain. 'I apologise – but can you get yourself off my chest – while you were gone I was in an accident.'

Maya realised that she had subconsciously put her body on his and she moved away, suddenly embarrassed. Ever since kissing Seth and having the awkward conversation with Tahani, the last thing that Maya wanted was to have everyone else noticing.

'Sorry. Wait – I'm not sorry – well for the pain, but you have a lot of explaining to do. About that little stunt of yours known as telepathy.'

'How did you–' The pieces connected and Seth shot a cold look towards Tahani. 'I should've known. She would never keep that from you.'

'What does that mean?' Maya demanded, folding her arms in protest. 'Seth, you have no idea how angry I am with you. Were you ever going to tell me?'

Seth appeared alarmed before he answered, 'I had my intentions of telling you – I promise.'

The scowl deepened in Maya's features. 'Then why, Seth? Why keep it from me? I thought we were closer than that.'

'I wish I could give my reasons,' Seth told her and Maya's eyes still remained harsh on him. 'But I was worried of how you would react… could you really blame me?'

With a scoff, Maya shook her head. 'I can't… but it was still no excuse.' Immediately she stood. 'Now, I got to make sure my other friends are okay.' She felt Seth's stare on her as she went to Laria, smiling in relief as she realised that everyone was okay.

***

'Brodie… Come on, we need to get out of here.'

Recognising the voice, Brodie grunted in annoyance as the history teacher gently shook his shoulder.

As soon as Brodie opened his eyes, pain flooded his leg

and he recalled the trap. 'What happened?' He looked around, realising that he wasn't alone. All he remembered was a shadow coming over him.

'You guys were taken by the hunters,' David said and patted his back. 'But I'm glad we got to you on time.'

'This isn't something to celebrate Mister Embers,' Laria said, scowling at her hands. It was the first time Brodie saw her since their fight. She either hadn't noticed him yet or was too distracted, though Brodie was leaning towards the latter. 'We have bigger problems.'

'What's going on Laria?' David asked. Next to Brodie, Jason slowly recovered from his state.

'Zanobi is the one pulling the strings,' she told them with a cracking voice. 'He is possessing Susan Cana.' Brodie's eyes widened and his blood turned cold. The pieces were coming together – now he understood why the hunters were targeting them.

'The less shifters in town, the easier it was for Zanobi to find the remainder of the stones.' Heather looked at her hands. 'I'm sorry we couldn't do enough.'

'Don't worry,' Takon said with a reassuring smile. 'You did everything you could. I suppose now, it's time to be on the lookout for Susan Cana as well.'

'But there's something else,' Jason added and with a grunt, he slowly pulled himself up. 'There was a shifter with the hunters.' Brodie gritted his teeth at the thought. So there were shifters that were against them as well? Just what was Zanobi's plan besides finding the stones?

'Takon,' Tahani spoke up. Brodie realised that she hadn't said anything since waking up. 'I'm gonna see if I can find him.'

Takon looked over to Tahani with a frown. 'I don't think that's a good idea Tahani.'

'I'm just gonna follow him,' Tahani protested and crossed her arms over her chest. 'I need to find him Takon – or at least try.'

Takon sighed quietly. 'Very well – keep your distance and

watch him from afar.'

'Hey guys…' Maya's voice came in and Brodie frowned as she was skimming through her phone. 'Jenna messaged us. She believes that we aren't the bad guys.'

Hearing the confirmation, Brodie felt something akin the gratitude. What could've changed her mind? He didn't know, but hearing the news did lift his spirits. After pushing Laria away, he needed all the friends he got.

'But there's also a message, that was only just sent to us now.' Maya frowned and she looked conflicted. 'She wants us at Brodie's place. Why there?'

'Easiest place to access I assume,' David said with a slight shrug. 'But I'm happy that she's willing to make amends.'

'Our phones should be close by,' Laria said to Heather. 'She probably messaged all of us.'

'These must be yours then,' Tahani pointed out and she showed the devices. 'Yer gotta make sure yer more careful.' Laria took her phone and within a few taps, she was beaming.

'Yes, I got the message too,' Laria announced.

'That's certainly good,' David said and he flashed a smile. He then scratched the back of his head. 'I would join but I think it's better off if I head out. Need to check on the family.'

'Thank you for your assistance David,' Takon said.

'No problem.' David returned the nod and he headed out. Once he left them, Maya helped Brodie up to his feet. From afar, Seth was still watching and he finally pulled himself to his feet. Judging Seth's expression, Brodie could tell that he and Maya had another argument.

Laria cleared her throat and checked her phone. 'Alright then – let's go to Brodie's.'

'Unfortunately I have my own duties to attend to,' Takon reminded with a deep frown. 'With Tahani tracking Zanobi, I have to inform the other duxes of this new information – please try to be careful.'

'Got it,' Brodie muttered unenthusiastically. How was he meant to predict that the hunters were going to capture him when he was at breaking point?

As Takon and Tahani left to do their errands, the small group headed back towards the car. Being a five-seater car, Laria was the one that had to be squashed in the back with Maya, Seth and Jason.

They were in silence when they recognised Brodie's house. Heather pulled the car over in the estate and Brodie was surprised that Jenna's car wasn't in sight.

I need to leave. Brodie thought before discharging the thought. Where did that come from? He couldn't abandon his friend, after everything that happened.

'That's not Jenna,' Laria replied as she looked around with a frown. 'She would've told us otherwise. And her scent is still around.'

Seth stepped in between the pair with an observant frown. 'I can't hear her thoughts... but she has been here. Shall we go inside and call for her again?'

Brodie ignored the group and he unlocked the door to his house. It was true when he recognised Jenna's sweet scent, but every fibre in his body told him not to step into his house. He ignored the tiny voice in his head, opening the door and as soon as he looked up, his arms dropped to the side as if they stopped functioning.

No... this can't be happening...

Seth stepped in as he heard Brodie's thoughts and the Forte made no move to snap at Seth. He looked up and stiffened with alarm.

'What's going on?' Maya demanded as she appeared. Immediately Seth wrapped his arms around her form to stop her from stepping inside. She gave him a look of disbelief and struggled to escape. 'Seth, come on. Let me see.'

'You won't want to,' Seth warned her in a heavy voice. Brodie's mind had yet to function or react, even when he heard the protests coming from his friend. He didn't react when Jason appeared by his side, his eyes growing wide when he stared at the scene.

'Seth!' Maya snapped angrily and with an angry shove, she broke out of his grip.

'Maya, no!' Seth tried to reach out, but it was already too late. She was next to Brodie by the time Seth caught up to her, and she was seeing the same thing that Brodie was seeing.

Maya's horror coloured her features. 'Jenna!'

***

Laria was still outside the Forte Estate, recalling Zanobi's taunts. Knowing that Zanobi was close by once again caused her blood to boil. If Zanobi was within the town, did that mean Lucien was too? Laria let out a sigh. Perhaps it could be a tomorrow problem.

But all those thoughts went out the window when she heard Maya's voice that sounded like a scream of denial. Adrenaline overcame Laria and she dashed into the building for an investigation. As Laria came after her friends, Laria's body became immobilised.

Their perky friend.

Laria swore that her eyes were merely deceiving everyone from the truth. It was impossible to have their friend hanging from the ceiling with a rope around her wrists. Jenna wasn't supposed to have dried blood from the gaping wound in her stomach and chest. Her skin wasn't meant to be so pale and there was meant to be life in her eyes. There shouldn't be a piece of paper stuck to her with it addressed to Brodie.

The only thing Laria could hear were her short breaths leaving her lips. Her heart raced in her chest, but it just felt as if it was torn out. As the seconds passed on, heat flooded in Laria's cheeks as she struggled to catch her breath.

In that moment, everything felt still. 'Jenna...' Laria whispered as tears stung her eyes. After all that happened these past months, Laria thought that she could handle everything. But as soon as she saw Jenna's *dead* body, Laria couldn't take it.

She took one step. And another. Her body trembled in protest.

'Laria.' Jason's shaky voice broke her.

'No, no, no...' Laria looked around at the others for

confirmation, hoping one would say it was a sick prank of some kind, but their faces showed the same shock and despair she felt. 'She can't be gone. Please Jenna!'

'Get her down!' Maya demanded with rage flashing in her eyes. The boys made no noise and it was Seth that managed to bring Jenna's body down with one of his knives.

As soon as Jenna's limp body was lying on the floor, Laria stumbled weakly to her friend and she trembled.

'Please don't be dead, Jenna,' Laria begged desperately and knew it was pointless. She didn't flinch at the contact from one of the boys; she assumed Jason.

Maya knelt next to her, eyes glistening with angry tears. 'I was in Maine... I couldn't do anything...'

'It wasn't your fault.' Seth crouched to her side, his emotions in check.

Laria grasped Jenna's hand and squeezed it. 'Nick did this... it had to be him...' She never should've let him leave back at the Halloween party.

'Do not jump to conclusions,' Seth told Laria firmly. 'Besides, this note is addressed to Brodie – it even has a 'C' on it. It was clearly Charmi.'

Seth's confirmation didn't allow Laria to feel better. If anything, she felt worse. Laria had the chance to kill Charmi and to stop the madness. Yet her hesitation got in the way again and Jenna paid the price.

A shout of anger cut Laria's thoughts off. She sharply turned, realising Brodie was on his hands and knees with a trembling body. His eyes were bright, lips were pulled back into a snarl.

'Brodie.' Seth's eyes didn't show any emotions, but Brodie refused to look back at him. 'This isn't anyone's fault.'

'It is my fault!' Brodie fumed with denial. 'My dad died and the first thing I do is kill the brother of a psychotic bitch so that she can declare her vengeance on me! I will kill her myself – I will make sure she suffers every damn second.'

'Jenna!'

A new voice interrupted them and they instantly

recognised the owner. Taro rushed in with Clark, their eyes grew wide as they saw Jenna's body. Clark looked like he just lost the life in his brown eyes, the ones so similar to Jenna's, while Taro snarled viciously.

'This is your fault!' Taro declared and grabbed the collar of Laria's shirt and pulled her to her feet. Her chest didn't recognise the tightness and Laria forced herself to meet the quarterback in the eyes. 'You did this – you hurt her! Why didn't you protect her?!' When Laria didn't say anything to defend herself, Taro's eyes lit furiously. 'Why don't you apologise? You heartless monster!'

She tried to apologise, but nothing came out. What could be said that hadn't already been said? Laria knew it was her fault, but she couldn't find her voice. Her guilt consumed her.

Another moment passed and she felt a blunt force knock her off her feet. The shock hit her before the motion did and Laria dropped to the floor with a cold thud. Her first reaction was to reach for her jaw, before feeling a sting and realising that Taro's punch cut her lip. Much to her surprise, Laria didn't feel much pain to his punch – she wasn't sure if it was related to her adrenaline.

Before Taro could hit her again, Maya shoved Taro roughly. 'Back off you idiot, before I punch you back!' she shouted protectively and Taro glared back at her. 'We tried to keep Jenna safe from this business but you had to involve her, didn't you? You went against us when you don't even know half of the damn story!'

Laria didn't move from her spot, she wanted to apologise to someone. Tears forced their way out of her eyes as the guilt flooded in her chest. Why? Why couldn't she find the strength to say something? She deserved to suffer for her mistakes. Jenna's life was not the price she wanted to pay for peace.

Jason was the one who grabbed Maya, pulling her away from Taro. 'Maya's right. We were too busy being ambushed by you bastards to even consider hurting our friend.'

For once, Laria had to look over to Jason. It was in the moments like this when Laria knew that she needed him to be supportive. She wouldn't know what would happen if he or any of her friends weren't around.

'We're going to find the killer,' Brodie declared with a hoarse voice. 'And I will kill her myself.'

CHAPTER 23

'So why should we help you, Ungue Dux?' Jyle questioned, leaning back into his seat of his medical lab as Tahani slammed an angry fist on his desk. 'As if that's a convincing argument.' His job at the morgue gave the Scientia Dux an opportunity to examine the bodies of the deceased.

'My trail went dead for Zanobi, but I've got a theory about–' Tahani quickly spun on the spot when she felt a chilling presence and noticed that Nadia was staring suspiciously back at the Ungue Dux from the open doorway. 'Nadia – just the dux I need to see for today. We need to have a chat.'

'What do you want?' Nadia asked with annoyance colouring her tone. Her deep expression turned flat when she placed the paperwork on top of Jyle's desk. The mortician sighed in depression. 'Here's the report for Jenna Sommers – fill this out.'

'How disappointing,' Jyle huffed and took the paperwork with a lazy gaze. 'A mere human and I can't even use her carcass as a lab rat.'

He earned himself another glare before the two women headed out of the office. 'I will come back this afternoon to collect the finished paperwork.' Tahani used this chance to catch up to Nadia, who didn't bother to slow her pace as she said, 'There better be a good reason why you're trying to talk about – let me guess... someone stole your flask.'

'Not funny Nadia – I don't have one though I am missing a few shot glasses,' Tahani said with a snide smirk. Instantly Nadia stopped and she shot a demanding look in Tahani's direction. Once Nadia's eyes met with Tahani's, she lost the smirk and her face turned serious. 'Whatever happened to ya kids?'

Nadia's eyes narrowed distastefully and Tahani thought that she actually felt cold for once. 'That's none of your business, Rosa. How dare you ask that question?'

But Tahani wasn't one to back down from a challenge. 'Well I dare ask it because I was attacked,' she sharply replied and showed off her uninjured arm. 'This arm had a cut and when I encountered this stranger... the wound was gone as soon as we crossed paths – exactly like the way Hugh heals. Hugh is the only one with that power so I connected the dots.'

Nadia looked around quietly before she edged herself closer to Tahani in order to whisper, 'Our children never died, Rosa. They disappeared into thin air; whether someone kidnapped them and raised them as their own, I don't know. I hoped so, rather than the alternative. We searched endlessly for trails but we never found them... I don't know of their situation today but leave me out of it – we've put ourselves through enough pain.' The dux left Tahani to her own devices.

Surprisingly enough, Tahani felt sorry for the other woman. Nadia lost her damn kids and she had to live with the fact for the rest of her life. If it was possible, Tahani was determined to reencounter the one that healed her arm.

But that was in Cheyenne. Unfortunately, Tahani had no intentions on travelling any time soon. At the moment, her main concern went to Zanobi.

***

The low music hummed in the church walls as David's grey eyes watched Father Jonathon. He felt the comfort of Diana's hand brushing his. Their little girl was at school, hopefully ignorant of the situation.

But it felt like someone had ripped out his heart. When

David met Jenna, she was a curious freshman with grand opportunity to succeed. Along with Laria, the pair worked together and their history grades were almost flawless. Now that the years had passed, David got to know Jenna as a kind, intelligent individual who had a lot to live for.

However now she was gone – killed by the one who wanted to make Brodie so miserable.

And it worked. Sitting at the front of the room, Brodie looked like he was ready to punch whatever was close to him at the time.

Laria sat next to Maya and Jason. Laria's eyes were hard, like she was only trying to put on a mask to seek comfort with herself. Maya had a similar expression but the anger in her face was more obvious while Jason showed his depression.

Seth was with them as well, but his face was hard to read as usual. He kept near to Maya, occasionally eyeing her whenever she balled up her fist with anger.

With them was Maya's grandmother, David only heard of her but this was his first time seeing her. The woman was standing with them, squeezing each of their shoulders. With the way she interacted with each of Jenna's friends, she seemed like the perfect person to comfort them.

David didn't protest when they took her coffin away. He felt like if he did, then her death would've been far more realistic. It shouldn't be like this – if only the hunters saw things the way that he did then they could bring proper justice to the one that did this. Everything was planned like this; the killer used the hunters as an advantage and Jenna paid the price.

Angrily David spread his fingers out on his knees to stop himself from clenching them. Why didn't he say something to convince her about the shifters? Why didn't he fight harder for her? Now that she had lost her life, her dad was probably going to take it out on the innocents.

Once the service was over, David forced himself to remain in the church and Diana allowed him to stay with a sad smile. He shouldn't take it out on her, and he wasn't trying to but the sensation of losing one of his students still remained.

But David quickly realised he wasn't alone. With a sudden turn, he recognised Clark and Susan re-enter the church room. Clark's brown eyes were dull and David could only imagine his devastation over his daughter's death. Even with everything that had happened, Clark was still his friend.

'Clark–' David began, but the other male cut him off.

'We're going to capture them,' Clark announced with a glare towards the history teacher. David's head shook once he understood who he was referring to. 'Those are our orders and then they will pay dearly.'

'No, Clark, this isn't the right way!' David insisted and surprised himself when the other hunters looked at him. 'It was not their fault!'

'Why do you bother defending them?' Susan questioned and David froze with alarm. This wasn't Susan. When the group were discussing Zanobi's power then it would only make sense that he would keep using her as a puppet. 'It's too late, David – they had their chance to give up their powers... now we're taking everything with force.'

'These guys have lost more than just their parents! They have to live with something darker than both you and I,' David defended, standing up to Zanobi in Susan's body. 'You lay a single finger on them and you will regret it.'

Susan merely smiled. 'David – you're too soft when it comes to this job. Which is why I only answer to Clark now – he's unlike you, loyal and he has purpose. You have none of those things, David Embers.'

'We will hunt them,' Clark announced and David's fists curled up tightly to contain his rage. 'They killed her, David, and I'm doing this – with or without your help.'

And that's when David snapped, 'Wake up, Clark!' His eyes grew angry as he grabbed the tie of his grief-stricken friend. 'Your daughter is dead because the rest of you chose not to believe the shifters! I cared about her as well, but is killing them going to solve anything? Her friends just blamed themselves that she was dead, isn't that meant to give you a crazy hint that they still care about humans?!'

'Brodie was the reason why this all began,' Clark muttered and pushed the history teacher away. 'Maybe once he's gone, you'll realise the difference.'

'You bastard!' David shook his head warily, sensing the threatening tone of the other male. 'What the hell happened to you, Clark? You weren't this person until we started going against the shifters.'

'He took this chance when you didn't, David,' Zanobi continued and he ushered Clark to leave them alone. Clark glared back at David for a second before he complied with the wish. As soon as they were alone in the church, David felt his stomach twist into knots.

'You are aware of my identity,' the traitor stated with a bored tone. 'You say a word and you'll be sorry.'

'What makes you say that they don't already know?' David challenged darkly, glaring at Zanobi through Susan's eyes.

Zanobi scoffed lightly at the challenge. 'Your daughter is cute, David – Kim... isn't it?' David's eyes narrowed in disgust. 'I'm not afraid to hurt a child to get what I want – or maybe I should leave her as an orphan, it is rather trendy these days.'

This wasn't Susan. David had to keep telling himself that the mayor was under possession of this madman who wanted power. However no matter how many times he told himself, David's mind kept referring her to Susan with their expressions.

Zanobi's eyes flashed with amusement at David's anger. 'You're no longer a part of the S.H.O., David – you have twenty-four hours to return your licences, your fancy gadgets and your ties with any of the shifters. If I find you near or talking to any of the shifters in this town when these twenty-four hours are up – you will regret it.'

David's eyes grew wide with disbelief when Zanobi left David alone. His body was shaking with violent tremors and with that, he wanted to break down in the middle of the church.

The phone rang with Ruddy's number on the top. David

huffed quietly to himself and answered the number. He had twenty-four hours and he had to figure out a plan to stop Zanobi.

'Ruddy – please tell me you have some good news because I would kill for something good right now.'

'*Unfortunately, we don't,*' Ruddy replied through the other line. For once, his tone indicated that it was heavily strained from stress. '*There's been another killing and this one was a message to the hunters in particular. Maybe you can try to convince them that it was the shifter that they held.*'

'I can't Ruddy,' David replied with a slow groan to himself. He failed. All this time he wanted to help the innocent lives and he couldn't. 'I'm not a hunter anymore; Sus- Zanobi kicked me out of the organisation.'

'*That's the worst thing I've heard you say – if you believe that then it's clear that you're dumber than the rest of your hunting friends,*' Ruddy replied bluntly and David caught his own breath. '*You lose your authority and you're not a hunter. Don't be stupid – you are a hunter as long as you have the will, David.*'

David almost smiled in surprise. 'I think that's the first time you called me by my name.'

'*Don't get used to it,*' Ruddy replied curtly. A real smile crawled onto David's face at the thoughts of his companion brushing off the compliments. '*Now, this changes things, but I believe that we can get our way if we play the cards right.*'

***

'I'm surprised that you didn't want to be with Seth,' Jason muttered when he and Maya walked down the street. After the funeral, Seth offered to drive them back to his house but Maya wanted to walk back to her house. Jason tagged along because he knew it wasn't safe for her. Or anyone, really, these days.

'I would've,' Maya admitted with a small shrug. 'I just wanted to think to myself for a bit.'

Oh. 'So you know,' Jason figured it out and shoved his hands in his pockets. 'He really does try when it comes to you. He believes that you have a right to your own thoughts as well as our own thoughts. Apparently mind reading is a hard power to control, especially if we're close with him.'

Maya fell into a comfortable silence and she continued to move alongside Jason. 'How does it work?'

'I don't really know,' Jason admitted in return and scratched the back of his neck. 'But I think if you want to know more about Seth, you should ask him yourself. He won't keep it from you if you ask.'

'He probably already knows...' Maya muttered with a light scoff to herself. Her features remained unclear as she took her anger out on a small pebble. 'He knows everything that I've ever thought of... and that includes Jenna.'

'No one asked how you're feeling,' Jason realised and stopped his friend momentarily. 'How are you feeling, Maya? With everything that's been going on?'

Again, Maya was silent. It almost felt like a lifetime until she spoke. 'I'm not well – I found nothing about Azu. I have to stay in the background as usual, all these secrets being kept from me and then I come home to find out my best friend was killed by one of Brodie's sadistic cousins. One of *your* cousins.' She glared out into the distance. 'How am I meant to react with all of that?'

Jason lacked an answer and Maya finally huffed in annoyance in order to leave Jason behind. He rapidly followed and stopped her by grabbing her arm. She spun around the spot automatically and Jason flinched when he saw tears in her blue eyes.

'I can't take it, Jason!' Maya finally cried, collapsing into him, and Jason remained quiet as she sobbed into his chest. Raising his arms around her, Jason realised that he couldn't speak for her. 'I used to think of Jenna as the one who would always be with us. She annoyed the hell out of me with her ridiculous attempts to set me up with a boy – hell; that back and forth stuff with Taro, so damn annoying.' His shirt felt damp from her tear stains and he only tightened the hold. 'And now she's dead... she didn't deserve to be killed so ruthlessly for a stupid reason.'

'I know,' Jason whispered softly. He felt her fist bunch up his shirt for support and her sobbing only fell quiet with sniffles. 'The shifters live in a messed-up world – we might be unable to help Jenna or our parents, but we can help the ones in future.'

'That's what I want too,' Maya whispered painfully and she let go of him. Despite everything, her power still hadn't come to her. Why her? Where was her bloodlust? Jason let her go but he walked beside her back to her house.

Her silence indicated that she didn't want to have the discussion anymore, though Jason should've been surprised that he managed to get her to talk this much.

It hadn't been long until Jason found his way walking onto Maya's driveway and she brushed her curly hair back. 'Thanks for before,' she whispered. 'I don't often do that and I promise I won't try to do it again...'

'It's no problem.' He felt great that Maya wasn't going to face her problems alone anymore. 'And just so you know... we are here to listen.'

Before Maya got into the house, she paused in consideration. 'Jenna always liked the Acer Opacare. I remember when we went dress shopping – Jenna loved it but Laria and I hated it... Yet despite that I hate it, I would do anything to back to that time. Now she will never be able to go.'

'That fancy dance?' Jason frowned.

'To announce the treaty with shifters and humans,' Maya answered softly. 'It's meant to be a legend, but apparently my mum was the one who was responsible for this.'

Jason wanted to say something to comfort her. 'Are you not going?'

'No, it's not that,' she said quietly and she smiled like she accepted her new fate. 'This is something that Jenna would've wanted and as her friend I want this – I'm going to get a dress and I'm going to go to the Acer Opacare for her.'

CHAPTER 24

Brodie didn't go to Jenna's house for the wake – not that he was sure if Clark would allow him. The memories would've been too fresh on his mind and it still haunted him. His thoughts went into the empty glass and he ignored it to grab a bottle.

A part of him said that maybe her death had been nothing but a horrible nightmare. He just returned from going out to a stranger's funeral.

Once he grabbed the phone, Brodie recognised the black screen and his heart sank. His eyes darkened at the lack of messages, and the pain quickly returned. She was really gone. Her face was going to be only in his memories, as well as everything that made her important to him.

He took a swig of his drink. Brodie was so desperate to forget about Jenna: her smile, her cheerful brown eyes and her optimism. Yet a voice cried in the back of his mind, telling him that he couldn't bear the thought of not knowing her. A life without Jenna's existence seemed empty. Could he really fathom the idea of forgetting Jenna?

Charmi warned him and Brodie was too stupid to listen. They should've ended Charmi the first time they met, and then it would've saved the lives that were effortlessly wasted. Jenna would've still been alive.

Jenna... Brodie wanted to cry like he had with his father's death. But it was wrong. Brodie knew that there was a way to make himself feel better and it wasn't by drinking.

'I'm gonna kill Charmi,' Brodie announced with a strained voice. 'I'm going to make sure that she doesn't kill anyone else.'

Now that's a surprise, Orgul commented from the back of Brodie's mind. Immediately Brodie tensed at the feeling of his darker counterpart taking over him. *Are you really capable of killing her without falling into the darkness?*

'I am already in the darkness,' Brodie said in response. He took another swig of his drink and slammed the bottle down. 'And I will destroy her. The remainder of my friends can choose if they're with me or against me – I won't let Charmi get away with this.'

'That's a well thought out answer Brodie.' Laria's voice cut him off. Brodie whirled from his spot on the couch to see Laria's black dress. 'And I am going to be with you on this one – they took it too far by bringing Jenna into this.'

Brodie was still surprised that Laria was willing to openly admit it. She was willing to stand with him after everything that happened between them. If it was her rage or grief speaking, Brodie only hoped that she didn't come to regret it later.

Instead of getting into a monologue, Brodie gave a short reply, 'Are you sure?'

'At first I was against it,' Laria admitted and her tone still indicated that it was hard. 'After you nearly killed me, I wanted to help you by stopping you from killing Charmi and even Lucien. I was going to say that on my way here... but then Tracy spoke to me about the Acer Opacare.'

'You're going to that?' he asked suspiciously.

'After calling Maya, she's coming as well. I think Tracy wanted the both of us to go for Jenna – honestly I never thought of her as the sentimental type.'

'Neither did I,' Brodie added with a scoff.

'I don't know how Charmi got to her,' Her eyes flashed amber to indicate that she was ready. 'We're going to hit them hard.'

Satisfied with her answer, Brodie showed off a smirk. 'Good.' He got up from the couch and met Laria's determined gaze. 'Follow me.' Brodie gestured for Laria and she obeyed obediently.

They reached his father's former office and Brodie went down to the safe. Laria remained quiet as Brodie typed in the pin code and swung the heavy door open. He grimaced at the sight of the yellow glow next to the dull, red stone. Brodie pulled out Rel and he immediately went to cover the stone with a small cloth.

He showed the stone to Laria. 'I felt her presence,' he muttered and tightened his hold. 'She's pleased with everything that happened. I wasn't able to sense Nick for some reason.'

'We won't let her get away with it,' Laria declared and she watched the stone with wary eyes. 'Is it possible for us to be able to find her now?'

'No,' Brodie replied and placed the stone on the table. 'She's managed to snag some witch to put a protection spell over her and possibly Nick. We can't touch her until she steps out of the boundaries or she makes herself known.'

'I'm going to help you then.' She gained Brodie's full attention with her honest tone. 'Whether it was Charmi or Nick or both – there is no stopping them.' She looked like she was set with her thoughts. 'Both of them will be faced with us and we will not let them get away with their crimes, even if that means we have to step into the darkness.'

Brodie's eyes narrowed in agreement. 'And let's make Charmi's death painful.'

***

She was actually going to kill someone willingly. Maybe it was Lux talking to her, but Laria didn't disagree with her dark counterpart.

Laria wanted to kill Charmi. When they had their last encounter, Laria's strange vision about Jason stopped her from killing Charmi. Yet things were different now – Laria wasn't going to hesitate.

She pushed the current thoughts aside, tightening the hold that she had on her bag. As soon as she entered the school building, every pair of eyes went in her direction. It had been a week since Jenna's death and they knew. Everyone knew Laria's friendship with Jenna.

Yet as she walked through the halls, all Laria could feel were pity stares. Why did they have to stare at her so much? They should take a photo since they lasted longer. It was a miracle that Laria managed to keep her untamed temper in check.

Surprisingly, a loud angry voice cut the whispering off. 'Don't you blubbering idiots have anything better than to do than spread bloody rumours?!' Instantly, Laria followed the sound of Maya's angry yells and she noticed that her friend was yelling at a small group of seniors from their class. 'Shut the hell up for once and get to freakin' class!'

One of them spoke back to her, and judging Maya's irritated look, it wasn't a nice comment. Maya grabbed the one who spoke and she slammed him against the locker.

'I'm sorry.' Maya's voice was drenched with sarcasm. 'My friend just died – so forgive me if I don't know how to take a chill pill.' She pulled back her fist to make contact with their face when Laria told herself to step in.

'Maya–' Laria tried to call out to her friend and grabbed Maya's arm. Had Laria been a second later, the student would've been suffering from a broken nose. Immediately, Maya froze at the contact. 'You have to calm down.'

Maya's eyes flashed in denial as she glared back at Laria, but she settled down. The classmate slinked away from Maya's grip and went off with the rest of his friends. Now the other students were keeping their distance from the pair.

However, despite her annoyance, Laria felt a small smile form on her face. Maya was strong – Laria knew that she would be alright after letting out some steam. But when they heard someone clear their throat from behind, Laria turned with a scowl and recognised the face.

'What do you want, Sara?' Laria muttered darkly, even as she considered that Sara Maraca looked different. While her appearance hadn't changed since the last time Laria saw her, she didn't have the usual snide grin or the hateful spark in her eyes.

Sara didn't snap back at Laria's cold tone surprisingly. 'That person who killed Jenna... it's linked to everything right? You guys missing from school?'

Laria remembered when she unlocked her bloodlust for the first time. Even though they hadn't had much interaction since then, Laria realised that Sara knew that Jenna's death wasn't done by a human.

'It is,' Laria replied honestly and Maya sent her a surprised glance. 'I am going to finish off what they started.'

'I'm not sure if he would,' Sara replied awkwardly. 'We broke up on bad terms about Jenna and I feel like this was the final break up.' Sara looked truly sincere. 'I know we aren't really friends... but I hope you get to the bottom of this.'

'I hope so too,' Maya agreed with a strange frown directed at Laria. Meanwhile Laria was still trying to figure out why Sara was acting strange. It was almost like she was distracting them from something–

Laria noticed a hooded figure was by her locker. The figure turned and Laria's eyes widened with fury once she recognised the face. She tried to call out on him but a large crowd of people blocked her.

'Laria?' Maya frowned in confusion. 'Is he one of the guys we need to find?'

'He is,' Laria hissed and struggled to push past the students.

The memories came flooding back as Laria tried to squeeze through the crowd. He attacked her, threatened her and Heather's life. At the Halloween party, Nick mentioned that he was going to go on a hunt. What if mocking Laria was his hunt?

He spared a look at them, before shoving a slip of paper into the locker and retreated out of the building. By the time Laria managed to break through the crowd, she left Maya behind to race after the blonde.

However the second that she got out of the building, Nick was gone. Angrily, Laria clenched her fists and slammed them against the post. Her knuckles stung from the contact of the cold metal, but her anger evaporated her pain.

The bastard was going to pay for hurting Jenna. Laria knew that she couldn't follow him, especially not alone. But the one question still remained. Why did he bother coming out in the open so recklessly?

It had to do with whatever he put in her locker. As soon as Laria went back to Maya, she found her standing loyally back at the lockers with a hard gaze.

'What happened?'

'He's gone,' Laria cursed to herself and banged her fist against her own locker. 'I can't believe he would come here to taunt us. She focused her attention on unlocking the locker and inside she found a slip of paper on top of her dusty books. Laria picked it up and frowned at the text.

In the morning glad I see, my foe outstretched beneath
the tree.

'What is it?' Maya asked to read the text. 'Sounds like some poem or something that Shakespeare would write – why would he give us this?'

'I don't know.' As she dialled Brodie's number, Laria sent a look towards Maya. 'Can you let Seth and Jason know about this? I'll call Tahani as well since we need all the strength we can get.'

Maya pulled her phone next to her ear 'I'm on it.'

***

'Alright,' Seth spoke on the phone while Jason flipped the knives through his hand. The blade danced in his palm awkwardly, but Jason knew it didn't just take one day to master a weapon.

After a muffled voice came from the phone that Jason recognised as Maya, Jason noticed a small smirk on Seth's face. However Jason paused from his training when he saw Seth's face turn rather stern like he heard something discouraging on the other line.

'I will keep an ear out,' Seth promised softly and his gaze turned gentle. 'I'll talk to you later.' As soon as he hung up the phone, he turned to Jason with a frown.

'What's up?' Jason asked casually and he went back to his knife training.

'The girls are at school – but Nick was there,' Seth explained curtly and Jason's features suddenly turned hard like Seth's.

'Judging from your lack of anger,' he noted, trying to calm himself, 'it seems that they weren't hurt.'

With the roll of his eyes, Seth continued, 'But there was something strange – he gave a note to Laria but neither of the girls understand what it means.'

Why on Earth would Nick of all people give a note to Laria? Nick had clear disdain for her after she broke his wrist – even though it was mostly her bloodlust that was in control. 'A note? It's not a love letter is it?'

'That's a tad ridiculous mate.' An English voice broke the air and the boys froze with alarm at the familiar accent. Immediately, Jason and Seth turned to face one of the large windows where the devil in mention was leaning on the sill. 'She's not my type of girl – she's too timid to take on the world.' The silence between the three was almost deafening, but Nick mocked the surprise. 'Oh, I'm sorry – I would've gone through the door but I wanted to give a bit of a scare.'

'What do you want?' Jason demanded and he tightened his hold on the blades.

'Easy there, mate.' Nick shrugged off Jason's threat and raised his hands peacefully. 'I give you lads my word that I am not here to harm you.'

'How come I find that difficult to believe?' Seth wondered dryly, and he appeared unaffected by the presence of the sadistic killer.

Nick shrugged calmly once again and didn't move from his spot. 'Why don't you read my mind then? I promise you that my intentions are here for your behalf.'

'That's bull and you know it!' Jason cut Nick's promise off. 'You're the reason why Jenna's dead right now.'

At the sound of Jenna's name, Nick's gaze turned dark.

'Keep Jenna out of this. I had no part in her death – I was in my own personal hell while my sister stabbed her.' He lifted his chin like he was trying to rise above some ugly emotion. 'You're right, I hate the rest of you lot, but I don't... I will never hate Jenna...' His eyes flashed gold to show his grief. 'I come here to help you. If you don't believe that then I can't help.'

'He's telling the truth,' Seth announced and Jason sent him a confused glance. 'While he could be using these thoughts currently – I prefer to hear him out. So Jason, lower the knives.' Jason's arms dropped to his side and glared at the enemy.

'What do you want?' Seth asked impatiently.

'That line: *In the morning glad I see, my foe outstretched beneath the tree*, is not for you to assume that I'm striking you guys next. But in order to throw my sister off course, I sent that line to Laria Alfero's locker. It's so you would know that I'm going to assist you in killing her, but I suppose it was perhaps a little too sophisticated for your illiterate tastes.'

'Why?' Jason asked slowly, still suspicious of Nick's plan. The last time he saw the sibling pair, they were strictly loyal to each other.

'Jenna believed that I could be redeemed,' Nick admitted and his eyes turned hard. 'Even when she found out the truth… she still saw that I could walk my own path. I made a mistake. It was my plan – to pretend to care about her feelings, to tell her everything to get her to trust me. However when she did… I just couldn't go through with it. Each day, I wanted to try again but I couldn't put myself through it.'

'You actually liked her?' Seth questioned with a frown of disgust.

'Wait.' Jason's eyes grew wide with alarm. 'What did they do together?'

'That's none of your business mate,' Nick snapped and his eyes turned furious. 'Charmi has so completely lost herself to vengeance that she didn't consider my thoughts about leaving Jenna alone. I couldn't protect her in the end – Charmi stabbed her and used her power on me.' Nick's eyes were filled with a mix of anger and sadness. 'And you two are well aware of the rest of the story.'

Maya and Laria were in tears when they found Jenna's body. There was no way he could forget that moment. Naturally, Jason felt his fist tighten. If only Nick wasn't so far away, then Jason could've easily punctured an artery for hurting his friends.

'What's this got to do with us?' Seth asked with a frown. 'I still don't see how you're helping us with anything.'

'Oh, but I am.' Nick's eyes returned to their mocking gaze and a smirk formed on his face. 'I know when Charmi wants to end it all.' The pair suddenly froze with realisation at Nick's confidence. 'She wants Brodie to attack with Rel so that she can take the stone.'

'Why would she want that?' Seth questioned as his frown deepened. 'Zanobi and Lucien both want that stone – they will know when it's out in the open. We already know that she's aware of them two coming after her. In fact I bet Zanobi knows just as we speak – since he has taken the comfort of being the mayor.'

'Typical of that body-jumping pain in the arse,' Nick muttered dryly. 'As I was saying – Charmi wants Rel and she plans to give herself extra power. If she has enough power, she will be able to kill off the remainder of your friends.'

Seth's eyes remained hard. 'We won't let her touch Rel. When does she strike?'

The teasing smirk widened on Nick's face. 'Now look who's the Curious George? I'm surprised that you care about Brodie's friends... or is it that Rosa girl?' In response, Seth's eyes flashed yellow as if to warn him. 'Very well – I shall give you two a deal.'

'You've got to be joking,' Jason scoffed in disbelief.

'Not really,' Nick replied. 'I will give you your information, and in return you make sure that I get easy access to the same place.'

'To what?' Jason wondered, sparing a glance at Seth whose

eyes showed his scepticism.

Finally Nick walked up to them. He was close enough for Jason to touch but he made no move towards Nick. It seemed that the other male was aware that Jason wanted the answers too much to bother attacking.

'Charmi will attack your group at the Acer Opacare.'

CHAPTER 25

Brodie fixed his tie and grunted in annoyance when he realised that it wasn't done properly. He redid the tie and nodded in approval at his new conditions.

For a moment, Brodie's hazel eyes glanced down to see Rel still wrapped in its cloth. So far the only person who knew of his plan to kill Charmi was Laria. But the rest of their friends were aware of the fact that it ended after today. Charmi wanted to strike at the Acer Opacare, where she would have to draw Brodie out so that she could grab Rel.

Unfortunately, it had to be at town hall and after Jenna's death, Brodie wasn't sure how the hunters would react.

And Brodie's only way of being successful was if he didn't know her plan. He agreed to be Laria's date so that they could pretend to be normal and avoid suspicion. Together they agreed that they would work together to take Charmi down.

'Your father is proud of you Brodie.' Tara's voice in the background gave Brodie momentary pause. He quickly shoved Rel in his pocket before his aunt could see him.

'Do you really think that?' Brodie replied, combing his hair with his fingers as he glared at his reflection. It felt like too much gel.

'Why do you question your intentions?' Tara quested gently.

'I hate my twin; I nearly killed my best friend and I lost another person close to me because I was reckless to begin with.' He turned to face his auntie with remorse in his gaze. 'How could my father ever be proud about that?

'Because you didn't choose vengeance,' Tara answered

sternly. 'Instead, you're going to a party and having your Acer Opacare with one of the closest people to you.'

Brodie always thought about the Acer Opacare as a good thing. He wanted to go ever since being a freshman of Golden Cliff. He wanted to dance with Laria, laugh at her clumsy attempts at dancing and even dance with Jenna.

Right now, Brodie could feel his father's disappointed gaze from the afterlife. But he couldn't afford to deal with Leon's silent judgement. Even though he was killing Charmi for vengeance, he was also doing it to protect the rest of the lives at stake.

Finally Brodie returned to his reflection in the mirror and he still saw himself. Not Orgul – the bloodlust didn't even grin in excitement when Brodie looked at his reflection.

'I guess so,' Brodie muttered blankly and he felt his insides coil in anticipation. Was it normal to feel nervous over a dance?

Brodie got a text from Laria and he picked the phone up with reluctance. A sigh of relief escaped his lips when the message didn't have anything to do with their plan – except for the location of the Acer Opacare this year.

***

Brodie pulled his car to the town hall and he sighed to himself. Unfortunately, they had to put up with hunters watching them as well as Zanobi.

With a huff of annoyance, Brodie stepped out of the car and shuddered with the cold weather. He felt the comfort of Rel in his pocket and nodded in greeting towards Tracy, who was standing at the entrance with a stern nod of approval.

For once she didn't look like a principal but a woman who was at a formal party. She had a long white dress with her blonde hair in a fancy bun. Now if Brodie saw her like this more often, he probably would've been more distant with her. She would've been a beautiful woman with a tone that matched Death's – not a nice combination.

'I didn't expect to see you here,' the fallen angel

commented flatly.

'This isn't a school event,' Brodie told her, shoving his hands in pockets. A moment passed and Brodie sighed. 'Can I get inside?'

'I know why you're here today. Laria's inside.' Once Tracy turned away to greet another guest, Brodie hurried along inside.

He recognised many faces of his classmates. Most of them were complimenting their looks, but Brodie blocked out the voices. There was a part of him that wanted to find Jenna, but his insides kept telling him that she was gone.

'Brodie.' Seth's voice drew Brodie out of these thoughts and he turned to see the Laurence in a suit similar to his. His brown eyes remained focused as they met Brodie's. 'Don't worry – we won't let anything happen; they are safe.'

'It would be nice if you got out of my head for once,' Brodie retorted and it took him a moment to realise that he wasn't alone. Jason was in a suit, staring back at him with disgust in his eyes and Brodie didn't flinch from the glare.

With a sigh of annoyance, Seth stepped between them. 'The both of you need to grow up – your thoughts give me a migraine.'

'So where are the girls?' Brodie changed the subject and ignored Jason's presence altogether.

Seth answered, 'Maya's going to find Laria and the Ungue Dux.' Now that was a surprise. Why was Tahani with them? 'Since Charmi plans to attack today, we need all the muscle we can get – I saw Mister Embers before and I believe that Nick is roaming around somewhere within the crowds.'

'Do you honestly believe that Nick is on our side?' Brodie doubted the other shifter, recalling the sadistic killer. They didn't exchange words or speak much, but Brodie didn't trust the enemy that had a strong connection with Charmi.

'I don't trust him for a second but he's our best shot at winning,' Seth admitted and he raised his eyes to look behind Brodie and slowly his stern brown eyes softened. Brodie turned to see what Seth saw and he felt his limbs lock up with nerves once more.

Maya was the first to be seen. She wore a bright blue dress to bring out her eyes; with a single strap over her left shoulder. Her curly black hair was straightened, and it was much longer than Brodie thought he would see it. However Brodie could see the hair threatening to return to its curliness so Maya had it in a fancy ponytail.

Out of the trio, Tahani was the only one who looked normal. The dress she wore was cobalt blue; darker than Maya's dress but there were no fancy redesigns. Unlike Maya, Tahani didn't do anything much with her hair except for brushing it. It cascaded down to her shoulders and Brodie had to admit that it was a nice look for the Ungue Dux.

However, Laria appeared like Maya, unrecognisable at first glance. She wore a scarlet dress with a similar design to Maya's except Laria's went down to hide her feet as Maya's went down to her knees. Her hair was wavy, but only wavy at the bottom half of her brown hair. Honestly Brodie was baffled to how she managed to pull it off. And unlike Maya, Laria left her hair to bounce harmlessly on her shoulders.

'Hey, fake date.' Laria smiled slowly at the sight of her friends.

'Yeah,' Brodie said lamely. 'You girls look... different.'

'These were both my mum's,' Maya explained with a grin. 'But we had to change the designs since she was a bit smaller than our sizes.'

'Well it suits you,' Seth complimented with a small smile in Maya's direction. She seemed hesitant at first, finding herself looking at her dress awkwardly before taking in a deep breath.

'I prefer a pair of sweatpants and a fat jacket,' Maya replied sheepishly. 'But unfortunately, I'm stuck as a normal girl that's dreaded this event ever since she was seven.'

'You don't have to,' Seth commented, ignoring the looks from the twin brothers. 'You're look nice either way.'

Maya rolled her eyes to dismiss the compliments. 'Lame.'

Seth didn't express his reaction, but it seemed like they were still having issues over Seth's secrets. Brodie knew that

Maya would forgive him eventually, but naturally she was being stubborn.

Besides, Brodie knew the reason Maya came to the party was for Jenna. They had to get along and try to find Charmi.

After the awkward silence, Maya finally offered a hand. 'Shall we get this stupid thing over and done with, my fake date?' From her spot, Tahani let out a snort of disgust at the pair and she snickered at Seth. 'Wait, I got the perfect nickname... my mind-reading fake boyfriend who is the most anti-social boy in school because he's a telepath.'

For a moment he looked flustered at his nickname. 'You do not need to offer yourself to me, Maya,' Seth commented as he regained his posture. He offered his arm like some sort of gentleman, leaving the group slowly dropping their jaws. Maya didn't smile or react verbally, taking his arm in a stoic silence to step into the crowd.

It seemed that so far, their plan of looking like a bunch of friends was a good sign. Yet it was Tahani who finally cleared her throat to show her annoyance and boredom with the party already.

'I'm gonna go get something to drink,' Tahani said, earning herself a look from Jason and Laria. Just because she didn't go to school anymore, it didn't mean that people forgot that she was a student of Golden Cliff. 'Don't worry,' Tahani's voice cut Brodie's thoughts off. 'I've gotta silver tongue – I'll get my drink.'

Brodie envied that ability.

The Ungue Dux snickered at the trio's shocked expression and she went into the same crowd that the previous pair entered. It left Laria, Jason and Brodie alone to stand around awkwardly – well Laria was the one who appeared awkward. Jason was glaring at Brodie and Brodie was too busy in glaring at the distance to acknowledge Jason.

'We should start searching for Charmi,' Brodie suggested in a whisper to Laria.

Laria nodded in agreement. 'Right.' Just as Laria went to walk with Brodie, she was pulled back by Jason who grabbed her arm. 'What is it Jason?' His eyes flashed with uncertainty, but he was glaring fiercely into Brodie's eyes as if they were searching for something. 'Jason.'

Jason snapped out of the trance and he shook his head to dismiss Laria's concern. 'I'm fine, as long as you're not gonna be thrown out of glass windows.'

Brodie looked away, ashamed and angry, as Laria scolded him with her own glare. Eventually Jason announced that he was going through a search of his own date and he wandered off. They had to search for Charmi – wherever the madwoman had run off to.

'Let's go, fake date,' Brodie offered back and Laria smirked at his teasing. They went through a bunch of people, linking arms when the people started to notice them together. It was their set up, Charmi needed to see that they were together and friends again.

'So are we going to dance or hang out like this?'

'We do the dancing in an hour,' Laria replied with a frown. Her eyes weren't on him, but she was vividly searching through the crowd. 'I'm sure you practised it earlier this year when we had those dance classes that Leon and Mum forced us to go to.'

A pain shot through Brodie's chest at the mention of Leon, but he didn't show it. Charmi first, and then he could put his energy into Lucien.

'You would think that the school would provide lessons to the ones they accepted?' Brodie wondered dryly, sparing a glare in Tracy's direction.

'Well, first of all – they do provide them which brings me to my second point – we haven't exactly been in school for any of the times they would've provided the lessons for us.'

Brodie smirked again. 'Touché.' His expression dropped when he saw something within the crowd. It was a brief passing – a haunting image that scarred his mind to this day. And Brodie knew well that it wasn't Seth.

'Brodie?' Laria frowned when she noticed that something was wrong. 'What's wrong?'

However Brodie could barely register her voice. His eyes were trained on the image that reappeared before Brodie, forcing his anger to come back to him.

Lucien. It was the man who murdered his father – the same man who happened to be the father of the girl standing next to Brodie. The image dissolved as quickly as it appeared, but Brodie was left shaking with anger.

'Brodie.' Laria's eyes were filled with concern. 'Brodie, what's wrong?'

You need to kill her. Orgul's voice was a whisper in his mind. In a haze, Brodie tightened his grasp on Laria and his fingernails dug into her skin. *Get revenge. Kill her in order to make Lucien suffer – falter his plans. For your father that you lost.*

'Brodie, you're squeezing me,' Laria whimpered, trying to pull away. 'You have to let go.'

Leon's death flashed in his mind's eye and Brodie could see Lucien; the bastard that killed him in the first place. Instantly, all Brodie wanted to do was kill Laria for everything that Lucien did to him–

This wasn't right. Brodie's body stopped shaking, and he let out a shaky breath as the realisation dawned on him. He hurt Laria once more. How could he? She was his friend and she would do anything for him, and that meant it was the same from him to her. He wasn't going to be a puppet anymore.

'I need to go,' Brodie stammered, and he dropped Laria's arm to move away from her. It was Orgul that was talking, but it was Charmi who was doing the influencing. She must've peeked through his subconscious memories of Lucien and Brodie hated it. Why didn't he think that she would use her power against him? It was the perfect way to reawaken his obvious hatred for Lucien.

Brodie reached down for Rel and made skin contact with the stone. His mind focused on Charmi and he figured out where she was. Now all he had to do was kill her.

***

During the hour, Jason contemplated the last few days. It

started off with a nearly successful kidnapping, then learning that Jenna was killed which was followed by Nick helping them. Yet there was a tiny voice in the back of Jason's mind that told him that he wouldn't go back to his old life.

Back when he was living in Cheyenne, Jason always felt like he was an outcast. It had been as if someone had always been watching his every move. The second Mae announced that they were moving to the isolated town known as Golden Cliff, Jason felt as if he was breathing fresh air.

Looking around, Jason was beginning to see why.

The people around Jason didn't make him feel uncomfortable, but rather the thought of leaving Laria alone with Brodie. His mind went rigid and Jason wanted to stay with her to protect her, but the second he heard her voice, he just couldn't disagree.

But he needed to find Seth; Jason looked through the crowd with a frown. Only Seth knew what Brodie's plans were, and he was the only one that could track Charmi down. However Seth was hard to locate when he didn't want to be found. He was most likely checking out for Nick as well.

However, Jason was surprised as he found himself bumping into Tahani. The Ungue Dux had two glasses of champagne as she merely smirked when she recognised Jason.

'Hey, yer look parched,' Tahani teased. She offered a glass and Jason took the glass instantly to taste the drink. The bitter taste almost made him throw up, but he kept drinking. 'Wow – yer not yerself if ya drinking like a goldfish.'

'We need to find Charmi,' Jason muttered in frustration and placed the glass with another waiter's tray. 'How did you get these drinks?'

'I told ya, silver tongue.' Tahani commented momentarily as she took a sip. 'Let's just say that anyone is willing to do anything for the deadly sin of lust.'

'Is everything about sex to you?' Jason asked, shooting a frown towards the crowd.

'No – only when yer around.' Tahani grinned lightly and Jason groaned. 'I'm kidding kiddo – lighten up.' But her smile dropped when she looked around the area. 'The dance will be starting up shortly – go find Seth and I'll go find the other two.'

Jason didn't need to be told twice. He rushed through the crowds of people when he saw the pair that he was looking for. Just as he was about to call them, he noticed Laria looking through the crowds.

Yet much to Jason's surprise, she was alone. Instead of going to Maya and Seth, Jason went up to Laria. 'What's wrong?' Suddenly, Jason saw the markings on her arm and he bristled. Brodie hurt her again?!

Laria was startled at the sight of him, before she looked around to drag him into a secluded area. As soon as they were alone, Laria faced him with panic.

'Brodie's missing,' Laria explained quietly. 'He was fine one moment, then he got tense – that's what caused this.' She showed the arm and Jason gritted his teeth. Didn't Laria realise that it angered Jason to see so much as a scratch on her? '…But he's gone, Jason. I think he left the building because Seth can't track him down.'

Seeing the desperation in her eyes, Jason found himself calming. It wasn't the time to get angry. He had to make sure Laria was okay first.

'We'll find him,' Jason promised, hating the taste of the words in the back of his tongue. The last thing Brodie deserved was for Laria to watch out for him. 'If anyone can find him, it's Seth – you know that.'

'But it doesn't change the fact that we don't know where Charmi is,' Laria argued back fiercely and avoided Jason's stare. 'I knew I should've gone with him... I have to find him!' Just as Laria prepared to flee the scene, Jason had a sudden thought and grabbed her unmarked arm.

'Wait.' His voice seemed to stun her.

But Laria didn't let him have it. 'If anything happens to Brodie while I had a chance to protect him-'

'You need to care for yourself for once,' Jason told her, pulling her closer. Laria's surprise was obvious in her face, and

Jason used that chance to continue. 'I know that you need to go to him... put yourself first for once. You said it yourself, we don't know where Charmi is and she could easily target you. Once we find her, we can go after Brodie.'

As Laria stared at him, he felt his grip tighten on her. He knew he couldn't force her to stay, but the last thing Jason wanted was for her to be in danger. After everything Laria put herself through, Jason felt like he owed her. She really did flip his world upside down, yet it was for the best.

And much to his surprise, she smiled softly and her muscles relaxed in his arms. 'You're right, thank you...'

'Now let's get this dance over and done with,' Jason declared as he linked an arm with Laria to take her into the dancing room. Soft music played in the background as they appeared with the other dancers, catching the attention of Maya and Seth.

'You know how to do whatever this is?' Laria asked dryly as Jason held her hand gently. She eyed the remainder of the dancers and rolled her eyes. 'This looks like something that's done in the medieval times with all the princesses and balls.'

'You watch too many Disney movies. It's called a waltz,' he corrected her just as Laria gave him a strange look.

'It still looks old-fashioned.'

'And there's only one rule,' Jason whispered back, moving along in sync. 'Try not to stand on my feet.'

'And what movie did you steal that quote from?' Laria smirked as she moved with him.

'Who knows?' Jason felt a matching smile grow on his face, but seeing Laria's curiosity made his drop. The memories came rushing back to him. 'My mother... taught me this when I was younger but it's always stuck in my head.' His chest bloomed with a familiar pain and Jason tightened his hold in search of comfort. 'She wanted me to be the charmer sort — that really didn't work out but at least I can be a pretty good friend.'

Laria's eyes softened at the mention of his mother. It had been a conversation that they were meant to have, but with the recent events, they hadn't had much time to talk about it. Mae still looked alive in his head, however whenever he thought of her, Jason could only recall the last memories he had of her. Her pained screams while Jason was helpless to fight against Edward's hold – that was when he wanted to kill someone for the first time in his life.

'When this is over,' Laria decided with a light nod. 'We will have a nice sit down and talk.' He crouched low for Laria to spin around him.

'You look stunning by the way, Miss Alfero.' Jason changed the subject and Laria looked down at the red dress with embarrassment. 'It suits you.'

'Glad that one of us thinks so,' Laria grumbled as she gazed back at him. 'And you do clean yourself up nicely, Newbie.' They ended up in their arms again, and Laria's eyes turned serious as she stared behind Jason's back.

'What's wrong?' Jason asked, noticing her reaction.

Finally, Laria met Jason's eyes harshly. 'Nick's behind you.' With a tensed body, Jason believed her words. If Nick was around, it meant that something was about to begin.

***

Laria saw the blonde-haired male glare at them; there was hatred for Laria.

'I need to speak with Seth,' Laria whispered, looking across the room at the telepath. Seth quietly spoke to Maya who looked up to glance at Jason and Laria.

Jason slowly led Laria closer towards Seth through their dance. When Laria did let go of Jason, she felt Maya's body pass hers. Before she knew it, Laria was in Seth's arms. He was warm just like Jason, and Laria was surprised that she managed to slip into his arms so easily.

'You want me to find Charmi,' Seth muttered blankly. Without Laria asking, he closed his eyes with a look of concentration. It was interesting to see how Seth was able to multitask with a complex dance. 'Stop thinking about it,' he said bluntly and Laria obeyed his words instantly.

Finally his eyes snapped open and the dance was over. 'She's not here – at the school campus. I assume that Brodie is with her to take her down once and for all.' With that, he let her go.

'Thanks Seth.' Laria offered a smile to the Laurence heir but he grabbed her to stop her.

'Be careful.'

The warning stunned Laria and she watched him with cautious eyes, before she felt her head nod. 'Will do,' she said and walked out of the Main Hall. As soon as the cold air hit her face, Laria slowly undid the strap of her dress to run to the forest.

As much as she loathed admitting it – this was the one time that she was going to be glad to turn into her wolf form.

CHAPTER 26

Everything was working so well for Charmi.

Concealed within the empty school campus, she knew that Brodie was on his way. Soon she would have him alone and rip the stone itself from his grasp.

A scoff escaped her lips when the doors of the school building slammed open. Even though he wasn't in her sight just yet, she could practically feel Brodie's desire.

'Hurry up and show yourself!' he shouted, storming through the building. His rage coated his words. 'I know you're in here, you psychotic bitch!'

Finally, Brodie's face came to view and he halted in his tracks. She didn't bother to move and smiled with amusement as she faced him.

Immediately, his anger returned and Brodie clenched his fists. 'Charmi.'

'Good job, Brodie,' Charmi sneered in delight. 'You found me – and here I thought that the Rel you possess was a dud.'

His eyes flashed brown. 'I will make you pay.' Before Charmi could respond, Brodie pulled out a gun out of his suit and shot her through the arm. Pain erupted through her body, forcing the female to groan.

'You brought the gun with you,' Charmi whispered with a snarl of agony. She reached for her arm and gritted her teeth. 'I never thought that you would've had it in you.' This definitely wasn't what she had in mind. 'We fight with our bare hands, not with weapons like a mere coward does.'

'That's funny,' Brodie scoffed and approached her with a scowl. 'I recall my friend was stabbed to death. You're the last person to call me a coward.'

'Are you referring to your present a week ago?' Charmi wondered slyly, squeezing her wounded arm. She had to admit that he got her good. 'What was her name? Jamie? Janis? Jennifer? Well it doesn't matter to me – she was in this fight to begin with after you selfishly killed Brad.'

'Jenna had nothing to do with this!' Brodie snarled. 'You and your brother forced her to turn against us!' His eyes were brighter now, ready to lose his temper. 'You should've gone after me, I was the one that killed your brother!'

'That's right!' the woman screamed back in agony. The memories of Brad's death were still fresh. 'You killed Brad! How dare you think that you can walk away peacefully when we went through hell as a family?!'

'What we went through as friends was just as strong!' Brodie snapped, slamming his fist into the locker with a force of his anger. The door bent with his will. 'With your petty threats, you took her life!'

'You and I both know that my threats weren't petty,' Charmi added and felt the disgust in her chest as she stared back at Brodie's angered features. 'I told you that you would eat your words.'

'It doesn't matter anymore,' Brodie said and he raised the gun to point it back at her. 'This is for you, Jenna – I can't redeem this monster so she has to die.'

He was ready to kill her.

Charmi raised her hand and forced her mind to explode into his with his regrets. Brodie hesitated with his shot and it gave enough time to dodge the bullet. The gunshot was loud in her ears, yet she wasn't going to let him get off that easily.

Dashing towards him, Charmi used her uninjured arm to strike a Brodie. He took in a sharp breath in shock, but she used the opportunity to slam her palm into his chest. The force of her hit knocked him backwards and he dropped the gun in surprise.

'Face it, Brodie, you had no chance against me.' She raised her uninjured arm, recognising her blood coating her hand.

'Let's make this easy, give me Rel.'

Brodie let out a shaky breath and he rubbed his chest. 'Like hell I will,' he told her and his eyes flickered towards the gun on the floor. His eyes began to glow like a savage animal's. 'You need to be stopped, Jenna was the first and last person you hurt in this town.'

What a foolish boy.

Flashing a grin, Charmi realised that the pain in her arm was numb. Perhaps it was her bloodlust's way of protecting her or maybe it was the adrenaline. Either way, she didn't care.

It was time to fulfil her desires.

Brodie charged at her with a cry leaving his lips, aiming a punch towards her face. In response, she grabbed his fist but she wasn't expecting Brodie to slam his other fist into her stomach. The force of Brodie's punch knocked the air out of her lungs, causing her to bend from the blow.

'I thought you had more punch,' Brodie taunted as he freed his hands from her grip.

Through her rapid breaths, Charmi forced her eyes to meet with Brodie's. 'Don't... get... cocky!' She used the opportunity to use her injured arm for an uppercut and satisfaction filled her as her fist connected with Brodie's jaw.

Her hit caused him to curse, but Charmi recovered from her recent injury. As Brodie nursed his jaw, Charmi used her palm to strike Brodie again. Before he could retaliate, Charmi grabbed a fist full of hair and slammed a knee into his gut.

Brodie lost his footing but she only tightened her grip on his hair. 'I told you that you had no chance,' Charmi said and slammed Brodie into the floor.

The impact caused him to groan and he tried to recover but Charmi dug a heel into his spine. He let out a cry and despite through the pain, he still struggled to move.

'My, you're persistent,' she confessed and put more weight into his spine. She could feel him squirm from the extra pressure. When she lifted her heel from his back, Brodie was left in a heaving mess. With him on the ground, it caused a cruel smile to crawl on her lips. Her revenge was right in front of her.

'Shut up…' Brodie's voice was hoarse and Charmi's smile didn't leave. 'You talk too much.'

Instead she kicked him in the ribs, causing him to cry out again. She chuckled in amusement and kicked him again. With each groan he let out, it felt like music to Charmi's ears. After a third kick, Brodie rolled over and exposed his torso.

Reaching down, Charmi patted the boy's pockets. When she felt the warm presence of Rel, her grin grew wider. It was true what they said about the stone. With the contact of Rel, she could feel every Forte and she could tell that the Forte in front of her was suffering.

'I win, Brodie,' Charmi sneered and the power of the stone coursed through her veins.

'You think you've won?' Brodie muttered through his pained voice. He tried to pick himself off the floor, but lost the strength. Clenching his fist, Brodie met Charmi's eyes with a harsh stare. 'I won't be going down this easily.'

'Very well.' Charmi's eyes glowed as her sneer formed. 'It looks like I will have to kill you-'

A growl from behind Charmi made the woman jump back. Standing behind her was a grey wolf with familiar amber eyes, snarling back at Charmi's figure.

Back away from him, Charmi,' Laria's angry voice declared as she snarled. Slowly, Charmi sneered in delight of Laria's fierce gaze.

'Well, well,' Charmi replied sadistically and her mood was lifted upon seeing the beast in front of her. 'This is my lucky day.'

∗∗∗

'We need to get these people out of here.' Jason observed the group of humans. 'If hunters are around – I don't think that they will be safe from our interactions.'

'Mister Embers.' Seth's eyes widened when he saw the serious gaze on David's face. At the sound of his name, David shook his head to dismiss the quiet comments.

'It's David now – I quit my job a few days ago,' the teacher corrected, and the boys exchanged a surprised glance. 'Where's the rest of your group?'

'Laria and Brodie are with Charmi,' Jason replied and he felt his gut twist into uncomfortable knots. If anything happened to her – no he had to trust her. 'Maya's with the crowd of people trying to keep a low profile and Tahani's disappeared.'

'Because she went to search for Susan,' Seth realised and a scowl deepened in his features. 'I cannot hear Zanobi's thoughts.' Seth glowered around him to search for her. 'I can find her if that's what needs to be done-'

'No.' David cut Seth off instantly with a stern expression. 'She's the Ungue Dux. Tahani will be fine – I want you to be safe.'

'And the last thing we need to do is repeat history,' Seth murmured softly to himself. 'Very well – just let me know where these hunters are.'

'Ruddy is in the garage right now, taking care of the vans – you need to go to the upper floor and do a clean-up. You remember where you were kidnapped, don't you?'

He scowled, but nodded. 'I will have it done.' Seth stormed off into one of the rooms in order to finish his task. As soon as Jason was alone with the former teacher, he looked surprised when David checked the time.

'David?' It was too strange to call him by his first name but he easily responded to it.

'We need to get these humans out of here,' David announced and he pointed to a single room. 'I'm going into the security room and collect the data from the shifters that lived in this town. I may not be a hacker but they make it painfully easy.' He departed from Jason and he went into the room he was referring to, leaving Jason to his devices.

Jason froze as he saw Taro in the background. Suddenly Jason felt his body move on its own and the quarterback saw him from afar. Taro fled the scene and Jason followed him immediately.

As soon as they got into an isolated area, Jason found Taro standing by himself. It caught Jason off guard of how Taro's expression was unreadable.

'What do you want?' Taro asked, throwing off his coat. 'Want to kill me off? Is that why you followed me?'

Despite the threatening tone, Jason raised his hands. 'During the first day of school, you tried to pick a fight with me…' Taking a step towards the quarterback, Taro's eyes narrowed but Jason kept calm. 'But now… you seem to be avoiding any sort of fighting… did Jenna change you that much?'

'I liked her…' Taro confessed, nodding slowly. 'But after she found out the truth, she didn't trust me… She stayed by my side, but in the end, she was more willing to trust a *shifter* than me. Why?'

'I don't know,' Jason responded and the guilt came flooding back. 'I'm sorry that we couldn't save her.'

Taro's confusion slowly morphed into an expression of sorrow. He dropped his chin and avoided Jason's stare. 'I'm just as responsible for her death. I shouldn't have left, I should've stayed with her or at least stuck by her.'

Hearing this side of Taro was foreign, even to Jason. 'The shifter that killed her isn't going to get away with this.'

Finally, Taro locked eyes with Jason again. 'I know.' He then looked behind Jason and let out a sigh. 'That's why I'm letting you go. Because I know that you guys will stop that monster.'

Jason blinked. 'You trust us?'

'Don't think that for a second,' Taro dismissed and scowled. 'This will be the last time I spare you. The next time we meet, we will be enemies. Now make sure that your friends are safe.'

'Thanks Taro,' Jason said, but the quarterback didn't respond. Instead, Jason turned back in the direction he came from. Maybe the first thing he should do was help the people leave the party.

CHAPTER 27

As soon as David left Jason to help the humans, he entered the small room and went to the computer monitor. The computer was filled with video footage and everything he needed.

Without thinking, David pulled out his hard drive from his pocket and plugged it into the computer. He used it to put as much data as he could and tapped his fingers impatiently. After copying whatever he needed, he then needed to erase all of it.

But despite his plan so far going well, David couldn't fight the bad feeling in his gut. He immediately picked up his phone and desperately searched for Diana's contact details.

Luckily for him, Diana's phone answered within the first ring. *'David,'* her voice sounded through the device. *'I'm busy with Kimmy, is there something wrong?'*

'We need to go,' David replied with a strained tone. 'Zanobi is in town and he threatened you guys – I can't protect you from him...'

'David...' Her tone sounded like she had just lost a difficult battle.

'I know we discussed waiting, but I don't think it's safe to do so anymore.' David's tone cracked with pain and the mental images of his dead wife clouded his mind.

'It's okay David – as long as we're together, I would go to the ends of the Earth with you,' Diana replied softly. *'I haven't seen signs of Zanobi – I'll get Kim and we'll meet you at the town's border.'*

'Thank you,' David muttered gratefully. With a light ring on the computer, David noticed that the files were uploaded. 'I will see you then.' After hearing a confirmation from Diana that she would be ten minutes, David hung up the phone. What was Zanobi planning?

David wasn't expecting something to hit the back of his head. His world spun around as he dropped to the floor. David's first reaction was to reach for his head, grateful that the force wasn't enough to cause him to bleed. As soon as the shock disappeared, David could only feel pain in the back of his skull.

'You're not supposed to be here,' Clark said coldly from behind, holding a fire extinguisher. Slowly, David turned to face his companion with pain in his grey eyes.

'Clark...' In the midst of his confusion, David was grateful that the blunt force hadn't knocked him out. 'You can't go after these kids. These are Jenna's friends.'

'It doesn't matter!' Clark snapped, tears forming in his eyes at the mention of his daughter.

'Listen Clark.' David tried to negotiate, pulling himself to his feet. A wave of dizziness overcame him, but David leaned on the table. 'Susan isn't the mayor! She is as much of a victim as the rest of us.'

'I don't believe you,' Clark replied, but David didn't buy it.

He tried to stand again, but his body wasn't co-operating with him. Mentally cursing, David settled back in his spot. It was most likely a concussion – which was the last thing David needed. 'Isn't it strange that Susan suddenly wanted to take out shifters after Zanobi revealed his true colours? You have to trust your gut, because I know that you feel it.'

Clark said nothing, taking a step towards David. David quickly checked the deleting files behind him, realising that they weren't finished.

Finally, Clark spoke, 'you tried to delete the information regarding the shifters that lived in this town. Any that weren't registered on this system was classed as an outsider, which is how we could tell the difference between a friend or foe. Nowadays, they are all foes.'

Clark approached the computer, ignoring David's presence.

'Clark… don't do this…' David tried again. Desperation coated his voice. 'We can't be killing shifters, or people who might be shifters…'

'You're lucky you deleted most of it,' Clark said to him coldly. 'Had I come a few minutes later, your plan of keeping us blind would've been successful.'

'What's your plan then?' David demanded, 'I can't understand it. Do you want people to realise that people live in a supernatural world? It can't work, people are always scared of things they can't understand.'

'I guess you're scared then,' Clark confirmed and met his stare again. 'Since you've sided with the shifters, we're going to treat you like one.'

David waited for Clark to hit him with the extinguisher once more, however the door opened and stopped Clark from going through with his threat.

Yet the anger in Clark's eyes returned. 'You!' It seemed that Clark recognised the shifter. 'I'm surprised that you have the guts to show your face after remaining in hiding like the coward you are.'

The shifter wasn't one David recognised. With golden eyes and a wide sneer, it occurred to David that it was the outsider that came into town. Nick Forte, according to Takon and Ruddy.

'It seems that living in a world filled with black and white runs in the family,' Nick exclaimed without flinching. 'Did you really think that you would get away with locking me up? Jenna didn't seem pleased about that.'

Clark's anger deepened with rage. 'You have no bloody right to call her by her name!' He hissed. 'You are a bastard that deserves to be put down for good.'

However, David was still trying to decipher Nick's intentions.

'It seems that we have a lot to discuss.' Nick continued blankly and Clark remained glaring in silence. 'I never killed her, nor had I wanted to in the end. She wanted me to prove that I could be good as well.'

Clark snarled. 'Did you know the last thing she said to me? That she loved me, only for me to wake up and find out that she was dead.' He spat back at the shifter but Nick looked unfazed. 'You were the only one that was there. I know how to connect the dots you damn monster.'

'Jenna didn't believe me to be a monster.' It took David a moment to realise but Nick slowly moved away from him. Briefly, Nick's blue eyes met with David's and the hunter understood. 'She told me that I could prove to her that I could be redeemed and that's what I'm going through right now.'

'You can never be redeemed,' Clark replied and once he was out of David's sight, he moved back to get behind Clark. 'I know your type, you used my daughter and now you're free from the cage that you belong in.'

'She said something to me... even a monster like me could be read and you're no different.' Nick continued casually. 'But if you really feel the need, then do your worst to me. Just remember you will live the rest of your life running from the demon known as vengeance.'

Before Clark could reply, David was close enough and tapped Clark on the shoulder. With a frown, the brunette turned only to earn a punch in the face. David's fist slammed against Clark's face and knocked him out instantly, leaving Nick to be mildly impressed.

'I have to admit, mate.' Nick shoved his hands in his pockets casually. 'I never thought you would've done anything without my power influencing you.'

'Wait...' David frowned when he realised. 'You put me under your control?'

'You weren't really getting the picture mate – you looked like you were ready to faint,' Nick answered back and David rubbed the back of his head. His head was still pounding, but it had to wait.

'Thanks for that.' David gestured at the unconscious Clark. 'I think he's too consumed by his pain to understand.'

Immediately a frown formed on Nick's face. 'You know that I'm not a good guy – I don't care what happens to you.'

'And I wasn't always this guy,' David replied with a light shrug. Nick still had the sceptical look in his eyes but he didn't say anything. 'No one's perfect – in the end, we have to use those flaws to bring ourselves to the surface. Now I've got to go.' Reaching for his phone, David requested an Uber. When Uber confirmed his ride, David's phone began to ring.

It was Diana's number, thank goodness. He picked it up without hesitation and pressed the phone in his ear. But what he heard from the other line was enough to make his body freeze in horror.

***

It started off fine; Maya was making the people get into their cars safely. With the event over, Maya wasn't sure how the hunters were going to act. While she wasn't able to fight off the hunters, she had some trust that the rest of her friends would be alright.

However, while she was taking these people away, someone grabbed her arm roughly. Just before she could protest angrily, she felt something sink into the skin of her neck. A wave of dizziness overcame Maya and she lost her footing. Someone caught her before she could hit the ground and she got a glimpse of the hunter tattoo.

'That was easy.' The gruff voice of the hunter pulled her closer. Her muscles were limp in his hold, but Maya struggled against the hold. Nothing affected him and the hunter dragged her relaxed body away.

Her vision became blurry, but she couldn't see any more people within the building. In a desperate attempt, she tried to talk but her throat was dry. After everything she went through in Maine, Maya felt shame return to her. Once again, she was danger but this time – she couldn't protect herself.

She didn't know where exactly she was, but she heard a door shut behind them. As soon as the door closed, the support Maya had suddenly disappeared and she hit the ground with a cold thud. A yelp left her throat, before staring at the blob that appeared to be the hunter.

'Why...?' Maya moaned, regaining a twitch in her movement. The dosage was probably not enough to knock her out completely. 'Why are you doing this? I'm not a shifter.' Though it would be a good time to become one at the moment.

'Your bloodline is a Rosa,' the hunter answered. 'Despite you are a mere human, there is a chance that your future generation will be shifters. I can't allow that to happen.' He came closer and Maya tried to move but only her hand moved.

'Get away from me...' She said through her teeth. Her head slumped back on the ground after another wave of dizziness overcame her. 'I'll kick you into next week.'

'Cute.' The hunter crouched closer to her. 'But it won't save you-' Maya heard the door swing open. She could see another blur and her heart started to race, in a panic she never knew she could feel. However her strength left her and everything went black.

In her dreams, Maya was standing in a black void. It seemed endless, stretching as far as she could see. Maya looked around her and discovered she couldn't talk, or move. Maybe it was due to the drug still in her system.

'Can you hear me?'

Suddenly, Maya froze and she tried to move once more. The voice echoed within the void. Who was that calling for her? It sounded familiar, but Maya wasn't sure. Nothing made sense.

Who's there? Maya cursed when the words didn't leave her lips. She couldn't see where the voice was coming from. Instead of feeling panic, Maya felt calm – strangely enough.

'I guess you cannot.'

Wait. Her voice was still in silence. Maya squirmed uncomfortably and tried to regain some sort of movement. Like in her consciousness state, only her arm twitched. She gritted her teeth and tried to move again, only to remain motionless.

'Maya.'

Suddenly, Maya was blinded by a bright light. It only took

a few seconds for her to adjust the light, only to realise that Nadia Cyler was using a flashlight on her eyes.

'You seem fine,' the sheriff pointed out but it was a mutter. 'Can you hear me Maya? Do you know what happened?'

Maya blinked herself into awareness. 'Someone drugged me… I passed out before I could do much.'

Nadia lowered the flashlight, nodding slowly. 'Tahani Rosa managed to come in.' In that moment, the sheriff gestured towards Tahani who raised two fingers as a wave. 'She nearly killed the hunter, until Seth Laurence stopped her.'

Realising that the telepath was in fact with them, Maya tried to push herself into a seating position only to feel her stomach churn. The bile threatened to come up and Maya covered her mouth in disgust.

'Maya!' Seth called out, but Maya didn't respond to him. Her attention was on controlling any bodily fluids that she didn't want to leave her body.

Note to self – don't get drugged again. Maya took a deep breath and the upset stomach seemed to calm down.

'Be careful.' Tahani approached Maya to rub her back. 'Yer clearly not used to the drugs enough kiddo.'

'What now?' Maya asked after regaining her composure. She did her best not to move from her spot. 'I mean, if the hunter isn't dead then… where is he?'

'I arrested him just earlier,' Nadia explained and Maya felt herself relax. A part of her was grateful that the hunter lived, however the more submissive part of her wished that Seth didn't stop Tahani. Realising her sudden thoughts, Maya shook her head dismissively. Despite what the hunter did to her, Maya shouldn't be wishing for anyone's death – even if the hunter could've done anything to her while she was unconscious.

'But you should get home.' Sheriff Cyler, pulled herself back to her feet. 'Seth, can you make sure she gets home? She probably won't be well enough to walk by herself.' Maya was about to protest when she realised that Nadia was right. Her body felt like jelly and she nearly threw up after moving quickly.

'What about me then?' Tahani demanded, crossing her

arms. 'I can take her home.'

'I actually have some information for you,' Nadia said and Tahani's eyes widened. 'I would rather discuss it in private, if you're willing of course.'

Tahani looked conflicted, clenching her fists to the side as she looked towards Maya in silence. It was then, when Maya understood why Tahani didn't react right away.

'It's alright Tahani,' Maya told her and Tahani hesitated. 'Truth be told, I'm dead tired and I feel sick. You're better off listening to the sheriff.'

'I can't,' Tahani said with a slow shake of her head. 'I can't be letting yer on ya own, especially after everything that's happened.'

'I promise I will be there for Maya,' Seth said and Tahani froze. 'You would need to hear it.' Maya eyed Seth, trying to resist the urge to roll her eyes. There was no point in Nadia trying to hide the information with Seth around.

'Fine,' Tahani said through her teeth. 'Just make sure she gets home.'

Maya felt Seth grab her and slowly ease her to her feet. At first, Maya stumbled but Seth was there to keep her stable. As much as she wanted to keep standing on her own, Maya knew that it was pointless to argue with him. She didn't even have the strength to walk on her own.

Slowly, they trudged out of the building and Maya got herself into Seth's car. Like always, he was quiet as if trapped in his own thoughts. It wasn't until Seth got into the driver's seat and he let out a sigh.

'So much for doing something for Jenna…' He reached for the steering wheel and Maya frowned towards him. 'I'm sorry this day didn't go as planned.'

'What is it Seth?' Maya asked, tilting her head as his eyes remained staring in front of him. He hadn't started the car yet and his blank expression wasn't reassuring.

'While David managed to delete some of the files, he didn't get all of them.' Seth's answer seemed rather strained. Finally, he turned to her. 'Ours were saved and sent to each hunter –

they know our name and faces.'

'Including mine?'

'You're safe.' Seth seemed a bit more relaxed with that answer. 'But it means you could be in danger, the best option would be to hide in Cheyenne with the other shifters-'

'That's not happening,' Maya told him firmly. Her response caught Seth off guard and Maya chuckled dryly. 'I've never been safe, my own mum died because the bastard thought I would become a shifter. I wasn't scared of him, not even when he held me and threatened to kill me – so I'm staying. Besides, I couldn't bear the thought of being away from you.'

Seth's jaw dropped, before regaining his composure. 'Maya-'

'It's not just you,' Maya told him. 'Grams, Laria, Brodie, Jason – even Tahani. I can't leave them, because I know they wouldn't leave me. I'm prepared to stay.'

Seth sighed again, looking away from Maya to stare at the front of the car. 'I was foolish to think I could convince you.'

'It's about time that you're learning,' Maya replied back with a wink.

After the conversation, Seth began to start the car. 'I suppose it's time to take you home-'

'No.' Maya cut him off. When he raised his eyebrow back at her, Maya leaned back into her seat. 'At least, not yet. I want you to stop by somewhere first.'

***

What on Earth was Laria doing?

Brodie remained on the ground, staring at his friend as she growled at Charmi. In her wolf form, Laria's eyes flashed with certainty as she attacked.

They were going through the same fighting routine as Laria lunged at Charmi and she dodged. It was obviously one-sided, and Brodie hated that thought.

'You really are stupid girl,' Charmi commented as she looked back at the wolf. Laria snarled in response, showing off her vicious canines. 'After what Brodie did to get away from you – and you followed him.'

'*Shut up,*' Laria ordered and the pale hair on her hackles rose. '*You killed Jenna – and I will make sure that you don't get away with hurting any more innocent people.*'

'Good luck with that,' Charmi taunted and showed off the glowing Rel. 'I have more power than the both of you put together; I don't even need to use my power to get you two screaming.'

Laria leaped at Charmi with a menacing growl, attempting to rip into flesh but Charmi was faster with the presence of Rel. She jumped away and sneered when Laria bounced back on the ground without any harm. Using the opportunity to grab his gun, Brodie crawled towards it and found comfort with holding it.

'Laria!' Brodie called out and Laria turned back to face him. 'Don't do this! This is my fight to begin with!'

'*I'm sorry Brodie, but Jenna was my friend too. I am going to finish what Charmi started.*' Her tail instinctively shot up and Brodie cursed when he found himself useless once again. He didn't want Laria to fight Charmi on her own – especially with Rel's presence.

It could do more than just give extra power and he knew it.

'We'll see who really started this mess, Laria Alfero.' Charmi smiled in Brodie's direction and he froze when the buried memories uprooted in his mind. 'Don't you two remember what it was like before Laria became a shifter? She was carefree and innocent... wasn't life perfect? Now that she has turned, your life has gone upside down, Brodie.'

The nagging feeling in his brain made him hesitate. He clenched his jaw to force out the memories from his mind. He hated the feeling his mind was emitting. During those times, Brodie did care about her like she was his sister. And back then, he was willing to protect her with his life – even now he was willing.

'*Stop it!*' Laria ordered. '*Stop using Rel to manipulate him!*'

'Screw you, Charmi,' Brodie replied with effort and he picked himself off the ground. 'I won't let you of all people to control my bloodlust.' He aimed the weapon towards her and she remained still.

Charmi ignored their words and chuckled sadistically. 'I must add something important – Laria tried to kill me, that pathetic witch even gave her the chance to kill me. But she didn't, she claimed that she couldn't kill me. She thought she could let me go and think I owed her my life. But Laria didn't consider one thing – I couldn't care less about being spared; I wanted my revenge. The best way to do so was kill someone you both cared about deeply.'

Jenna.

Brodie froze, processing the information. All this time, Laria could've killed Charmi and when given the opening, she let her go? Was Jenna dead because of Laria?

'How could you do this?' Brodie demanded, glaring at the wolf. 'How could you not tell me this?!'

I wanted to,' Laria whimpered, flattening her ears. *'Brodie, I was ashamed of it.'*

Kill her. Orgul demanded and Brodie tried to keep his bloodlust at bay.

'Jenna didn't deserve to die…' Brodie's voice trembled. His body was shaking in protest as he tried to deny it. 'You attacked her, then you let her die.' Was this even him speaking? Or was it Orgul? *I can't kill Laria… can I?*

'Laria is the reason why your life is hell,' Charmi said to Brodie, flashing a grin. 'It was her father after all, that killed yours. Take revenge, you should make her suffer like you had.'

Brodie broke. Orgul took advantage of his anger, taking control of Brodie's movements and thoughts. He was forced to watch his body's claws extend from his fingertips.

'Brodie!' Laria panicked, but Orgul wasn't listening.

I should be better off letting Laria die… Brodie considered. It was a sacrifice that Brodie didn't want to take, but in the end, it could probably protect his other friends. They would probably hate Brodie for allowing it, but it meant Jenna and

Leon could rest in peace.

'This isn't you!' Laria tried to defend herself. *'Charmi is taking advantage of your grief!'*

'You brought this upon yourself Laria.' Brodie couldn't even recognise his own voice anymore. Without warning, he lifted his gun and fired bullets throughout her body. Much to his surprise, Laria dodged a few of them, but one punctured her thigh.

A loud yelp escaped Laria's throat, crumbling to the floor as blood matted her fur. He was having his revenge, the bloodlust was thrilled with the idea of Laria in agony. It appeared that she couldn't handle the pain and with slow cracks, Laria turned back into her human form.

She whimpered weakly. 'Please come back to me...'

'You will die, Laria,' Orgul promised and pointed the gun directly at her head. 'So there's honestly no point to beg for your worthless life.'

Her eyes were wide with fear, blood covering her leg. However her expression changed and her eyes flashed amber. Brodie was surprised as her fear disappeared and was replaced with determination.

So in protest, Laria got back to her feet. As Brodie watched her, he questioned Orgul's motives. How could he kill her if she was willing to stand back up, even with a bleeding thigh?

'I know you can hear me, Brodie,' Laria whispered desperately and her body trembled. Charmi was watching in the background, sneering at Laria's attempts. 'I'm not begging you to spare my life – I'm begging for your forgiveness, for leaving you alone and for what Lucien did. It was wrong and I hate myself that he still gets to live while Leon is gone. But please Brodie, you and I both know that I would die for you – but I can't die with you blaming me for someone's actions. You are my link to humanity and I will always be yours.'

With that, Laria jumped at him. Brodie wasn't expecting her to strike, but he felt no pain. She held him in her arms like they used to when they were younger. With the warmth, Brodie felt another presence within him, like someone was standing by his side. Then it hit him; Laria had to ability to take away his spiritual energy, and she gave him hers to fight against Charmi.

The realisation dawned on Brodie. What was Orgul thinking? This was wrong, even for Brodie. He grew up with her with the silent promise to protect her, even when she became a shifter. They played together, ate together, grew together. In that moment an image appeared in Brodie's mind, he found himself staring at the night sky in bliss. Beside him, Laria with her short pigtails and chubby cheeks flashed a smile.

'We'll always be friends right?' the young Laria had asked.

In response, Brodie remembered nodding back, grinning back as he lifted a pinkie. 'Of course.'

And their fingers latched.

The image faded from his mind and Brodie was back at the school grounds in Laria's embrace. He didn't want to kill her – she and Leon were the reasons he wanted to protect the people.

'That's the Brodie I know…'

Laria's voice went quiet and she fell. Brodie didn't realise he regained control of himself until he reached out and caught her. He watched over her face, with his panic resurfacing.

This is my fault, Brodie realised, and felt Laria's energy boil within him. *I need to save her.* He pulled off his coat and placed it over Laria's bare form. 'I won't ever hurt you again, Laria,' Brodie whispered.

She wanted him to fight against the vengeance and by gambling her life it worked. He shot a warning glare towards Charmi who suddenly realised that her plan of manipulating wasn't going to work.

'You think that you can handle me?' Charmi taunted and tightened her grip around Rel. 'I have the power – your power won't be able to break into my head.'

'I wouldn't be so sure,' Brodie replied with a smirk forming on his face. 'I don't need to kill you to get what I want.' Without hesitation, he shot at Charmi's hand and she dropped Rel.

As soon as Rel clicked on the ground, Brodie felt the strong urge from Orgul pull away. He fired his final bullet to pierce through the enemy's shoulder and she yelped.

'It looks like I'm out of bullets,' Brodie mocked with a scoff.

Charmi snarled in agony. 'Don't think that you've won this. I'm still alive and I will take someone down with me.' She turned around and morphed into a large falcon, screeching in protest as she flew away from the pair to escape the school. Her clothes dropped into a pile as she transformed.

Brodie didn't even spare her a second glance, because he turned to Laria, crouching by her side and felt for her pulse. It was faint but it was still there.

He grabbed her hands gently. 'Laria – you have to take your energy back.' Brodie tried to whisper her awake as she squirmed uncomfortably. 'I won't let you die in my arms... I've already lost Dad and Jenna – losing you will be the end of me.'

Nothing was happening and Brodie felt rising panic. She had to come back.

'Now it's time to use my power, to save you.' Brodie forced his mind into Laria's and commanded her to take her life energy back. Brodie never liked using his power, similar to hypnosis by using the deeper part of someone's mind. By using the subconscious part of their mind, Brodie was able to feel Laria like he was in her body. In his mind's eye, he could see that she was slipping from life.

In seconds, Brodie could feel her twitch under his hold and she went with his command, taking the energy that she gave him. The effect was strange – he felt dizzy and confused.

Yet, it was worth it when Laria's chestnut eyes fluttered open.

Suddenly, Laria lurched with a gasp. She heavily panted but looked towards Brodie with gratitude in her eyes.

However, Brodie's jacket fell off and Brodie's happiness immediately went to embarrassment. His cheeks were flushed and he froze. No matter what, he never thought his childhood friend would look so womanly under clothes.

However it seemed that she didn't notice she was naked in front of him. 'Brodie, you're alright!' Laria tackled him into a hug, and Brodie was screaming internally.

He couldn't think straight with her holding him. No. Nope. It couldn't happen.

'Laria *please*,' Brodie begged and stopped Laria momentarily. It seemed that she finally noticed why Brodie was so flustered and she screeched in humiliation. Without thinking she pulled Brodie's jacket over her body. 'I can't unsee that.'

Laria's eyes softened with a smile, even though her cheeks were still brilliant red. 'You did it, Brodie – we're still alive thanks to you.'

'Are you kidding?' Brodie replied with a scoff. 'It was the both of us that did it. Speaking of that stunt you pulled – if you ever do that again, I will seriously lock you in my father's basement.' Laria merely scoffed in response and Brodie stood up to his feet to offer her a hand. 'Come on... we need to track Charmi down.'

Just as Laria grabbed his hand, Brodie felt a smile form on his face. Even though he was smiling on the outside, Brodie knew that this was a step closer to darkness. Just because he was ready to forgive Laria, it didn't mean Lucien was off the hook.

'But first.' Laria wore Brodie's jacket and her cheeks flushed. Brodie's mind returned to the current situation of Laria wearing only his jacket. 'Let's put on Charmi's clothes – they might be a bit bigger but they may fit.'

CHAPTER 28

Picking up Rel and wearing Charmi's clothes, the two friends walked out together. It was a good feeling for Laria; she hadn't seen this side of Brodie in a long time.

'So what happened with your dress?' Brodie asked, sparing a look towards Laria who suddenly looked sheepish. She knew this question would've popped up sooner or later.

'Ripped it to shreds when I turned,' Laria muttered. 'I didn't mean for it to happen, but Adelle is going to kill me.' Suddenly Brodie stopped walking and Laria realised that he looked like he was having troubles with his thoughts. 'Brodie? What's wrong?'

Finally Brodie found the strength to answer, 'It was my fault that Jenna's gone.'

But it wasn't his fault. Were they really going to have this discussion again? It wasn't Brodie's fault that Jenna was killed – it was Charmi's reasoning that she wanted to stir Brodie up.

'But it was also my fault that we didn't find out about Zanobi sooner,' Brodie continued with a frown and slowly his fists clenched up. 'It was my fault that Jason didn't know about his heritage sooner and I was the reason why you nearly died today. It's like a storm and I started up everything, you should never have forgiven me for trying to kill you.'

Laria frowned in return, recalling her last-minute stunt. She used her connection with Lux. It was pure luck that she gave Brodie enough of her energy to keep herself alive, but he was the reason why she was alive as well.

'Brodie – you can't just keep blaming yourself for everything...'

'I can't say sorry for everything that will happen.' Brodie ignored Laria's voice and he lifted the newly concealed Rel. 'But I can show you of how much I trust you.'

Recognising Rel's glow, Laria suddenly stepped back in alarm. 'No. I can't.' If he gave her a discount card – that would've been fine. However Brodie was offering her Rel. This was one of the two stones with their location known. 'Brodie this isn't what you should do-'

'I want to, Laria,' Brodie replied softly and cut her off. Laria stared back at the yellow stone with shock as if she expected it to grow a head. 'This is a symbol of our friendship – I don't even need Viri... even though none of us know where it is. But I just want you to know that I will always be with you in that stone.'

Laria's eyes went to Brodie. Her heart was pounding recklessly in her chest as she realised what Brodie was telling her. He trusted her – just as she trusted him with her life. They were both willing to die for each other, and this was what her bond with him was about.

'Okay.' Laria accepted the stone with its cloth and the glowing stone dulled from her touch. 'Wait a minute... If we need our bloodlust to support the stones and these stones can influence bloodlust... then why don't Zanobi and Lucien just do that in the first place?'

'Because.' A new deep voice behind them stopped their movements altogether. 'We have no intention of using the bloodlust. Zanobi does need you to be aware of it however.' Slowly the pair turned around and Laria felt her heart jump out of her chest.

It was him.

Laria recognised him through the vision.

'Lucien.' Laria's voice trembled and she took a step away from her father. Her eyes went down to his belt and she noticed two white hilted blades attached to their sheaths. That was why Chris trained her with swords.

'Hello, Laria,' Lucien greeted and smiled softly. It wasn't a sneer, or some sadistic grin but an actual smile. 'It's been a long time since we last saw each other, though I doubt you remember me.'

Laria wasn't even aware of Brodie's quivering form until she heard him yell, 'Lucien!' Brodie lunged towards the older Alfero and Lucien scoffed in protest.

'I believe that you remember me clearly.' Lucien brought out one of his blades. It was pure white, like the snow that was threatening to fall above them. Laria screamed out for her father to stop, but it was to her surprise that Lucien attacked with the hilt. As soon as the hilt smacked against Brodie's face, he fell to the ground unconscious.

Glaring at him, Laria didn't hide her disgust. 'Why?' Laria was desperate for answers. 'Why do you want the rectocs to come back?'

'Do you think that's what I want?' Lucien questioned back calmly. Slowly, Lucien raised his other hand and showed of a bright green stone. The stone, Viri – it was calling for her. 'The stones are the only things that can help us now – I simply want to do what's right.'

What was right? His answer made her blood boil. *How dare he consider what was right for any of them?!*

'What was right about sending Edward to ruin my life?' Laria demanded, clenching her fists tightly. Lucien's expression remained unfazed and it only gave Laria more anger. 'I lost my innocence that day! I lost my mother! How could you put a daughter through that? You made Edward ruin my friends' lives and then you hunted Leon down. I've lost so much because of you!'

She didn't realise that she was crying until she noticed Lucien approach her. His chestnut eyes glanced down at Laria, and she refused to move.

Returning his blade back, Lucien gently brushed the tears away with a thumb. Laria flinched from his contact, disgusted that he pretended. She wanted to say that she hated this man that stood in front of her, but it was a lie. In reality, she hated the bloodlust that took over her father.

'You will understand one day,' Lucien explained with a

frown. 'But for now – you just have to play along and give me Rel.'

'I'm not giving anything to you,' Laria barked back as her eyes flashed amber. She immediately stepped away and brought Rel to her side. 'If I have to, I will kill you so that no one will be able to touch the stones again.'

Lucien sighed softly. 'I'm proud of you – even if you don't believe it.' Laria wasn't prepared for Lucien; not one bit. Within seconds, she felt something smack into her gut and she dropped Rel as she flew back. Pain laced through her body as she smacked into the pavement. He definitely hit her with the hilt of his sword.

Depending on her bloodlust, Laria pushed herself back to her feet and she growled at Lucien's calm posture. 'Keep away from Rel!' As Laria tried to attack again, she didn't notice that Lucien passed through her angry movements.

'I can feel everything from you, Laria,' Lucien said, forcing Laria to jump back when he was literally behind her. Right now, he had a grip on Viri and the other was with one of his blades. 'You're in pain, your loneliness and even your anger directed at me... but deep down, I can even see that you are wishing that you can do what's right.'

Before Laria could comment, Lucien bent down to grab the yellow stone.

'Stop, Lucien!' Laria demanded furiously. Much to her surprise Lucien stopped in his tracks. 'I know that my father is still there. I might not remember him... but I know that he wants to fight, just like me.'

'You look like Lesley.' Lucien offered a smile in Laria's direction once he picked up Rel. 'It was nice to see you so grown up. I'm sorry for everything – but I cannot let you chase after me.' Without warning, Laria realised that Lucien appeared by her side to hit the side of her neck. Her world darkened as she heard his voice again. 'But you will learn when the time is right.'

***

Seth pulled the car up to the cemetery and spared a glance of concern towards Maya. She stared silently at the area filled with tombstones in front of them.

'Are you sure you want to come here?' Seth's voice drew her out of her trance.

'I do.' She stepped out of the car with a determined look on her face. A shudder from the chill escaped Maya's lips when the cool air brushed against her skin.

Fortunately for her, Seth noticed and shrugged off his jacket to place it around Maya's shoulders.

The pair walked through the similar graves; it wasn't a big cemetery since it had a lot of the family tombs from the founders. Maya recognised the grave with a fresh clump of dirt by a small tombstone. She felt her heart twist with agony as she looked at her friend's name and a shaky breath escaped her.

'It's okay,' Seth whispered with his gentle encouragement. Maya spared him a surprised glance when Seth reached for her hand. 'I will be here with you. It was never your fault.'

A smile formed on Maya's face as she looked back at Jenna's tombstone. Finally, Maya tightened the hold she had on Seth and huddled to him for the warm.

'Hey, Jenna...' Maya began awkwardly. 'I know it's definitely not like me to talk to nothing like a damn lunatic.' She chuckled to herself quietly and she read her friend's name. 'Well... to tell you the truth – it kinda sounds okay. I'm not sure of your location right now and since you ain't a shifter of the Rosa family I wouldn't be able to talk...'

The grave remained silent, and to Maya's surprise the breeze brushed her face as if it had been Jenna trying to communicate with her.

Slowly, Maya looked back to her feet. 'It doesn't matter. That monster that killed you is getting the justice she deserves... and I heard that you managed to tame one of the crazy killers.'

Seth scoffed lightly from the side. 'More than enough. You really gave us a surprise when we found out about your final moments.'

'Anyways – that's all for today... I don't have any flowers since they would be dead by tonight. Our friendship was one of the greatest things that happened to me.' Letting go of Seth's hand, Maya crouched down to the ground and gently placed her fist against the clump of dirt. 'So fist bump for that.' Standing back to her feet, Maya grabbed Seth's hand to regain the warmth. 'I'll see you later Jenna...'

'*I'm sorry, Maya…*'

Suddenly, Maya pricked up in alarm. 'Jenna?'

Seth grabbed Maya as she stood, but he seemed confused. 'What's wrong?'

Maya looked back at the spot, but she returned the stare towards Seth. 'Did you not hear that?'

He shook his head. 'I heard nothing – but did you say you hear Jenna? How is that possible?'

Maya realised how ridiculous she sounded. Of course she didn't hear Jenna, it must've been a part of her imagination. 'Sorry… let's head back. We need to find a safe place to hide from those hunters.'

She led them back, ignoring the strange voice she heard. It seemed crazy that she heard Jenna. What would Jenna apologise for anyways? From what happened to them?

However, Maya hesitated when they passed the Rosa tomb. Her mother's grave was in there. There was a small part of her that wanted to go inside, to pay respects. Then again, Maya let her mother go a long time ago. Wherever Kaeylin Rosa was, Maya only hoped that her mother was doing the right thing. Until she figured out clues to her mother's story, Maya was going to be strong in her own way.

'We will find Azu, Maya,' Seth promised and Maya immediately smiled at his promise.

'And promise me one final thing,' the Rosa requested just as Seth merely raised an eyebrow in her direction. She faced him seriously and held his hand with both of hers. 'Promise me that you will never leave me.'

Seth's eyes were hard but his tone was gentle. 'I promise.'

***

Jason opened the door to the Forte estate. It seemed that Brodie had not returned yet.

Surprise flashed in Jason's features when he noticed the lack of smashed glasses. Tara came or Brodie cleaned up – Jason doubted the latter. He went into Leon's office and froze when he realised that he stood in his father's private space.

Jason went into the safe and pressed the key code he had from memory of the last time. The door clicked and Jason swung open the door. His heart pounded nervously as he pulled the heavy door open, but he only felt his stomach drop at the lack of Rel. While Verm was there as a dull red rock, Rel wasn't to be seen which only meant one thing.

Brodie took the stone.

Just before Jason could slam the door in a quick rage, he noticed a photo within the safe and he picked it up. It was a photo of two people, one that Jason recognised as Leon and the other looked eerily similar to Mae... but had her own features to make Jason realise that this was Deborah Amarel.

She was probably the nice kind of mother. He pictured she would've been clumsy sometimes, while Leon would tease her attempts to be tough. Perhaps Mae would've come over occasionally and the three would often hang out like a small group of friends.

Jason didn't realise that he was experiencing nostalgia until he felt the irritating throb from his jaw. He didn't usually have the habit of clenching his jaw. Finally Jason put the photo back in the safe and locked it.

However a knock at the door halted his thoughts. While this wasn't exactly his house, people knew that he came around occasionally. Sure he hadn't been in the house for at least a month, but that was between Jason and Brodie. He stood up and exited his father's office in order to answer the door but Jason was astounded when he realised who stood behind it.

'Jason.' Heather's breath left her with a frown.

And now it was awkward.

'Hey,' Jason muttered uncomfortably and scratched the

back of his head. The last time he saw Heather, she broke up with him. 'So why are you here?'

'I was looking for Brodie,' Heather replied stiffly and avoided Jason's gaze. 'I wanted to tell him that I was heading to Cheyenne... the witches are trying to find a way to stopping the uniting of the stones. All I know is it starts with the Uniter.'

Jason raised an eyebrow. 'What is that?'

Heather shook her head. 'I can't say much... They're the only one that can stop the stone's reunion. To protect the future for everyone, I can't afford to show weakness now of all times.'

That was when Jason realised he couldn't take it. With a shake of his head and a scoff, Jason asked, 'Is that why you dumped me?' Heather flinched at his voice. He didn't hesitate with her anymore. 'Or is the reason more personal?'

Heather's eyes suddenly flashed with pain, as if she was trying to get rid of a burden. 'Jason,' she whispered with a weak tone. 'I shouldn't have to explain myself-'

'You do,' Jason shot back. 'Heather please – let me finish what I need to say.' He saw that the witch fell quiet and it gave Jason his chance to continue, 'I just need to know.'

Heather looked like she was filled with guilt. Jason desperately wanted to comfort her, become her friend like they were but the second he approached her, Heather seemed to distance herself away.

'I can't...' she whispered, slowly backing herself away from him.

He grabbed her wrist, halting her movements completely. 'Heather, I just need to know!'

'Please stop it,' Heather frantically said. 'You won't like it.'

'Not until you tell me.' A dark voice crept in the back of his mind, telling Jason to pin Heather until she answered. Yet he knew it was his bloodlust and Jason didn't want to hurt Heather of all people.

Jason wasn't expecting Heather to return the force. She whispered a chant and Jason was flung off his feet to hit the ground. The air was knocked out of his lungs and Jason gasped at the sudden force.

He wouldn't lie, he deserved that. But it didn't mean that he was going to let her run without the answers he craved. Jason forced himself back to his feet, but he didn't approach Heather.

'You can't just keep secrets from me!' Jason shouted, shaking his head. 'You did it when you met me, you did it while we were dating and you're doing it now! For once Heather, just tell me the truth and don't be subtle about it.'

Heather seemed hesitant about it, but she responded, 'your bloodlust was the reason I dumped you.' The answer caused him to hesitate. His bloodlust didn't come around until after they broke up. 'Don't you find it strange you were able to control it instantly? Your bloodlust is intense – stronger than a normal bloodlust. I saw visions of it each night – it's going to be more powerful and you're not going to be able to stop it. You're going to kill a lot of people, that will begin the domino effect…'

'The domino effect? Of what?' Jason demanded.

Heather looked hesitant. 'It's what leads to your death… and Laria is with you.'

It felt like she had punched him in the stomach. 'No… that can't be true…'

'What I'm doing, breaking up with you is to protect you from the witches.' Heather's voice continued to ring in his ears. 'Witches from my family aren't like me or Liza – if they found out about your power, they would use your body as power. Despite everything, I care about you Jason and I couldn't allow that to happen to you.'

As Jason allowed the new information to sink in, Heather used this chance to escape, pulling herself away from him to leave his sight. Jason couldn't move, his eyes losing focus as he stared at his hands.

His desire to slaughter would cause his own death. What if it was because of his thoughts of Laria? Or… what if Laria was the one that killed him in the vision?

***

'DIANA!' David's screams escaped his throat as he ran back into the house, seeing that the door was left open.

His heart lurched in his chest as soon as David rushed inside his house. He didn't even think, recognising his beautiful wife in a bloody pool with life-threatening injuries. There were cuts all over her body, and a gaping stab wound in the centre of her stomach. She was still alive; David could see her weak breaths visible in the chilly air.

'Where's Kim, Diana?' David begged his injured wife, taking her hands and realising how cold her hands were. 'Stay with me please...' he whispered desperately as tears of agony stung his eyes. Zanobi warned him and he didn't listen. Why was it that every time he did something right for someone, it had to end up hurting him from the inside?

'Daddy!' David sighed in relief when Kim ran towards him. The girl that looked like Diana wrapped her arms around her father. 'Mummy told me to hide with the pelt while the bad man hurt her.'

The father nodded gratefully, however he called the emergency number.

'What's your emergency?'

'My wife...' David replied in agony. 'She's hurt badly with stab wounds and I need an ambulance right away!'

'Alright, can you give us an address?' David agreed without hesitation and he said it as calmly as he could. *'There will be an ambulance dispatched for you immediately. In the meantime, I want you to hold her wounds.'*

'I will save her,' David swore to himself. David let the phone drop on loudspeaker and he relied on his first aid training by placing his hands on the largest wound. Beside him, his young daughter watched on with shallow breaths.

'I love you, David Embers...' Diana flashed a smile and she tried to keep her eyes open by keeping her breathing at a steady pace.

Immediately, David felt his composure break. 'I love you too, so stay alive. Do that for us.'

If Diana didn't make it, David wasn't sure if he could ever

go back to being this man. She was the reason of his change and little Kim... Kim was the reason he managed to hold himself together as wife was on the verge of dying.

***

Pain raced through Charmi's body as she morphed back into her bare human form in the middle of a deep forest. Her feet didn't make a sound as she opened the old door and stepped in for recovery.

The only one alive that knew this place so far was Nick. He often played here with her as a child and when he didn't want to go back to their father.

But Charmi was infuriated – she didn't expect Brodie to gain control over his bloodlust. Now her plan was ruined. She couldn't win for today but their war was not over.

As soon as she slipped on the clothes, Charmi cursed to herself over her failure. Brad would've been disappointed in her. Everything that Charmi did was for him. That stupid human was dead, yet it was only going to inspire the rest of her friends to fight harder.

Just as Charmi fixed her messy hair, a twig snapped from the outside. Her body went stiff with alarm as she couldn't see the intruder. The pain on her leg reminded her that she needed attention on it before infection.

'Who's there?' Charmi demanded fiercely and opened the door.

'It's alright, sister.' Nick stepped up and smirked devilishly. 'It's just handsome old me.'

'Nick,' she whispered with a raised eyebrow. 'How was the party? Did anyone cause you any trouble?'

'None at all really.' Nick flashed a grin. 'I ran into an old mate – I didn't expect to see him so soon, but it seems that life is full of surprises nowadays.'

'What's going on?' Charmi asked sceptically as she took a step back from her brother. Now there was something about his presence that didn't sit well with her. 'Nick. Who did you run into?'

'Remember when I asked for you not to kill Jenna?' Nick asked with a dark smile and Charmi's blood went cold. His tone reminded her of death itself. 'What did you do to me, big sister?'

'I did it for Brad,' Charmi answered lowly. 'Brodie's suffering is what mattered to me.'

'Was it worth it?' Nick wondered and he was still smiling. No – Charmi realised that it wasn't a smile. 'Was her dying breath really worth your pathetic plan?'

'What the hell are you talking about? What got you thinking like this?'

'I believe he is referring to me.' A deep voice interrupted them and immediately Charmi froze with recognition. She turned into the cabin, where Zanobi Adkins stood. 'Hello, Charmi.' Zanobi pushed his shades up to cover his green eyes. 'You've been convinced that you're a bold girl.'

'How could you?' Charmi shouted in Nick's direction. 'We went through hell together and you betrayed me!'

'Because you killed Jenna,' Nick replied darkly and he took a threatening step towards his sister. 'I told you to not kill her. I did not want you to lay a finger on her.'

'She was manipulating you.' Charmi resisted his glare and tried to fight back. 'Brad's vengeance is far more important that whatever plans you had for her.'

'I was going to change my life with her!' Nick snapped viciously and his eyes glowed dangerously. 'I want you dead, but I will never kill you, sister. So I found the next best thing – since Zanobi was unhappy that you tried to take the stone, he offered me a deal that I couldn't refuse.'

'Soon enough Rel will be in our hands,' Zanobi explained and Charmi jumped at his voice. 'We know that you plan to remove Brodie and Laria from the picture. We can't have that.'

'They don't know why they're the chosen four,' Charmi hissed back at the man with shades. 'The only way you can reunite the stone is if you have an immediate relative to the ones who sealed up the stone in the first place, like a child... or a sibling in our Rosa case might have to do.'

'I'm glad that you know why you nearly ruined our plans,' Zanobi stated with a small sneer of satisfaction. 'Which means that you know the first four we need alive. The other four – the original sealers – must die.'

She knew what that meant. A majority of the original sealers were dead but the only ones that weren't dead were...

Zanobi finished her thoughts. 'Takon Falls and Lucien Alfero, but he doesn't know that he has to die just yet.' As he stepped forward, Charmi knew that she was next in the dead list.

'You think that you're going to get what you want?' Charmi sneered to stop Zanobi momentarily. He wasn't put off by her attempts of intimidation. 'I also know about the conditions of reuniting the Corvena. You need your four sacrifices to be able to control their bloodlust – but that won't work if someone can't contain it.'

'And you think that they won't be able to handle it? You pushed Brodie and Laria in the right direction. Tahani already knows how to control her bloodlust as does Seth.'

'We'll see about that,' Charmi spat back and shot a glare towards her brother. 'Farewell, Nick – I hope you enjoy being in a group of those puny children.'

'Why, I never said I would work with them.' Nick merely chuckled and folded his arms over his chest. 'I'm leaving this wretched town, to search for someone.'

She didn't protest as a hand from Zanobi pinned her by a tree, arm across her neck. However, her powers activated and she saw some of the hidden memories he blocked. A blonde-haired woman was the first image in his mind.

Then it struck her.

'I know who you really are...' Charmi wheezed, sneering towards Zanobi. His green eyes narrowed in irritation. 'And now... I know why you want to reunite the stone!' A sharp pain came from her neck, then everything numbed as her world turned black.

***

'You are finally leaving?'

Tahani glanced back at Tracy. 'I am,' Tahani confirmed and held her packed bag. 'This is Haroni's house – but I feel like it's not right to freeload in someone's house when they're not around.'

'Laria will not like it,' Tracy said coolly and glowered at the bottle of bourbon in Tahani's hands. 'You have trained her, and she cares about you. That is why my brother let you stay.'

Taking a swig of her drink Tahani showed off a snide smirk. 'It's alright.' She slurred lightly from the effects of the alcohol. 'I wrote a note... and it's not like I've been the best magister for her.' A sigh of irritation escaped the blonde-haired woman. 'Besides I thought yer better off without me staining up the mansion.'

'I care for Laria and want to protect her. I care for her best interests which includes you – as much as the idea sounds ludicrous.'

'Well – she can visit me whenever she wants,' Tahani responded lazily and took another drink. 'Adios, angel.' She turned away from Tracy; got into a rental car and drove out of the driveway.

Tahani thought back to her reason of leaving the mansion. Recalling the way Nadia addressed to her and their privacy.

'My sources don't lie Tahani,' Nadia told her when they were at the town hall.

'Why would Zanobi want to target Cheyenne?' Tahani asked in return, crossing her arms. 'The stones are here aren't they? At least, two of them are.'

'I don't know,' Nadia answered the question honestly. 'But think about it – the shifters that fled this town probably hate the hunters. It's the best time to start influencing them, whether in his original body or another person.'

'I can't leave Maya or Laria,' Tahani protested and tried to think of any other cons to the idea of her leaving for Cheyenne. 'Besides, Takon didn't want me to target Zanobi, usually you would be on his side.'

Nadia paused, before exhaling. 'It's true, the Mandati

Dux's orders are there for a reason, but it's rumoured that angels are there.'

Tahani narrowed her eyes. 'Who cares? The only two angels I know happen to be cowards, they don't care about anything but their selfish desires.'

'If Zanobi manages to take possession one, then we're all screwed.' Nadia was firm on the idea. Now it made sense. 'Please go to Cheyenne and try to stop him from getting them.'

Tahani didn't need much convincing afterwards. Nadia did a lot for her when Tahani just got out of jail. She destroyed any other evidence, despite it being against the law. Her records of ever being the Beast were gone forever.

As much as Tahani hated it, she did owe Nadia one.

But that part of her life was over, Tahani didn't realise how empty it felt from the inside. As she drove through the border of Golden Cliff, it became a lonely road with no evidence of human contact.

What was I doing? Tahani thought to herself, she pulled over on the side of the road with a deep breath. The world seemed quiet, quiet enough for Tahani to remember how her life was like after she abandoned Kaeylin.

'Tahani, please understand!'

Speaking of the dead sister. 'It's not real.' Tahani pushed away Kaeylin's voice with a curse and snarled in agony. The image of her murdered parents appeared and Tahani forcibly stepped out of the car.

Before she realised it, Tahani was no longer standing in the middle of the road but in the forest. Her eyes grew wide and the pain kept growing. It was like she couldn't interact with the image of Laria crying over Tahani's wounded body. Tahani swallowed nervously when she recalled the scene; the day that she nearly died from Edward.

'Laria.'

Tahani's eyes grew wide as Zanobi stepped into her sight and the dux cursed when she realised she couldn't move. 'Zanobi...' It wasn't real, yet it felt like it.

Zanobi's eyes grew wide to show his shock. *What happened?'* he asked, as he spared a glance at Tahani's unconscious body.

'I was stupid.' Past Laria sobbed as he approached them. *'I told Tahani not to kill him and she paid the price... It's my fault she's like this... I want to save her...'*

'No...' Tahani realised when she realised that Zanobi was trying to set her up. Deep down, Tahani didn't want to believe that her best friend betrayed her.

'But Laria, don't you know? Tahani really killed those people! She's the Beast that was willing to send you to the enemies.'

'Come on!' Tahani shouted at her own panic. 'Stop being so damn afraid of everything!'

He set her up, stole her body to kill a pair of shifters just because he felt like it. She didn't want to watch this memory anymore. Immediately, the dux shook her head to dismiss the visions, but she could still hear their desperation.

'Come on!' Tahani shouted at Charmi from wherever the rogue was, wincing at the ear-splitting agony that rang in her head. 'Just leave me the hell alone! I don't care anymore! They're not a part of my life!'

'I don't believe it for a second. Tahani saved my life – if it wasn't for her, I would've been dead. We've got to save her. You of all people should be up for saving her life.'

The reply that Zanobi gave was enough to shatter Tahani. *'We can't.'*

He left her to die. Agony shot through her mind and Tahani felt all the regrets piling on top of her. She wasn't strong enough to protect Kaeylin alone. Tahani didn't bring people together, she was nothing but toxic to them.

It wasn't fair!

Tahani couldn't breathe. In a panic, she reached for her chest, choking and gasping for air. Why was it so hard for her to breathe?

A gunfire blasted next to her ears and Tahani yelped like a child.

She couldn't take it anymore.

Her body dropped on the ground in response, no longer aware if it was a dream or reality. Snow sank around her, and Tahani couldn't even feel the cold. However, she saw a shadow move in the corner of her eyes.

Was this over for her?

To my friend who rests within the stars, to my
friend, Brodie Saint. I have waited so long for this
dedication to you.